MAGIC'S GENESIS: THE GREY

Book 1 of the 30 Stones Saga

Rosaire Bushey

PI·01·C

Printed in the United States of America

First Printing, May 2018

Independently published

ISBN 9781982962272

ONE

Death was creeping in.

The violent winter trapped the island town of Thrushton. Isolated from the mainland, an unexpected early freeze caught most of the boats still in the water and the ice crushed their fragile wooden hulls, and the early onset of winter did not relent.

With the cold came sickness, and the rutted dirt streets were practically deserted. Those who braved the cold moved quickly and the fires were kept stoked for as long as those inside the crude wooden houses could find the strength to lift fuel to the fire. Soon, however, sickness became plague and Wynter watched from the window of his small shop where lengths of wood lay cradled in vices and bundles of goose feathers waited to be shaped and fastened to straight wooden rods tipped with steel. The bowyer wasn't carving, shaping, or fletching today, however. He sat by the small window and counted the victims as the smoke faded and disappeared from chimneys up and down the street. For days Wynter stayed in his shop with his son, Sol, making arrows and leaving full quivers outside the door for those who could still move and hunt.

Several days before, when people first showed signs of sickness, Wynter's wife, Ellaster, begged him to take their son and hide in the shop. Wynter provisioned his home and his shop to get through two weeks and kissed his wife and said a tender goodbye to his newborn daughter, imploring the nursemaid to spare no fuel to keep the home warm. He would leave wood, food and water at the door if the weather didn't break. But after nearly a week, the weather was as cold as ever, so when the smoke faded from his own home, Wynter wrapped himself in a long hunter green cloak, thick brown leather gloves lined with fur, and a woolen scarf which he wrapped around his nose and face.

"Sol, stay here, I'll be back soon. I'm going to check on your mother." Wynter wanted Sol to come, so he could cheer his mother, but he was still young, having just passed his eighth year, and in the

3

shop, he was safe. There was food and it was warm and Wynter did not want to risk his son becoming sick. The older man lifted a pack of food and a small bundle of wood and told Sol he would be back within the hour.

The draft coming through the thick maple door to his shop was nothing compared to the fury of the wind that caught his eyes and made them water in seconds. Burying his chin to his chest, Wynter fought against the gale that whipped up bits of dirt and debris along with the snow and ice. It was unlike any weather he had ever seen in nearly a decade on the island. Every year winter was difficult, and every year people died of exposure, hunger, or sickness, but usually they were very young or very old. This year death took no heed of circumstance and claimed everyone with equal measure.

On the street Wynter passed prone bodies half buried with snow gathering in drifts with the wind. Giving them a wide berth, he could see some with swollen limbs bearing signs of sickness and plague that Wynter had seen in other places as a younger man. A few of the bodies were nearly naked despite the cold, dressed only in light linen tunics or bedclothes, a sure sign they suffered from exposure before they died, convinced they were hot and sweaty, even as their bodies froze to death.

Wynter shivered and pulled his thick oiled leather coat tighter around his neck. The bodies were the last straw; he would check on his wife and daughter and bring back more supplies later that day and then he and Sol would pack their belongings, and against all sense, traverse the ice. Crossing to the mainland tempted death. Staying on the island assured it.

The lake surrounding Thrushton was enormous, extending hundreds of miles to the south and several miles east to west. It would take hours of slow and careful walking to make it to the ferry shack on the northeastern corner of the lake.

Staring at his home, Wynter noted the door had shrunk from the cold, leaving a gap around it he could fit his finger in. As he lifted the latch, his heart raced as the battered door creaked open easily. Small, narrow drifts had crept into the house along either side of the door, and underneath and it all scattered like dry leaves when

4

the wind took hold of the door and Wynter was yanked inside. It took a moment for his eyes to adjust from the brightness of the snow outside to the almost total darkness inside. The windows were covered, and the fire had died, but he stayed by the door, dropping a log on the floor and leaving the door open slightly so he could see clearly over the wrap that still covered his face. As his vision adjusted he saw his infant daughter lying motionless in his wife's arms. The nurse-maid was in a chair near the cold, still fireplace, a chunk of wood on her lap, dried blood streaked down her face, and leaking from her eyes and mouth.

Wynter started to move toward his wife and was startled when she held out her hand to stop him. Her hand, he saw, was covered with blistery, puss-filled mounds and her eyes were red, not from crying, but from the growths that had formed there. She was dressed and covered with blankets over her shoulders, but her pale face was tinged with a blue that belied the warmth of her coverings.

"Wynter. Wynter, where is Sol?" she asked.

"He's fine. He's in the shop with the door shut tight and a roaring fire." He nodded toward his daughter and the old woman, "When...?"

"This morning. Wynter, you need to do something for me." Ellaster should have been shaking, her lips and voice quivering from the cold, dead air in the house, but she wasn't. Her shallow breaths caused tiny, wispy, white tendrils of vapor to form with only enough strength to escape her lips. She lowered her hand to her lap and held up a knife. "I can't do it myself," she said. She nodded to a bow and quiver by the door. "You need to stay away. Do it quickly and then take Sol and leave."

"No, Ellaster, I won't."

She pleaded with him and showed him the still form of their newborn daughter. A girl who didn't even have a name.

"I can't."

"You must." Ellaster's words weren't the weak cry for mercy Wynter had heard before. They were a cry for help, but Wynter shook his head against what she begged him to do.

"Don't make me do this myself," she pleaded. "I don't have the strength to do more than linger here and die … in time and in pain. Please, Wynter, help me. Let me rest with our daughter." She stopped pleading only long enough to draw breath and cough up a mouthful of blood that barely moved along her clothing before freezing in place.

Ellaster's pleading continued. His gaze was drawn to her bloody lip and chin as he reached for the bow and fitted an arrow to the string, feeling as if he were watching someone else move his body. Her pleas continued and Wynter realized that what she asked was reasonable. It was the one thing he could do to prove his love and save his son. It was practical. It was necessary. "Do it. Please. I don't want to die like this. It hurts. Our baby is gone. She needs me. Help me. I love you."

Sol pushed open the door as Wynter lowered his bow and he reacted only just in time to stop the boy from rushing to his mother's side. "Sol, I …" but the words didn't come. Sol glared at his father and fled from the house, running down the street away from his father's shop and to the north, to the small bay where the ferries docked in summer. Wynter instinctively grabbed the quiver by the door, shouldered his bow and ran after his son, leaving the bodies of his daughter and wife lying on the bed in a pool of blood, a goose feather arrow still quivering in time with the last pulse of Ellaster's heart.

Wynter called to his son, but the wind blew the words back into his face. Sol reached the shoreline and he looked back once before lowering his head and starting across the lake leaving Wynter no choice but to follow. Had the journey been on land Wynter would have caught his son quickly, but on the ice Sol, who was light and ran with the nimbleness of youth, gained ground on his father leaving only rhythmic clouds of breath as a trail.

But light as he was, Sol's grip on the ice was tenuous and every time Sol fell, Wynter paused, holding his breath and sending a silent prayer to whatever gods might listen that the ice would hold.

Had this been a normal lake, the ice would be feet thick and easily crossed by men and beast. But the Great Lake was fed from an unknown underground source and the water's warmth and odd currents caused the ice to vary greatly in thickness. Rarely was it solid enough for men and never for cattle or horses.

Sol scrambled back to his feet and Wynter heard echoes of his sobs reach him on the wind. The heavier man lumbered on, carefully, slowly making his inexorable way across the expanse linking the island to the mainland.

Wynter didn't know how long he had been chasing Sol, with every fall or crack of the ice, time seemed to stand still. Wynter paused often when the ice shifted or cracked and moved more slowly each time. Sol's cries had stopped, and the boy no longer looked behind him.

After a punishing amount of time, Wynter started to think his son might make it to land. He was three-quarters of the way there, and as the lake got shallower, the ice was more solid, but the lake was very deep – even the shallows were close to shore, dropping off quickly into water far deeper than any man stood. But he was making good time and Wynter believed he would make it to land in a score of minutes if not sooner at the rate he continued to run. Believing this, Wynter slowed his gait, taking care on the ice so that he might join his son on land.

The wind had died down and the lake was still which made the crack sound sharp and painfully loud when it came, like a tree the moment before it breaks its last connection and falls to the ground. When the sound reached Wynter's ears, Sol's arms were already flying up to the sky as his legs were swallowed by the lake. Before his scream died on the ice Wynter was sprinting to save his son.

Closing the distance Wynter slipped and slammed onto the ice, causing a crack to spread several feet in all directions, small spots of water visible near his knee. Unheeding, he scrambled to his feet, propelled by the sight of a small hand, fingers splayed, slowly sinking into the water. Wynter ran several strides and dove toward the hole in the ice, sliding through the water brought to the surface by Sol's collapse, and plunging his left arm into the blisteringly cold water. His arm went numb instantly. Even if he were touching Sol, he doubted he would have felt him. Withdrawing his arm Wynter stared into the water, and as the ripples ceased he thought he could see Sol's face; the young boy's eyes and mouth wide open staring straight up – accusing him of ... everything.

Slowly, carefully, on his hands and knees, Wynter wept, his tears turning quickly to ice as he began his journey to the mainland thinking only of his failure. He crawled toward shore with no feeling in his hands. His eyes were almost closed, eyelids frozen together from the tears and cold. He had failed to protect his daughter. He had failed to protect his wife. He had failed his son so miserably. Wynter vomited on the ice and lay next to the mound of bile, watching the steam rise, reminding him of the guts of an animal, or worse, laid out to the elements.

Part of him wanted to lie there and die, but that was not his nature. He had seen death before and he knew the finality of it. There would be time for remorse later. He would have the rest of his life to deal with the guilt. In the end, it was the guilt that drove him to the shore. Death was too easy – he had to survive so he could live with the guilt. In that way, he might atone for his failures. But he had to survive.

Dragging his bow, he moved forward and paused at every creak and shift in the ice. He spent agonizing breaths in perfect stillness, studying the surface, determining where the ice was thin and where it might hold him. He remained still until the curls of vapor marking his breath were steady before creeping forward again.

Wynter stood only when he made the shore. The hole his son had fallen through was gone, replaced already by a thin layer of ice. He was wet and cold and needed to find warmth, but he stood and mourned for several minutes before his mind reached into his past, to part of his life he had thought buried, and resurrected it, pushing his feelings to the back of his mind and focusing on his task. It was a mental adjustment, he realized, that started when his wife asked him to end her suffering. Wynter's past was never really buried, he knew, it was only waiting for a reason to reassert itself.

On land, Wynter's first action was to hunt – first for dry clothes and then for food, starting with the ferryman's shack where he found empty bottles and flint and tinder to make a fire, and a small stove which he fueled with floor planks from rickety structure, and he ate some moldy food he found in the shack's single cabinet. When he tried to sleep, he was haunted by images of his family and sleep would not come, so he lay awake replaying the events of the day over and over. He couldn't close his eyes without the images of Sol's outstretched hands and his wife's pleading face to torment him. The next day he moved inland thinking perhaps to make his way to the sea, stow aboard a ship, perhaps become a pirate. He was disoriented, hungry, and sleep deprived, and sleeping in the woods on the second night, his haunting dreams gave way to a voice, "*murderer. Killer. Murderer. Killer...*"

When Wynter awoke, he didn't open his eyes. He was warm and could smell bacon and porridge. For a moment he thought he had succumbed to the cold and would end up like those in Thrushton, half-dressed and frozen on the streets. But he pried his eyes open, determined to meet his fate. He was in a small wooden house. It was plain, with dirt floors, and low ceilings, but it was well patched against the cold, and covering him were thick wool blankets that made his skin itch. Underneath the coverings it was so warm he was tempted to go back to sleep, but he listened to the snapping of dry wood on a fire and smelled the pine and smoke. The sounds of the woods were muted by the thick walls, and he could hear the whispered tones of voices conversing nearby. He flexed his hands, happy he had lost none of the feeling in his fingers. On a small stool nearby, he saw his clothes were clean and piled neatly, and his boots were underneath the stool, also clean. He lifted his head to help clear his thoughts and the voices became clearer. They belonged to several people, three at least, he thought, and their tone seemed like that of people whispering for the sake of being considerate. Despite the warmth and comfort, he was thankful for the voices and so he lifted himself up to get out of bed and relay his well wishes and thanks. As he hoisted himself up, a satisfying crack punctured the air as his elbow locked into position. The noise was almost immediately followed by the arrival of a large, bearded man with a wide grin and a mouth half full of grimy teeth and red gums.

"Well, I'm glad to see you're alright then, that was some scare you gave us, it sure was."

"Where am I?"

"You're in Wellsville and you're darned lucky to be here as well. I don't know where you come from, but someone's looking after you. I'm Ned, by the way. Who're you and where you from?"

"Wynter. From Thrushton. How did I get here? Wellsville is miles away from the lake."

"Miles? I should say, more like days. I heard a noise last night and grabbed a big ole rusty spear, thinking maybe you was a bear or something as we could kill and eat. When I opened the door, there you were, lying like you'd crawled to the door, muttering something about Sol, and ice, and arrows. Figured you must have been near dead from the cold so I bundled you up and brought you in here by the fire. Got some breakfast on if you're hungry."

Wynter was famished and he readily accepted the hand Ned offered to help him out of bed. He dressed quickly, relishing the feeling of clean, warm clothes, and then left his room, by moving a piece of cloth hung from the ceiling. He looked at Ned's family and sat on a log bench by a crude cooking fire and rested his elbows on roughly sawn boards. His mouth watered at the food set before him. He ate the boiled fruit, cheese, bread, and bacon and then looked up sharply when he felt the family staring at him. "These here are my kids, Will and Jesra and their mom, Eula, who's cookin' you're tucking into. You sure are hungry Mister Wynter."

Wynter said nothing, but stared at the two children, each older by several years than Sol. The voice came to him as he looked at them, *"Killer. Murderer."* Wynter thanked Ned and his wife and got up to be on his way, looking for his things and reaching for his bow and quiver in a corner.

"Nah. You can't go today," Ned said. "You've slept half the morning; the weather is still storming and you're still only half standin.' Why don't you get some proper rest and tomorrow you can get an early start and make best use of the light. We'll lend you a pack with some food and you can be on your way."

It made sense. He had slept most of the day, but he didn't feel rested. Wynter wasn't sure he ever would be. But he looked at the fire and at Ned, nodded once and silently walked back to his blanket and drifted off to an uneasy sleep.

His wife was waiting for him as he closed his eyes, staring at him. Their daughter wasn't there, but Sol was, sitting on the edge of the bed in their cottage on the island; sitting where his daughter had been, still and lifeless. His wife and son looked at each other once before turning back to him. "*You murdered your son,*" said his wife. "*I asked you to kill me and save Sol and instead you killed us both. What have you done? I only asked you to kill me. Kill me. Kill me. Stop the pain. Make it go away. Let me be with our daughter. Save your son. Please. I love you. Stop the pain...*

The dream was relentless. Wynter saw arrows fly from his bowstring and strike home into the chests and throats of dozens of people. He saw himself through the eyes of unknown people, collecting small packets of coins. He saw himself gutting deer and bear and watching others work with similar skill on those he had killed. Behind all the images, was the incessant voice of his wife, calling out for death to avenge his family. But he knew there was no vengeance unless it would be had on him. "*Kill them, then. Kill all of them. You don't care.*"

Wynter awoke with a start and tried to get his bearings. The full light of the moon through the cabin's small windows created shadows and silhouettes. He wasn't by his own bed. He was standing with a single arrow in his hand, and he strained his eyes and realized there was a pallet in front of him. The thin silver light showed several reedy sticks standing up from the pallet as if they were planted in the ground. Wynter didn't want to accept what his eyes were telling him but all the same he moved forward and out of habit, reached to collect his arrows from the throats, and hearts of Ned and Eula. In a state of shock, he cleaned each shaft and blade on the woolen blanket that covered the couple and then, lifting it by the hem, he covered their heads and made his way to the patch of floor where the children slept. It was silent there too. He examined and

11

removed from their small lifeless forms two kitchen knives and drew up their blankets as well.

Wynter walked, almost as if he were still asleep, back to the cooking area and took as much food and supplies as there were and stuffed it all into the sack Ned was going to prepare for him. Ready for travel, he looked coolly around the cabin and restoked the fire until it blazed orange, and then he lit another fire on the bed of Ned and Eula and another in the kitchen. In a few minutes, the cabin would be a beacon to any neighbor who happened to be awake and Wynter would be gone.

"*You killed the whole family,*" Wynter's wife's voice muttered emotionlessly to him as he walked toward the woods. "*You killed our whole family. Killer. Murderer.*"

Wynter smiled as he walked dismissing his wife's voice in his head as he would ignore the cries of someone else's baby. That's right, he thought, that's what I am. Just what you've asked me to become. Again.

TWO

"I'm heading to the outpost at Steven's Folly with a small supply train. The captain says if there are people who will be useful, I can take a few along."

The words, Lydria knew, were an invitation. Her father, Cargile, was a soldier of Wesolk, and since she was a baby she had followed him wherever he went. She eagerly accepted his invitation and started gathering her needles and thread, and some bits of leather and cloth that might be useful at the Folly.

Since her mother had died bringing her into the world, Lydria had worked in some capacity with her father. When she was young, she carried water or helped the cooks. She was brought up by the wives of soldiers, especially when the army was on the move, who nursed her as a baby and provided for her as they could. But it was Cargile who raised her, and he did it the only way he knew how – like a soldier. She was taught to hunt and fish, how to fight, how to handle a knife and a sword. But her real skill was with a needle, although not in the making and repairing of garments, although she was quite skilled in that regard, but in helping the surgeons sew flesh and muscle. No one was finer with a needle and thread. Soldiers bragged about their fine white scars to peers who possessed huge white masses where their skin had been sewn roughly and hurriedly together by less skilled or more drunk assistants.

A trip to the outpost as seamstress meant work and money, which she saved to help her father for when he was no longer strong enough to swing a sword or wear armor. The trip came on the heels of an unusually long winter that kept both healers and gravediggers busy. After such a hard season, being with the first supply wagons was a wonderful opportunity for Lydria, who would be kept busy every waking hour repairing the uniforms and other clothing of the men at the Folly.

"We'll be leaving in the morning. There will be others with us," Cargile said, winking at his daughter as she sifted through a basket of fabric.

The 'others' were sometimes the betrothed of the soldiers at the Folly, sometimes shop keepers, tinkers, peddlers, cobblers, or cooks. But more often, they were simply women who would make a lot more money over the course of a few days than Lydria ever would. Still, she would make use of her time on the way, making those women loosely-sewn clothing that would turn her a fair profit from their profession as well.

Cargile seemed to read the expression on his daughter's face and smiled. Lydria was a pleasant woman, but not fair. Her fingers were long and thin, perfectly suited to her work, but she would never be mistaken for a frail or fragile woman. She was shorter by a forehead than most women her age, and her hair was dark and straight, matted to her head as if she kept it covered with a helmet. Her mouth was generous, her chin was strong but not masculine, and her cheeks were low, which often made people think she was sad, unless she was smiling.

Being raised in the army Lydria had sensibilities more common among soldiers than wives. Cargile made it a point to often tell her she was pretty, but she knew better. As a seamstress she'd seen the curves that made men think women were pretty. She possessed very narrow hips and a nose that had been broken at least twice. She was, she knew, unremarkable except for her eyes. Her father had often said her eyes were exceptional – "the right as blue as a perfect summer sky, lit by flecks of silver like moonlight; and the left the green of a pine tree in front of a rising sun." It was the closest her father had ever come to being poetic.

"This will be a small company," her father said. She realized he had stopped for a moment as she drifted into her own thoughts. "After this miserable winter, we will be the first of several early wagon trains," he said at last. "Bring what equipment you need. We will be staying at the Folly for a couple days and returning directly. That's our orders."

14

Lydria smiled. One of the things she loved about her father was his simplistic way of looking at everything. It was either this or that, black or white and there was no room for anything in between. He explained to her as a child that orders were to be followed, not questioned. There were people with long titles in grand tents and wearing uncomfortable shoes who asked the questions. When they arrived at the answers, they gave orders. It was simple that way. When too many people had a say, he had told her, competing interests and personalities and emotions, especially emotions, got involved and nothing of note was accomplished. He was a soldier, and simplicity made his life easier. He had opinions, but he didn't share them often with anyone other than Lydria.

The next day they were heading north along a road that followed the Great Lake's shoreline leaving Bayside, the capital city of Wesolk and its relative comfort, to life on the road, hunting, sleeping under crude tents, and living with the land. Lydria knew that life suited her father better than life inside the town's walls. Cargile was telling her of how Wesolk had been created with the help of their ancestors. It was an old story Cargile told every time they left the city, and Lydria was happy to listen if only to watch her father smile as he told it.

Decades earlier Bayside had been a small fishing village, but wars and refugees had brought farmers and trade and some measure of wealth to the area. It had also brought a king - Aric who was the first King of Wesolk.

Aric had united several communities south and east of Bayside and created Wesolk, a sizeable kingdom for himself and his people. Cargile told Lydria that her great, great-grandfather, Carg the Younger, had fought by Aric's side at the Demigod Hills, a small series of foothills to the south of the city, and the scene of the battle that created Wesolk. Soon after Aric took his throne, two princes from the east saw in Aric an easy target. A young king rumored to spend most of his time buried in books, who had just finished a war for existence, would be an easy target, they thought. "They thought wrong!" Both Lydria and Cargile made the announcement in unison, eliciting laughter from the wagons behind them. Cargile always made

15

it a point to say the phrase when he told the story of Carg. The two princes, her father continued, joined Aric in battle in the foothills of the Godsmouth Peaks, at the eastern edge of the plains that marked Wesolk's border at the time.

Learning of the plans for invasion, Carg helped Aric set a series of traps and deftly moved his own army up into the Godsmouth and back along the slopes to come down behind and flank the princes, catching them between the well-provisioned and battle-tested army of Wesolk on the plains, and a mobile force coming down from the mountains behind them, cutting off their supplies and reinforcements.

The battle raged for two days and during the second night, three of the enemy prince's commanders stole away from their lines to meet Carg and sue for peace. Aric told the three commanders to hold their forces from the field, and the next day, the combined might of Wesolk descended upon the fractured army and destroyed it. The princes were taken captive and hung, and the commanders given dukedoms in the lands of the former princes in return for fealty to Aric. The borders of Wesolk now extended east across the Godsmouth to the shores of the Eastern Sea.

Now, with Aric's great-grandson, Ahlric, on the throne, Bayside was developing into a large, walled city with a small but capable standing army. At the center of the city was a great keep and what would soon be the largest castle north of the palaces of the kings of the southern deserts.

Lydria leaned across her horse and patted her father on the knee and thanked him for the story before turning away and riding to the back of the wagon trains.

From a distance, Lydria could be mistaken for a man. Her shoulders were broader than most women, and the way she sat a horse, and even walked, gave her shape no distinctiveness from a distance. There were two other women in the party, who rode on the supply wagons to 'keep the drivers company' and they wore plain linen dresses with the sleeves pulled up above the elbows, tied with bits of colored yarn. Neither wore shoes, although Lydria knew the luggage they shared contained dresses and shoes and even some face paint which they used while they worked. Lydria laughed to herself as she considered that sitting next to the wagon drivers they might be at work already. She nodded to them and they smiled back, happy to have another woman along who wasn't in competition with them for money.

The trip to Steven's Folly would take more than a week. It was a pleasant journey and the weather atypically fine for the middle of spring; a blessing after the devastatingly cold and long winter. By the lake shore the fires of Bayside were kept strong for months in the face of severe snow. In the Godsmouth's to the east, even as the land hinted at the edge of summer, the snows were still far lower on the peaks than they generally were for the season.

The riding was uneventful, broken only by the occasional visit from a scout, a hunter, or a resident of an outlying town looking for news and an opportunity to sell wares or food. Cargile was always ready and generous to townsfolk who approached the wagons and he never failed to tell his soldiers how the people outside the city provided the food and labor that made Wesolk possible. "We can never forget," Cargile would say, "that when we kneel to the king, we also kneel to his subjects."

The group moved slowly across the muddy track following the contour of the lake and it was another three days before they arrived at the ferry launch, the closest point between the mainland and the island town of Thrushton. Despite the amount of cargo that transited the dock to and from the island each year, it was barely more than shack that the merchants of Wesolk had begged their king to enlarge for years. Still, it served its purpose, so the king saw no reason to spend money to make it larger, and the merchants couldn't decide among themselves who would pay for repairs, so the launch remained a perpetual ruin.

As the road beyond the ferry was narrower and less well maintained, Cargile ordered the wagons to stop while he spoke to the ferry master who was sitting near a dilapidated dock that looked as if the past winter had only just left standing. The docks tree stump pilings were rotting and tilting in odd directions, causing the deck to roll in much the same way a ferry might in rough waves. There was no ferry in the water, but Cargile could make out the outline of the craft underneath heavy canvas sheets, pulled a short distance onto the shore nearby.

Cargile took a small flask from a pocket Lydria had sewn on the inside of his tunic and offered it to a bearded old man staring out at the water. "A little something to take the chill off, eh?"

The old man hardly moved, only his arm and hand made their way up to grasp the small, hardened leather container, which he lifted even further in thanks before taking a long pull. His eyes never came off the water line – even as he emptied Cargile's flask.

"What are you looking for, Lem?" Cargile's tone was gentle with the old man, but he was genuinely curious. Old Lem had run the ferries for years and was usually good for a story, a bit of fish, and a smoke if one had the patience for the stories. But the old man continued to watch the water like a statue.

"Thing is," Lem said at last, in the whistling punctuated voice of an elderly man with a shortened capacity for breath. "T'aint seen a boat yet this year. Should'a been boats by now. Always boats as soon as the ice breaks." And then he looked up, and Cargile met the man's eyes and together they looked back to the water.

Lydria watched the exchange between the two men as she hitched her horse to a tree. It was mid-afternoon, and they had only a few more hours of daylight so it was unlikely they'd find a better spot to rest for the evening. The landing also brought the possibility of trade and news, so even the women riding in the carts were busy setting up camp for the evening, gathering wood for a fire and preparing food. Still not being able to hear her father's discussion, Lydria moved to join her father and ask Lem if he'd like to join them for supper.

"I thought a'first the weather musta damaged their boats some," Lem supplied to Cargile after a thoughtful silence. "When a storm as ter'ble as what we got here comes through and as fast as it did, chances are boats aren't in, and some are gonna git crushed in the ice." There was a pause as if Lem were contemplating what he was going to say next, and Cargile let the pause run a long while before the old man continued his thought as if uninterrupted. "That dohne 'splain though why they ain't used their spare boats. They got plenty a' spare boats. Always 'ave spare boats, do islanders."

Lydria had joined them but Cargile was so engaged he didn't hear her approach. Lem turned to look at the girl and saw she was intent on the island, and he saw the brow above her blue eye arch upwards and her mouth open just a little as if she wanted but were afraid to say something. "Your girl figured it out Cargile," Lem said with a gap-toothed grin. "Tell him what you see, girly."

"There's no smoke."

"That's right." Lem nearly shouted the words, as if excited to have his guess confirmed and not be thought a lunatic. "The ice broke up more than a week ago, so I say to my wife, 'Murnah, I've got to get to the landing to see what it is the islanders will be needing'."

Lem was at the landing every year as soon as the ice broke, waiting on the first small boat from the island with a list of provisions. He'd have someone, usually his son, go to Bayside to gather the supplies while he got the ferry ready for the trip to Thrushton.

"No one has gone out there, have they?" Cargile asked, an edge of concern and firmness in his voice that demanded a no-nonsense answer.

Lem was back to staring at the island and humming lightly to himself, his tongue kept his bottom lip in motion as if he were trying to work a piece of food from between his teeth. "T'aint nobody been out there from this landing since fall. Our only boat is there," he said, pointing to the canvas roof Cargile had noted earlier. "And between us, young Cargile, I t'aint stupid. I know the signs of a plague when I see it." He handed the empty flask back to Cargile who mutely accepted it, gave it a wistful shake, and tucked it back into his tunic.

The camp was set up and a fire lit. The two women and the wagon drivers were becoming fast friends and Lydria noted the women didn't have their own tents set up. She gave them a smile and a wink by way of congratulations which they returned with wry smiles. While she didn't want to be in their line of work, she didn't disapprove of it altogether. You worked at something or you didn't eat, as her father had told her. It was as simple as that.

After giving Cargile back his flask, Lem took two fishing lines from his shack which he and Lydria's father cast into the water from the edge of the decrepit dock. Lem happily assured the group that if he couldn't catch dinner he would clean the dishes. Within minutes the wagon drivers and soldiers were placing bets on who would catch more dinner, Cargile or Lem. The last bet was barely in place before Lem had two large trout flopping on the dock and had cast his line back into the water for a third. "I t'aint got no 'tention of doin' dishes," he whistled to Cargile.

The drivers had bet on Lem in the hopes that the king's uniformed men might pay for their nights' diversion, so when the old man called out that he had a big one on the line, they cheered out loud. Lydria laughed as she raced back to the dock to gather the fish flopping in a small bucket near her father's feet.

"What in the name of every bastard in the kingdom do you have there, Lem?" Cargile reached down to help the old man bring the line in and he called to Bracknell and Josen, the soldiers who traveled with them. The soldiers were on their way before Cargile finished his sentence and he soon fell to his stomach and thrust his hand into the lake, dragging something to shallower water where Lydria and the soldiers were waiting. As Cargile moved toward the shore, they all saw the pale, bloated body of a person. The torso, legs, arms and even the face were large and expanded from water, but the skin was mostly intact, save some from the fingers and nose where most guessed the fish had had a nibble.

Moving the body gently to shore, Cargile ordered Bracknell to fetch an old blanket. Handling the body was delicate as the waterlogged skin collapsed under all but the slightest of touches, and the smell was like a farm at slaughter time, and worse for knowing where the smell came from.

"This looks like a boy," Cargile said. "But I don't see any visible signs of plague on him. Do you think he was trying to find help?"

"Or escape," offered Lem. "Musta fallen through the ice."

Cargile looked to his men to see if they had any other theories before carefully searching the boy's clothes. He found several bits of string, a few feathers, and a small, much-used knife which he placed on the dock. Using a piece of hemp canvas, he gingerly rolled the boy up and onto a small makeshift pallet Josen had put together. As veterans of several campaigns the soldiers knew how to bury people, even if they couldn't care for them. The men carried the pallet inland and set to work digging a shallow grave in the still hard ground and covered the body with rocks.

Cargile gathered the contents of the boys' pockets and after Josen and Bracknell finished with the grave, they gathered around the fire where Cargile passed the items around for everyone to examine. The items reminded him of something, but nothing he could put his finger on. Likely, it didn't matter. Any family the boy had was likely dead in Thrushton. There were no suspicious holes in the body that would point to murder. It was just bad luck and a poor decision to cross the lake.

"I've seen this before," said Barn, the eldest of the drivers. A short man who had become hunched from sitting over a set of reins for more than 30 years, Barn was quiet and known within his trade as being an honest man who wouldn't take a half copper more than his load was worth. It had made him enemies among the less scrupulous wagon masters, but it won him many friends among those who paid for the service. Lydria knew from her father that silent patronage had kept him alive on at least two occasions. "I've seen many a bundle of supplies and weapons loaded onto and off my wagons, and unless I'm very much wrong... he walked to Josen's tent and picked up a short arrow meant for the small cavalry bow the man had tied to his saddle. He handed the arrow and the pocket's contents to Cargile.

"There was a bowyer on the island who did work for the king's troops supplying arrows and some of the nicest bows you've ever seen. It was likely he had made the arrow you're holding now, but I don't know his name," Barn said. Josen studied the items and his own arrow and after a moment's consideration provided Wynter's name.

21

"There are only a few bowyers worth a silver in Bayside and most use feathers from the wild turkey that roam the countryside," Josen explained. "Wynter used mostly goose feathers. It's possible this boy knew Wynter."

With the matter settled, the company ate the fish Lem had caught and sat by the fire for a long time speculating on what may have happened and what the situation on the island was now. "There's nothing we can do about it," Cargile announced. "We'll make our report when we return to Bayside. We can't do much for the dead, but the living need sleep."

THREE

The next day they left the docks and continued their journey, their path curving to the northwest following the taper of the lake into a flat land of fields marking the subtle beginnings of a steady incline into a series of small hills.

Small stone walls carved grey scars into the landscape in the flat space between the lake and tundra to the north. Generations of farmers divided the land into small holdings. While nominally part of Wesolk, the northern areas, including the tundra and the small fishing villages in the more northern wastes, were free, but had been given the protection of Wesolk to spur trade and prevent hostile kingdoms from creating holdings in the sparsely populated area.

In the summer cows grazed among the red clover, wildflowers and the patches of wild blackberries that created their own thorny barriers in the flats, but now they buried their snouts in the ground, gathering what early spring grass they could find. Across the fields to the west and past the Folly, the woods were largely unexplored. Steven's Folly was meant to be a first tenuous step into expanding Wesolk's reach. To the north past the fields, the flat land continued, and forests became less dense as the ground slowly turned to tundra and eventually perpetual frost and snow.

As the western hills began to take over from the lowlands, their travel along the road slowed as mud gripped the horses' hooves and sucked at the wooden wagon wheels. Small paths broke off the main road leading to farms where women and boys chopped and stacked wood for their homes and for large fires in small buildings near the wood line among stands of maples.

On the third day after leaving Lem they started to notice the incline toward the hills. The pitch of the land meant less pooling of water and so while the ground was slick, it wasn't as bad as the thick mud that had slowed them previously. However, the trail narrowed as it entered a forest that grew thicker as they moved further from the shore of the lake. Lydria knew the trail well enough to understand they were within two to three days of the Folly. They would travel and sleep under these trees until they reached a clearing that was the beginning of a series of small farms leading to a hamlet outside the garrison.

In the morning sun, the buds were just starting to open in the trees and soon the forest road would be covered under a canopy of leaves and feel much more confined. Lydria was enjoying the warmth of the sun that filtered through the trees onto her face and arms when she felt a subtle shift of the horse underneath her. Her father and the soldiers noticed it too – as Bracknell started to put some space between himself and the others. Lydria calmly stroked the brown coat of her horse, "you feel it too, don't you," she said quietly to the animal. "There's something out there." As she spoke Cargile lifted his hand, telling the wagons to stop. It took several moments for the horses and wagons to stop their movement and for the creaking of wood and leather to fade.

Lydria looked at her father not daring to move the two horse lengths to his side. He cupped a hand to his ear, but she heard nothing. That was the point, she realized. No birds, no slight movement of small animals in the undergrowth – even the breeze seemed to have stopped. It was spring, and the smaller animals searching for food wouldn't be so easily silenced by a small group of people and horses.

Cargile motioned for Josen and Bracknell to take out their bows, but he needn't have bothered, the pair were already sliding their weapons to the fronts of their bodies and pulling their first arrows from the quivers by their sides. The wooden shafts of the arrows scraped against the sides of the hardened leather quivers and seemed to scream into the distance even though it was a small noise. Josen's attention was drawn to a spot in the trees and Lydria tried to follow his gaze. She caught a glimpse of movement that was followed by the sound of an arrow striking home and then the sound of Josen falling from his horse. After that the forest was full of sound.

Bracknell spurred his mount and bolted forward, missing by a heartbeat a second arrow that buried itself in a tree after his passing. Cargile shouted orders for the group to take cover. Putting the wagons between themselves and the forest where the arrows had come from, the wagon drivers and women took cover, looking to Cargile who had turned his horse behind a wagon and was removing everything that hung from his armor that might get caught in a bush or hinder his movement. The soldier was murmuring to himself as he worked, counting Lydria realized, and he offered his daughter a wink to reassure her, but his lips never stopped moving.

Lydria understood his plan. They couldn't continue with a killer in the woods at their backs so he and Bracknell were going into the woods to find the archer. He motioned with his hands that he wanted her to get the group to the Folly.

The archer was shooting from a slight rise in the woods, so Cargile and Bracknell would be running uphill, but from different directions. Bracknell had moved down the road and would have, Lydria knew, dismounted and started moving toward the assailant. Cargile's job was to wait a certain amount of time and attack from the front to give the archer an immediate threat to focus on. It wasn't the best plan, but Lydria knew it was the fastest plan to execute in an ambush. Now all her father had to do was not get shot.

Cargile sprinted off up the hill and into the trees never running in a straight line for more than three steps and passing behind as many trees as possible on his way up the hill. Lydria saw two arrows sink into trees within a stride of her father passing them, but she was able to discern the archer's general location from the flight of the arrows and yelled directions to her father based on forest landmarks like a fallen elm or a large boulder.

Her shouts caught the attention of the archer who sent a shaft in her direction. Lydria ducked her head behind the wagon wheel she knelt behind as an arrow buried itself in the rim of the wheel she was holding. The arrow didn't sound like it impacted the wheel at first. The noise wasn't the sharp solid sound she thought it would be – it was as though the arrow hit a waterlogged wheel and not the dry wheel she was gripping with her left hand – was still gripping with her left hand. As Lydria tried to move her hand, a sharp pain told her an arrow had caught at least one of her fingers.

Peeking around the wheel and looking up, she saw the arrowhead had all but removed her left index finger, going through the bone and pinning the finger to the wheel by a small chunk of skin. Not being able to move her finger Lydria pulled out the arrow and brought her hand near her chest, watching as the wreck of flesh above her knuckle pulsed blood. With little choice, she took a small blade from her belt and finished the arrow's job, slicing off what remained of her finger, trying to stifle the pain growing inside her. Without thinking why, she wrapped the finger in a piece of cloth and put the loose digit in pouch and set about wrapping her blood covered hand. While she did, she saw the arrow she had dropped by her knees and noticed for the first time it was made with goose feathers.

Lydria was tying off the bandage on her hand when she heard her father speaking with Bracknell in the woods as they came down the hill. Their tone suggested the danger had passed and several minutes later three men made their way down the hill, the two soldiers flanking a thin man being held and pulled along by his biceps. As they walked toward the wagons Cargile saw his daughter's blood-stained and bandaged hand and pushed the prisoner forward, tripping him at the same time so that the bound man landed face-first on the hard-packed path. "Are you hurt badly?" he asked.

"Just a finger," Lydria responded, deciding not to tell him she had lost it completely. With Josen dead and the murderer caught, any additional revelations at this point might push her father to institute 'field justice' here and now. She didn't think he'd be wrong for doing it as the man had obviously killed Josen, but though her father would never admit it, killing people didn't sit well with him.

Cargile at home was a different person than Cargile in camp. He had terrible dreams and woke in cold sweats, sometimes shouting, sometimes swearing, sometimes swinging, but always, when it was over, crying. Always. He taught Lydria by, and he lived by, black and white principles. His dreams, he believed, were merely a black and white response to those decisions. The price one had to pay for the actions they took.

Cargile and Bracknell inspected the prisoner's bonds and tied his ankles. Setting him by a tree away from the main group before checking on the drivers and women and then tending to the task of wrapping Josen's body in a blanket and gathering shovels to dig another grave.

Lydria took a short sword from her horse and sat by a tree near the bound man to guard him until her father or Bracknell decided what to do with him. It was likely that he would be bound further and secured to the inside of one of the wagons and taken to the Folly. Lowering herself slowly with her right hand so as not to hit the tender flesh of her left hand, Lydria remembered the man's name. Wynter was short for a man, but still several inches taller than her. His face was gaunt and hollow, it was the face of a soldier who had spent too much time in battle, too much time without food, and too long without a night uninterrupted by violence and pain. The skin around his eyes was dark, limp and deep-seated, but they were focused. His brown eyes moved back and forth around the camps, settling for a moment on a person or thing, and then moving on. Wynter was taking in details, and Lydria tried to follow his glances to see what he was looking at.

The group was small, weapons were few, and most of the company could be disregarded in a fight. It was obvious they were from Bayside based on the uniforms of Cargile and Bracknell and the direction of travel and loaded wagons would make the Folly a likely destination. As Lydria watched him return again and again to the wagons, she thought he was estimating how little money the group had as there were no carriages, no tables or chairs, none of the trappings that go along with traveling nobility. There were no servants. He then turned his attention to the forest and Lydria noticed the stillness in the woods, like a shadow descending among the noise. There were still no birds singing, and no small animals moving in the underbrush. Looking down from where they had come, there was a gap in the trees that showed a meadow in the flatlands. Cows could just be seen through the gap, like looking at a farm through a hole in a fence. It was a lovely scene, Lydria thought, although it was odd the cows were lying down in such fine weather.

27

Lydria's gaze left the cows and moved back to Wynter who was closing his left eye and working his way through camp again with only his right eye open, as if sighting an arrow. The man took no notice of her as she tried to guess his age. He was not young – the beard covering his neck was streaked with grey and it was full along his jawline and chin but mostly ignored his cheeks. Finally, as she moved up Wynter's face to his eyes, Lydria noticed that he noticed her.

His gaze was empty. Despite his methodical accounting of the camp, his eyes betrayed no emotion. They were the eyes of the hunted, who knew the end game and only waited for it to play out. "Yes, I will kill them all, dear," he said, looking directly at Lydria. "I'm a killer, a murderer." His eyes never left Lydria's and his face was expressionless, as if he were reciting words back to someone.

"Who are you talking to?" Lydria asked, gripping her sword hilt more tightly than she was taught and looking at his bound hands and feet which hadn't moved. He wasn't trying to escape.

"Oh, I'm talking to her," he said. "She wants me to kill you all and I have to do it. I don't have a choice. She won't leave me alone otherwise. I owe her that much."

Lydria opened her mouth to ask who the woman was, but before she said a word, Wynter's eyes grew wide as if startled, his pupils enlarging and crowding out the brown to leave his eyes nearly black. Lydria followed his gaze to the meadow beyond the trees and a growing darkness in the sky that left a trail of dense smoke in its wake. "You have to let me go," were the last words she heard.

FOUR

Lydria opened her eyes and raised herself to a sitting position and sneezed. Her nose and throat were dry and clogged with dirt. She stood up and held a finger to her nose to clear each nostril and then cleared her throat and spit up more dirt. Around her the forest was mostly gone. The sky was dark, as dirt and dust fell from the sky. Her body ached from being thrown but it was difficult to say how far, as points of reference no longer existed.

The devastation was immense. In army sieges, she had seen acres of land burned by retreating forces and then made worse by conquering ones who tore it up with feet and hooves, filth and waste. But nothing prepared her for what was left of the rolling hills and the gap that opened to the meadow so far away. Trees for furlongs were lying on the ground as if pushed down by a giant foot making a path in the forest and a deep trench stretched from the distant meadow to end in a pit nearby.

Lydria staggered in the direction of the pit and halted halfway as a wave of dizziness washed over her. She reached a hand to her head and felt blood, she was still reeling from the impact and noticed her footsteps were almost silent – everything, in fact, was muted. The only sound she heard clearly was the rapid, deep thumping of her heart. Staggering on, she tripped over half-buried tree branches and ducked under the roots of pine trees that reached out for the sky. Stopping briefly to clear her nose and throat again, Lydria rested her hands on her knees recoiling from the pain of her finger as it lanced into her knee and looked away from the pit. The trench that had devastated the forest was at least a hundred feet wide, and the walls of the trench got deeper until when she reached the pit, she could see the bottom at least ten feet below at the bottom of dirt walls that were nearly vertical.

As she cleared her nose again, the smell of soil and bark reached her, and the sun hung in the sky like a dull yellow smudge, hidden behind the dust that continued to fall. Lydria pulled a cloth

29

from inside her tunic and tied it around her face. How did she survive? There was no sign of her father or Bracknell, or the others. No horses, no wagons, no fire, no tents, no bodies – nothing except an upturned forest.

The dull crack of a branch startled Lydria and she jerked her head up to try to find the sound, excited that she had heard anything at all. Across the crater before her she saw a movement, and a shadow. Hope grabbed her, and she stood on her toes hopeful to see something more telling. Someone was still alive, and finally she made out the blurred silhouette of a figure through the falling debris - dropping to its knees in the unnatural twilight. The figure raised an arm and dropped it again. Hoping it was her father, Lydria shifted her weight in preparation to run around the rim of the crater to join him, but instead, her weight triggered the collapse of the crater wall and she tumbled to the bottom.

The fall seemed to take far longer than the mere seconds it must have been, and when she came to a stop she lay on her back coughing and staring at the brown sky above her. Within a minute of her fall, from the corner of her eye, Lydria saw something slide down the far side of the crater wall from where she fell.

Pushing herself to her knees, she noticed the figure stumbling toward a blue glow at the center of the crater and she started moving toward it herself, forgetting the danger the unknown person may pose to her. At that moment, for reasons she didn't understand, the only thing that mattered was reaching the glow. Crawling on her hands and knees, oblivious of the sticks and rocks and the driving pain of her left hand, she neared the crater's center and lunged.

There were two dense areas of light and as Lydria's hand reached out to one, another hand collapsed over the other. As she closed her fingers around the light, she was thrown away from the center of the crater to land with her back against the dirt wall. Lydria's breath left her and she lay in the dirt, staring at a stick the width of her arm that had narrowly missed impaling her, but giving it no more than a seconds' thought because her attention was again

30

drawn to a blue glow laying in the dirt near her left hand. It was a small pulsing sphere and it seemed to invite her to take it.

The bandages of her left hand were mere tatters of cloth, but most of the bleeding had stopped. Using her three good fingers and thumb, she reached out and wrapped her palm around the sphere and her world changed again.

Her vision was clear and well-defined as though she could see further into the distance. The dirt that continued to fall was moving very slowly toward the ground, and she opened her mouth in wonder as each grain of dirt drifted slowly past her eyes as it fell, tumbling and losing pieces of itself as it made its way to the ground.

In her hand she saw a stone, a brilliant blue sphere, and watched as it slowly broke, a piece of it falling onto her palm and passing through her skin in a faint blue mist. The remaining stone turned to liquid in her hand, swirling once before reforming into a complete, slightly smaller sphere, with a series of fine silver lines segmenting the stone into fourteen pieces.

As quickly as it started, it was over, and time returned to its normal speed and Lydria's vision was once again clouded by falling dirt. Across the crater she saw the figure who held what she presumed was a similar stone, but it was not Cargile, as she had hoped, it was Wynter, who looked more injured and beaten than before. His body was contorted like something was broken and he seemed to be in a great deal of pain. Lydria was encouraged by the thought.

Struggling to stand, Lydria made out the details of Wynter's face as he stood opposite her – separated by dozens of feet of blackness and waves of heat that rose from the center of the pit. Wynter leered at her and wiped a wrist, a torn rope still hanging from it, across his lips to clear them of dirt before licking them with a bloody tongue. Lydria gripped the stone in her left hand and reached for her sword. Before she moved her arm an inch, she realized it wasn't there. She had been holding it when she was thrown, and it was now likely buried beneath the trees.

Wynter's eyes were wide and his mouth hung open, not in the disgusting lecherous way she had seen from men in the taverns, but in the awe-struck way children look when they see something for the first time. Lydria was now sure he had a piece of the stone and had seen the world as she had seen it.

"Kill the girl." Wynter spoke the words, not to Lydria, but to himself, she realized. Lydria cast her gaze around the pit for a weapon and finding none she started to look for paths of escape when Wynter spoke again. "No, too tired. Injured, and I just used my last arrow." He said the last with a smile directed at Lydria and looked down to untie the frayed rope from his wrist.

His voice lowered and sounded grittier than she thought it should have from someone in his condition. "No, not now. It will have to wait, unless - you, girl, be a good girl and fetch my last arrow." He inclined his head toward where Lydria had seen the silhouette earlier and he gave her a wicked smile and looked her straight in the eyes. "I won't kill you yet. But I will find you. You can't hide your eyes. I will find you. I've given my word and I will find you and I will kill you. All of you."

He glared at Lydria for long seconds before turning to walk down the trench, holding his glowing blue sphere in his left hand and stooping for a branch to use as a walking stick with his right. As he began to move away, a burst of light broke through the haze around Wynter's head and Lydria saw a bright band of blue outline Wynter's neck. He turned briefly, raised his hand to his neck, raised an eyebrow and then shuffled on, limping down the trench on his makeshift crutch. As he walked his features disappeared in the haze, but the dimming blue glow around his neck allowed Lydria to follow him as he stumbled on until he was far enough away where he could step over the shallower walls of the trench. The light soon faded from his neck, leaving only his shadowy figure haltingly struggle over the mass of broken trees on his way toward the boreal forests of the frozen north.

Lydria was used to judging people underneath their rags, seeing the person underneath the cloth and Wynter's ragged clothing and malnourished face did not haunt her thoughts. Wynter was not what was under his clothes, but what was behind his eyes. His eyes were those of a dead man, yet they were alive in awareness and suspicion. Wynter was a mystery but she was sure he was a thing borne of malice. Lydria knew everyone had a weakness to be exploited, but Wynter was different. He was savage but not in the way of animals. He was intelligent and thoughtful and deliberate. It was a dangerous combination and Lydria couldn't suppress a shiver. For the first time in her life, she feared a man.

A tingling sensation followed by a bright light similar to the one that lit up Wynter pulled Lydria's thoughts away from him and to herself. Lifting her hands to her throat she felt her skin under her chin and moving her hands lower, she contacted a smooth surface about three fingers wide over her throat. Tracing the surface around her neck with her fingertips she realized she was wearing a collar, only it wasn't a collar – it was part of her as much as her own skin. She held her right index finger with the pad of her thumb and flicked the collar with her fingernail and was rewarded with a sharp rap, like she had banged it against stone. She picked up a rock and scraped it against her skin and then against her throat. She could feel the sharp edge of the rock make its way down her sweaty, grimy neck until it reached the collar where she felt nothing but heard the click of two hard objects making contact.

Confused but with nothing else to do, Lydria looked around the crater and began a scrambling ascent of the far wall using half-buried tree roots to climb. When she reached the top, she surveyed the carnage again and spied a small movement from a pile of debris a few yards away. It wasn't wind. The movement was unmistakably something mostly buried under the trees and dirt – most likely it was someone's hand or finger, but as she moved closer, she half stopped in surprise. Amid the destruction, there was a small animal, a bobcat cub she would have never noticed had it not moved.

Bobcats were rarely seen in the wild and Lydria knew most hunters went their entire lives perhaps only glimpsing one as it ran away. Smaller than catamounts, bobcats were still deadly hunters, but as Lydria moved branches and dirt, the sound that came from the cub was anything but ferocious. It was mewling with rasping breaths. She took it by the scruff and removed it from the rubble and sat down with the small kitten in her lap, moving her fingers carefully along its body, looking for broken bones.

"Well, boy, what's wrong with you?" Lydria spoke out loud to hear herself and found the sound still thick and low. "You've broken a bone in your back leg, but I'm not sure what I can do. I can splint it, there's enough wood, but I've never splint a cat before." Lydria was exhausted. With Wynter gone, she knew she had to find food and water and a place to rest; but first she had to tend to the cub and suppress a desire to curl up and sleep herself. She lowered her head toward the cat who was purring lightly as it relaxed in her lap and thought about what she would need to do to help the animal. She closed her eyes and stroked the cat absently, thinking about how she would set the bone of a man, when she felt a warmth in her hands and saw a warm yellow light behind her closed eyelids. She wondered for a moment if she had missed a wound and whether her hands were bleeding. Not wanting to see her own hands filled with blood again, Lydria opened her eyes in time to see the dimming of a faint blue glow around the cub, and feel a painful pressure behind her eyes, before closing them again and falling to her side.

FIVE

A splash of cool water startled Lydria into wakefulness and a voice broke through the dullness of her ears telling her to wake up. By the time she had wiped away the light mud on her eyelids created from the falling dust and the water, she felt a small warm weight on her stomach. She pushed her arms underneath her to lift her torso and blinked away the water and dirt to reveal the cub resting on her stomach. When she stopped, the bobcat rose and licked her nose, rubbing his forehead under her chin. Lydria noticed he was walking well and that he had a thin blue collar like a tattoo of gemstones barely perceptible under his fur.

Standing next to Lydria, holding a dripping water skin in one hand a hunting spear in the other, was a willowy female wearing leather breeches. She had a delicately curved bow on her back and she smiled when Lydria's eyes found her own. The woman's own eyes widened as they glimpsed the blue and green orbs staring back at her, and she proffered a hand to help Lydria to her feet and said simply, 'friend.'

The women stared at each other for some seconds before they were interrupted by the cub that jumped onto Lydria's shoulders, startling both women. Lydria reached her left hand to stroke the cub's chin and the newcomer pulled back half a step, looking from Lydria's neck to the cub's.

The cub was kitten-like in his appreciation for Lydria and purred loudly when she stroked him. For a cat that relied on elusiveness and cunning, she thought it was out of their character to remain in the company of humans regardless of how much help she had provided.

"He must have lost his mother," Lydria declared, trying to reassure the strange woman with a friendly tone.

"You are his mother now. You must name him. I am called Haidrea and in this place of desolation, you are the only two living. You must come with me to my home in Eifynar."

35

The mention of Eifynar startled Lydria who had heard of the place only rarely from her father. Although known to the people of Wesolk, the Eifen people were much like the cub on her shoulder - rarely seen, preferring to stay deep in the woods and interact little with the people of the Wesolk. Lydria looked at the woman more closely, and saw a story come to life. The Eifen were said to be slim and graceful, blessed with a cunningness of woodcraft that was unmatched. Lydria's father had told her stories of how the Eifen moved nearly silently through the forests and helped Aric win his kingdom by protecting their homes, and therefore Wesolk's northern flank. The Eifen did not fight for any but themselves, but their reputation as archers of unmatched skill was the stuff of legends.

Haidrea's face was delicate but hard, fine lines mixed with a rugged determination, and her ears were not rounded at the top, but extended further from the woman's head than did Lydria's. As she stared, Lydria was startled and amazed to Haidrea's ears move, back to front, much like those of the cat on her shoulder.

"Am I the first Eifen you've met, then?"

"Yes, I'm sorry. I don't mean to stare. Your ears…"

"And your eyes. We are what we are made and no more. Come, we can speak more when we are away from here."

Lydria steadied the cat on her shoulders where it lay easily, its small, needle-like claws finding purchase in her clothes and skin. In a few months the cub's claws and size would make riding on her shoulders impractical if not impossible, but for now he was small enough that it was only a slight discomfort. And his purring was very soothing.

Haidrea motioned that they should walk east when Lydria paused to look at the wasteland of trees, dirt and rock. "There is something…" Lydria said, and Haidrea turned and followed her back toward the pile of rubble just past the crater. "I saw someone here before I fell into the crater…" Lydria picked her way through the tangled mass of branches and dirt to the place she had seen.

"What do you hope to find?" Haidrea asked.

"My father. Someone. I don't know, but I saw someone here."

"How did you see someone in all this?"

Lydria didn't answer. Her eyes were locked on an incongruous site among the wreckage – a thin piece of wood sticking straight up amidst the tumbled branches. It was an arrow, and she remembered the shadow's arm raising and falling, she knew what the find meant and retched a little before moving forward. A little closer and she saw a dirty and bloody hand and then the neck where the goose-feathered arrow was buried. It was her father, and from the fresh pool of blood sprinkled with the still falling dust, Lydria realized he was alive when Wynter found him. Was this why Wynter let her live, she wondered, because he had already killed her father and wanted her to live with the pain of knowing who was responsible?

Cargile's face was bruised but intact. Stroking his grey hair, Lydria murmured 'father' and uncurled the dead fingers to hold them in her own. The cub, sensing her emotion, climbed down from her shoulders and sat quietly to the side.

"Your father's spirit is part of the world now," Haidrea said after several heartbeats of silence and stillness. "He will watch over all who come here, and it will be a sacred place. There is power here. I can feel it, as can the cub."

Lydria mutely nodded. She was preparing to rise when her hand reached out and snapped off the feathered end of the arrow and tucked it along with the stone into the pouch on her belt. She tapped her shoulder for the cub to jump up. "Why did you come to me in the crater – how did you know?"

Haidrea paused before she spoke. "I heard your group and made to see who passed along the trail. I was there," she pointed to the east and south where the standing forest was closest. "I was there in the nearest standing trees behind a large rock when the earth was thrown into the air and the trees fell. I too was thrown but was not seriously injured. When I got up I saw the man moving and then you. I watched as you ran into the hole and as he followed. I waited. When he left, I let him go. And then I saw you gather this cub in your arms and … fall. So, I came to help."

"Why?"

"The land and the animals can tell us much if we take the time to listen. It is the same with people if we are open to the signs Eigrae provides and take the time to watch. The man has a dark spirit that seeks to harm. You have no such spirit for destruction … though I believe you capable of it."

Lydria nodded slowly. She had made up her mind to trust Haidrea, as she knew she could do little else. If she had meant to harm her, she could have easily done so. "The man's name is Wynter and he has killed several people, and he promises to kill more."

"Then we will go to Eifynar and you will speak to our chief and our Graetongue and they will provide guidance for you."

"May I bring my cat?" Lydria looked at Haidrea with a smile, the animal curled happily around her neck, its nose pressed against her chin, thumping her nose and mouth as he banged his stubby tail against her face.

"We do not own animals – they have spirits of their own and they will do as they will. It is more likely to say that this cat has you. I'm sure you both will be received well, for it is not often we have visitors, much less someone with two souls." Haidrea looked pointedly at Lydria's eyes. "Nor have we ever seen a person or a cat who wears a collar such as yours, although I feel it is safe to believe the man Wynter may have one as well, as each of you were bathed in a light for a short time before the blue glow left your neck." Haidrea motioned at the small animal and Lydria nodded for her to touch him. She stroked the animal lightly but Lydria noticed she took great pains to not touch the cat's collar.

Lydria reached for a stick to help her travel. She was sore and the pain from the impact that destroyed the forest and the bruises from being repeatedly thrown to the ground had begun to make her stiff. "What do you mean, two souls?" She pulled herself upright on the stick and the cat shifted slightly to maintain his balance.

"You have twin souls. The caring soul of a blue-eyed spirit, and the dangerous soul of a green-eyed spirit. It is very rare. Most people have the brown-eyed soul of balance." She said no more about it.

Haidrea led the way with Lydria struggling to keep up. The Eifen made barely a sound, walking lightly on the balls of her feet through the limb-strewn landscape along the trench and into the standing forests beyond. Her head moved slowly and ceaselessly from side to side, her spear pointed always forward, and her arm loose but coiled and ready to shift grip on the wooden haft of the weapon.

Lydria's father made many of the same motions Haidrea made, even when walking through peaceful lands. The motions came from years of training and awareness. Cargile had often said, when you cease being aware, you quickly cease being alive. The memory caused her to suppress a gasp as the reality of her situation struck home. She was wounded and sore, although whatever healed the cat draped over her neck seemed to have helped ease her pain. She had lost a fair amount of blood despite her bandaging, and her head swam somewhat. But despite these physical injuries, she realized that she was alone in the world. With her father gone, she had no one to look to for support or comfort. As if reading her thoughts and offering consolation, the cat around her neck pushed the bridge of his nose into her chin and licked her own bent nose before resting his head again around her neck.

Trusting that Haidrea had awareness for both, Lydria focused her attention on the slim Eifen and how gracefully she moved across the terrain. Even through her clothing, Lydria could discern taught muscles ready to respond to any threat. Despite that, her neck and shoulders were relaxed as if out for an afternoon walk. Although, she thought, stalking would be more accurate. The effortlessness of her posture and movements were a thing of beauty and Lydria's father would have been in awe of the sparseness of motion she used to complete a task. Her skin was a radiant black, so dark that in the right light, it was almost blue.

Lydria wondered if the Eifen were like the people of Wesolk who came in many shades, with darker or lighter skin appearing at random like the color of one's hair, or eyes. Haidrea's hands were unadorned and shifted subtly on the haft of the spear, the paleness of her palms contrasting against the dark wood of the spear. She

39

exerted minimal effort as she carried the spear, but she kept it poised to be brought to bear in any direction at a moment's notice.

Her hair, liker her skin, was black like onyx and straight, but tied simply with string in an intricate braided pattern that produced a stunning oak leaf effect that started from the back of her head and continued past her shoulder blades where it was tucked under her snug top. The tunic itself was a work of art, made primarily of light brown, supple and flexible leather, it fitted her body and hugged her torso to fall over her hips and waist freely. The design was clever and would have taken a long time for even a skilled seamstress as it seemed to be made specifically for Haidrea's form.

On her back Haidrea carried a short bow, like a cavalry bow. It was unstrung and hung so as not to impede her movement in any way. Like her clothes, the weapon looked to have been made to fit her form. Sewn into the back of her tunic, there was an extra layer of hide, where the black feathers of six short arrows were cleverly placed. It was not a situation that would allow for the rapid deployment of the weapon, but it spared having to carry a quiver and the noise it would cause.

Unlike many women, but like Lydria, Haidrea wore her clothing in the fashion of men with leggings instead of a dress. It made practical sense for a warrior or a hunter. Exposed skin in the forest was susceptible to everything from insect bites to thorns and a dress made noise and caught on foliage.

"Where are we going?" Lydria asked after noticing the faded yellow sun settling in the sky. "It must be getting late."

"The moon has risen over the hills and the sun is on its way to bed," Haidrea answered. "We will camp here. You are tired, and we have some distance to travel." With no more said, Haidrea stopped to gather sticks for a fire in a small clearing. After their sparse camp was made Lydria lay down with her back to a tree and when she woke up, Haidrea was smiling and holding out breakfast. "The sun is up, and we should be on our way."

Still stiff, but feeling better with the food, the two traveled east and slightly north. The cub occasionally wandered into the woods but if he was fed, he seemed content to spend most of his time riding on Lydria's shoulders.

They walked the whole day and the next and as the sun started to set for the third time, Haidrea stopped and waited for Lydria to stand by her. "We will soon be challenged by our scouts. Keep the cat close."

Their pace slowed, and the tree roots were a nuisance to Lydria who tried not to jostle the bobcat too much lest she become a pin cushion for his claws. Occasionally she thought she heard Haidrea whisper for her to be careful and so she tried to follow her guide's lead. Haidrea never missed a stride; she flowed like smoke over the terrain and finally came to a full stop and turned her head to Lydria. In the growing darkness the whites of Haidrea's eyes shone brightly and she closed one quickly, winking at Lydria and warning her to pay close attention.

"You can come out Nethyal, I can smell the rabbit you had for dinner. I hope you saved me some; I bring guests and we are hungry."

Almost imperceptible footfalls announced a man who stepped out of the forest. "Ah, sister, your skill continues to amaze me." The tone was caring, chiding, and respectful all at the same time. After hugging his sister, he turned toward Lydria and stopped, pausing for a moment to stare at her. Taking a step backward so he was next to Haidrea again, he spoke to his sister in the language of the Eifen, a gentle and soft language that made Lydria think of a spring breeze. There were few harsh sounds as they spoke, and she realized even the language of the Eifen was quiet and at home in the forest.

The cat around Lydria's neck stopped purring and Haidrea laughed. It was the first time Lydria had heard her laugh and unlike all her skills and muscles, the laugh belonged to a woman; it pealed across the trees like a small creek released from winter's embrace. But it was short lived and replaced with a less delicate snort when the cat lifted his head and Nethyal took a quick step back, instinctively raising his spear to a defensive position.

"Are you going to kill our guests before I can introduce them properly, then? I think father would find disgrace in such a welcome. Come, let us get home so I can tell you of my journey."

Lydria followed as quietly as she was able and watched Nethyal make quick, uneasy glances in her direction, finally stopping in the trail and turning to her just as the cat opened his mouth and let out a crackling, barely audible mewl of a noise. "Gods how is this, then," he turned to his sister. "How is it that you walk from the ash rain and come back with a kingdom woman who carries a bobcat like a cloak?"

"First fire and food, and then we will speak. I will tell our story to Wae Ilsit, for I fear there is more here than a cub who has lost its mother." They walked, treading lightly but no longer silent as Nethyal and his sister continued to converse in the language of Wesolk. After half a mile, Lydria guessed, she began to see the soft glow of fires as if they were hidden by a piece of cloth. A man came out and spoke to Nethyal briefly before running back through the trees to signal their arrival.

When they reached the edge of the village, the people of Eifynar were waiting in two lines that provided a path to the center of the village where they met a man wearing clothes very much like Haidrea and Nethyal. Unlike the others, however, he also wore what looked like an amulet around his neck. It was not gold but shimmered in the setting sun and firelight. The amulet captivated Lydria. It fit the man's shape almost perfectly, covering his collarbone under his tunic, and the base of his throat.

Only the sound of Haidrea's voice dragged her attention away from the man's neck. "Wae Ilsit," Haidrea said clearly, formally hugging the man before turning to another, older man beside him who wore a tunic with long sleeves and who leaned heavily on a carved staff, and offered him the same, deliberate, respectful hug. "Drae Ghern. I bring to Eifynar a woman with two spirits and a cub who has befriended her. Lydria, this is Wae Ilsit, the leader of the Eifen east of the Great Lake, sire of Nethyal and Haidrea; and this is Drae Ghern, our Graetongue, oldest and wisest of us all, keeper of many stories, sire of Wae Ilsit, and my grandfather."

SIX

Haidrea stepped aside and motioned for Lydria. The cat stopped purring and sniffed hopefully at the air, catching the scent of food drifting across the street from different directions. As he sniffed, he stood by Lydria's head kneading his claws into her shoulders. The woman held back any indication of pain caused by the cub, sensing a show of strength would reflect well upon her host. Following the lead of Nethyal whom she had watched greet Wae Ilsit and Drae Ghern, she touched her right hand to her heart and lips and extended her fingers, palms up toward the elders. The older of the two men smiled faintly and motioned her forward to greet her as he had Haidrea.

With formal greetings finished, Wae Ilsit looked at Lydria and then past her down the street. "It is time for food and then we shall hear what stories Haidrea and Lydria have to share," he told the people gathered outside, who parted and went to their homes, leaving small trace of their passage on the ash-covered path. As they left, Lydria got her first good look at Eifynar. The Eifen town was similar to Bayside only in that they held large numbers of people. There were no roads, but clean and natural dirt paths that lead to homes built inside of trees. No, Lydria realized, they weren't inside of trees, they were made of wood as were the homes of Bayside, but they were skillfully and thoughtfully crafted so that they became a part of the forest instead of a replacement for the forest.

"You have never seen Eifynar?" Haidrea stood by Lydria's side and stroked the cats' ears. "You should see it in the height of summer or when the snow is banked high. It is a lovely place. I will show you more of it tomorrow, but for now, we must go into the chief's hall." Lydria turned and smiled at Haidrea and they walked down the road where Wae Ilsit and Drae Ghern were already entering a building that to Lydria looked like a path into the forest.

Inside the hall it was bright and warm with firelight and torches. Everything Lydria saw seemed to be made of wood and stone and soil, and it was created with exacting craftsmanship that allowed the light of fires to stay inside, but smoke to drift out through unseen vents. Men and women were moving carved chairs and wooden stumps into positions around planks that served as tables. Others brought food from a kitchen at the back, and some brought food from outside. When the chairs were settled and planks in place, those who didn't have a seat made themselves comfortable on the ground or around the walls.

Haidrea leaned close to Lydria and pointed upward and around the building to small spaces where shutters were being opened. Outside on tree branches those who couldn't fit in the hall were finding seats until it seemed like everyone must be waiting to hear what the newcomers had to say.

Drae Ghern sat on a chair at the far end of the room, indicating Lydria should sit between he and Wae Ilsit while Haidrea sat to Drae Ghern's left. As they reached their seats, women and children served meat and fruit, root vegetables, and a corn-based bread from wooden bowls. Each place at the plank had metal spoons and knives that were among the most delicately carved and beautiful pieces Lydria had ever seen. Skins and bowls of fresh water were passed, and horn and bone cups were given to the four in honored positions.

The cub, whose tiny claws were drawing blood from Lydria's shoulder by this time, was far better behaved than any wild animal could hope to be, and it was a great surprise when a dish of raw meat found its way to Lydria and the cat launched itself off her shoulder and onto the plank, his small tail swishing back and forth as it worried its dinner. Lydria thought she heard a voice say, *thank you,* and turned to add her own thanks to that of Drae Ghern to the child who had brought the cat's dinner.

Wae Ilsit's voice grabbed her attention and he indicated with his hand the bobcat who was by now making low, growling noises as he ate. "Your friend looks hungry." Wae Ilsit smiled at the cub and then gently to Lydria as the cat continued to growl in warning to anyone who might be tempted to steal his meal. As more meat appeared, his growling stopped and, ignoring the audience that watched, he turned his back to the rest of the hall and ate his meal in peace on the table next to Lydria's own plate.

Drae Ghern and Wae Ilsit looked across Lydria to each other and the graetongue put down his cup. "Haidrea, come forward. You have brought us two remarkable guests and we would hear your story."

A young girl brought a finely carved wooden chair with a deep cushion and placed it in front of the table where Wae Ilsit and Drae Ghern sat. Haidrea sat down, placing her elbows on her knees as if considering her story, and soon, Lydria noted, the crowd had gathered, children to the front, in a great semi-circle. The noises of dinner began to fade as the Eifen pushed aside their plates and turned their attention to Haidrea who waited only for the graetongue to finish speaking with Lydria.

"The telling of stories is very important. All stories told here will be written down and put aside in the tree of knowledge. As the years pass, some of this information can be re-examined. Some of our oldest stories, traditions, myths and legends have been created from stories that start just as this will. They provide guidance, and a link to our past, and are useful to look upon in times of trouble."

"Do you think there will be trouble?" Lydria asked, sure of the answer as she remembered Wynter at the crater.

"Trouble happens when people who have lost their way, meet others who have lost theirs. When these two souls find each other, neither can be sure of the other and great sadness often follows."

As Drae Ghern finished, the crowd settled and Haidrea began her story, telling the quiet ranks of Eifen how the kingdom men and the wagons made a tremendous crashing noise along the forest road which she heard even from a great distance. She told of how she noticed the strange behavior of animals in the area as they fled and could be heard no more. She recited Lydria's story of how the kingdom men chased the archer into the trees; and the grit of the woman who calmly pulled an arrow from her hand and deftly pocketed her finger and dressed her wound. At this she paused as all eyes turned toward Lydria and she somewhat proudly held up her left hand, wrapped in leafy bandage of Haidrea's making.

Haidrea continued Lydria's tale of the bowman's cowardly murder of the horse soldier followed by his own capture, before pausing again to take up her own story. "The air became numb and the hairs on my arm stood up as if searching for the sun," she told her audience, paying special attention the children. "My chest was heavy as if the air were water and then, at the same time, the sun was no more and the forest in front of me vanished."

The villagers had heard the impact and had seen a very light dusting of ash filter through the trees of their homes the first day. It was not as thick in Eifynar owing largely to the wind which pushed the ash to the west. Aside from the ash, however, there was no evidence in the city of what had happened. Hearing of this strike from the heavens, all the Eifen rested more easily knowing the source of the ash rain.

"When I lifted my head from the wall of rock that shielded me, I saw a forest the size of many grazing lands cut down as if by the scythe of the gods. The kingdom men were gone. Their horses were gone. The wagons were gone. I moved forward through the broken forest and I saw a man rise from amongst the trees. He looked as if he had come from the ground, so covered with dirt and mud were his clothes and skin. Even from where I crouched, I could feel a dark presence about him, as if a spirit not his own moved his legs forward. I prepared my bow to rid the land of his darkness and then saw another rise from the ash," and she nodded again toward Lydria, and smiled, showing a set of beautiful teeth perched delicately below cheekbones that, under the firelight, made Lydria feel warm and cared for, as if her father were staring at her.

Haidrea told the Eifen of how Lydria and Wynter met in the crater and after a few minutes, how Wynter had left limping toward the north, and how Lydria had climbed out, found the bobcat and then fallen asleep under a golden light. "This woman stood up to and cowed a murderer, and then she turned to her other spirit and comforted this broken cub, and his body shone as if the sun hid behind him instead of behind the clouds of ash and ruin. When the

46

light ebbed, the cub jumped to his feet, but Lydria fell to the ground. That is when we met. When she awoke, I could see she was possessed of two spirits – the strong and the gentle."

The crowd was unsure if the story were finished but turned their heads slowly to Lydria who seemed to be asleep. She was sitting with her eyes closed, thinking of Haidrea's story realizing that the light was real, and that she had, somehow, healed the cub. It didn't make sense and the Eifen shifted uneasily as they waited for the story to continue. Lydria opened her eyes and found scores of men, women and children staring at her. Where they had looked at her with curiosity and compassion earlier, they now looked at her with interest and respect.

"Our guests are tired. We will speak more of this in the cleansing light of day. Lydria," the word came easily to his tongue as Wae Ilsit spoke it. He was clearly fluent with the language of Wesolk. "You will stay in our home this evening with my daughter and Drae Ghern."

"My son," Drae Ghern interrupted before Lydria could find her feet. "Let me first speak with this child. She is tired, but she is also wounded. She has lost a part of herself and bears the marks of a warrior's courage. We owe her a debt for the story."

"You are wise and teach me still, father. You are correct. Lydria, my manners are lacking. Please, tend to your wounds. Tomorrow we will speak again." Wae Ilsit embraced her with the greeting he shared with Haidrea and turned away to his home at the opposite end of town from where she had entered.

Haidrea waited as the children were coaxed away from her by their parents. Drae Ghern led Lydria to a small building between two large maples. Although made of wood and stone, the chief's home was soft and comfortable. Inside it was warm and thick with the smell of smoldering wood from a fireplace in a back corner where the remnants of a fire glowed red, and a chimney made of a dark stone funneled the smoke out. Around the small house there were several chairs and a bench near a handsome wooden table, carved around the edges with leaves and small animals. Nearby there was a reed basket with blankets and animal furs. Stairs led to an alcove of a second level where Lydria guessed Drae Ghern kept his bed, and the old man explained that his rooms were attached to those of his son and grandchildren through another door.

Motioning Lydria to a soft, low chair by the fire, Drae Ghern sat next to her on a plain bench and they faced one another with their knees nearly touching. The bobcat had made himself at home in the basket of furs and was just settling down after kneading his bed as Lydria began to relax.

"You'll be fine."

In the dimly lit room Lydria didn't see Drae Ghern speak, but in the time they'd shared, she thought his voice was thicker and deeper than what she had just heard. It had been a very confusing day. The old man murmured to himself as he crushed together several plants and liquids in a bowl. Having seen army surgeons do similar things, she knew he was creating a medicine or poultice, probably for her finger, so she waited patiently not wanting to interrupt the rhythm of his song, for almost surely, he was singing rather than talking.

His voice was low and slow as he chanted words that were strange but made her think of trees and plants, sun and rain, and the smells of a spring morning in the sunshine. As he finished his song, he took her left hand in his and carefully unwrapped her bandage. "You are not unskilled in the healing arts." He said it as if confirming the information to himself, but Lydria offered that she had some experience with needle and thread with the wounded but that Haidrea had tended her wound while she slept the first night.

"Soldiers work is tiring and requires muscles and skill, it is true. A healer's work, however, is tiring and requires skill, empathy, plant lore, body knowledge, and compassion. It is far more worthwhile and far less understood. Yet we seem always to turn our attention to fighting. It is a shame that we learn to hurt so much more easily than we learn to heal."

Lydria nodded. Drae Ghern presented his opinion as a fact and not a question, but Lydria didn't agree. Soldiering had provided for herself and her father and it was what taught her how the body works, how wounds were healed, and how she could make the body heal faster. "Surely, the two are part of the same," she offered, explaining her reasoning. "If not for the soldier, the healer would learn little and would be less skilled for the benefit of the children and the rest of the community?" Lydria raised her voice to present her thoughts as a question so as not to offend the graetongue.

Drae Ghern was quiet as he cleaned the wounded finger stump so carefully Lydria hardly felt his work against her still-raw nerves. He chuckled quietly and applied a paste from the bowl and rewrapped her hand with a material so fine Lydria wasn't sure what she saw was real. It was thin and light, and she was sure she would be able to see through it in daylight.

When he was finished he continued to hold her hand and stared. She stared back, searching his eyes to determine his intent. His hands were supple, yet rough. Heavy lines of age and work ran along his skin which was lighter than Haidrea's, but far darker than the bronzed skin of his son, Wae Ilsit. Drae Ghern's hands felt like they might tell a story of their own if they were held long enough. A story about work, building, pain, experience … life.

"Haidrea was correct, you do have two spirits in you," he said finally, releasing her hand and adding some small sticks to the glowing coals of his fire. "What you must do, is determine which spirit you will follow."

"Can I not choose to follow both?" Her question was not adversarial, but inquisitive. She shifted her garments and felt the stone in the pouch at her side. Taking it out she held the small sphere in front of her and stared, waiting to see what Drae Ghern might say.

The old man stared at the stone and leaned backward, extending his arm for a small sack on the floor nearby. The sack was bare of any decoration and made, Drae Ghern told her, from the pelt of an ancient beaver who dammed the river to the east of Eifynar.

"The beaver who belonged to this skin was so old, we would bring wood close to his lodge, so he didn't have to swim far or work long to cut timber for his family. Animals, like men, need to feel useful," he said, nodding with a small grin toward the curled bobcat breathing fast, regular breaths behind her. "By helping the beaver

49

retain his youth with his den, he lived many long years and I'm sure he passed his stories to his family for many seasons. One day, we found him outside this very house. He had come here, a good distance from his river home, to die and repay us with all he had. This lesson we must remember as well – that our actions in life will much longer be remembered if our actions in death are for the benefit of others."

He paused for a moment, his hands tracing the stitching along the beaver-skin bag, lightly following the patterns that held it together and feeling the old smooth skin against his old roughened skin.

"This skin has seen many seasons and built many lodges and dams. He has sired many young, told many stories, and lived nobly amongst the beings of this world. His spirit resides within this skin, for he gave it as a gift to us." As if to punctuate the importance of the bag, he silently searched Lydria's blue and green eyes, both of which were locked onto the bag he held.

"I give this bag now to you so that you may always remember the story of the great beaver. In it you can place what you will - pieces of your life's story to protect you and help those who will come after you."

Lydria blushed as she accepted the gift and placed it on her lap, laying her hand, still holding the stone, on top of it, moving the stone between her fingers, searching its bright silver lines.

"The stone you carry is unlike any stone I have seen in all my years," Drae Ghern said. "Haidrea must have sensed this too as she chose not to include in her story how you came by it. How this stone is special, however, is hidden from me. Together, perhaps, we can determine if the spirit it carries is light or dark."

To prove Drae Ghern correct, Lydria pulled back her hair and lifted her chin, showing Drae Ghern clearly the band of blue skin that encircled her neck. "Soon after I touched the stone, this appeared, as it did with Wynter, and I believe with this bobcat as well." She took the stone and touched it to her neck, expecting the clicking sound of stone on stone, and surprised when she heard not only the noise, but also saw a light that penetrated the shadows of

Drae Ghern's house with a pale blue light. Touching her neck with her fingers, however, the blue collar felt as supple as her own skin, and no joint could be felt between skin and collar.

Drae Ghern thanked Lydria for showing him both the stone and her collar, and then moved quickly to his feet with a nimbleness that startled both Lydria and the cub, trotting up the stairs to his sleeping area and returning seconds later with another bag, slightly larger than the one Lydria held, and darkened with age and weather. It was decorated with a delicate inlay of silver and gold in the shapes of leaves and trees. Drae Ghern gently shook the bag to indicate something inside and the noise was enough to perk the interest of the cat who moved to the side of Lydria nearest the fire. His paws were to his front and his eyes locked onto the old man's.

"May I hold the stone?"

Lydria offered him the stone without hesitation and Drae Ghern held it carefully as if it might break, turning it over and singing his chant once more. This time there was more inflection and occasionally a high note would escape as he lifted his head to the rafters which were thick with hanging herbs and vegetables. His singing rose and fell for long minutes before he suddenly stopped and locked eyes with Lydria once more. Not taking his gaze from her, his lined hands felt along the stone as if searching for a crease and stopped, his eyebrows arching sharply. Placing the stone on the ground, he stood again and busied himself looking through several baskets and bundles and then built the fire higher and hotter, placing upon it succulent plants and leaves that gave off a thick, pungent smoke.

Returning to his bench he quickly picked up his chant again, opening his bag with deliberate care, retrieving a thin bone pipe and packing it with a weed from a special pouch before turning to the fire and lighting the pipe with a glowing stick. He sucked in his leathered cheeks until they seemed to touch and blew out the resulting smoke in a series of short wisps, murmuring a word or phrase with each release. Finally, he took in the smoke once more and picking up the stone he pressed his lips to the curved face and blew. A thin stream of smoke, barely visible as a haze in the firelight,

51

flowed over the stone and engulfed it for a moment in a sphere of grey before continuing.

"Your stone has stories of its own," Drae Ghern said. "Take in the smoke and let it fill your body. Let us see what the smoke tells us about your stories and your path."

Lydria took the pipe and hesitated, never taking her eyes from the old man. Drae Ghern laughed and patted the woman's knee. "You do not know much about me. I am sorry," he said. "I am a graetongue, that is I speak with and for the earth on behalf of the Eifen. There are among the Eifen those who can keenly sense the world around him in a way that goes unnoticed by all others. That person becomes the voice of the earth, the graetongue. I have felt the earth's sorrows and joys all my life; she tells me when her rivers will overflow, when the time is right to plant crops, which trees can be used for homes or fires, and much more besides. To me, it is obvious, but to everyone else, what the earth says goes largely unnoticed."

"Are women not graetongues, then? You said, a child could sense the world around him." Lydria didn't want to offend Drae Ghern, but she was tired and wanted him to keep talking. She thought the question might entice him to tell her more about the Eifen.

"As far as I know, only men have been graetongues." Drae Ghern smiled appreciatively and looked hard at her eyes before continuing. "There is, however, The Haustis, who is always a woman, and it is said she possesses a connection with Eigrae that is to the graetongue what the graetongue is to the rest of the Eifen. But there is only one, and she does not make her home with her people. She is betrothed to Eigrae."

Seeing sadness in the old man's eyes, Lydria didn't press the issue, and instead picked up the pipe and mimicking Drae Ghern, sucked her cheeks together and inhaled deeply, pausing shortly before coughing it all out again, eliciting a laugh from the graetongue. "Draw from the pipe more slowly and let the smoke live for a time in your mouth. When the smoke has accepted you, swallow it, so it becomes part of you. It will take some time, be patient and let the spirits come to you to tell their stories."

Lydria drew deeply and held the smoke in her mouth and immediately tasted flavors of fruit and earthy loam. It wasn't disagreeable, but she was glad when she heard Drae Ghern tell her to swallow the smoke and let it settle inside her. His rough hands lifted hers again with the pipe to her mouth to repeat the process. After several breaths, Lydria was becoming used to the smoke and its taste became more pleasant. It was like nature, rich with grass and tree and soil. As the power of the smoke took hold, Drae Ghern brought out a set of tiles, crafted of bone and carved into different shapes with ebony inlay. He selected several of the tiles at random and placed them in front of Lydria and himself. He sang all the while, not stopping until the last tile was placed. Then, his chant became slower as he turned each tile over, sometimes switching a tile with one he had not turned before continuing until all the tiles reflected the light of the fire from their black inscriptions.

Lydria closed her eyes and felt warm inside from the smoke and her skin warmed as the embers in the fireplace began to lick up around the sticks and small pieces of wood. She felt each individual bead of sweat burst forth from her skin leaving a trail in the dirt that still covered her as it made its way down her body. She felt as if she was seeing all this from a position outside and above her sitting body. The graetongue, the sleeping area, the fire, the bobcat, – all floated beneath her in a pleasant drift and she was beginning to enjoy the experience when she heard the word 'kimi' in her dream.

The bobcat pressed himself up and arched his back to stretch before curling again on her lap. A voice interrupted her pleasant drift across the house, but Lydria didn't hear it with her ears. It was part of her, entering her directly like the rumble of thunder, filling her entirely.

"You and I have been chosen and are marked by the collars we wear. Through the stone, I can speak with you, through the stone we are bonded."

It was unlike any dream she had ever experienced. Lydria continued to drift above the room. She could see and hear Drae Ghern chanting. She watched as the old man helped her raise her hands and she felt the pipe being pressed to her lips, and she welcomed the smoke, letting it envelope her like a warm bath.

The dream shifted from the lodge to the far north where forests grew tall, narrow, and sparse. She watched a man bathed in blue light walk among the trees. He carried a stick and a wore a blue collar like her.

"*You must find him,*" said a different voice, a more ethereal, whispering voice. "*His soul is corrupted. The stone enhances the essence of those who are bonded to it so that the light and darkness within each wielder is magnified and made purposeful.*"

"How?" Lydria asked the dream voice, but she was met with silence and opened her eyes to a dark room.

"Welcome back," said Drae Ghern, handing her a skin of water and a bowl of fruit, making no move to relight the cold fireplace. "You were gone long – longer ever than I have watched someone travel. What the spirits have shown is for you alone, unless you would share it."

"Should I?"

"No one other than you can answer that. But if you do, I will use the wisdom of my years to provide what counsel I may. However, you may not like it. If you do not want counsel, then keep what you have learned to yourself and trust your own counsel. It is often the wisest choice."

Quickly, fearing she might forget some important detail, Lydria told him what she remembered from the feeling of looking down on the room to the voice of the bobcat, to a second voice, and the man in the north.

Drae Ghern was silent and Lydria could not judge his expression in the dark but finally, his voice reached her as a wisp of wind close to her face before reaching her ears. She smelled upon him the odor of the very old and dying and felt sorry for the man and his people.

"The voice named you wielder, one who carries. Perhaps this refers to the stone which you carry, or the blue ring you wear on your neck. It is encouraging. Dream voices, when they speak, do not always speak as friends," he explained. "Kimi, I believe, is the cat, and it is a good name, for it is an old word for a secret. I believe your furry companion has a secret ... or maybe he has shared his secret with you already?" Drae Ghern smiled like a grandfather who has shown a youngster an old trick for the first time. They both knew he was correct and that, however impossible it seemed, the cat had talked to her in the dream.

"As for the rest of your dream, I would advise caution and strength. You must find this man Wynter and retrieve his stone. When spirits talk of evil and darkness, it is best to listen. At the same time, dream voices often speak in riddles, and we cannot so easily accept the words they say. We must each use our power, whatever it may be, to the benefit of that light which guides us."

Lydria struggled with the questions racing through her mind, finally making her decision. "Drae Ghern, what did you see when you touched the stone? Did your world slow and turn blue?"

"I saw many things, as is the way when I seek the spirits' help, but the colors were those we see outside and around us, and things moved too fast, like they do in life. I also saw the Haustis, and you should seek her counsel as you prepare to meet Wynter again."

"Who is the Haustis and where can I find her?"

"There are many stories that follow the name of the Haustis. Some say she is older than all the Eifen; others say she can fly; some few believe her to be a legend, a tale to help us discover for ourselves what we need." Drae Ghern paused as if deciding if he should tell a great secret and looked for a long time at Kimi, whose ears perked up when he sensed the old man's eyes lingering upon him and yawned to show his teeth and pink tongue. "Haustis is no spirit or legend. How she comes by her great age, if indeed she is ancient, none may know. The Eifen live longer than the men of your kingdom, but if stories can be believed, she has eclipsed all the Eifen and has walked the land for generations. As to where she lives, I do not know. It is said the wisdom of the Haustis finds you."

Lydria was exhausted and now she was apprehensive as well. Meeting Wynter was bad; having to search for him and take his stone, having to find a legendary figure who has no home – these were not things Lydria had considered as she made her way to Steven's Folly.

If she found Wynter, what was she to do? Kill him? Lydria didn't think Drae Ghern would answer that question. She lowered her hands to steady herself in the darkness and felt the cool roundness of the stone against her palm. She wondered if Drae Ghern would relight the fire. Light would help her make sense of everything. As Wae Ilsit had said, the light helped to cleanse. She closed her eyes before rising, thinking perhaps her motion would encourage Drae Ghern to relight his fire.

"*There it is.*" It was the dream voice again, the one she had heard first, and its suddenness caused Lydria to open her eyes and instantly shut them again as they instinctively adjusted to the bright light of the fireplace. She dropped to one knee, nausea threatening to overcome her and outside she could hear startled voices reacting to the sudden bright shaft of light coming through the small windows of Drae Ghern's home. The fire burned like daylight but without smoke and, it appeared, without wood. Drae Ghern smiled at her and repacked his bag. Kimi, all signs of tiredness gone, put his front paws on her bent knee and licked her nose. "*Your stone will help you reach for the light.*"

Lydria stared at the cat and wondered if the dream voice really could be coming from the bobcat, and no sooner did she think it then the voice responded, "*Of course. I told you we were bonded by the stone.*"

Lydria felt weak in her stomach and her head throbbed with pain. Trying to look at Kimi, she realized she was slumping.

"*Wielder, wake up.*" Kimi's tongue persistently licked Lydria's nose and face until she moved her head and held out her hand for him to stop. When she rose, the cat was sitting between her and the graetongue, the fire had died down to its normal state with several pieces of new wood being licked by the orange flames. Drae Ghern called for Haidrea who entered at once, as if she were waiting on the doorstep.

"Come, Haidrea, sit with us, we have much to discuss."

SEVEN

Drae Ghern made a bed of blankets and furs for Lydria a few paces away from the fire. "Lie down and rest peacefully, wielder. You have had a long day. You will make history as one of the few among the kingdom to have their story become part of the Eifen history. Sleep, while my granddaughter and I discuss your vision and what the coming of the stone and Wynter could mean for our people."

Lydria dragged herself to the makeshift bed and thanked Drae Ghern. She didn't think she'd be able to sleep despite being bone tired. Every muscle ached, and her body cried out to be prone among the soft furs, but she was nervous and curious. She put her head on the bag Drae Ghern had given her and watched the fire. The flames snapped peacefully as the aromatic herbs Drae Ghern added made the house thick with the smells of jasmine and wildflowers.

Kimi moved to Lydria's bed and kneaded the furs before turning twice in a circle and lying down with his spine resting against her stomach and breasts. *"Good night, Kimi,"* Lydria thought absently, scratching the cub's ears.

"Good night," he replied. *"And don't scratch so hard, your claws are not as soft as you think."*

With that, both surrendered to their dreams, while several feet away Haidrea and her grandfather spoke quietly.

When morning came, Lydria woke feeling better than she had in ages. Kimi was nowhere to be seen, but judging by the noises outside, he was entertaining some of the children and she could hear his low growls punctuated with laughter and the running of small feet in mock terror.

"Come out and get some breakfast before I eat it all." The cat's voice entered her head cleanly, but more quietly than normal. Perhaps, like a real voice, the further away he was the fainter would be his voice. Lydria wondered if one could yell silently.

"Of course. You just have to think how you want it to sound."

"Can you read my mind? I wasn't talking to you." Lydria tried to sound indignant, but she enjoyed the cat's presence, both physical and mental.

"If you concentrate, you can tell what I'm thinking too, but that won't get you far unless you're interested in food or sleep. So, in some ways, yes, we can read each other's minds. But, I believe you could also stop me from doing so if you wish."

Lydria laughed out loud. She couldn't imagine blocking out Kimi.

"So, you are awake, nearly in time to watch the sun begin its descent toward the western hills."

"Good morning, Haidrea, I must have been very tired."

"And so you were. Grandfather says rest is often the best of all the medicines. The Eifen council waits in the great hall. When you are ready there is food as well."

As she turned to leave, Haidrea stared at Lydria for a few seconds as if she wanted to say something, but the moment passed, and she pushed open the wooden door.

"You'd better hurry," Kimi said. *"The council is gathering, and I've only got to make it past three stern looking ladies to have a second breakfast – yours."*

Lydria left the house and found Kimi in the street. She gently pushed him to his back and rubbed his stomach. "You're not such a bad kitten, are you? Little kitten." The children laughed when they saw how gentle Kimi was and as Lydria moved toward Drae Ghern and Wae Ilsit, the youngsters moved in.

"Don't hurt them, Kimi."

"I'll get you…" The rest of his thought was buried in a wave of happiness as small hands eagerly sought out his belly, ears, and chin to tickle and scratch until the cat's purr could be heard by anyone nearby.

"Good morning Wielder." It was Drae Ghern who approached first and greeted her with the formal greeting he had shared with Haidrea. Following the graetongue's lead, Wae Ilsit also greeted her as did Haidrea and her brother Nethyal. The formal greeting from the siblings was unexpected.

Indicating the great hall where they had eaten the previous evening the four entered and found most of the tables and benches had been removed. Now there was a long table with only a few chairs clustered at the far end. By one chair there were bowls of food and Haidrea invited Lydria to sit. The hall was dark and cool, lit only by the light from cleverly designed windows. As it was near mid-day the foliage of the trees blocked most of the light from entering the hall. Only in early morning and before the sun set did the room have full natural light.

"Father tells me the spirits call you wielder. We will call you Lydria, but do not be surprised if many among us choose to call you wielder in deference to the word of the spirits. So, you have two souls, you now have two names." Wae Ilsit, in the light, was not much older than Lydria's own father and the two shared the same rugged intensity and even temperament that marked the leaders of men. But where Cargile had grown large and heavy as he aged, Wae Ilsit's frame was thin and taut like a well-made rope. Age seemed to have done little to impede his movements and his motions were as supple and easy as his daughters'. Wae Ilsit was a warrior who one underestimated at one's own peril.

"Tell them you'll take the name and honor it."

"I gladly accept this second name and will do honor to the Eifen with all who speak it," Lydria said, silently thanking Kimi for his intervention.

Drae Ghern, who had watched Lydria's expression could tell she was listening to something outside the lodge and he laughed out loud, a short, sharp laugh, but with a smile that showed his mostly full set of teeth and set off his deep, brown eyes. The others looked at their elder and waited as he slowly rose and went to the doorway which opened on silent hinges.

"Kimi," Drae Ghern called. "Pardon an old man's manners – please come join us. It's not often we have such a guest."

Answering the blank expressions of those around him, and with Lydria's permission, Drae Ghern told the story of the previous evening, to include his presumption of the connection between Lydria and Kimi.

Lydria watched the ears of the chief as they moved back and forth as if trying to detect some falsehood in what Drae Ghern had said. "Is this true? You can speak to this bobcat?" Wae Ilsit was stunned, but also deeply impressed. He turned to Drae Ghern and asked, "how then, father, are we to help one who can heal with a touch, bring flame from nothing, and speak with forest cats?"

"As best we can. First there are things we must know or guess at. Last night, with Haidrea's help, I sought the guidance of the spirits and for my troubles was given a word; but there is no way to repeat the word as it was told to me. This power of Lydria's, the spirits call it 'magic'."

"You're saying I can do these things on purpose, then? It wasn't an accident?"

"*There is one way to find out*," Kimi interceded. "*Light another fire.*"

Lydria realized she was staring at the cat and the others had turned to him as well. When she looked up all eyes were on her, waiting to hear what she had been told.

"Kimi says I should try to make a fire again."

Drae Ghern jumped from his chair to stack small kindling and branches in the hall's large central fireplace. "I think there is no need to make fire from nothing," he said by way of explanation. "I have seen a path. All I need…" Drae Ghern turned where he stood as if looking for something, before taking the knife from beside Lydria's plate and quickly opening a large wound in his left hand. He moved around the table and sat beside Lydria never taking his eyes from hers. "Take my hand."

Overcoming her shock, Lydria took the old man's hand in hers and felt once again the calloused and deeply lined texture of his skin. Beneath it though, she felt a vibrancy she had not felt before. The smell of death, too, had receded, replaced with an essence of spring and hope. She looked at the wound and saw the white bone underneath and understood how it would be mended with needle and thread. She cradled his hand in her two smaller, paler hands and pressed her thumbs together on either side of the wound. She closed her eyes and saw the wound and how it should be. Seconds later there were gasps and she could see the yellow light through her eyelids.

Lydria opened her eyes and sought first the silent Haidrea, who smiled knowingly. She had seen this light before and was happy to see it repeated. Wae Ilsit took his father's hand and rubbed the palm, smearing the warm blood, but finding no gash. Nethyal poured water onto his grandfather's hand and touched it himself before sitting again next to his sister and apologizing for his disbelief.

"Are you tired, Wielder?" It was apparent to her that the shaman knew the answer.

"I am weary as if I've been up for several hours, and a little stiff, but I do not ache, nor am I hurt. Why do you ask?"

"It is what I saw while you slept. Now, light the fire."

Lydria made to get up to approach the pit, and Kimi put a paw on her thigh. *"There is no need to move closer."*

Looking at the fire pit again, Lydria spent several minutes thinking of how she managed the feat the previous evening. The longer it took, the more worried she became and more quickly she lost focus.

"Take a deep breath, Wielder. Imagine the smoke filling you and becoming one with you. Breathe deeply, achieve balance, and then call the fire." Drae Ghern's voice had a steadying effect on her and she did as he said.

Without the pipe it was difficult, but Lydria's experience and memory of the spirits calmed her. Thinking only within, she moved her hands forward and out toward the pit and released a small ball of fire that seemed to float like a leaf on a turbulent stream toward the wood where it set the dried timber alight. Almost instantly she tilted sideways and had to reach out a hand to steady herself. She was dizzy, nauseous, and the good feeling she had when she woke up was now a distant memory. She wanted to lay down and possibly be sick, but a sharp, stabbing sensation above her knee helped her recover some of her alertness. Kimi was dislodging his cub teeth from her leggings.

"Don't be sick on me — I'm not washing your sick out of my fur."

Nethyal, Haidrea, and Wae Ilsit slowly turned their gaze from the fire.

"It is as I have been shown," Drae Ghern said. "The Wielder's power to heal comes from within. She has the healer's art and it speaks through this gift, taking little of her magic." Drae Ghern was talking to everyone, shifting his gaze between them. "Your power to harm is real as well – but it takes more from you. We all have the two sides within us, the dark and the light, ready to be called upon in time of need. This is the line you must walk. I cannot say what might happen should you use your gift in the cause of the darkness," he said. "That sight was not for me."

"Why then, did I pass out when I healed Kimi?"

Drae Ghern laughed a shallow, understanding, and protective laugh. "Daughter," it was the first time he used the term and it caused the goose flesh to stand up on Lydria's arms. She had lost her father, her only family. To be called daughter by Drae Ghern reminded her of that fact. "When you healed Kimi, your world had been ripped apart, and your body nearly so, you were threatened by a mad man and you held a nearly dead bobcat on your lap. Anyone might be forgiven passing out after all that."

"Grandfather, forgive me, but can this be true? Can one person contain so much power?" Nethyal's enthusiasm to see more was palpable.

In Lydria's mind, Kimi spoke quietly, indicating she was to give no outward sign he had spoken. *"Nethyal is a warrior, and he has yet to learn command as has his father."* For her part, Lydria observed Nethyal more closely. For all the time she had spent inspecting Wynter, and Haidrea, and even Drae Ghern, she had given barely a thought to Nethyal. There were thin beads of sweat above his brow that were not caused by the new fire. His veins stood out along his well-muscled arms and without a tunic, it was obvious his heart was racing, thumping against his slim, angular chest. His ears were pitched forward, eager to hear more. *"He's considering the possibilities of what this power could do for the Eifen. Do not fault him for that."*

"You have witnessed it for yourself Nethyal," Drae Ghern replied. Lydria guessed he could also sense Nethyal's rising appreciation of her power.

"Nethyal. We speak of this to no one." The command in Wae Ilsit's voice was not that of a father, but of a commander that left no room for questions.

Turning to Lydria Wae Ilsit's voice lowered and he looked genuinely sad to say the words he spoke next. "We will provide what aid we can, but I am sorry, Lydria, you may not remain in Eifynar." There was a finality in his voice that even Drae Ghern could not openly speak against.

Haidrea looked at her father as if ready to speak but was cut off by her grandfather. "You are correct, of course, Wae Ilsit." The old man spoke the words with respect and an inflection that bestowed wisdom to the chief's words. "Please join me by the fire and provide your counsel as I ask the spirits the shape our aid shall take."

EIGHT

The walk out of the crater was miserable. Everything hurt – even the parts of him he thought strongest stabbed at him as he walked. Each step was agony built upon despair, but until he was out of sight, pride dictated he continue. Pride was a selfish bitch, he thought. The sightline from the crater was easily more than a mile and for a long time he thought he would make an easy target for even a moderate bowman.

"But there are no arrows trained on you, my love."

"All arrows will be trained on me. You've seen to that." He answered the voice in his head out loud. He needn't have bothered, but he felt doing so kept him planted in a reality he could control instead of the waking nightmare his life was becoming. "Why do you continue to torment me? I did as you asked and relieved you of your suffering to be with our daughter."

"You killed our son."

It was by now an old conversation. It always came back to the death of Sol. There was nothing he could do to placate the spirit of his wife. He had tried bargaining. He had tried killing himself, only to find her fighting against him in his mind. Part of him continued to resist her intrusion, but his body had given up. It was too weak, and he knew it wouldn't be long until his mind gave up as well.

"Admit it, Wynter, you enjoy the hunt. You enjoy the killing. The begging for mercy, the power, the sound as your arrow strikes home and the body is thrown backward to land like a stone in the mud. You love the smell of the blood, fresh as it pours out of a small wound, or several. You are a hunter, Wynter. You always have been, but you've managed to hide it all these years. Even from me, you've hidden your past. What you're capable of. What you once did with relish and satisfaction."

Wynter was stunned by the revelations she made and stopped as he reached the cover of the forest. "How do you know?"

"I know everything you know. There are no secrets between us anymore. I live now through you, Wynter, and we shall use your skills to create a new home."

"For what?"

"Why, for us, of course."

"But, you're…"

"Dead? Yes, I'm dead, thanks to you. As is our daughter and our son. But there's a new day coming, Wynter. I can feel the change. Can't you? Listen to the world, husband. It is crying out for a ruler."

Wynter stopped by a small birch tree and emptied what little was in his stomach. The bile was thick on his tongue and he could smell it as well as taste it. It was acrid and foul and lingered at the back of his throat and in his nose. The voice in his head had politely gone quiet so he could savor the unpleasantness with all his senses.

It would be some time before darkness fell completely. As he walked north, the ash lessened as the winds blew it west and south. The moon should be full enough to walk by, but the fouled air made it only a glimmer. Regardless, he thought, it would be best to rest and perhaps find some small thing to eat.

Gathering sticks was easy. Even in the standing trees the impact had caused shock enough to disturb the branches and the ground was littered with small pieces of wood for kindling. He reached into the small sack he had retrieved from the soldier who chased him into the woods; the soldier he had put out of his misery as his body lay crushed beneath a tree. Inside the sack were the stone he had taken at the crater, some line, bandages, a small flask, a needle and fine thread, a short filleting knife and a tinder box – everything a soldier would need for a night in the woods in one package. So very thoughtful, Wynter mused to himself. He opened the flask first, and lifted it to the sky, "to you, soldier, you've been the best thing that's happened to me in weeks." The liquor in the flask was strong and none too fine, but it helped give him enough energy to light a fire and set a string trap a distance away for anything small and unwary enough to become dinner.

The next day Wynter woke sore and stiff. Between the cold ground, the damp air and the beating he had taken the day before, he just wanted to lie in a bed and sleep. But there was nothing to be done but move on. He gathered his meager supplies, ate half of what remained of the rabbit he had caught the evening before, and headed north. There was nowhere else to go.

"Let's say I head north and see what's going on in the flatlands, eh?" He had spoken aloud to hear himself talk, and he thought Ellaster would talk back. It struck him that he hadn't said his wife's name, nor thought about it, since before that day in his home. She was always 'his wife' and the more he thought about it, the more he thought that was how it should be. "You stopped being Ellaster the day you died," he said to the trees. "I stopped being me then as well."

"No. That's when you became you again," came the voice, sending a shiver of disgust down Wynter's neck. The voice was unrelenting, but he also missed it when it wasn't there. Loneliness drove men to do unusual things. *"You never told me what you did in Bayside before we met. You never mentioned the time you spent in the castle with the king; the dark nights on the road, at taverns, in ditches, wearing black, hiding in shadows, filling shallow graves. You never mentioned to me or anyone in Thrushton what Wynter did before he became a bowyer. Why do you think that is?"*

"It wasn't important for you to know. Do you think I was proud of those things? Do you think anyone chooses to do that work?"

"Work! Ha! Even now you see it as work, as just another chore to pass the day. Or should I say, chore to pass the days — weeks sometimes. You were very good at your job, Wynter. Tell me, why did you leave such an exalted position?"

"Piss off."

"Tell me about the women and the children who so enraged the king that he sent you to them. Tell me how they looked, sighted down an arrow shaft, moments before they were silently cut down. Tell me how children died of poisoned milk, or how men and women were found with their throats cut. What did you tell yourself to stop from going mad? That it was a job? That someone had to do it? Or was it really because you just enjoyed it?"

Wynter was shaking in rage, her words bringing back memories he had long ago suppressed, digging into a history he had thought removed from the world.

"You were a paid assassin, working for the king," her information was as accurate as the memories buried in his head. *"You lied to me, to your children, to everyone. A simple bowyer and fletcher, you said. Ha! How many have you killed, Wynter? Including myself and your son, how many…"*

"Stop!" The word exploded from Wynter's mouth. He was near a small stream and when he shouted even the water seemed to stop for several moments before he heard the splashing again. The leaves in the trees around him rattled as if they had been shaken and there was silence. Tears that had not fallen on his own behalf for years came to him now as he stood as still as the trees surrounding him. But they were only tears. They did not rack his body and he did not sob because he could not move.

It took several minutes for him to realize his paralysis was not a simple matter of the heady rush one sometimes gets in a fight. He was frozen on land in much the same way his son had been in the lake. Aside from blinking, he was immobile.

Panic like he had never experienced gripped him. He felt his heart racing in his starving frame, and the blood rushing in his ears blotted out the sound of the water making its way over its narrow course, but he couldn't turn his head to see it. He was sure if he were pushed, he would fall on his face, unable to stop. And so, he stood, because he had no choice. And his wife did not come back to taunt him. Eventually, animals returned to the clearing near the stream. First the birds who looked upon him with hesitation, not trusting this new thing. The small animals were next. Squirrels and rabbits walked up and sniffed his boots.

"If a bear or mountain cat comes along, I'm finished," he said in a whisper to himself, thankful at least that he was able to speak. Still, he thought, what could he do? Yell for help? There was no one to hear him, and in his present state he was unlikely to fare well with strangers. Speaking out loud was dangerous and so he waited, and the day passed, and the sun started to fall. He was hungry, and he needed to vacate his breakfast. The pain of not being able to do so was very real. All pain was real, he found. A bird found pieces of cloth from his ragged clothing suitable for a nest and in the process of pilfering it from him, pecked him several times. Mosquitoes were starting to find him as the sun set. "I'm going to die standing up," he thought. "Of all the ways one can die, this is one I've never thought of." It was, he concluded, far less desirable than an arrow that left one dead before hitting the ground.

As he stood he considered the conversation he'd had with his wife. She was right. He had enjoyed his work. It was difficult at first, as a young man so full of life to be staring down a shaft of wood at a stranger. At a rich man, or an old woman, an eldest son, or a faithless spouse. But after a while, one stopped thinking of them as people; stopped seeing the blood; stopped wondering what their families felt. After a while, one started to examine the target and practice degrees of precision; fine-tuning weapons to ensure a job done quickly and quietly. One became, professional. Work, whatever form it took, was something to be proud of and do well. Ask anyone in any kingdom and they would say so, he rationalized to himself. Work done well was a noble and honorable thing. Unless the work involved selectively killing people. Most people took exception to that.

Wynter had no such softness. Early on, he would take jobs for next to nothing, or shoot peasants that no one would miss. At first, he found the homeless, or the drunks – those with no families. He found artists who would pay him to bring corpses to quiet places, so they could study muscles and bones. He found healers who would pass a few coins to likewise learn from the dead. Wynter watched them attentively as they used small, fine blades to cut into the corpses. He saw the organs they removed, and in this way learned exactly where to most effectively place his shots. As he began to be paid by kingdom officials, he earned extra money from the armory's blacksmiths who used the dead to try new armor or weapons.

He was very good at his job and because of it, society had benefited, not only from the artists and healers, but also from the removal of 'ugly' elements. That was how he rationalized his actions. That is why, when the target was a child, or a family, he was able to draw back his bowstring, or casually slip poison into a bucket of milk, without hesitation or interruption.

And now, he stood in the early dusk, unable to move and wondering if his last moments on earth would be spent as dinner for some passing forest cat, or bear, or, and he shuddered internally at the thought, a small fox or raccoon who would take ages before finally eating the part of him that would result in his death.

After a time, Wynter's thoughts turned to the silence that enveloped him. The only voice in his head was his own. The trees were still, and the birds had stopped twittering. The realization caused him to focus all his attention on his ears, even going so far as to close his eyes to hear more clearly.

"Hello there."

Wynter's first instinct was to spin around to see who had come upon him, but he couldn't. He considered speaking, but waited, hoping the voice would go away.

"Are you all right?"

It was a woman's voice. An older woman by the sound of it. That meant there was lodging, and possibly a town within a day's journey. The crunch of her steps was getting closer. Her voice was old, but her steps were firm and quick, even as she skirted to the side to avoid coming at him directly from the back. Eventually, he could see her shadow move between the trees. She had kept her distance and approached from the stream, with the setting sun behind her. She was smart. He was in full view, and he could make out nothing of her.

"Blink if you can hear me."

"I can hear you."

She drew a long thin blade from her belt catching the fading sun on its polished edge. It was a weapon not a tool, that much was clear. She held it firmly, and Wynter appreciated at once that this lady was very familiar with how to use such a blade. Given his health, he doubted if he would have moved even if he could have.

"What's the matter with you, why don't you move?"

"I seem to be rooted to this exact spot." The tone of his voice was one Wynter had used on many occasions. It was the voice he used when he'd been spotted before making a kill. It was a friendly voice. A voice that put people at ease and got them off their guard. The old woman was having none of it. She sniffed the air as if mocking his attempt at frivolity.

She approached him and poked him with the blade and when he made no movement after she drew a drop of blood, she pushed him with her hand. He fell straight back and landed like a freshly cut tree.

"Are you satisfied?" he asked as she stood over him, one eyebrow cocked skyward. "Well, I've never seen anything like this in all my years. I'm going to start a fire. You, well, you can just lay there for a bit."

She came back several minutes later and started a small fire before taking out a pack and mumbling to herself.

"Interesting," she said.

"Who are you?" Wynter asked. He could see she was Eifen. He was familiar with the people but had seen few in his travels. The woman before him was as dark as night, but her eyes shown like gold and her ears, so different from those of the men of Wesolk, protruded about two fingers distance from the side of her head and moved backwards and forwards to catch all the sounds of the forest.

"Well, it seems as if I should ask that question, but you beat me to it. My name is Haustis.

NINE

This woman, Haustis, was a dervish, Wynter thought. He had been laying like stone for an hour and she had been in constant motion. First, she made a fire, started a stew, and then she finally seemed to settle down when she took some oddments from a bag and began singing to them. She sang for a long time. She paced and walked around the fire in larger and larger circles, always singing, stopping only briefly to look at Wynter, or take a drink from a water skin. Wynter wanted to tell her to stop, but he had nothing else to do but watch. When she did stop, his relief was momentary as she put away her bag and turned her full attention toward him.

"You are a troubled spirit. Perhaps more than one," she said. Moving with a quick, efficient grace that belied the crow's feet crowding her eyes and the light gray hairs that stood out on her top lip, stark against her dark skin. She ladled stew into a small wooden bowl and wafted the aroma to her nose. "Nothing like day-old meat for stew is there?" She smiled and arched both her eyebrows as if daring him to disagree. "So," she started, holding her mouth open for several seconds to let the food cool before continuing to chew. "That's hot. You'd think I'd be a better cook by now... I'm not going to be able to taste anything for days."

"Who are you?" Wynter's voice inflected the second word more than he had planned. He didn't like people to know he was curious. But, he decided, he didn't like being paralyzed either.

"I told you, I am Haustis." She said nothing more as she ate, first with a wooden spoon and then after several minutes, she lifted the bowl to her mouth and shoveled the stew in with her fingers. When she was done she walked to the stream to clean her bowl before coming back and refilling her pack.

"The big question, really, is who are you?" There was no denying the change in her voice. The woman who minutes earlier had seemed to be forgetful, mumbling over her stew and eating with her hands, turned serious. She crouched so her knees were less than a foot from Wynter's head, forcing him to go cross-eyed as he tried to see her face. Instead, all he saw was a knife blade resting on her leg, just above her knees, the hilt in her right hand. She was sitting on her heels, both legs tucked underneath her, and she stared straight through him.

Wynter considered his options while they stared silently at one another. In Wynter's life, hiding himself had usually resulted in the most effective, even pleasing outcomes. Even after giving up his life as an assassin, he hid that life from everyone else. Given his current physical condition, however, the situation presented candid truth as a reasonable option, and so he told her about his life in Thrushton, the plague, and even about his wife's request to be put out of her misery and his son's meaningless death.

"Yes, that would explain the darkness that surrounds you," she said finally, after considering his words for a time. "But that doesn't explain the darkness *inside* you. You will soon recover your motion, Wynter," Haustis said dismissively. The knife twitched ever so slightly in her hand. It would have been missed by anyone not forced to stare at the blade from mere inches away, but the twitch told Wynter his life was being considered.

"Your spirits do not tell a noble story," Haustis said after a lengthy pause. She didn't relax her grip on the knife, Wynter noted, but her fingers shifted subtly, as if she were trying to decide how to gut the animal in front of her. Chest or throat. "You tell a story that, in its own way, is noble and sorrowful. You were asked to do cruelty to be kind, despite its effect on your own spirit. Many would consider that a warrior's choice, to end the suffering of a brother on the field who is soon destined to fall to the animals or to his own misery. But your spirit... your spirit is divided. It pulls you and you follow."

Everything Haustis said had been lost on Wynter who fixated on her statement that he would regain his motion. Since those words crossed her lips, his defenses went up and he dismissed the notion that she might kill him. Surely, she would have done so already, he thought, and so he decided to try another tactic - belligerence.

"What do you know of me, or my spirit, old woman Haustis?"

More quickly than he thought possible, Haustis unfolded her legs and stood before him, leaving him staring at her boots. "You should show more respect to your elders, young man."

"I have no reason to respect you."

"Perhaps not, but a deer that fails to know its place in the herd will be set upon by the leader of the herd." She moved slowly as she spoke until her feet were opposite his groin. "When that happens, the leader will often wound the youngster. Not so that he will respect the leader, but so that he will not endanger the herd." Haustis continued to move around the prone form of Wynter until her toes contacted the back of his neck.

"Are you going to injure me then, to keep this magnificent herd that surrounds me safe?" It was a bad move, and Wynter knew it, but bravado made as much sense as lying on the ground.

Haustis paused and chuckled, lowering her head so that her dry lips were just above his ears. "I'm not going to hurt you, Wynter. I've spoken with the spirits and they have told me what I should do." She paused again waiting for a response that Wynter didn't provide. "The spirits tell me, as they rarely do, to send you to your wife so that your family can be together again, and you can be whole."

"Then, do it."

"Among my people, I am known as a wise woman," Haustis went on, lowering her voice to a whisper and causing the hair on the back of Wynter's neck to stand up. "But many years living in the wild and communing with the spirits has made me trust my own instincts perhaps a little too much, so I choose not to kill you."

"You don't obey your spirits?"

"The spirits do not control us. They guide us and bring us to the path we were meant to travel. I do not know what path you are meant to travel, Wynter. The spirits believe it to be a dark path. But knowing that, you can now choose a different route."

Between the frustration of not being able to move and the nonsense of the spirits, Wynter was losing his composure. He knew his path and he was content with it. His path was dark. He was embracing it as his only hope to regain his freedom from his past. "Why don't you just kill me or leave me here?"

"Because I know something you need to know." How it was possible, Wynter didn't know, but Haustis' voice got so low he thought it may have entered directly into his head when she said, "I know *why* you cannot move."

Wynter's response was stuck in his throat. How could she know this? "Why is that?"

She considered his request as she completed the circle around his body and methodically folded herself back into the sitting position she had abandoned moments before. She once again readjusted her grip on her knife and this time brought it alongside her right leg, held to be ready to thrust straight forward into his lower gut – not a fast death, but an inevitable one, he knew. "Your darkness is very deep," she said. "If I were a true friend of the earth, I would cut you open and leave you to the scavengers."

He studied her eyes and saw there the strength and conviction of her words. The shock of Haustis saying she knew why he was unable to move, coupled with her knowledge that he would regain his movement, had worn off. Wynter regained his mental balance and realized it was time to tread lightly. A wrong answer at this point and she would make good on her threat, with the spirits' blessing – he had no doubt.

"But, you're in luck. My path tells me that for every time of darkness there must be a time of light and for every hill to climb, there is another that a free spirit may run down with joy. You, Wynter, represent a challenge to that balance."

Haustis pushed her blade point into the dry ground and reached up to her neck and removed a necklace he hadn't noticed from his restricted vantage point. It looked to be made of woven hair, probably from a horse, and each end was capped. One end with bone and the other with a stone that could have been made of darkness itself.

"Do you understand the concept of Grey, Wynter?"

It wasn't a rhetorical question and she waited patiently for an answer. He tried to shake his head and realized he still could not, so he clearly and quietly said, 'no' with as much humility as he could.

"You understand good and evil, though, yes?"

"Of course."

"Many people think of good here," and she held out the necklace and offered him a view of the bone cap which was separated by a finger's width from its opposite, "and evil here." She traced her hand along the length of the braided hair until she reached the black cap. "The Eifen have known for generations the truth; that is, that good and evil are more accurately understood as an incomplete circle, like this necklace, with the farthest reaches of evil and the farthest reaches of good nearly, but not quite, touching. The further you move from either good toward evil or evil toward good, that is the cloudy area where almost all things live. No one is wholly good, and no one is wholly evil. Even you, Wynter, are not entirely one or the other."

"What about the space between good and evil where the necklace is broken?"

Haustis smiled. "That, Wynter, that is the Grey. That area where the most noble and the most evil, live side by side, each doing what they think is right; because they believe they have been blessed with answers the rest of us are too common, or simple, to understand."

"What if they do?"

"They never do." Haustis took the hilt of the knife and flipped the blade casually, probably unaware she was doing it. The point was now away from Wynter, but her fist was wrapped around the hilt and the blade's edge slowly pivoted to lie parallel with his prone body. He knew she watched his eyes follow the weapon and he didn't care. He couldn't do anything about it, but he would be damned if he were to be killed by surprise.

"The Grey is not for mortal men, Wynter. It is certainly not for the likes of you. It takes great fortitude and strength of character to live in The Grey and not be seduced by its lies."

"Are you calling me a coward?"

"No. I'm calling you a man."

Wynter choked back curses that crossed his mind as he felt the flat of her blade land squarely on his testicles. "Should I call you not a man, then? Be careful, Wynter, for pride is a selfish bitch."

Haustis said the last with an inflection and raised eyebrow that made Wynter think she might have heard him the previous day, or somehow read his thoughts. Had she been following him? No, that was ridiculous, he thought. That had been in the wasted trench and there was no one around – except the woman with blue and green eyes.

Haustis unfolded herself once more, collected her small possessions and built up the fire so he could feel its warmth. She turned to walk away but stopped and looked at the still and rigid man one last time as if she were reconsidering the spirits' request. She had again placed herself where he couldn't see her, but he noted her feet and her mid-calf deerskin boots, tied with laces made from cured animal guts. They were worn and repaired many times over.

"Turn from your path, Wynter. Go south, away from here. The north holds only darkness and ultimately, leads to your destruction. The spirits have bid me slay you, and I do not. We are not slaves to the spirits or anyone else. As I have not taken your life, you do not have to follow the path they have chosen for you."

Wynter listened to the faint crunch of dried grass and bare earth beneath her feet as she walked away, trying to judge which way she went so he could track her down and kill her when he regained his ability to move. He strained his ears to listen and heard Haustis singing, her voice seeming to come from all directions at once as she walked away.

TEN

Wynter woke up, rubbed his eyes and rolled onto his hands and knees before he realized he could move again. His joints tingled with pain and the less comfortable awareness that his body had taken care of all its needs as he slept. He ignored the food Haustis had left and made his way to the stream where a cold bath cleaned his body and clothes. It did nothing, however, to cool his temper. Trudging back up the rocky river bank he threw his clothes onto a large rock and hoped the sun would dry them quickly and turned his attention to the food the old woman had left.

He leaned his body forward and situated his feet under him, resting his arms on his upper thighs and taking stock of his situation. In addition to the food, Haustis had left a small water skin, but nothing else. South or north? To the south, he knew, were people, towns, the hope of a new start. He was young enough to start a family with the right woman, but too old to see any children grow into families of their own. He would have to go far south to avoid towns where people might know him.

The problem, he knew, was that he was known by some people in many towns. People who would not be comfortable at his taking up residence nearby.

"Then go north. That's where the old lady doesn't want you to go. Obviously, that's the place to be."

"I thought you left." Wynter didn't say the words out loud this time, he was done trying to pretend to be thought less mad. If he were seen talking to the air, he believed, then he would be known as mad by all who saw him.

"You need me. You said so yourself. It wasn't very kind of you to throw me out like that, but I'm not surprised you let me back in. How did you become an assassin when you're so needy of other people?"

"Did the old woman leave a knife I could stab myself with? I don't need you. What I need is for my clothes to dry so I can walk ... somewhere."

"Light a fire."

77

"I don't have anything to light a fire with." He knew it was true without looking. Haustis had gone through his small pouch of belongings and taken the needle and thread, the small knife, even the empty bottle of liquor. She had only left the stone, which sat untouched. *"What good is a stone here? Why did I take it and why did Haustis leave it?"*

"Do you want an answer?"

"Do you have one?" Wynter was certain she did, and he wanted to hear it.

"If you have an answer, I have an answer, and you have, perhaps, an answer." His wife's voice, even in his head was irritating. She was trying to sound soft and sweet but all he could see was her wrapped in a shawl, holding their dead daughter, and signs of plague breaking out along her neck, face, and around her eyes. Her voice, to him, was becoming a thing of death and decay. He could almost smell the mold rot as if she were breathing on him as she spoke.

"What do you remember from when you picked up the stone at the crater?" The question came as if it were being asked of a child. It was condescending and necessary all at once, and it forced him to think. Wynter remembered smelling the woman's sweat and blood and looking into her green and blue eyes for the fear he would surely find there. But he didn't find any of that. He found two eyes that stared through him as if they were looking at something miles away.

When Wynter held the stone, the world turned dark, as if the dirt falling from the sky had redoubled and only the hint of a moon behind storm clouds lit his path. A trail of light, meager though it was, had a quality that couldn't be denied. Like a river of milk, he saw a path leading straight down the trench and into the woods, heading north.

Considering the small sack in his hand, he reached forward to hold the stone again, expecting a similar path to light his way, to provide a sign that he couldn't ignore.

"Do it," his wife said. *"It holds all the answers you need."*

Wynter almost pulled his hand back. He didn't want to do what his wife said; he wanted to be difficult and free himself from her orders, but he had no better options, and so he took the stone again, and let the darkness envelope him. It was different this time, the darkness had an ambient light that didn't exist before as if it were somehow alive, pulsing with energy and waiting.

"Well?" His wife sounded excited and nervous, just as he felt himself.

"Where should I go?" The question came into Wynter's head unbidden, and barely with his realization. Almost at once, the light changed and again, the milky path pointed the way. Again, it pointed north.

Wynter stuffed the stone back in the bag and fell back slightly onto his bottom, like he'd just run a dozen leagues. He was tired, and he looked at his clothes by the rock, disappointed to see the sun was doing little to dry them as it lay hidden behind fists of clouds that dotted an otherwise clear sky. Not knowing what else he could do, Wynter gathered small sticks and placed them in the fire pit, painstakingly coaxing the remaining lingering coals into a small flame.

After drying his clothes and finishing his food, he started off again, consulting the stone occasionally before eventually leaving it in his bag, and continuing north. In this way he passed several days, eating what food he could find, mainly early spring berries, some edible plants, and more bugs than he ever would have considered. So many in fact, he started to become choosy, developing a taste for some over others. On the rare occasion he came across people, he hid and tried to pilfer supplies from them as they camped for the night.

"Are you going to leave them, dear?" Through his entire footsore journey, the scenery changed, becoming flatter and the forests thinning, but the voice in his head never seemed to run out of things to say.

"I don't need to leave a trail of bodies for people to follow," Wynter replied after relieving a small group of traders heading south who had drunk themselves to sleep, of an assortment of clothing, a pack, some food, a serviceable knife, and a passable spear. *"I don't want to be chased. I want to rest and recover."* Wynter realized he was starting to

think like an assassin again, putting needs ahead of wants and looking at every decision as a move in a longer game.

"And then what? What happens when you're fit and strong again? What happens when you've equipped yourself with the finest weapons you can find in the bedrolls of peasants? Will you find a town and take up a trade, get married, have children?" Her voice was ratcheting up and Wynter could tell his wife was getting impatient.

"You can play these games all you want, you know, but the truth is, I'm right here with you. You can't turn your back on yourself."

Wynter groaned out loud. Of all the things she had said so far, he knew beyond a doubt the last was true.

He turned his back on the small campsite and the lifeless bodies he left there and continued his march north. *"Right now, I'm just trying to survive. Maybe I will take up a trade and settle down,"* he said silently but forcefully to his dead wife. *"But I damn sure won't get married again."*

ELEVEN

It was more than a week before Lydria, Kimi, and Haidrea were prepared to leave Eifynar. Lydria lingered, unsure of how to find Haustis or Wynter and what to do if she found them.

"Maybe he will be dead along the road and it won't matter," Lydria said to Drae Ghern, who had become a spiritual confidant and a father figure to her as they spent time every morning doing small tasks with magic such as lighting fires and mending small objects. This morning the old Eifen had her moving items in his house. The force necessary to lift and move a physical object with magic was, Lydria thought, more taxing than lifting the thing by hand.

"You are doing well, Lydria. Drae Ghern is wise to have you practice. As you are becoming aware, the tasks get easier as you learn to gather and use your magical energy." The small cat's voice had become so normal to her over the last few days Lydria sometimes had to ask Kimi to repeat himself. Today, however, she heard him clearly as she moved Drae Ghern from a chair by the fireplace to another across the room.

"Maybe I should have started by moving you instead of a fully-grown man." Lydria's voice in Kimi's ears was stressed, but not without compassion. Just then Drae Ghern patted his lap inviting the cat to jump up as he floated an arm's span in the air. Kimi jumped onto the old man's leg which caused him to drop slightly as Lydria reacted to the new weight. *"It was your idea,"* the bobcat said in answer to her exasperated sigh.

As soon as Drae Ghern and Kimi were settled gently on the ground, Lydria slumped to the floor and put her hands on her knees. She was exhausted, as if she had tried to pick them up herself. She reached into a small bag on her belt and ate some dried meat. She had discovered that food helped keep exhaustion from becoming nausea but did little else. The dressing, drying, and curing of the meat had been an exercise in magic as well; one which the Eifen charged with such chores encouraged her to practice.

Drae Ghern got up and put his hand on Lydria's shoulder and encouraged her; at the same time the door to his house opened and Wae Ilsit stood silhouetted in the frame. "Father, it is time," he said. Drae Ghern helped Lydria to her feet and together with Kimi, the three went outside where the Eifen gathered.

Nethyal and three warriors were facing their chief, Haidrea, and three other men. Drae Ghern took his place next to his son, and Lydria to his left. Kimi was curled on Lydria's shoulders.

"Today we send a party to watch over the land. Ever it has been the role of the Eifen to watch over Eigrae and protect it as best we can from those who would despoil it. Wynter, may or may not be such a person, but there is reason to believe he should be watched carefully," Wae Ilsit said. "The warriors before us are not preparing for battle, but to determine if Wynter is a man who may use his power for the good of Eigrae or toward its peril. Nethyal, you were chosen to find Wynter. If it can be done, you have the will of the spirits, the Eifen of Eifynar, and Eigrae herself, to do what must be done to prevent him from using his power as a stain upon the earth."

Wae Ilsit paused and considered the faces of the tribe. "Is there any among you who would go in their place?"

Lydria started to lift her arm and was instantly aware of Drae Ghern's hand on her elbow. "This is not your time, Wielder."

Around her the entire town, save Wae Ilsit, Haidrea, Drae Ghern, and herself, stood with their hands raised.

"Is this pleasing to the spirits, Father?" Wae Ilsit spoke the words with pride as he glanced to the graetongue.

Drae Ghern nodded lightly, let go of Lydria's arm and started the chant that had become so familiar to the kingdom woman over the past few weeks. The tone in his song today, however, was different; it sped up and slowed like a bird, moving from place to place, eager to find somewhere to roost. He moved as he sang, among the villagers, stopping at every adult and child old enough to plow, shoot, sew, or chew, to hold the head, arm, or chest of one of the Eifen. As he passed each person, they did not follow him with their eyes, but rather they looked toward the four warriors who stood straight and still with their eyes closed and chins jutted forward.

"What is happening?" Lydria asked. *"I can't keep my eyes off him, but they act as if he's not there."* She was mesmerized by the singing man who seemed to have grown straighter as he walked among his people, years dropping away from his shoulders like raindrops.

"Close your eyes, Wielder, and think about me, see through my eyes."

Lydria obeyed and after a moment, she nearly cried aloud for she could see Drae Ghern move through his village, but the image was different. There were no strong colors, and everything looked closer, sharper than it should have.

"What is this?" she asked.

"This is how I view the world, and our connection means you can view it through me. Drae Ghern is doing the same spiritually for Nethyal and his warriors. He is gathering the vision, wisdom, and strength of the community which he will pass to them to help them on their journey."

As the shaman moved through his people he began to move toward Wae Ilsit and the waiting warriors and stopped. Looking for a moment toward Lydria and Haidrea, he smiled, and bowed his head. When his eyes came up they were alive with inspiration and he immediately took four steps backward and lowered himself to one knee where he lifted into his arms a baby, the youngest of the Eifen. A small pale girl whose ears peaked from behind a head of hair the color of sunlight. Drae Ghern held her tightly to his chest and then kissed her forehead lightly before handing her back to her mother who looked pleased her daughter had been marked in such a way.

Moving lightly to Wae Ilsit's side he faced his son, the chief's strong arms encircled with bands of metal above the elbows and his skin marked with the small white lines of scars that told the story of his battles. Father and son embraced quickly and Wae Ilsit knelt before his elder who took his head in both his hands and began to sing once more.

Kimi inhaled as if he was going to interpret what was taking place, but he was interrupted by Lydria. *"Wae Ilsit gives the experience of the Chief. But what of the baby?"*

83

As Drae Ghern finished his song, the town began to clap in unison until Wae Ilsit rose once more and ceded the place of honor to Drae Ghern.

"I have lived many seasons and heard many stories," he said loudly for the town to hear, but for the benefit of the four warriors in front of him. "Only once have I had cause to gather the wisdom, strength, and love of the Eifen to send a party into the wild. The hunt these warriors undertake is perhaps the most important in the life of our people, and they will need all your gifts as they proceed. With that, he nodded to Wae Ilsit who resumed his place and motioned for Nethyal to come forward.

"Father, I have chosen these three warriors to join me. If it is the will of the Eifen, we will do as you bid."

"It is the will of the Eifen," Wae Ilsit said gravely.

"It is the will of the spirits as well," Drae Ghern added. He then moved to each of the four men and held each of them by the head, the arm, and the chest. "And to the leader of these warriors, I also add mercy," and with that he took Nethyal to him and hugged him in the same manner he had the baby.

The ceremony was unlike anything Lydria had witnessed among the kingdom armies where men made their good-byes to their families in private, if at all.

With Drae Ghern back in his place, Wae Ilsit presented a knife with a handle carved from a brilliant white bone and a blade so black it made Lydria gasp. She had never seen anything like it and as Nethyal turned the blade in his hand she could see he too, was honored and surprised by the gift. Wae Ilsit held his son's face between his two strong hands for several seconds before leaning forward so their foreheads met. Lydria could see Wae Ilsit's lips move but what he said to his son was for his ears alone.

In turn, each of the other three men who had stood by quietly during the ceremony approached one of Nethyal's warriors. The older men were the warriors' fathers, Lydria knew from her time in the town. Each presented a small weapon as a gift to their son. Each also touched his own head, arm, and heart before touching the head, arm, and heart of his offspring. Each also hugged his son.

Finally, Drae Ghern raised his left hand and began a low, rumbling chant. *"He asks the spirits to watch over these men,"* Kimi said. *"And he grants them the peace and goodwill of the Eifen and Eigrae, so they may remain strong until their safe return."*

Lydria noticed Nethyal was no longer paying attention to his father or grandfather. His eyes were locked to hers, and while he nodded his head in acknowledgement of her, his cheek and lip crept modestly upward – a look not lost on Lydria or Kimi.

"As marvelous a gift as he has been given, Nethyal is not pleased with his weapon or his warriors," Kimi said.

"Did he not have his choice of men?" Lydria asked, somewhat surprised by the bobcat's assessment.

"He did, yes," came the reply. *"But the weapon he really wanted, was you."*

As Drae Ghern finished his song, the men looked at their chief and turned to move through the town on their way to the forest. As they left, a hundred hands touched their shoulders.

"The touch of the Eifen tells the group that they will watch over them; and that if they do not come back, that they will avenge them."

The men and women of Eifynar were still and silent until they were sure the men were too far into the forest to hear them. When Drae Ghern and Wae Ilsit turned to move, the rest followed, returning to their tasks, knowing that the warriors were on their own and the town had work that needed to be accomplished.

"Why did Drae Ghern say he had only once witnessed such a ceremony as this, when hunting parties must surely be sent routinely?" Lydria asked Kimi.

"They are sending these warriors to hunt a man," the bobcat said. *"To hunt a deer is something done to feed the town. This is something more, and it is treated with more...dignity. I think they are correct to treat such a decision this way."*

Standing in their places while the rest of the people melted back into the town, Drae Ghern spoke softly to the chief, but Kimi's sharp ears heard his words and relayed them to Lydria. *"His heart is hard, my son. He has seen the wielder's power and it has taken a place within him. He needs to find a path under his own power, with his own strength. It is good that he goes now, for the spirits tell me, this journey will show him his true heart and bring him back to us. But when our daughters go into the wild, they must go by a different path."*

Lydria and Haidrea worked together for several more days preparing for their journey, and consulting Drae Ghern on the best path to find the legendary Haustis. Lydria's magical strength continued to grow and she became skilled in basic tasks that, she thought, were no more useful than having the right equipment or skills. Each night she, Haidrea, and Kimi would join Drae Ghern to speak with the spirits and through these journeys Lydria began to understand how magic took a payment from wielders – sometimes physical, sometimes emotional – but always in relation to the difficulty of the task. A small task, practiced often, took less of a toll, just as a skill practiced often could be accomplished quickly and with ease, but not altogether without cost. But still, she felt, Nethyal was wrong to think it was such a great power. Other than healing, it seemed there was nothing she could do that Haidrea could not, given enough time.

On the night before their departure, Drae Ghern called his daughters and Kimi into his home. "We will prepare your bag. Bring out the old beaver and let us refill his body with items to take you on your journey and protect you."

Lydria placed the bag gently on the ground between herself and Drae Ghern, carefully opening the gut laces that held it closed, and then took from another small pouch several items she had gathered. As she laid them in front of her, Drae Ghern chanted and moved around the room encompassing all the company in a circle as he did. Slowly, and reverentially, Lydria placed into the bag the feathered end of the arrow used to kill her father, and a thin white bone – her finger. Drae Ghern stopped chanting after the first item was placed in the bag.

"Aside from the stone, these are all I have," Lydria said.

"I have something for you, daughter." Drae Ghern smiled as he presented the pipe he had shared with Lydria during their first spirit journey together, and he gave her as well a small pouch of weed. The woman smiled and gripped Drae Ghern's hand in thanks.

"The women of Eifynar have asked you to have this," he said and brought out a small package wrapped in leaves. "It includes herbs and berries for healing. You have been a great help to us this last moon and the women would have you be spared from harm with the healing spirit to look over you. And there is one more thing, but I cannot say what it contains; it was left on my doorstep last evening."

The final package was slightly larger than an acorn and wrapped in a finely detailed linen with images of trees and with beautiful curved lines worked around the edge. "It says, Lydria, friend of the Eifen, and Wielder," said Drae Ghern. The old man added it to her possessions and sealed the bag with a short, low song.

The three humans and bobcat were silent for a moment as Lydria took the bag and placed it over her shoulder. "Father," Lydria called Drae Ghern the name out of respect as he had called and treated her, like a daughter. "Nethyal believes my magic could be used as a weapon. How?"

Drae Ghern had his back to Lydria when she asked the question, and she could see his shoulders slump slightly with her last word. As he waited to respond, time in the room seemed to freeze. Haidrea and Kimi, who had been rising to go back to their own beds, froze as well to await the answer, for the question was theirs as well.

"Sit," Drae Ghern said. It was unlike him to command in such a way, but it was not loud or demanding, but said with a tone and resolve that left no doubt as to his authority.

"This question I had hoped would not be asked of me, but of Haustis." He turned to them and slowly sank to the floor, his old joints creaking with exertion. He sat with his head down and when he at last lifted his eyes, Lydria could see sadness in them. "I'm sorry, Father, I did not mean…"

"No. No, you are right to ask. I am a fool to have not told you more of what has been shown me. But I am not the right person … Haustis must be the one."

"So, I can use magic as a weapon?" Lydria absently sent her message to Kimi though a quick look told them both that Haidrea was thinking the same.

Haidrea, who did not speak often of magic or question her grandfather, spoke quietly when she asked, "Grandfather, what have the spirits shown you?" The pleading quality of her voice convinced him to speak.

"The spirits have shown me light and darkness in such contrast that it can only be the work of magic. You said Wynter has a stone alike to yours, and the spirits tell me that he too, is capable of magic. Perhaps more so, for his heart is not well and it is unlikely he will use his magic to heal."

"But if you can heal with little cost, what can he do...?" Kimi's question made Lydria's eyes widen and her heart race as her head snapped up to look at Drae Ghern.

"Kimi was wondering..."

"What Wynter is capable of?" Drae Ghern smiled again at the bobcat who lay across Lydria's lap, his head up and staring at the old man. "Magic, as the spirits have shown me, has very few limits, Wielder, and I do not know what those limits might be. You may be able to fell an oak in the forest and build a lodge without moving. You may, as you have demonstrated, clean a deer, tan a hide, or make dried meat."

"Or..." Lydria offered. She was almost certain what the final 'or' might bring, but she couldn't be the one to say it.

"Or kill...," offered Haidrea with a whisper. As she said the words, Drae Ghern bowed his head and muttered only, "perhaps." The women could tell Drae Ghern hoped he was wrong.

"But what would that do to me?" Lydria asked. "The things I've done here have all had some effect on me, and they were small things. Killing is certainly no small thing?"

"I do not have the answers you seek, and the spirits do not provide them to me." Drae Ghern lifted his head again and placed his palms on his knees and straightened his back and his arms, locking his elbows as if to hold himself up. "I believe there would be a price for such an act. A severe price. But I do not think it is the stone's nature to destroy itself by destroying its possessor." He let the statement linger before continuing. "What have you noticed with your magic since you've arrived?"

Lydria thought, and instantly knew the answer. She shuddered, and Drae Ghern nodded gravely. "The more I do something, the easier it gets and the less of an effect it has on me," she whispered, her voice barely audible in the stillness of the room. The realization of what they all knew, when held up against the terror of Wynter, made everyone pause.

Haidrea lifted her head to speak before Lydria's breath had faded into the darkness that enveloped the house. Only the embers of a fire were visible, and they cast a heavy shadow across her sharp features. Finally, Drae Ghern's granddaughter gave voice to their shared concern, "given enough time, a person with this power could kill with ease."

"If they *can* kill. But, now at least, you understand why you must seek Haustis first," Drae Ghern replied. "As long as Wynter walks the land, there will be no peace. His shadow will fall over all kingdoms, and all people until he is destroyed."

"Would it not make sense, then, for me to prepare to fight him – like your warriors prepare, through practice?" Lydria was breathing faster and her voice rising in pitch. Kimi sent soothing thoughts to her to keep her calm. He faced her so the others would know he spoke to her.

"What would you do, Wielder? Kill for practice? For sport? Each creature in the forest does what he does best to survive. Not all creatures have claws and teeth. Some are fast, some fly high, some are cunning. Each uses the strengths he was given, and in this way, fights. Do not try to become that what you are not – that is the surest path to defeat."

Lydria took a deep breath and relayed Kimi's message and then she thanked Drae Ghern and excused herself for the evening to do as her father had taught her – examine the options and then sleep. In the morning, along with Haidrea and Kimi, she would speak again with Drae Ghern and Wae Ilsit and leave the town and search for a legend.

TWELVE

Lydria and Haidrea left Eifynar the way they had come, heading back toward the crater. Haidrea knew the way as if she were walking to the house next door, and Kimi ran off ahead, as a silent scout, sending back word to the women of what the terrain held.

"There are rabbits here! Lots of rabbits."

"Kimi is hunting again," Lydria told her friend. "I don't think he's going to be much use to us until he's full."

"He is embracing his nature. Bobcats are very cunning and rarely the prey for others, yet they happily indulge in everything from mice to animals many times their size. He is small, yet he is, in his way, formidable." Haidrea surprised Lydria by saying so much in a single breath.

"You are talkative today," Lydria teased.

"Kimi is ahead of us and I trust his instincts and his senses more than my own. I have no doubt if he hears or smells anything, you would know right away."

"If he isn't thinking about food."

"Grandfather and I have had many long talks about the animals in the forest and your connection to Kimi; Grandfather has wondered if you might be able to take part in his senses if you wished."

Lydria could tell Haidrea was not sure if she believed her grandfather, but given Lydria's other talents, she was willing to accept the possibility. "Have you spoken with Kimi about it?"

Lydria smiled and told Haidrea of her experience seeing through Kimi's eyes at the ceremony with the warriors.

Haidrea stopped. She didn't seem surprised by the admission, but she sounded concerned as she spoke to Lydria. "You walk away from a destroyed forest, turn back a man who would kill you, speak with the forest animals, move objects with a thought, and now you say you can see through his eyes as well. Does this gift, too, have a price your body must pay?"

Haidrea's question receded as Lydria kept walking, only stopping as Haidrea's voice finally tailed off through the trees.

"No." She turned to look at Haidrea who was walking toward her again. "No, there wasn't. It requires some concentration, but the connection takes nothing from me." Lydria paused and explained to her friend how the world looked through Kimi's eyes, as if everyone were different, with less color, but more distinctiveness. "If anything, I think I felt better when I was finished, but I didn't really give it any thought."

"You must give all of your efforts thought from now on," Haidrea admonished. "You have a power without equal, and you must make yourself aware of it, and be the one who holds the reins, lest it control you."

Lydria smiled and impulsively reached out to hug her friend, who at that time sounded so very much like the old shaman. Kimi chose that time to bound back toward them, hurtling through the trees, the mottled fur of his snout stained a dark red. He stopped several feet from them along their path, and ran a paw across his nose, alternately licking it and wiping away the blood of lunch.

"*You can see through my eyes, and I believe you could hear through my ears and even taste that delicious rabbit, and not quite so filling squirrel I just ate. But I would discourage it.*" Lydria relayed the message and then turned her head toward the cat again, who spoke before she could verbalize her next question. "*When you look through my eyes, I am ... not blind, but nearly so; I cannot see clearly, as if I were looking at things under water.*" Kimi said no more but wandered over to Haidrea and rubbed his head across the woman's buckskin trousers. "*She smells like a herd of deer and it makes me hungry.*"

Lydria watched Haidrea scratch Kimi behind the ears and laughed. The bobcat was still a kitten and just as playful. With his stomach full, he might allow himself to be scratched for hours.

Soon they were walking again and Haidrea was more alert, her spear held as Lydria had seen it when they first met and her eyes glancing at the ground. She whispered Lydria's name and held her hand to signal a stop. Kimi, fluid and silent back amongst the thinning trees, continued forward and moved south of the pair, staying in denser forest.

"Kimi says you have seen something?" Lydria whispered, crouched on one knee behind a small birch watching Haidrea examine the ground around her.

"We are fortunate the rains have not come yet," Haidrea said, her voice rising to a more normal level. "Come, see. You can still make out the prints of a small person's booted foot."

Lydria was impressed. Her father had been a reasonable tracker and she learned a little from him of the subtle signs to look for when searching for the passage of others – bent tree branches, scratches on bark, crushed leaves and, of course, prints. But on his best day Cargile would never have spotted what Haidrea casually observed. Only when she pointed them out by circling them with her finger, did Lydria see them, and even then, not clearly. They were, Haidrea insisted, made after the rains several days earlier and had dried into their shape making them an easy track to spot for someone who knew what to look for. "Whoever it was, is lightly encumbered and in no hurry," Haidrea said, looking at once to Lydria, and unconsciously shifting her spear to a defensive position.

"Do you think we should be worried of a single person traveling through the forest?" Lydria's attempt to not sound worried came out instead as deeply concerned.

"*Lydria, tell Haidrea I think whoever it is, it is not Wynter,*" Kimi said and bounded off to the west.

The two women ran ahead, their worry lessened by Kimi's frenetic passage through the thickening ground cover. Lydria followed Haidrea, who picked the best paths and easily moved among the rocks and tree roots. As they traveled the trees thinned noticeably and the light became brighter, until they stood along the edge of the forest where piles of trees and earth led to the trench and the crater. To the west of the crater, Kimi lay upon a small pile of stones, one of several that had been placed recently judging by the damp lines indicating they had only recently been pulled from the ground.

Haidrea moved toward the crater while Lydria went to Kimi. "Those are graves," she noted quickly, and she saw her father's remains had been moved from where she had last seen them. Moving toward the bobcat and the burial mounds, she noticed a crushed helmet placed on top of one of the stones. It was her father's. She had more than once mended the leather straps that lined the metal, and hefting its weight, she moved as if to put it on, and stopped as the faint but still familiar odor of her father raced into her nose, silencing all her thoughts. Holding the mangled metal in front of her face she felt a wave of grief as the smell of oil and leather brought back a flood of memories from her childhood in the army camps, running to her father after a battle, or learning how to inspect a weapon or piece of armor.

She did not cry, but her lip trembled as she thought of his face amongst the dirt and stones and trees with an arrow shaft sticking out of his throat. Lydria started to place the helmet on the rocks of her father's grave and hesitated. Holding her palm to the inside of the helmet and pushing, a white light left her hand and poured from the steel helmet like a waterfall. The metal gave a satisfying pop as the largest dents were pushed out. There was hardly a seam to show it had ever been damaged. Lydria staggered a little and placed the helmet on Cargile's crude grave as Haidrea and Kimi, stood respectfully nearby.

"You honor the dead, Lydria. That is good. The dead deserve to be remembered for their actions, and through their stories. You will tell the story of your father one day." Haidrea looked at her friend warmly for a moment before moving to recover the trail. "Our prey does not try to hide their movement," she said. "They went this way back to the woods and toward the road that heads west to the small kingdom fort."

"Steven's Folly," Lydria sighed. She took one last look at her father's resting place and stumbled forward landing heavily on a bank of dirt. She took up a large stick and used it to pull herself back up and continue walking.

"Perhaps you should have something to eat?" suggested Kimi. *"You've done something new and it has weakened you."*

"Thank you, my furry friend, I'll be fine," was all the reply the bobcat received.

For the rest of the day they rarely spoke. The air had become warm and small flies gathered around their heads as they neared the shores of the Great Lake. The smell of dead fish washed upon the shores reached them soon after and as the sun made its lingering descent, they made camp early. Haidrea left to hunt, while Kimi and Lydria set up camp and prepared for a light meal. Lydria turned her thoughts to her companion, *"You worry too much, Kimi. I will be fine. I'm tired and hungry."*

"I'm glad. I'm going into the trees more where the flying pests aren't so bad. Really, what's the point of having a tail so short I can't swipe flies from my eyes!"

Lydria laughed and soon after Haidrea returned bringing a small, freshly gutted young deer into camp where she cleaned the animal and set venison to cook for the two women, and to bleed for the always-hungry Kimi.

"The person we follow continues to walk west and her pace has slowed," Haidrea said as they finished their meal and Lydria used magic to artfully preserve the deerskin to be sold to the soldiers at Steven's Folly.

"You said 'her'."

"Yes. The prints are narrow and shallow. The stride is also short and the path she travels continues to the west. Beyond your folly, there are great forests. Grandfather says far beyond those forests, there is an enormous city of the Eifen – a city that make Eifynar look like a collection of huts." Lydria kept silent hoping her friend would continue. She had never heard more than small tales of the Eifen and their city north of Bayside; she had never heard any about other Eifen cities.

"The Eifen, according to grandfather, have been in Eifynar for many of our generations, and even more of yours." Haidrea gauged Lydria's expression and nodded. "We live a span of years greater than your people – not a huge span, but it is not uncommon for Eifynar to have a dozen or more who have seen six score of years or more. Many of the Eifen live very long lives compared to our neighbors. Still, grandfather says the cities of our forebears far to the west, hold many times the numbers residing in Eifynar and many more of these had seen more than seven score years. During their years, the Eifen of the west built great buildings of stone and buried their hands deep in the earth, as Eigrae shared her secrets with them."

Haidrea paused, looking at a handful of dirt she seemed to have collected without noticing, pulling small stones from the pile until it was just dirt which she lovingly sifted through her fingers. She brought her hand to her face and inhaled deeply before turning back to Lydria.

"I can smell Eigrae and from that smell, I know she is trying to heal from her recent wounds at the crater. I can also smell the Farn'Nethyn, but only rarely do I get a hint of its presence."

"What is Farn'Nethyn?" Lydria asked before Haidrea could continue. Haidrea seemed sad as if she had lost a friend, but her spirit picked up somewhat as Kimi rolled in the dirt she had recently turned over in front of her. Haidrea rubbed the cat and smiled as Kimi licked her fingers.

"Farn'Nethyn is the darkstone. It is a very rare stone and the reason Eifynar exists. The blade my father gave to Nethyal represented all we could find in a handful of Eifen life-times of searching. Many generations ago, well before grandfather's time, a small group of Eifen set off east from the great city in the west, spurred on by a graetongue's vision. In that vision, a wall of warriors with spears of Farn'Nethyn filled a valley as the last defense against a great power. The lost city, grandfather says, is in a faraway place where there are no mountains, and so the graetongue looked for those who would search to the east among the fabled mountains and valleys and build the army of spears that would protect Eigrae from this danger.

"But no Farn'Nethyn was ever found. Father believes we are the last Eifen, and that the city of the west must have long ago fallen to the danger the graetongue foresaw."

"Has no one gone west to look?" Lydria leaned forward, hoping for more.

"The woods to the west are vast and wild. The Haustis believe we belong here between the great lake and the great sea of the east. The spirits tell grandfather the same, yet no longer do we search for Farn'Nethyn. Sometimes, I can smell a trace of it on the wind, but never have we been able to find it."

"You are the last of the Eifen?" Lydria asked as she stroked the small space between Kimi's ears. She had moved to sit beside Haidrea, hoping that by her closeness she could learn more of her people. All the time they had spent in Eifynar, Drae Ghern had never mentioned the darkstone, or their ancestors' cities.

"There are many people who are not of your people, nor of mine, but who dwell in the forests. Many roam from place to place as the herds move. Some stay in small groups, hoping to one day grow to a hamlet; very few grow into anything larger. These people are not always friendly with the Eifen and to go west would be to court war as we traveled through their lands.

"The stories we share tell us the Eifen of the west are gone, and only we remain. We have grown, and continue to do so," Haidrea explained. "We stay remote and stray not into the world of Wesolk and the southern princes.

Haidrea paused and held her toes which were each under the opposite leg as she sat near the fire. Reaching for a small stick, she stirred the flames sending up bits of ash, reminding Lydria of the ash that was falling when they met.

"I am not convinced that Haustis exists, and I feel I betray my grandfather even as I say it," Haidrea declared, her head hung lower than Lydria had ever seen, in the dusk, only the whites of her eyes giving her position away. Her voice cracked, as one who has come to grips with the truth in her own mind. "It has been many generations of my people since the Eifen traveled east. No one can live so long. I have asked my father many times if he met Haustis when he was made chief, as the stories say must happen, but he does not answer plainly. He tells me Haustis is a legend from which we can take comfort. He says the legend of Haustis helps us find a place for the power we wish we had but do not; and in that person we can look for guidance. In the end, he says, we find the answers ourselves."

The words hung drying and drifting away in the flames of the fire with neither woman eager to dispel the silence that remained. Kimi stopped purring and looked at Haidrea with his chin rested across Lydria's knee, his paws extended and hanging limply on either side of her leg. "*Say something*," he prompted.

"Having such a person does not seem like such a bad thing," Lydria said, hesitatingly at first, but more forcefully as she made connections in her head. "The kingdom people have gods whom they say have powers above mortal men. No one is faulted for not seeing these gods, or for the gods not responding to a summons."

"But, don't you see, Lydria," Haidrea's eyes were wide and her voice thin in the still night air. "Haustis is *said* to have these powers, your gods are *said* to have these powers. But you...you *do*. You have these powers and more."

"I can't call upon the wind and rain." Lydria's voice did not carry the conviction it should have and Haidrea stared at her friend, unconvinced of her dismissal. "At least, I don't think I can. But still, what does it matter? Drae Ghern believes Haustis exists and he asks us to find her for the sake of your people." Gently and with a dip in her voice that told Haidrea she was honest in her desire to honor the wishes of Drae Ghern. "Should that not be our concern right now?"

Haidrea reached toward Lydria's knee to scratch Kimi's ears and put her other hand reassuringly on Lydria's shoulder. "You are right, friend Lydria. We must honor our grandfather. And when we find Haustis, we will get our answers. Sleep well. Kimi has first watch."

"*What? What just happened?*"

"*You heard the woman, you have first watch.*"

THIRTEEN

Haidrea recovered the trail the next morning and they continued to follow it west, where it joined the road leading to Steven's Folly. Lydria remembered the border outpost as not much more than a small collection of shacks that had built itself into something resembling a small community with farmers and others who wanted to live away from Bayside.

Families had moved to the community as part of King Ahlric's plan to grow the outpost into a proper town before pushing the kingdom's borders west into the deep forest and onto the western bank of the Great Lake. Trade was scarce but evident and farms were starting to take shape as men and women worked the fields, gathering their seemingly endless crop of stones to use for buildings, field fences, and as the foundations of a large gatehouse keep and fortified walls.

Kimi went into the woods at the first sign of people, pledging to circle the town to see what he could learn from a walk around the settlement. He believed it shouldn't take more than a few minutes, but it was hours before Lydria heard his voice again.

"Have any of Haidrea's people come into this part of the forest? I swear I could smell them in the woods far south of the fort." Kimi sounded as if he was sure the answer would be no.

Lydria relayed the information to Haidrea, who was curious. "I thought the woman we followed was heading here. I have heard stories of people who live in the western forests, but Grandfather says they are recluses from Wesolk or the desert kingdoms of the south"

Lydria and Haidrea continued to Steven's Folly to find a place to rest and visit the commander to confirm the deaths of Cargile, Josen, Bracknell and the others. Tomorrow, they would follow Kimi's nose to the south.

As they walked toward the fort the smells of spring were running toward summer and the air was thick with pollen that gathered in the rough fibers of their clothing. The wind also brought the smell of sweet red clover and wildflowers which grew unchecked in fields outside the burgeoning walls and along the dry, grassless, and caked earth that passed as a road.

Among the women and children of the fort, Haidrea and Lydria were a curiosity worth staring at. A tall Eifen warrior with skin that glowed like midnight and strange ears and a kingdom woman with what looked like a vibrant piece of blue jewelry around her neck. They were not farmers, nor were they among the king's court for their shoes and clothes were dirty and spotted with sweat from long on the road. Lydria knew they would be the subject of conversation at every pub and table that evening. People stared but they didn't let their eyes linger.

Through the wall gate, which still stood somewhat higher than the actual wall, they passed hovels with roofs of thatched reeds and grass, a section of rickety stalls that served as a market, and just beyond those was the guarded door of the fort itself, an unimposing wooden structure surrounded by sharpened stakes and a wide, shallow ditch whose sole purpose was to delay an attacker just long enough so that they could be cut down by the archers who manned posts along the top of the fort's inner walls. Lydria stifled a laugh as she took in the defenses. Of more use than the stakes or ditch for stalling attackers, were the people of the village who would be plundered by invaders.

The soldier at the gate was young and officious, trying to do his duty and not stare openly at the exotic Eifen. Lydria smiled, knowing Haidrea was oblivious to the lecherous intent in the man's eyes. She felt almost sorry for the boy; if he tried anything with Haidrea he would be apologizing through a mouth full of blood and loose teeth. Sizing up his undersized arms, poor posture, and weak legs, the outcome wouldn't even be in doubt.

"I'd like to speak to the captain of the garrison," Lydria said. "Tell him Lydria, daughter of Cargile, has news."

The boy seemed startled to find Lydria standing there, her long, straight and unkempt hair clinging to the sides of her square, almost masculine face. He glanced quickly at her face and when his eyes started to go down they quickly stopped at the blue collar around her neck before returning to meet her own eyes. "Lydria, daughter of Cargile to speak with your captain," Lydria repeated. The soldier was young, but he wasn't stupid, at least; the name Cargile had opened his eyes, and something registered in his head when he finally recognized her – perhaps because of her eyes.

Cargile was liked and well respected among the soldiers and his daughter with two-colored eyes was a minor legend among the barracks. Once, when she was much younger, a soldier like the one before her now thought he would come see the little girl with the blue and green eyes. Cargile beat him like an unbroken horse. As the soldier turned to find the garrison captain, Lydria smiled at the memory of her father and his loving, overly-protective nature.

"I think he likes you," Lydria teased her friend. "He seemed very interested in your… clothing."

"Boys are the same, even among my people," Haidrea said. "They carry a weapon and think all women should believe them courageous and worthy because of it. I've met very few who are – and certainly not that boy who could not tell you even now what color my eyes are."

The two women laughed easily and passed the time waiting for the commander by Lydria explaining how life was lived in a kingdom village; from the distribution of chores, to feeding, cleaning, and raising children.

"Each family eats its own food and does not share with the rest of the village? What happens then if one family has a poor hunt, or sickness? How do the children eat?" Haidrea's questions flew at Lydria as she tried to answer each casually, finally understanding that for all the benefits of defense and education and training that her society prided itself on, it was not, perhaps, the most humane system. Lydria tried to explain that people did help others and that there was a measure of charity within the system, but even as she said it, the words sounded hollow and insufficient. She let the conversation lapse into silence.

Finally, the guard came racing back toward them with another man following at a brisk but unhurried pace. Lydria thought it was nice that the commander came at once, but she could tell he did not hurry for her. He merely walked like he had somewhere to be, and she doubted his stride changed much for anything.

"Welcome to Steven's Folly," he said when he reached the women, stepping in front of the guard who had positioned himself in front of Haidrea. "Please excuse Driscol," he said directly to Haidrea. "He's a good lad, but not … not very comfortable where women are concerned. I am Captain Edgar Branch, and I'm commander of the Folly."

Captain Branch was cordial and friendly, not at all like what Lydria remembered the last captain of Steven's Folly to be. He excused himself from the women and took a step back, tasking Driscol with seeing to lunch for him and his guests. "We'll take food outside by the unfinished walls – I assume that would be more comfortable for you both?" Haidrea nodded her assent, and over the course of the next two hours they ate and spoke about the message Lydria brought regarding her father and the wagons, and the event in the forest that had brought ruin upon them. As to Wynter, they told Captain Branch only that a bandit killed Josen and was taken prisoner just before disaster struck, and who had, apparently, Lydria added, also perished in the wreckage. By good fortune, Lydria had been at a stream nearby and down a hill and was spared the full effect of the devastation. Haidrea had found her and brought her to Eifynar where she was made well before arriving at Steven's Folly. The captain, though he undoubtedly noticed it, was kind enough not to ask questions of Lydria's exceptional neckwear.

"Well, that answers many questions," Captain Branch said. "Now, I take it you are home with us and will return to Bayside?"

The women paused but did not answer right away.

"I think," Lydria said, "I must help my friend find a member of her people who is also missing since the event. We have reason to believe she may have passed this way and we seek her to the west.

Captain Branch raised an eyebrow ever so slightly at the word 'west' and crossed his arms in front of him as he appraised each of the women. Lydria knew he was not inspecting them in the same way as had Driscol; he was providing himself a professional appraisal. Finally, after staring at Haidrea's eyes for several long minutes, he clapped his palms to his knees. "I would like to help and hope I may be of assistance in your search, but first, I would ask a favor of you." He spoke to Haidrea directly, and Lydria could feel more than see, the tension within her friend.

"I have seen many men in the king's service over the years," Captain Branch said, never taking his eyes from Haidrea's; "I like to think I can tell a soldier when I see one. I believe I see one now."

"And…"

"And I would like you to spend a day of your time and show my men your skill with a bow and how you fight. You must realize most of these men have never seen combat before, much less an Eifen. Many believe your people are just a story they heard from their mothers or grandmothers. Certainly, there has been trade and some interaction between our people, but it is scarce and such instances are far between. The skill the Eifen are said to possess with a bow is legend. It is something we would all benefit from seeing."

"Legend?" Haidrea was obviously flattered, and Lydria could tell by her voice that she was interested in the proposition, but she didn't entirely trust the captain. The captain could see it as well and so he told her a story.

"When I was a boy I lived far away. My parents and I were separated in a winter storm, and I was found nearly dead by an Eifen woman named Haustis, who brought me to a house where I was cared for. I lived among the people there and learned from them, and one day the old woman returned and sat with me and we smoked a pipe. When I awoke, Haustis was introducing me to a family in Stillwater, an independent town on the western shore of the Great Lake, far to the south of here. The people I lived with there could tell me nothing of where I had come from, and I remember little of it." He stared at Haidrea again and his eyes darted past hers to the tip of the bow strapped to her back.

"And you did not try to find your way back?" The surprise at hearing Haustis' name from the man was quickly overcome with curiosity and Haidrea hoped to learn more about this legend suddenly made real.

"Where would I start?" Branch laughed easily. It was apparent he had thought many times about searching for this place again. "Alas, that was where I was then, and this is where I am now. To my question, however, there are many within Steven's Folly, and even in Bayside, who know nothing of the Eifen. I've found that this kind of ignorance generally begets a certain belligerent attitude at worst, and misgivings, at best. I was hoping that by meeting with some of my men, they might see for themselves what is real and what is legend."

"You do not believe our people can shoot well, then, Captain Branch?" Haidrea was smiling, almost flirting, with the captain, but Lydria could tell she was eager to accept his offer and show the skill of her people.

Lydria, reached out to Kimi who seemed far away and relayed the discussion as the two women were shown to lodging for the evening.

"We may have an ally, my hungry friend."

"You may. Or you may have someone who hopes to learn how Haidrea's people fight to better fend off the Eifen on his doorstep."

The next day Lydria watched from a wooden bench near the gatehouse as Haidrea spoke with Captain Branch in front of an assembled company of perhaps two dozen soldiers. They were young like Driscol mostly, with several older men with white hair and soft bellies. Their equipment was worn but well kept, and they had obviously been in each other's company for many years. Lydria could see very little outward sign of the bearing that normally marked groups of soldiers. They were not in ranks, but in a cluster, talking amongst each other, and occasionally one would laugh loud enough so that those on the outskirts of the circle turned to his direction.

Several targets had been placed by a stone wall and three archers stood together at the edge of the cluster speaking privately but taking no pains to hide the looks and grins they sent toward the thin, muscular woman in front of them. Lydria relayed the proceedings to Kimi and let the cat use her eye for a time so he could appreciate the spectacle.

"Haidrea will show them more than her archery skills before this is over," Kimi said coldly as he scanned the crowd with Lydria's green eye.

The feeling of giving the cat control over one eye was uncomfortable. Kimi, aware of the disorientation it caused, tried not to overstay his welcome, but when Lydria finally got used to the cat's presence, Kimi would spend long moments on one spot, and Lydria clearly wanted to move to a different view. *"Kimi, what are you so interested in?"*

"Nothing. Your eyes are horrible – I'm just trying to be sure of what I'm looking at."

"Why do you think Haidrea will show more than archery?"

Kimi laughed, which sounded a bit like a sneeze to Lydria. *"Apart from the archers, do you see the three large men at the front and away from the captain? Watch them. They are trouble. Let me know how it goes, I'm going to get something to eat. Any longer in your eyes and I'll forget how to see properly."*

As Captain Branch made introductions, the men were polite. Several made rude comments and gestures to their companions, but none did so when the captain or Haidrea could see. Three archers lined up opposite their targets and fired off several volleys, most striking the hay bales surrounding the targets and a few finding the small wooden disc at the center. The entire target was contained in a small wooden cage so that it could be moved from place to place.

"That is good," said Haidrea, clearly enjoying her role as teacher.

"That's right, it's good, miss," said one of the large men Kimi had pointed out. "With this group behind their bows, an enemy doesn't stand a chance."

"Certainly not," Haidrea allowed. "At least, not if the enemy is twice as large as a man and standing perfectly still."

The comment made the group laugh lightly at the expense of the archers, as she knew it would, and as Captain Branch knew as well if his smile meant anything. Haidrea was enlivening the group and bringing them to her side slowly. The archers also picked up on the laughter, ceding her point, and Haidrea walked casually to the targets with three lengths of rope which she secured to the cages and gave the opposite ends to the three archers. "Pull these targets as fast you can."

The men looked at each other in disbelief. One said to the captain, "I'm not a horse. I'm not pulling…"

"Take a rope, each of you," barked Captain Branch. His authority was absolute, and the men immediately grabbed a line. Each of the men in turn recruited two of their fellows to pull the target very fast. As they began their journey back and forth along a long section of wall, Haidrea spoke to the remaining men.

"Every beast has a tempo and if you study it, you will be able to follow even the swiftest animal." With an effortlessness borne of years of practice she loaded an arrow and pulled the string of the short bow so that her arrow's feather brushed across her cheek. In the span of two heartbeats the arrow was away, and another had taken its place, followed by a third shortly after. Before the third struck home into the disc, she had already turned back to the assembled men. "Your enemy will be on the move and you must be able to hit the man who is moving." She paused for a moment for the men to return their gaze from the targets to her, their jaws slack and their attention now pinned to her every word.

"Also, remember, while you are shooting at them, they are shooting at you, so it is wise to be moving yourself." Haidrea mounted a horse Captain Branch had nearby and she wasted no time heading toward the targets. She fired two arrows and held back the last as she led the horse with her knees back to the waiting company. She was met with silence as the men noted the location of the arrows, both of which had just grazed the center discs.

The men pulling the targets dropped their ropes and rejoined the company. Nearly every man among them, including the captain, was humbled by what they had witnessed and stood silently processing the implications for their defenses. Finally, the largest of the three target pullers offered that Haidrea had only shot two of the targets. The mean-spirited jab drew scant, weak laughter from some of his fellows and a deafening silence from the rest.

Lydria relayed what was happening to Kimi as the men were waiting the storm the silence portended. Haidrea glanced at Captain Branch, who gave a nearly imperceptible nod and said, "Weaver," before Haidrea walked slowly and purposefully to the man who had spoken. When she reached him, she placed her face inches from his own, her eyes in direct line with his jaw. He was a large man, and Lydria was half afraid that the soldier would crush her friend before she could move. It was a pointless worry.

Haidrea's voice was soft but clear and each word resonated among the soldiers. "I didn't take the last shot, because it was my last arrow. Unless your enemy pays you the convenience of returning them, your last arrow is worth far more in your hand than in your enemy's neck. The soldier's smirk had only begun to form on his face when in a single fluid motion Haidrea shifted her weight and placed her right leg in front of his, punched his kidney with her left fist, took his left ear with her right hand and drew him down, leaning forward so that he fell over her extended leg onto the ground. By the time he realized what had happened her knee was under his chin, and her left hand held the point of the last arrow a finger-breadth from his eyeball.

"You are big. You are strong. But you are slow." The man was breathing hard, his eyes glued to the sharpened point of the arrow. "Speed, accuracy, and then strength are what a warrior need." Pushing into his chest with her knee, Haidrea placed a palm on the man's forehead and somersaulted off him, out of his range. Then she moved quickly back to him and held out her hand. "Thank you, Weaver, for volunteering for my demonstration." The man was not mentally agile, but he saw the captain nodding to him and understood. He smiled and accepted Haidrea's help to his feet. The men of the company applauded and laughed and Haidrea reached out and hugged the man before moving back to Captain Branch.

"She hugged him?" Kimi was incredulous as Lydria relayed what happened. *"She put her arms around him and hugged him? I don't believe it."*

"Believe it. She is very smart. She gave Weaver a way out of his humiliation and now his friends will merely tease him for the hug, and not the beating. Haidrea is very wise to not leave enemies in her wake."

The rest of the afternoon pitted the men against each other, shooting and sparring, with Haidrea giving them instruction and advice. Weaver, Lydria noted, was the most attentive and asked the most questions.

FOURTEEN

Summer days in the north were long, with light stretching into hours that were dark by the same time in Thrushton. Sleep was hard to come by, but the air was clean and the weather pleasingly cool at night and agreeably fine during the day. A low ridge of hills to the east helped Wynter judge distance and smoke on the horizon told him he was coming to a village, or at the very least, a camp. It had been days since he'd seen anyone. His theft of travelers had given him the tools to survive and his skill with his meager weapons began to return as he picked out distant targets along his route and practiced with the few arrows he possessed, collecting them as he passed. In this way, Wynter gathered his strength, honed his skill, and passed the long, miserable, and blessedly quiet hours.

The smoke continued to elude him, moving out of his reach each day, but he knew he was getting closer. He was in no hurry. Late in the evening the summer sun finally settled down, but Wynter knew it would only be down for a few hours. Holding his hand to the horizon, he knew the sun would rise only a couple of hand's lengths from where it set.

Using scrub brush and sticks he collected from the thin trees he passed during the day, he made a small fire and prepared his camp. Someone, he knew, had been following him for several days. Although he had never seen the person, Wynter was aware of something he could not see. It was an extra sense he credited to saving his life more than once. He had not had the sensation for years, but he knew exactly what it was when he felt it that morning. He was being followed, and whoever it was, was masterful at not being spotted. Throughout the day Wynter made subtle movements to scan the path he'd just walked without giving away that he was looking for something. He slowed his progress and deviated from a straight line. Even amidst the flatness and near-emptiness of the tundra, he saw nothing but seasonal grass and wildflowers with small stands of trees. They would be enough to hide in, but it wasn't a forest and the stands themselves could mostly be seen through - so great was the space between the trunks and so thin the ground cover under their weak canopy. Even the animals gave no account someone might be following him, but he knew better.

Knowing there was nothing to be done, Wynter made camp and curled up near his small fire with a blanket taken from one of his victims. Despite the season, nighttime on the tundra, when it came, was almost cold. A little sleep will serve me well, he thought. "If I am meant to die, then die I shall, but I won't be tired when death arrives." He chuckled to himself as he closed his eyes. Perhaps there was nothing out there. Perhaps he was seeing ghosts to match the one in his head.

"Wake up!"

"Go away, woman, just go away." Wynter threw off his blanket as if doing so would send the voice in his head sprawling across the grass, and when he opened his eyes, he saw dark legs with animal skin boots. He thought it was the old woman come to torment him again, but a quick look up showed a different face altogether.

"You are Wynter?"

Wynter made no immediate reply, studying the warrior standing before him. Sturdy but lithe, at this range Wynter knew the man could kill him if he chose; but he didn't fancy handing out his name to any stranger who asked. The warrior was an Eifen, a people Wynter had rarely seen, but was aware of; he was perhaps a messenger from the woman Haustis – there seemed to be a resemblance.

Wynter lifted his face to meet the eyes of the man, "I am known by several names, but I am not known by you." He hoped the tactic would help him gather more information than it provided.

"I have come to find a man of Wesolk by the name of Wynter. I have news he should hear."

Feeling at a disadvantage Wynter stood up, using his stick to help him, but also to provide a weapon should he need it. The warrior, for he could be nothing else, gave the stick an appraising look, and seeming unconcerned, turned his attention back to Wynter and stared at his neck in the poor light of the fire, moving to the side to catch the light more fully. "You are he, then."

Wynter paused and stared at the newcomer. His muscles were defined and developed. He wasn't a boy. He had a man's height and strength, it was obvious. But there was no tension in him. His eyes were wide, his shoulders at ease and his hands were not settled to make a quick or aggressive move to one of several bladed weapons evident on his body. There was no point in denying who he was, Wynter decided. If this man wanted him dead, he would already be dead.

"I am Wynter. Who are you who has tracked me through this desolate place without being seen or heard?"

"I will tell you my story. May I share your fire?"

The question was polite and disarming, and Wynter motioned toward the fire and rummaged through his things to find some food for the man who gave a grateful nod and accepted the plain meal earnestly and began to eat at once. Wynter said nothing as he ate. If this man were willing to tell his story, he was willing to hear it.

"You have chosen a good camp," the Eifen said. "The land is flat, and where you set your fire is just low enough to hide it from the south."

"Should I be worried about the foxes and rabbits who follow me from the south?" Wynter didn't appreciate the conversation and wondered why, if the man were going to kill him, he didn't just do it. Assassins, in general, didn't deal in polite conversation.

"The foxes and rabbits don't follow you. Much more dangerous creatures have been following you for some days. They've watched you hunt, eat, sleep, steal and mutter to yourself along your path. You presented for them a question."

"Presented? Do I no longer pose a question to these dangerous creatures?" Despite his instinct to not be near this man, Wynter was curious. This wasn't the type of conversation a killer had with his target. Some assassins, he knew, would try to get more money before killing their target. Some would try to get information that would lead to more work. Some just wanted the target to know who wanted them dead. This man did none of those things. He asked for nothing, he bragged of nothing.

"You no longer are threatened by three of them. My name is Nethyal. From the blue collar you wear, you are who and what I believe you to be."

Wynter raised his hand to his collar without thinking and felt the cool hardness of the ring there. "If I am 'what' you believe me to be? What if I am not 'what' you believe me to be?"

"Then you still have nothing to fear, for if you are not, my people have nothing to fear from you. For now, however, let us sleep and speak more as we walk tomorrow."

Nethyal laid back with his hands behind his head and quickly closed his eyes and was soon breathing steadily in sleep.

"Kill him now."

"Why? I don't think this man means to harm me. He seems to want to tell me something and I would like to know what it is."

"Fool. Your curiosity will kill you – and for what?" Wynter's wife's voice was getting deeper, as if she were afraid she would be heard if she didn't whisper.

"The worst that can happen to me is that I will die here in the tundra. If that happens I will not have to live a life in the barren cold and I will not have to listen to you any longer. I'll take my chances that this man won't kill me."

The next morning was crisp and cool, but the clear sky promised a bright sun and dry weather. Wynter woke to the smell of meat and soon picked out the sound of flames crackling on dry wood. Opening one eye he peered at Nethyal who was carefully cleaning the skin of a small rabbit, peacefully scraping the inside of the skin with a steel knife. He could have been at home in the middle of a family gathering, Wynter thought; he had no nervousness about the wild and seemed at ease in the camp of a stranger.

"You made breakfast?" Wynter offered by way of good morning.

"Sought, hunted, killed, cleaned, and made breakfast – yes." Nethyal smiled at the still prone form of Wynter to show he was in good spirits. "The meat will be finished soon, then we can continue our journey and talk."

"You say, 'our' journey, but I wasn't aware 'we' were on a journey. How do you come to know where I go or what I set out to do?"

Nethyal smiled again, using his knife as an extension of his hand, motioned for Wynter to sit up and carved him a slice of rabbit, holding it on the point of his blade. When Wynter took it, he hesitantly took a bite, and then another and then Nethyal began to speak. He told Wynter of a stranger who came to Eifynar soon after the night the sky rained ash; he spoke of the twin souls of her eyes, and her story of meeting Wynter at the crater. Wynter sat entranced, willing Nethyal to go on, but offering no confirmation that his story was true.

Nethyal considered the man's silence for a time and then told him of the power the woman he called Lydria could wield. The power to move objects, start fires, and perform tasks that would take hours – all in less time than it took to explain the task to be accomplished.

"Can you do these things?"

It was a simple question but one that demanded an answer. Nethyal's posture became more rigid and on guard. He didn't grasp a weapon, but Wynter could tell the man was considering all options for ensuring he couldn't escape. He looked at the remains of the rabbit and saw his fate in the steaming carcass.

"I don't know," Wynter answered, stalling for time to think of a way out of his circumstance. "I think it is possible, now that you tell me these things. Do you know how she accomplishes such …"?

"Magic. That is the word given to us by the spirits."

"Fine. Do you know how she accomplishes such magic?"

Nethyal explained as best he could how Lydria would think a thing and it would be but could offer no more elaboration than that. After a moment's silence, Nethyal picked up a small bundle of dry sticks sitting next to the fire and placed them between himself and Wynter. "Start a fire."

Wynter stared at the warrior and realized he was serious and after a moment, he stared at the bundle of dry leaves and twigs and thought about what he would do if he were going to start a fire. He considered how he would place a stick on the driest leaves and spin the stick back and forth through his palms until friction created smoke, and eventually fire.

It started slowly, the smoke curling up through the leaves and small twigs as if he had spent an hour with a hand drill. His palms seemed to hurt as though he had been running a stick back and forth through them, building up painful calluses, but the joy was the same – more so – as the wispy tendrils of smoke grew thicker until they burst into flame. Wynter fell back, exhausted, and when he went to wipe the sweat from his brow, he couldn't move his arms. He looked to Nethyal who had been watching him closely.

"I can't move my arms if that's what you're wondering," Wynter offered, silently considering his paralysis that seemed so long ago and wondering what magic he had caused that day.

"It is a good sign," Nethyal replied, helping Wynter into a comfortable sitting position and settling himself opposite, with the tiny flame between them. "Now, let me tell you what else I know."

Wynter was mesmerized by the story of the woman Lydria. How her magic affected her own being based on the power of the magic she attempted; and how by attempting a similar task repeatedly lead to a lessening of the effect on her body. Nethyal told him of how the woman healed with a thought and how it did her little harm. He heard the stories of Nethyal's grandfather, and even some of the woman Haustis. The story was long and full of useful information and by the end of it, Wynter had regained feeling in his fingers and could move his arms; although his hands were still largely useless. The healing power Nethyal spoke of would alone be worth a king's ransom, Wynter thought.

Wynter looked at Nethyal and realized the man had stopped talking and that he had been caught in his own thoughts, paying little attention to what was being said. "So," Wynter started, "why have you tracked me down to tell me this? You said I was being hunted by dangerous creatures, and yet you have not put a blade in me. You have not restrained me. You have not asked for anything. You may not know me well, Nethyal, but I know people well – wherever they come from, whatever they believe, whatever god they pray to – all men want something. What do you want, Nethyal?"

The young warrior's lip lifted slightly, and his left eyelid closed halfway as he nodded to Wynter. He was right, Wynter thought to himself, Nethyal did want something. "I will reveal what I want in time," he said. "For now, I offer you my help."

"What help would that be? You've just shown me the power of the gods and told me the story of your village, of Lydria, of your grandfather. I assume those who hunted me are no longer a danger because you killed them. I don't think you could go back to your village now if you wanted, Nethyal. Excuse me if I sound ungrateful, but how will you help me?"

Nethyal stared at Wynter for a moment before casually rising. His knees didn't crack, he made no noise of exertion; like Haustis, he simply unfolded himself until he was upright and like the old woman, he was almost instantly at his side with the pad of his index finger resting against Wynter's eyeball.

"This could easily be a knife," Nethyal said. "It could be a knife held by a killer or by a child. In your condition, the difference would be meaningless." The words contained no malice or emotion but were simply stated as one would notice the weather. "You cannot make a fire useful for cooking dinner without losing control of your arms; how do you plan to protect yourself as you learn what you are capable of? I have heard the stories from Lydria, and I've watched you make your way across this land. You are a capable bowman and you kill without remorse. I know a man such as yourself, knowing what he now knows, cannot go back to pulling a bowstring when he can command fire and objects by simply thinking of them. You are a wielder now, a user of magic, but until you learn and gain your full strength, I am all that stands between a world that will fear you, and death. Should that not be enough?"

Wynter laughed to himself. Nethyal wanted power and he was willing to be the shadow behind the throne. It was a useful arrangement and one, Wynter knew, that he could end easily when the time came. But for now, Nethyal was right, he needed to learn about his power and to harness it effectively, and he needed to be protected as he did so. Wynter knew the future would consist of many more days lying on the ground, unmoving and vulnerable before … what?

Nethyal felt the tension leave Wynter and moved back to the other side of the cooling ash of the small fire. "You have decided then." It wasn't a question. Wynter nodded and with some difficulty, lifted his arm to shake Nethyal's hand.

"What do you want, darling? You can have anything."

"I think I'd like to live somewhere grand," Wynter responded to his wife's voice. *"I think I would like to have people fear me again – but not from the shadows. I want people to know who I am and why they should be afraid."*

Wynter's wife started to say something and stopped after the first syllable. She had realized, perhaps, what the potential for this power could mean to her. The realization made Wynter smile. If his nascent power could have a quieting effect on the dead voice in his head, what kind of effect would it have on the living? How easy would it be to make them fear him and, ultimately, serve him? Yes, Wynter thought, I would like a new home one day and I've always rather admired Bayside – for starters.

FIFTEEN

Lydria and Haidrea stayed several days at the Folly where Haidrea spent a good deal of time with Captain Branch and Lydria gave her space by taking walks in the woods with Kimi and practicing small magic, leaving new or more intense magic for days of poor weather when she stayed inside the rooms the women had been given in the small keep.

Kimi spent a day when the women were inside to travel far to the south and scout the people he had smelled previously. He reported that they did not constitute a war camp, but more likely a hunting camp. Lydria told Captain Branch she had seen signs of people during one of her long walks, and the captain decided they should take a small group to meet with the strangers to avoid potential misunderstandings.

Branch, Haidrea, Lydria and Weaver, who had been a model soldier and citizen since Haidrea's demonstration, set off from Steven's Folly to meet the unknown group. Even with Kimi invisibly guiding them by the most direct route, it took more than a day and, not knowing of the cat, Branch and Weaver were keenly impressed by what they believed was the navigational prowess of the women.

"Do you see the big man, what he does, marking the trees?" Kimi spoke to Lydria as the group made their way through the forest.

"He marks the path to find his way home again," Lydria said. *"They think perhaps we may not go back with them, or that we may not be able to find our way back."*

"Will the strangers see it that way? Or will they see a path to their front door?"

"Remember Kimi, the markings work both ways. The captain has left a clear trail to his front door as well. I think it may be good each party understands this."

The hike through the woods was not silent, in fact, Branch argued, it would be good if they were heard coming from a distance, as it would lessen the opportunity for accidents.

As they creased a small hill into a relative clearing they were met by a single man. He was clad in finely woven breeches that clung to his skin, outlining lean, strong legs. His boots were tight to the middle of his calf and made of a leather so finely cured and sewn it certainly was not the work of anyone in Bayside, or even Eifynar. He waited patiently near a tree and wore a brown tunic that blended into his own skin as well as the forest around him. He wore no metal armor and by his side he steadied the hilt of a gently curved sword with a blade the length of his arm. On his back, Lydria could make out the black curve of an enormous bow, unstrung, hovering a foot above his head like a small tree branch.

The closer Lydria got the more she looked between the man and Haidrea, noting the man's ears – how they gently shifted forward and back listening for sounds in all directions. His deep brown eyes watched Lydria and her group walk steadily up a small rise meet him, but his ears continued to move slowly back and forth as if searching for something.

Haidrea raised an eyebrow but otherwise maintained her composure at the meeting of another Eifen. The man's dark, thick hair was tied at the back of his head, but he was bald from his forehead to the back of his ears. He looked older than Branch, and possibly older than Wae Ilsit, but it was hard to tell. He was fit and tall and as he stood, he could have been Lydria's age.

The party stopped almost at once and Haidrea greeted him in her own language. The man looked at Haidrea closely and opened his mouth as if he wanted to say something or ask a question. Instead, he looked to the others and said, "I speak the language of your kind." He then locked eyes with each member of the party before speaking again.

"It has been foretold that five would come," the man said. "Where does the fifth hide?"

"There are only four of us, I assure you…." Haidrea waited for the warrior's name but received only silence. "We have traveled lightly armed and without stealth. We wish to speak with your chief."

"The Haustis spoke of five. I see that you are lightly armed, and I have listened to your travels for some time, sister. I do not doubt you speak the truth. Yet I also do not doubt Haustis or the spirits she consults."

"It's me," Kimi's voice came to Lydria with a note of surprise and excitement. He had been largely on his own for days and was eager to be with Lydria and Haidrea again.

Lydria moved forward to Haidrea's side and spoke to her friend and the man facing them. "The fifth member of our party remains hidden in the woods. Not from any misgivings of your people, but for his own safety and to complement his nature. The two men that accompany us, have also never met him, but if you will grant him safe passage, he will come forward."

"It is the spirit's will there be five. Call your friend."

"Kimi."

As the bobcat left the cover of the forest, the three men were astonished to see the animal so openly approaching the group. When it leapt upon Lydria's shoulders, the man before them whispered, "it is true then."

He walked forward to Haidrea and Lydria, glancing quickly at the blue band embracing Lydria's pale neck and finally noticing her eyes. "Haustis foretold all, but I … I am…"

"Surprised?" Haidrea supplied.

"And more," he replied. "Haustis' foretelling brings both great joy and great suffering if all she says is true. As I see the fifth member of your party and the woman of two souls before me, I can no longer doubt. You are all welcome, although I wish it could be under a brighter star. We will go to our camp together."

It was obvious everyone wanted to know who both he and his chief was, but Haidrea responded to his offer without questioning him further. "You do your chief honor and we accept your invitation. We will follow where you lead." And with that, the man turned crisply and walked across the clearing. His pace was strong, and he knew his way as if he followed a road, although even Haidrea could not easily discern a path or track.

He was silent as the moved, and the others remained silent as well. Lydria moved close to Branch and he merely nodded to her and smiled. *"He does not fear betrayal,"* Kimi said. *"He smells of anticipation – he is happy and nervous although I don't understand why. Weaver is a tangle of odor and sights you cannot see. He trusts his commander, but he harbors a soldier's instinct to be wary."*

Lydria whispered to the captain that Weaver was anxious, and he responded to her with a look that asked a dozen questions before looking at the cat draped around her neck, and back to her. He pursed his lips and nodded, falling back to whisper quickly with Weaver; offering him some words of reassurance.

"What do you make of this, my furry friend," Lydria asked.

"I think, for the first time, I'm more interested in what we may hear than what we will have for dinner."

The conversation was long and Lydria and her party were treated like long-lost friends by the Eifen in the camp. Even Weaver seemed to enjoy the food and company outside by the light and warmth of a fire. Their guide from the forest was called Wae Relin and he was an amicable host.

"I have to wonder," Wae Relin said, "if the stories of our forebears come true before our eyes." He paused and dug up a handful of soil next to the rock on which he sat. "For many generations our people have stayed within our homes to the far west, rarely reaching out beyond our borders." Wae Relin stood before continuing his story and walked around the circle of the fire, stopping only to find a new seat on a log next to Haidrea.

"Generations ago a brave warrior named Wilmamen lead several families of our people east in search of a group that traveled before and did not return. She also sought the darkstone and to perform a task known only to our graetongue. Since that time, every generation leads a group east to seek our lost kin. Since that time, not one group has returned home." He took Haidrea's hand in his own and shook it, "it seems we have finally found our lost travelers."

Wae Relin turned in silence and looked squarely at Haidrea, his ears leaning forward to her, and his hands continuing their grip of her own. "Tell me sister, have any of them found you?"

Lydria could see that Haidrea had been on edge since meeting Wae Relin. Kimi too, had told Lydria he could smell the tension in both her and the man who spoke now.

119

Haidrea returned the grip of Wae Relin's hands and shook her head. "I am sorry, brother, but no one has come. Until now." And she lifted her hands and embraced Wae Relin as she did Wae Ilsit and Drae Ghern. No one spoke around the fire, but everyone smiled and turned to each other to share in the occasion of such a long-awaited reunion. The four men of Wae Relin's camp rose as one and gave a triumphant roar into the night air, and made their way around the fire, hugging each of Lydria's party and being especially joyful in the arms of Haidrea.

Eventually, they regained their seats to talk, but they sat closer now, and smiled more, and the Eifen of the west embraced Weaver and Branch as if they too were long-lost cousins.

Wae Relin settled back down to his seat and told his story of being chosen to lead the latest expedition to the east.

"The path from our city to your lands is not easy," he said. "There are many different peoples between our two lands, and not all of them share our visage. There are rivers the width of lakes, and forests that continue seemingly without end. Little of the way is friendly, and in the deep woods, small men did try to over-run us, but turned aside as we lifted our swords to defend ourselves, and for that we must thank Wae Wilmamen."

"Who is Wilmamen?" asked Haidrea, eager to learn all she could from her western cousins.

"The story of Wae Wilmamen is one of our greatest stories," Wae Relin began. "She was the Wae, the leader," he looked to the men of Wesolk and Lydria as he explained the word's meaning. "Wae Wilmamen was the first of the Eifen to venture east after the first company was lost. She has never seen the Great Lake of the east. After many weeks of travel, she and her company made their way across the Lang'Al, the Great River, which is so wide you can barely see the other side in places. Wae Wilmamen looked far for a place to cross before her people gave up and made small boats to cross.

In that crossing several died, so fierce was the river's current. Continuing through the rugged forest and into the eastern hills, Wae Wilmamen came to a forest that was more swamp than land. It was thick with blood-eating bugs, and large lizards and more of the company was lost to these creatures, but it was the short, misshapen men of the marsh who were her downfall."

Everyone, including Kimi, the Eifen, and the people of Wesolk, sat quietly transfixed by Wae Relin's story. He told the tale slowly and with great respect.

"The company of Wae Wilmamen walked through the fetid water huddled together with spears and swords ready to fend off the beasts of the water, but the marshmen, the Rargal, as we name them, were waiting among the low-hanging and leafy boughs of the trees that grew large in the swamp," Wae Relin had obviously told the story many times, and he moved his eyes to each of his audience to keep their attention. "The marshmen were short and stout, with dour faces and long beards and old weapons held together by rust in the damp swamp. They were poor fighters and many scores died as the Eifen fought, but their numbers were too great. Wae Wilmamen ordered her people to return west and she stayed in the swamp, swinging her great curved blade, hewing down swaths of the creatures and invoking the old gods of the Eifen.

Before she was slain, the last of her company to escape said that her sword wore the flames of the sun and burned man and forest together before the light was lost under the raging hordes of the Rargal. The last survivor of Wae Wilmamen's company, was my ancestor who wrote before he died, that even under the pile of bodies that brought down the great warrior, the blade continued to burn."

There was a moment of silence before Branch stood and raised a drink in honor of the gallantry of Wae Wilmamen. Wae Relin looked confused at first but when he realized the easterner honored his story and his people, Lydria thought she saw firelight glint on his eyes. He did not cry, but he was moved by the gesture.

As he sat down, Wae Relin began again. "That was long ago, and it is no surprise that our eastern kin do not know the story as it took place after your loss. However, even our path to the east began with dark omens. We were chosen and trained for our journey from the time we were very young and even then, the graetongue foretold that the spirits showed to him a world changing, on wings of darkness descending from the east and hurtling toward the west, shutting out all light, and leaving the world in an ever-lasting grey.

We did not understand this for the world is not grey, but a wondrous display of many colors; as boys, we asked him, and he would smile and tell us that omens from the spirits often can mean many things, and we need to look to nature for our answers.

As we grew, many of the elders said the graetongue misunderstood the spirits. As a boy the graetongue was different; he could speak to the spirits without a pipe and often without song. As a boy learning to hunt, it is told that he would stop in the middle of the forest and not move for man nor beast. They could not rouse him until he roused himself and when he did, he had a tale from the spirits to share. In this way, he earned his name, Farn'Eston – the deliverer of dark tidings. He was called upon to speak for our people while he was still a boy and he took no wife but traveled far and would often be gone for a season or more. His stories were always full of riddles and none were clear. His final story came a year ago when he sang over us on the dawn of our journey to the east, toward the snows and the rising sun.

Travel on to the rising sun
To the snowy hills that fade
Travel on to the forests thin
To find that which is unmade
Travel on to the fortress tall
To walls of blue ice and stone
Travel on in the light of day
Don't let The Grey be known

Wae Relin sat silently and then slowly rose to his feet. Looking to his guests, he said, "we have prepared beds for you in the trees. We will speak more tomorrow." As Wae Relin and his men turned to leave the fire, he looked to Lydria, Haidrea and the others. "I am proud and joyful to have found our people after so long, but we are not reunited yet. We must follow the song of Drae

122

Farn'Eston and continue north." Lydria raised her head as if to speak but Wae Relin shook his head slowly. "Tomorrow we will speak again. For tonight, let us all sleep with glad hearts at having finally found the lost Eifen. For us, the finding of Haidrea, has been like the discovery of a legend and only tomorrow will we have had time to appreciate that and speak again with clear heads, ready hearts, strong bodies, and merciful souls." With that he turned and made his way to a smaller version of the homes of Eifynar – carefully constructed from dead wood to blend seamlessly with the living forest around them.

With a dozen unspoken questions, Branch, Weaver, Lydria, Kimi, and Haidrea all went to their own beds to wait for the light. Weariness did not claim them readily as they each thought about what they would learn the next day.

Wae Relin's call for breakfast and meeting came early. Haidrea had been up, and Kimi as well, his hunting successfully accomplished before full light. As the party sat around the glowing embers of the fire pit, fresh logs were added, and food cooked as the Eifen enthusiastically greeted Haidrea again and maintained their joyful demeanor from the night before. Still, Lydria noted they were more focused and when Wae Relin came from his camp and spoke in his native tongue to the men gathered there, they said farewell to Haidrea and her party, saluted Wae Relin and left the area. "I have asked the men to hunt for it may be some time before we can again, and our conversation today is not for everyone – not yet."

SIXTEEN

The pipe was passed but it did not contain the same spirit weed Lydria shared with Drae Ghern, but a sweet-smelling herb that was pleasant and smooth on the back of the throat. Wae Relin said it was a good balm for days where there was much talking to be done.

For much of the day, the group shared their stories, with Haidrea giving a long account of her people, which contained little mention of the original group who settled in the east. Hours later it was Lydria's turn to speak and when she reached the point where she met Haidrea, she told the group everything to include how she found the sphere, which she showed them. To answer the incredulous stares from Wae Relin and Branch, she held out her hands and calmly lifted Haidrea from her seat and moved her across the circle and set her down next to Wae Relin. The silence that followed was interrupted by a hail of questions from everyone except Haidrea who explained what they had learned from Drae Ghern and through trial and error, as Lydria ate and tried to ignore the pain that gripped her swollen left leg.

While amazed at her power, Wae Relin did not question Lydria about it. He was very sure of himself, Lydria thought, and when no one else spoke, Wae Relin took up the pipe and began to tell the easterners about Eigraenal, the City of Earth, with its towering buildings built into the giant forests of the west.

"Our forests grow much larger, but not so thickly as your homes," Wae Relin said. "The trees of Eigraenal stand many times higher than your maples and oaks, and it would take more people than those we have here to reach our hands around their base; and they live for many generations of the Eifen. Our city is home to thousands of our kind and we are largely left alone in peace by others who live nearby."

Wae Relin told of the craft of the Eifen, "who are the only crafters of the Farn'Nethyn in all Eigrae. Alas, the master craftsmen of darkstone are gone many generations. So rare is the darkstone, that no new deposits have been found for generations and our people have lost much of their old skill. But we keep the knowledge alive by reworking old armor and weapons and crafting them anew. In the halls of our city, we have darkstone blades, and armor, and even arrows capable of slicing through any armor save darkstone itself. Because of this, we are enriched, as traders and kings pay handsomely for even a scrap of the stone turned into jewelry worn by queens. A darkstone ring would be a heavenly gift indeed."

"Are you not concerned these kings and traders will come to take your darkstone by force?" Always a practical soldier, Branch's question cut to the very heart of what everyone else was thinking.

"When outsiders are allowed in Eigraenal, we gladly show them the stone, and the works we have wrought from it," Wae Relin said, with a slow grin crawling across his face. "There are not enough Farn'Nethyn weapons to be worthy of war, and no king would attack a force that has even the amount we hold. Kings buy the stone so they may recognize it and search for it. If, by chance, one happens to find a vein of Farn'Nethyn, then they will seek us out again for the tools to mine it, and the skill to work it. Because of this, outside of Eigraenal, there is only one Farn'Nethyn weapon, and that is the Flaming Sword of Wae Wilmamen, lost to the swamps so many years ago."

Wae Relin ended his story and passed the pipe to others and before nightfall, his men came back to camp with their hunt. Wae Relin looked to Branch, who had not told his story and who declined when offered the pipe, causing the Eifen to turn his attention to other matters.

"From our travels east, to your Graetongue's insistence you leave Eifynar, one thing only is clear, and that is the involvement of Haustis."

"Surely, the Haustis of the west cannot be the Haustis of the east?" Branch's incredulousness was echoed on everyone's face and even Haidrea looked to Wae Relin to see if he had some answer they lacked.

"Haustis has been part of the Eifen since the beginning," Wae Relin said. "Knowing the difficulty of passing to these lands, it is unlikely the Haustis of the Eifynar is the same as she who serves Eigraenal. Before we left the west, Haustis came and spoke to me of the Grey," added Wae Relin. "That is, the space between good and evil." Only Haidrea seemed to comprehend what Wae Relin said as she nodded almost imperceptibly as he described what Haustis had told him. When the others didn't seem to fully understand, Wae Relin continued.

"Weaver," Wae Relin said, "You seem unfamiliar with our people, so I put it to you, which would you consider more of a threat – great good or great evil?"

Weaver, caught off guard, looked to his captain out of instinct borne of years of training. Branch placed his hand on the larger man's knee and said simply, "speak freely."

"Well, sir," the soldier said awkwardly, not wanting to make a fool of himself or his captain. "I would say great evil were most to be distrusted."

Wae Relin smiled. "So then, you are a farmer and an evil man wants to take over your lord's estate and have you slave for him. That is evil, I think we can agree. But, forgetting the evil man, there is still the lord, and to this lord you work and provide a portion of your yield. You bow to him and provide him with income, and the land you tend is not your own, it is his. There is no war, no fire, no rape, no destruction. But at the end of the day, you are still effectively, a slave..." He let the question tail off and no one answered.

Wae Relin let the subject drop and turned to Lydria, "I see beneath his fur, the cat Kimi wears a collar of blue as to yours. This magic you spoke of, does this extend to him? Can he hear and understand me?" Lydria nodded and Kimi lifted his head from the woman's knee to stare at Wae Relin, who gently ruffled the tufts of fur extending from the sides of the cat's mouth. "Remarkable. And can you understand him?" Before Lydria could answer, Kimi placed a thickly padded paw gently to the man's cheek and held his stare. There were no claws, but the cat held Wae Relin's face like one would a new borne babe. Finally, he lowered his paw and rubbed his head under the man's chin, before moving to his lap where he turned circles and kneaded a space for his nap once again.

Weaver, who had been thinking over the issue of good and evil, plucked up the courage to speak over the moment as Kimi sunk his chin into his front paws and stretched his jaw to show his young but impressive teeth. "Are you saying, then, there's no difference between good and evil?"

"Not at all," the Eifen smiled. "Not at all, good Weaver. Generally, people are good. Some are bad people with mistrust and greed in their hearts, but they are not evil. Just as good people who help others and are happy, are not entirely good in all they do. My point is this," and he took a green twig from the ground and pulled the two ends toward each other. "If good lies at this end, and evil at this end," and he moved the ends together to form a circle, "then what are they when they are linked in this way? Most of us, you see, are here, at the bottom of the circle, opposite the gap. Largely, we choose to go in one direction or another, but the way is always up, and very difficult, so most do not climb far. True Evil, like true Good, however, takes a strength of character most do no possess, and they do many things that may not seem altogether good – or altogether evil - along their journey. So, if they do make it to the top, whether truly good or truly evil, they continue," and here he opened the circle slightly. "That is when they enter this grey area, and this is of what Haustis speaks. The Grey is the defining point between good and evil, where acts of compassion and acts of belligerence are often the same thing."

"You believe Wynter climbs the side of evil?" Haidrea asked.

"From your story and the story of Lydria, he is a man capable of much disruption. So, it is likely that he is capable of doing so; but I am not Haustis, and I think you should do as Drae Ghern bids and find her."

As the night came upon them, the company shifted their conversation to stories of a more enjoyable nature, with Haidrea and Wae Relin and his company each telling children's tales or stories they were told by their elders. As the moon rose and a chill entered the evening air, the men and the Eifen said their goodbyes for the evening and retired to their beds. Lydria and Haidrea likewise went to their small cabin, chatting quietly as they opened the door, which as it cleared the frame, Kimi's voice came sharply to Lydria, *"We are not alone; someone is here."*

Lydria put her hand on Haidrea's shoulder and sent a ball of light through the air to land and ignite in the small fire pit across the room. All thoughts of sleep disappeared as they saw by the fire an old woman with buckskin boots, wiry hair and a smile that made them feel at home.

"Welcome. I am Haustis."

SEVENTEEN

The journey slowed considerably. Every waking hour, Wynter was performing magic. He had started small, with the fire and began moving objects, first by simply lifting them, then by hurling them, and then by sending them with a purpose toward a target. In this way, he learned to hunt with an arrow without ever pulling a bowstring. His first successful hunt was a small rabbit and when the arrow struck home, it was as if Wynter had been hit by a tree. The air was pulled from his lungs and his chest ached so, he was sure he had been ripped apart. As the rabbit fell, so did Wynter, an anguished cry echoing forth from lips instantly gone dry.

Wynter had broken bones before and he been sick before. He had been wounded by knives, clubs, and there were even scars on him from arrows. But the pain he felt as his arrow hit the rabbit was as if all the things that had ever happened to him, descended upon him at one time. From his hair, his eyes his teeth – every muscle ached with an intensity that betrayed logic. He couldn't curl up to ease his stomach, because his legs felt as if they were on fire, and he was sure his back was broken in many places.

Looking at Nethyal, his lips trembled, and tears flowed freely from his eyes, though they felt as though they cried blood. Wynter's hands were curled upon themselves and would not move from his chest, and it was little comfort when the Eifen told him that there was no blood, and his bones remained intact.

A moment of triumph had been replaced with the swift lesson that magic was not a gift given freely. For days, Wynter lay immobile, but not like in the forest earlier that spring. This time his body could move, but to do so was torturous pain. Every movement along the ground felt like his skin was being peeled like a piece of fruit, so he lay there, sobbing, his head pulsing with pain so extraordinary he was sure it might crack.

It was days before he could move again, and during that time, Nethyal fed and washed him, carefully turned him toward the fire at night, cleaned him when he could not move. The wisdom of Nethyal was clear, for without the Eifen's presence, Wynter realized he would have been dead many times over.

When he was able to move again, Wynter continued to practice but more carefully, never wasting an opportunity to do so, but never again trying to kill with magic. If faced with a stream to cross, he would send over their meager provisions one item at a time. He attempted to lift Nethyal across the river but was overcome by exhaustion before the man had moved a yard and it was he who was carried to the other side, slung over the warrior's soaked back like a sack of meal.

As summer came on, they continued moving north, finally arriving at a small village on the edge of a large bay. The ice and snow were visible in the distance along the water's horizon, but the bay itself was reasonably mild. A small community made their homes near the shore and for the first time in many weeks, Wynter heard children laughing and saw a community at work as they farmed their shallow fields and prepared their homes for the next cycle of ice and snow.

"Do the children remind you of anyone?"

The voice had been silent since Nethyal had come and now it was back.

"Why do you bother me, woman?" Wynter said to his wife's voice. *"Why now?"*

"Because you are tired, and you have relaxed your mind enough for me to get through."

"Where were you when I was lying broken upon the ground, unable to move and in constant pain?"

"I was making your pain bearable. Had I not been with you, your body would have been scavenged by birds along with the rabbit you killed." Ellaster moved smoothly from Wynter's accusation to continue her own line of questioning. *"This village, do you think this is where you will live your days?"*

"No. This is where I will build my power."

The voice in his head went silent, and Wynter turned to Nethyal and smiled. It was not a warm smile, but nor was it menacing, it was a smile that told the world change had arrived.

"Welcome home, Nethyal, my friend. Now it is time to work."

EIGHTEEN

Lydria, Kimi and Haidrea built the fire as introductions were handled by Haustis who seemed to know both women quite well, and when her eyes rested on Kimi, she immediately dropped to one knee and gathered the bobcat in her arms.

"This one is quite extraordinary," Kimi said. *"This is who left the tracks we were following through the woods."*

"The hour is late and I'm sure we will have time to speak more, but I wanted to tell you a story tonight that you may not have heard before."

With no ceremony or pipes, Haustis launched into a family history.

"I am the wife of Ghern, mother of Ilsit, and grandmother to you, Haidrea, although I left that title long ago."

The statement came with such clarity that both Haidrea and Lydria were struggling to react when Haustis continued, as if she had rehearsed her story many times and was in a rush to get it all out before she changed her mind.

"The Eifen say that Haustis comes to each new chief, and this is true. I came to Wae Ilsit when he became chief. I was so proud. And for perhaps one of the few times in my life, I was caught off guard. I took the mantle of Haustis when Ilsit was a baby and yet he knew me for his mother despite never having laid eyes on me. He said he could 'smell' it."

Kimi made an appreciative noise in the back of his throat and draped his front paws over Haustis' knee.

"Ilsit's wife, Majiya, the mother of Haidrea and Nethyal, did not die as you have been told. She was very ill and went to the woods to die. Her birthing of Haidrea was difficult, and leaving her child with her husband, she went to the woods, she told him, to rest. She walked far and long, eventually falling into a deep sleep. She was found by a man and taken to the city by the bay where she was treated well and healed, but she could not remember who she was or where she had come from. She was different, certainly, because of her Eifen ears, but she hid them with scarves and hats, and eventually she found a man to love again. A soldier, who treated her with respect and kindness. Sadly, she was lost for good while following her soldier husband on his campaigns. The life of a camp follower or wife is not easy with war a constant neighbor. Before her death, however, she bore her husband a daughter."

The women were leaning forward waiting to hear more. "Lydria, you are half-sister to Nethyal and Haidrea. Their mother is your mother also."

Haidrea was the first to move, grasping Lydria in her arms, "well met, sister." The three women smiled and cried and moved closer together in a circle, their knees almost touching and smiling like they knew no other expression. Kimi spread himself across the legs of all three women, enjoying three sets of hands scratching his ears, back, and tummy all at once.

And then, as quickly as the crying had started, it stopped, and while the smiles remained, the tone of Haustis turned serious once more.

"I know you must have questions and I have more to tell, but I will let you ask first, so we may continue with your minds at ease."

Haidrea spoke first. "How is it that you are Haustis who has been told of for generations? How is it you are wife of Drae Ghern who is appears so old and near his end, and you seem so young? How is it that Wae Ilsit knew you for who you are, but Drae Ghern did not? And are you the same Haustis who guides our kin from the west?"

"I will take the last question first," Haustis smiled. "I am not the Haustis of the west, for I watch over only the Eifen and the lands east of the Great Lake. However, the spirits have shown me walking toward the setting sun, and I have done so, entering lands new to me, and finding Wae Relin, and you. As to your other questions, I came to Ilsit as I must for every chief, and though I said nothing, he knew, and therefore I confided in him. In doing so, I broke a trust with those who came before me. But I made him swear an oath that he would not tell his father, and I know that oath bears heavily upon him. Even today his expression is dour and perhaps that has cost him much happiness, but I would not have Drae Ghern know the truth for it would torment him and I believe he would have died many years ago had he known."

"*The Grey,*" Lydria said to Kimi. "*She has done a terrible thing in the name of doing something good. That is what Wae Relin refers to.*"

Before Kimi could answer, Haustis looked from Haidrea toward Lydria, sensing in her face the connections she was making. "Yes, child, that is the Grey at its most common form. For a brief time, even those who sit at the bottom of the circle content to let the balancing hand of fate work with joy and misery, even they can journey up to the Grey. It is those who stay within the space who are in grievous peril. But that is a story we will save for the daylight. For now, let me tell you what else I know.

"The magic Lydria wields is a new and powerful magic, but it is not the only type of magic. The word magic has existed within the spirit world for ages upon ages, and some knowledge of it has helped the Haustis watch over the people for many seasons. The magic of the spirits is not tangible, and not really magic as Lydria knows it, but there is no more clear way for me to express the power of the Haustis.

"I cannot start a fire, but I have a window to a wider knowledge, that is perhaps useful. My body, despite its age, maintains a youthful and vigorous constitution, and I can use the spirits to help me feel Eigrae, and to help it heal its wounds.

"As Haustis, or more correctly, The Haustis, I am one of many in a long line. When the time comes, there will be another who follows me – one who shows an ability to interact with Eigrae through the spirits."

"How do you find the next?" asked Lydria.

"The new Haustis finds the old and when she does, her time is short. That is my quest – to find the new Haustis and train her, though she may be among the last. With the coming of this new magic, the spirits show a day where they will no longer be heard."

The tears of joy that had enveloped the lodge earlier, turned to sadness as Haidrea and Lydria asked Haustis why she would give up her role as the guardian of the Eifen.

"To live alone and grow old, watching the people you love grow old and die, is not an experience one enjoys," she said. "When I became Haustis, I asked only that the spirits give me a new face so that should I ever see my love again, he would not despair. But now, Ghern is preparing for his final journey into the spirit world, and I would join him soon, for he has been ever faithful to me and his love has never faltered. I am also tired and do not think I will hold up over the trials that are to pass in the coming seasons. The spirits have shown me many things, and few are good. But there is always hope.

"Lydria, please hand me the stone you keep."

Lydria untied her bag, the stub of her finger tingling as she held out the stone, clean and bright as if a light shown from within and pass it over the prone form of Kimi toward Haustis.

Haustis looked at the stone for a time and back to Lydria, but she did not reach out to touch it.

"The stone is whole?" she asked, with a look toward Lydria.

"Yes. There were two in the crater, this and a second that Wynter possesses. After I touched it, the stone shed a small piece of itself and then reformed, and I was left with this," Lydria indicated the collar on her neck and a similar blue band on Kimi.

"I am aware of Wynter," Haustis said. "I met him and sensed his power. The spirits tell me the stone's power is pure, and it can empower or corrupt. And yet, I find myself often at odds with the spirits of late. The stone in one piece, in the possession of a single person, presents the potential for ruin unlike anything we could dream, for even a pure heart may wreak unspeakable ill even if she thinks she is doing unimaginable good. A stone in many pieces, in many hands, may more likely offer a balance.

"It is late, and we are all tired. Tomorrow we will speak again and prepare for the bitter seasons that await. Your training, Lydria, begins in earnest with the new sun."

NINETEEN

The cold came soon. Summer in the far north was fleeting, but Wynter and Nethyal had made good use of their time. The people here were hardy, and profoundly superstitious. They moved about their daily chores with little thought for anything beyond what was in their sight. They were strong and looked to be made of leather themselves, with heavily creased faces browned by exposure to an unrelenting summer sun. They all had dark eyes and thick bodies, with extra weight that few in Wesolk carried. In the summer, they favored thin tunics or no tunic at all, and trousers made from the skin of deer, elk, or the large sea creatures they also used for food and fuel. Wynter didn't, however, believe they were simple. He admired their ability to remain doggedly focused on important issues such as food and survival. In fact, he counted on it.

The first day in town, Wynter made a point of moving through the village and meeting people. He found a family with a boy in great pain from an accident with a small harpoon and leaned over him to see if he could set his broken leg. Using his power, he healed the boy and walked away so the family couldn't see the way his left hand bent inward, his fingers pinned to his armpit. Nethyal stayed behind and made sure the family was aware of Wynter's name, and that he had the power of magic, a new form of power that had chosen this village as the center of a new age of Eigrae.

Wynter and Nethyal spent several days helping people in ways that defied all they had ever known, so that when the village shaman came to see him he was prepared. The shaman tried to call out Wynter as a charlatan and a crowd of people gathered to see the rare sight.

"You, old man, what have you done for these people," Wynter began smoothly when the shaman had finished. "Have you healed injuries, or brought in nets from the lake? Have you done the work of days in moments? You have done none of these things."

While Wynter spoke Nethyal gathered people to go and listen and soon every member of the village had gathered in a circle around the two men who stood in front of a large fire pit in the middle of the town that during the winter months was always kept lit to fend off the near-constant darkness.

The shaman was trying to respond when Wynter raised his hands and several pieces of wood floated from a pile near the pit and settled into the middle of the stone circle. Lifting his hands higher and then lowering them toward the pit, Wynter caused the wood to smolder and then burst into flame.

"Are the theatrics entirely necessary?" Wynter's wife asked. He had brought his hands back to his side, fighting the urge to hold his stomach which felt as though it had been hit by a log.

"For the common people, the theatrics make it real and show where the power comes from. If not for the show, the old shaman could take credit."

Wynter gathered himself as the people backed away from the fire and the shaman looked as though a demon had been dropped at his feet. "This man," Wynter pointed at the shaman, "is not a fit leader for you. I am willing to lead you and bring great prosperity to you. Will you have a leader, or will you stand for a miserable old man who cannot give you anything of what you need?"

The people spoke quietly amongst themselves for a moment before several men dragged the shaman away. "You may call me Lord Wynter and my companion the Lord Nethyal." The crowd looked at Wynter and for the most part walked away, content to know their new ruler's name.

Within a week he had the full allegiance of the community, for Wynter didn't just demand, he provided.

Meat appeared, rocks were hauled from the earth, and tasks the villagers thought impossible were completed easily. Magic, as Wynter found, could make him as stealthy as a woodland cat or as strong as an ox, but as he had surmised after he had killed the rabbit, killing a person would almost certainly kill him.

"What will you do, then, if you can't kill with this new power?"

"I will do what all kings and tyrants do — I will use my power to build an army to kill for me."

Wynter had been in the village for several weeks, and the weather was starting to turn toward fall when Nethyal approached him.

"Are you strong enough?"

Wynter turned to Nethyal with a smirk. The question was an honest one, and one he had asked himself for several days. His new kingdom was in its infancy and its people still needed constant reminding of his power. Word of Wynter, Lord of the North, had started to travel and people were beginning to arrive from nearby villages, looking for a fresh start for their families, to escape their old lives, or to share in the power said to be building in the frozen north. It was this last group of people Wynter was most keen to develop. They would become his army, his spies, his assassins, his sword to the throat of the south. But he needed to continue to show his power, and his latest scheme would cement his legend and buy him the time he needed to more fully develop his abilities.

"It could kill you."

Yes, Wynter nodded to his ally, it very well could. "But a Lord needs a fortress, don't you think, Nethyal? Something that will be visible for miles around and serve as a challenge to others. If we are going to invite war, my friend, we need to send a big invitation."

The invitation he had in mind would not go un-noticed. If he died and his attempt were successful, his name would live on for generations. If he lived and was successful, his name would never die, and people would flock to him.

"Your concern is touching, but you needn't worry," Wynter told his cautious aid. "I've been practicing." Wynter opened a door at the back of his home, a large wooden structure built for him soon after he took leadership of the town. While modest, it featured a walled courtyard in the rear. The labor required to fashion such a structure should have taken months, at best. The harvesting and transport of the wood should have taken weeks with scores of workers. Wynter provided the material in days and the men worked quickly to please their Lord.

Opening the door to the courtyard, Wynter proudly displayed a veritable forest of ice. Thick, tall blocks filled the space, some measuring a span that would require three men linking hands to encircle. "It's easier than you might think, actually," Wynter smiled at Nethyal. "Water forms into ice naturally, so I'm just shaping it to my purposes. These larger ones," he walked to a massive column, and touched it gently with an open palm. "These are the latest, and they came up smoothly yesterday morning. I was able to feed myself breakfast and do a full day's work afterward." Wynter smiled as he remembered the sensation of the monolith breaking the surface and realizing the cost to his well-being was minimal. He continued to smile as his tongue sought out the fresh hole in his gums where a tooth used to be. A little blood, a slight discomfort, but nothing damaging.

"How long do you expect it will take then?" Nethyal sounded more hopeful about the project, his voice expectant that a week or so would see the task completed without incident.

Wynter turned slowly and smiled again, the black hole visible in his lower jaw at the back of his grin. "I hope to have it finished before noon."

Nethyal quickly hid his surprise and countered in his emotionless rhythm, "I will see to it that hot food is prepared, your chamber is ready, and no one disturbs you."

"That's fine," Wynter said. He was aware of the nature of Nethyal, to follow through in a pragmatic fashion in any situation, but he was also aware of his warrior-friends' inability to grasp how things were seen by those who were not Eifen. What Wynter was about to do couldn't be done alone like what he'd done in his courtyard. It needed to be done in front of an audience and be a statement – something that would be talked about and turned into legend. "If this is to be the symbol it is required to be, I will not be coming back here," Wynter said.

"There are those within the village who still doubt me, are there not?" It was more a statement than question. Both men knew there was a certain group that had arrived with a large contingent from the south, who questioned Wynter's magic when their tongues were loosened with drink. The leader of the group, a burly man named Kelmenth, was allowed to speak freely, but Wynter and

Nethyal made sure he was watched closely and what he said always made its way back to them.

Kelmenth was a fit man who laughed at the head of a small group of simple-minded followers, young men and women who were all fit – perfectly fit, Wynter knew, for his purposes.

Before Nethyal left, Wynter told him that Kelmenth and his followers would be needed to move the contents of his home to the flat rise overlooking the lake where he would build his fortress. "I have cleared spaces for fourteen of them. Have them move the belongings to the center of the clearing and then stand on marked spaces facing south. They shall be the first to witness the birth of a new day."

Nethyal waited to see if there were more instructions, but Wynter turned away, walking among his ice pillars. Nethyal turned to find Kelmenth and his followers.

The next day was brisk, with a prickling frost tinge in the air. The sun had not yet risen, but the town had gathered at a respectful distance from the rise by the lake, to witness something, but what it was they had not been told. The night before Nethyal had given Kelmenth his task, and bade him say nothing to the town, for their Lord was to reveal an astonishment the next day. Knowing the man would spend his night in the small tavern that served the growing population, he was sure word would spread and the entire town would be on hand. He was not disappointed.

As the horizon glowed orange before the late rising of the sun, the townspeople could see Wynter, in silhouette against the lightening sky. Kelmenth and thirteen of his fellows, both men and women were moving objects on the rise, but when Wynter approached them they stopped what they were doing and gathered to listen to their Lord. As the crowd watched, Wynter finished and fourteen silhouettes could be seen moving along the flat rise before stopping and turning to face the south. Wynter raised his arms briefly and then moved to one of the fourteen where he stood for several seconds before making his way toward the village.

The distance between the people and the flat was no more than several hundred paces, but Wynter approached to within a few dozen paces and welcomed those who had come.

Sliding easily into his charismatic voice, Wynter wished the crowd a good morning and began a speech.

"This village has stood through your strong efforts, for many generations. It has withstood the most vicious of enemies – nature itself – and grown and prospered. You people are the strength and foundation of this land, and on this rise before you, stand fourteen – seven men and seven women - who represent the strength, the hardiness, the cunning, ... the nobility... of your people."

The fourteen of whom Wynter spoke had not moved an inch since Wynter had left them, but the townspeople didn't notice. Wynter's words fueled every prideful emotion and feeling of superiority they had over the soft men of the south. "Today, we start anew; today, we build a new kingdom to be known as Solwyn."

Without delay, Wynter turned and walked back to the edge of the rise. He heard murmurs from the village behind him. Most trying out the new name, and a brave few speaking to each other about kingdoms.

When he reached the edge of the rise, he quickly took note of his preparations. The fourteen were rooted to their spots, ice clamped above their ankles, their arms pinned to their sides, and their mouths frozen shut. Their eyes, however, were wide. Wynter made it a point to move directly in front of them, so he could watch their eyes, and so their eyes could watch him build an empire.

Holding his arms out wide for dramatic effect, Wynter began his silent incantation. The motions he had used early on to call forth fire, or throw arrows, or any task, were unnecessary he realized. Magic, he knew, rested solely in the mind. Only through pure will could he harness the power he needed. For weeks he had been preparing the ground beneath him. Bringing water up through the ground and imagining how it would need to be formed when called forth.

As the first rays of the sun touched what would be his front gate, he shuddered and bent his will toward the ground.

The ice rose quickly at first, in fourteen enormous columns that made the ice pillars in his courtyard look like twigs. Larger than any tree, the columns rose as crystal-clear ice encasing the men and women who lent their strength to the structure. Wynter avoided looking at their perfectly reflected faces buried beneath feet of ice. He would stop to enjoy that sight after he had finished.

When the columns stopped growing, he bent his will to the walls which rose evenly in every direction, glittering blue-green opaque walls shining in the sun like the ocean made solid. The structure left Wynter standing in a magnificently sized arched gateway that would serve as the grand entrance.

As the castle took shape, the rising ice slowed. Wynter's feet were numb and his body racked with pain. It took effort just to keep his arms lifted. He brought opaque towers up from the ground on the eastern and western sides of the building; and to the south, a small tower rose from above the arched gateway.

Amidst gasps of astonishment, the townspeople cheered as Wynter made his way out of the castle to walk around its western side, fully in their view to stand at the northern face of the structure. He had not stopped his incantation fearing that to do so would cause him to collapse, so he raised his hands again, the pain causing them to shake and his blue collar glowing faintly in the dawn, it's light visible in his peripheral vision. Finally, Wynter called forth the northern tower, which would be his home.

The tower came out of the ground as clear as the pillars inside, and the sunlight shone across it like a diamond, dazzling all of those who marveled at its creation. It grew higher than the walls, and higher than the roof of the building, continuing half again as high as the castle itself. As the tower reached its full height, Wynter took his stone and leaned into the fresh ice, its solid surface helping him stay upright, and he felt along its perfectly smooth facade until he reached the base of the tower. Thinking of what he wanted to achieve, Wynter held the stone cupped in the palm of his hand and resting on the tower wall, and he watched a piece of the stone drift through the ice and bury itself in the center of the tower's frozen floor. Within seconds, roots of blue reached out from the middle of the floor and worked their way up the walls like cobalt ivy wending its way through the essence of the ice. In moments the northern tower was a beacon of blue luminescence. Wynter pulled away from the wall and looked down, watching his stone reshape itself into a slightly smaller sphere once again.

It was as magnificent as the stone had shown him it would be. The tower would draw people and an army toward it like mosquitoes drawn to blood. Even as he admired the shimmering cobalt, Wynter could feel himself giving way, succumbing to his efforts, but he had more to do. This would be his last use of magic for proving his power, so he moved slowly back to the south and went inside the building bending his will to creating floors, torches, candle holders, carpets, rugs, tapestries – everything that made a castle splendid – and it began to appear as if weaved by thought and ice.

As Wynter felt himself on the verge of collapse, energy surged through his body and he stood tall and awake.

"You cannot be serious with those rugs."

As if watching his work rearranged by someone else, the interior of the space took form, telling touches from his home in Thrushton aggrandized to fit the larger space.

"I thought you were gone." Wynter wanted his voice to sound aggrieved, but it wasn't. He was grateful for the help and he no longer felt like crumpling to the floor.

"I told you, as you exist, I exist. You've made it difficult for me though," his wife's voice was tempered, as though she realized how much it grated on him to hear it. *"Your defenses stifle your abilities. By keeping me down, you limit yourself. We can work together. With me, you have access to such power ... well, look and see."*

Wynter raised his head and sucked in a breath of surprise, even he did not expect the magnitude of the creation in front of him. It was beyond grand and should have taken an army of workmen decades, and a mountain of gold, to produce the stunning structure around him. His lips turned up slowly at the corners of his mouth in a smile, not of joy, but of triumph.

The sun was now high, and he walked slowly from his castle and turned to the crowd who had gone silent as they watched the miracle Wynter had pulled from the ground. In moments, he heard their chant begin, and it grew louder until it rang across the north. "Hail King Wynter, hail Solwyn."

Wynter stood up straight, facing the crowd and holding out his arms again, as if daring them not to look at what he had accomplished. Soon, the chanting stopped, and as one, the people of Solwyn kneeled to their king.

TWENTY

Haustis was impressed by Lydria's magic but concerned over the woman's lack of proficiency at wielding her power as a weapon – as Wynter most surely would. Still, as Haustis convened with spirits over the course of the long summer, she began to accept that Lydria's unwillingness to use magic solely as a weapon signaled a strength that was perhaps more desirous in a wielder than physical power.

"Haustis, you know there is harmony in nature," Kimi spoke to Haustis as Lydria slept, regaining her strength from her exertions of the morning. *"Would you prefer wielders who think of nothing but power and conquest, or would you prefer those who heal and build?"*

The cat was correct, Haustis knew, but while good often prevailed over evil, it often did so at the feet of destruction and a pile of bodies. A strong wielder with good intent would be preferable. Haustis smiled at the motionless bobcat who didn't even bother to open his eyes. "You are remarkably perceptive for a creature who spends most of his day asleep," she chided.

"I'm not sleeping, merely conserving energy."

Later that day Lydria and Haidrea were in the woods with Wae Relin and Branch, learning about each other and from each other. Weaver had gone back to Steven's Folly early in the season to oversee continuing construction at the fort in Branch's stead.

"Would that more men could come and spend time with you to truly understand the ways of your people, we would all sleep easier at night," Branch said.

Wae Relin smiled. "I agree, but it is not within the nature of man to do so, nor is it within the desire of the Eifen. We live apart from men, even as we live among them. Like men we argue and like men we sometimes make war upon each other, although it is very rare."

When not in the woods, the group responded to Haustis' efforts to train Lydria by protecting her from falls and tending to her when she exhausted herself using magic. Haustis recognized that Lydria rarely engaged in harmful magic, instead focusing on the practical and beneficial, farming, construction, water collection … things that would make a community prosper in years instead of generations; and she encouraged them to provide Lydria tasks that would prepare her for war, or at the very least, preparing to defend against what might come.

In late summer, Weaver arrived back in the camp, looking leaner, stronger, and more confident. He wasted no time in finding and speaking to Branch, and later that evening, he spoke to everyone, happy to be amongst friends and delighting in the admiring looks his improved physique received, especially from Haidrea.

"When in the spring, I made my way back to the Folly," he began. "Work there had slowed to a crawl without the captain's influence, and so I spent some time getting the men back to their tasks. Several days after I arrived, a rider from Bayside came looking for the captain." Weaver glanced quickly at Branch who, out of habit, nodded for him to continue. "Explaining the captain was on a sensitive diplomatic mission, I was ordered back to Bayside in his place where I expected to meet the commander of the guards. Instead, I was escorted to the castle and brought before his lordship Krieger."

At this point, Branch interrupted. "Krieger," Branch began, "is an advisor and confidant of King Ahlric. He is a good man. Honest, loyal, and not averse to ignoring court politics if it means getting important work done. It's fair to say, however, that Krieger is rumored to be a spy, which I believe; and to have been an assassin in his youth, which I may not guess at. This reputation has allowed him to roll the slow wheels of politics more swiftly than they might otherwise move. Still, if he ever did, it is unlikely he has engaged in the latter work for many years, but he makes no pains to dispel rumors, which he thinks are more useful than harmful. Krieger is also the person to whom the king's spies report; and being called in by him usually does not bode well."

Branch stopped and looked to Weaver to pick up his story again but looks shared between Haustis and others stayed the man from continuing.

"Can Krieger be trusted?" Haustis asked.

Branch looked at the old woman. "Krieger was ambitious once, willing to use any methods to achieve his ends. The rumors say that if he showed up at your door you were grateful. It was when you couldn't see him that you had to be worried. No one can deny Krieger's youth was largely ill-used, but he is now considered a calming influence in Wesolk's affairs, and his voice is well heard and respected by the king and the lords who serve him. We would dismiss Krieger at our own peril, and we would be diminished if we did not listen to the rest of what Weaver has to say."

Knowing Branch knew the rest of the message whereas she did not, Haustis nodded and raised her hand to Weaver. "Continue, then Weaver, and tell us what this man has to say."

Krieger's spies, which operated in every direction, among other kingdoms and people of the north, were among the very best. Krieger knew intelligence was more useful than poison and he went to great lengths to learn information that would be useful in settling disagreements politically, rather than with force.

"There are stories coming from the North, and they tell of a tiny village of subsistence fishermen where great things are occurring."

"And what are these great things?" It was Wae Relin, leaning forward and eager to hear the tale in full as his desire was to continue north to fulfil his orders.

"Krieger did something highly unusual," Branch broke in again, signaling to Weaver that it was alright that he spoke of information the younger man had thought was not to be shared. "For some months there have been mutterings to the north; bandits, robbers, strange sights in the night skies, and of two men walking slowly through the tundra. Sometimes one man would carry the other and they did not travel as men who had a destination in mind. They went slowly and stopped often." Branch paused for effect and Weaver nodded slowly as if to confirm his captain's words.

"Krieger sent men to the north to investigate. His primary agent was a man named Kelmenth, who was part of a detachment that included several others posing as young families. Kelmenth sent word that a man named Wynter had taken up residence in the small town, and with him a tall Eifen called Nethyal."

Kimi, Haidrea, and Lydria all straightened at the mention of the name and looked at each other. *"Did he say Nethyal?"* Kimi asked. Not bothering to answer silently, Lydria said, "Yes, Kimi, he said Nethyal. What is this, Weaver? Branch? Are we supposed to believe these spies?" Despite herself she practically spit the word at Weaver.

Haidrea was staring hard at Weaver and Branch, her muscles taut and poised to spring to her feet. Wae Relin put his hand on her shoulder as he would any other warrior preparing to make an ill-advised move. "My brother Nethyal? How can that be? He was sent with men to find Wynter and return him to my father."

"Your brother was sent to kill Wynter," Weaver said. He was sorry to be the one to bring the news but seeing Haidrea so upset had caused him to want to tell her anything to be calm once again. More than anything, however, he didn't want the woman angry with him.

Weaver continued. "Krieger has it on good authority that Wae Ilsit bade his son to kill the rogue. And there's more. Wynter is known to Krieger. It appears the two were … in the same line of work at one time." Not wanting to say more, Weaver looked back to Branch who nimbly picked up the story.

"The barracks stories are that Krieger and Wynter were assassins on good terms with each other but in competition for …work. Eventually, Wynter, though the younger of the two, fell out and disappeared from that world. He went to live on an island and start a family, taking up a shop as a bowyer and fletcher. Some say he's gone mad. Krieger's spies reported he could be seen talking to himself from time to time."

"That fits," said Lydria, who recounted her story of how the party she was with when they met Wynter had pieced together that the arrow that killed Josen, likely came from Wynter. She also mentioned the body dragged from the water the day before her father and the rest of her party were killed and the contents of the boys' clothes.

When Lydria finished, the men and women said nothing until Branch broke the silence again. "The last word Krieger heard from his man was in mid-summer. The town was growing daily with men and families arriving from east, west, and south, and Wynter providing near-daily miracles. There was talk of kingdoms and lordships and of people who disagreed with Wynter disappearing.

"And then, there was nothing. Kelmenth, nor any of the others, have been heard from since. Krieger discusses the matter with King Ahlric even now, whether or not to march north before the snows come."

"Does the king or this Krieger, know anything of magic and Wynter's abilities?" Haustis who said nothing during the telling of the story, did not look up as she rubbed her hands together, and she did not wait for an answer. "I have met Wynter, and when I did, he was not sure what abilities he could command. I think, if he has learned to harness any of his power, part of that blame rests with me." It was Wae Relin who put out his hand to calm the shaking in Haustis' clenched fist.

"There is no reason to think so," answered Branch, looking to Weaver for confirmation that came quickly. "If Krieger knows of Wynter's magic, it is unlikely he would tell anyone. That kind of information is a currency all its own."

"Would he not even tell the king?" asked Haustis

"He would especially not tell the king!" Branch nearly laughed at the thought. "Krieger has spent years trying to use his influence to bring peace. He understands that a peaceful kingdom is a prosperous kingdom and it is his desire is to live to an old age with a warm house and plenty of food, and women who don't care how many wrinkles are in his skin. If King Ahlric, or any king for that matter, knew of the power wielded by Lydria, they would have their armies marching here now."

"To kill her," declared Wae Relin.

"To capture me," whispered Lydria.

TWENTY-ONE

The council lasted deep into the night. Soon after sunrise provisions were being packed and Wae Relin, Lydria, Haidrea, and Kimi were ready to head for Eifynar to discuss what they had learned with Wae Ilsit and Drae Ghern. Branch and Weaver would head back to Steven's Folly before turning for Bayside to speak with the king.

The remaining members of the camp would embark upon the perilous journey back to Eigraenal in the west to report that they had discovered the lost Eifen and to discuss sending a larger force back east to fight Wynter if need be. Given the season it was likely that if Wynter did make war upon the south, he would wait until spring. That might give Wae Relin's men enough time to return to their home and bring back a significant force.

"We will meet you in Eifynar after we have spoken with the king," Branch said. "Until then, let us hope that we prepare for storms that do not land on these shores." Branch and Weaver said their farewells and headed north.

"We should go too," Haustis said to Lydria. "We need to speak to Wae Ilsit and prepare the Eifen. It is Eifynar that stands between Ahlric and Wynter." Haustis' expression, however, revealed her true concern: what news of the betrayal of Nethyal would do to the village and its leader.

The group loaded food and gear onto horses Weaver had brought from the Folly. Considering going to war against Wynter, Lydria shuddered involuntarily, thinking of his cold gaze at the crater; how his eyes seemed to penetrate through her and find weakness where she hadn't thought any existed. She thought of how he so cruelly killed her father, and how he had promised to find her one day and kill her.

"'Kill you all', that's what he said," Lydria spoke to no one in particular.

"What's that?" said Haustis, fastening a bag on a horse. She wasn't used to riding horses.

"Wynter said he would come back and find me. It was like he was talking to someone else only he could hear – like I can with Kimi – but he said, 'I can't kill you yet. But I'll find you. You can't hide your eyes. I'll find you – I've given my word and I will find you and I will kill you all.' But I was the only one there."

"You had both suffered greatly when the forest was destroyed," countered Haidrea.

Lydria smiled at her friend, appreciative of her concern. Had it been anyone else, she might have let it go as the mad ramblings of a man who was wounded, tired, and alone. But Wynter was different. Lydria didn't think he would ever say something that wasn't calculated to be exactly the thing he wanted to say – and mean.

Before she returned to her horse, Haidrea heard Lydria say, perhaps out loud to Kimi, "He has the power and he intends to use it; why would he not use it against me?"

"He knows you have power too," Kimi spoke. The cat was keeping his distance from the long, strong legs of the horses and for their part they seemed to ignore his presence.

"If Nethyal is with him, we must believe he has told Wynter of your gift and what you can – and cannot – do. It is likely that Nethyal is helping him in the same way we help you."

After letting Haustis know Kimi's concern, the old woman echoed his sentiment. "I have thought for some time that you should focus your power in ways that will be useful should Wynter make good on his promise," the woman said. "Your gifts for healing and your kindness of spirit are what made you so valuable to your father and his men in the field. You have compassion, but you need to find the steel within yourself. You have never been a flower, Lydria. You are more than capable in a fight and with a bow or blade. You must now unlock your ability to strike first and decisively. A hard blow struck first may save many more painful blows down the road."

Lydria looked at her friends and could see they agreed with Haustis. "I will try," she said.

TWENTY-TWO

As they made their way east, Lydria attempted forceful magic and was met with wracking pain and discomfort. When she made plants grow quickly, she found herself unable to move from the waist up, and unable to control her mouth. Haidrea rode alongside her as Lydria controlled her horse with her knees, all the while drooling in her own lap, her lip hanging loosely on her chin.

'I'm sorry, I've been listening from the trees ... " Kimi stopped and looked up at his friend who was trying to look away and made a hissing sound at the back of his throat that the others quickly understood to be the cat's laugh.

"Gloating doesn't become you, Kimi." Lydria said aloud. The others looked at Lydria and Kimi and soon they too laughed until Lydria could not help but smile as well. And when she did, the saliva rolled steadily down her chin, which made everyone laugh more.

The ill effects didn't last long and by the time the group stopped to water the horses and have a meal, Lydria was ready to try again.

"What do you suggest?" Lydria asked Haustis who seemed the most determined to find a way to use magic practically in battle.

"As Haustis I can feel nature, sense it, and, in a way, speak with it though not in the way you speak with Kimi. Most things on Eigrae are alive – even things we don't consider so. Rivers, mountains, trees, these have an energy which we daily ignore." The old woman put down her wooden bowl and stared at her hands for a moment as if in them she might find the words she wanted to say.

"When I met Wynter, I was drawn to him because of his voice. I don't know who he was talking to when he yelled out, 'stop,' but in my head, there was a force as if I had been hit with a rock and for a moment I stopped – whether from his command or surprise I cannot tell. The river I walked besides, however was as still as a tree. Drops suspended in the air as they flew over hidden rocks, and the course of its movement halted. Two score paces from where I stood the river bottom was bare where the water before it rushed ahead. It didn't stay this way long. But a sizeable force could have crossed the river in the time it stood still. As I continued I made my way to where I heard the voice and found Wynter. He could hear and talk, but he was otherwise completely still. I doubt he knows what he did."

Haustis' voice trailed off, her face full of concern and awe at what she had seen. Turning her attention to face Lydria directly, she continued. "Do not limit yourself to what you would consider given the limitations of your hands and your tools, Lydria. The power you possess is no trifle." Haustis opened her mouth as if to speak again but abruptly closed it, mumbling only, "I must consider" before picking up her gear and moving to mount her horse. The others looked at each other silently, as if gauging whether to ask Haustis to continue. In the end, they did not, and within minutes were on their way east again.

Kimi suggested Lydria use her magic to try to find him as he lopped through the trees. After feeling for his energy which she knew very well, it took her only an hour before she could find the cat regularly despite the noise and movement of the horses, and the natural elusiveness of Kimi's kind. Considering Haustis' suggestion, Lydria began launching small thorns from nearby brambles to poke Kimi's short tale and bottom. It was difficult at first, and the yelp of the cat startled Haidrea and Wae Relin who immediately looked to Lydria. Lydria smiled widely before grasping her head and falling sideways onto the path.

Rather than continue, they made camp where Lydria had fallen. Summer was ending, and the night air was chill, so they made a fire without magic. Lydria was awake but her head throbbed with pain from her efforts and her shoulder ached from the fall. Still, Haustis, after hearing from Kimi what had been done, smiled.

Haustis sat next to Lydria near the fire and applied a salve to her bruised shoulder. Lydria's headache was so fierce she could do little but sit still as Haustis worked.

"Haustis," said Wae Relin, "what is it you were thinking when last we gathered around a fire?" It was a formal way to ask a simple question, but it was obvious, even to Lydria, that the respect the man had for Haustis demanded he be formal. Despite the time they spent together and the stories they shared, to the Eifen, Haustis was still a legend. Lydria put her energy into relieving the pain in her shoulder and was successful enough to be able to concentrate on Haustis' response. The pain in her head caused by magic, she could not dull.

"I have told of how people may, for short times, live in the grey," she said. "I have always believed so. And yet, since the last full moon, I have begun to think differently. Surely, people still walk a fine line between what we consider right and wrong, but they do so within the light or dark of good or evil. I now start to consider that perhaps The Grey is the domain of magic and only those who wield its power may live there. What is more, magic must exist solely in The Grey. That is my thought now. Who knows what truths I may unlearn tomorrow or what lies will fall apart under my gaze on the next full moon?"

Haidrea spoke after Haustis, hesitantly at first. "Because magic does not follow the natural way; everything is grey, and open to being both good and evil?"

Haustis smiled widely and clapped the young woman on the shoulder. "Yes. It is exactly so, or so I now believe. As Lydria tracked Kimi through the forest, she did nothing wrong, but she negated the natural benefits of the forest, dismissing its protection for Kimi. As she launched thorns into our dear young bobcat's hind quarters, she pulled away the natural defenses of a plant, and used them for offensive purposes against a creature far away, who the plant was unaware of."

"At the end of the day, however, it changes nothing," the voice, thin and distracted fell from Lydria's mouth like an accusation. "Knowing this doesn't make it easier to use. It doesn't make it hurt less, or get me any closer to, or farther away from, Wynter. So, what is the difference?"

Haustis and Haidrea, both reawakened to Lydria's physical pain, moved to either side of her. Haidrea clutching her unbruised shoulder, and Haustis holding her hands firmly between her own, thin, cold palms.

"Perhaps not yet," Haustis grinned with enthusiasm. "But, one day, as you master your gifts, you will be able to consider how using them effects the world around you. Knowing that, you can perhaps learn to harness the power of the earth, share the knowledge of the Haustis, and work your way to the edge of The Grey – to the colorless light, or the encompassing dark."

"Right now, encompassing dark doesn't sound like a bad thing." Lydria untethered herself from the two women and gingerly made her way to a bedroll beside the fire. Kimi joined her and despite her mood and discomfort, she quickly wrapped an arm around the cat and drifted off to sleep.

Haustis, Haidrea, and Wae Relin looked at the sleeping form of Lydria. "Will she be well?" Wae Relin asked. "Will she be ready when the challenge comes?" It was the question they had all been thinking since Weaver's news.

"Will we be ready?" asked Haidrea.

"We will have to be," Haustis answered. "As for Lydria, she is the daughter of a warrior. She knows what lies ahead only too well. She will be ready. Or we will all fall."

TWENTY-THREE

Wynter was aglow in his triumph and kept his head high as
the last echoes of his name drifted over the flats and away across the
lake as the people, his people, genuflected on the shore, the natives
of the village led in obeisance by the newcomers from the south. But
he could feel his energy slipping away and turned stiffly and marched
into the mouth of his new fortress as Nethyal gave orders to workers
who would be responsible for provisioning and serving the castle.

It would take the villagers weeks to build and outfit the
kitchens, sleeping quarters, and everything else necessary to finish
what Wynter had begun, but Wynter would let them do every bit of
it. He wanted them to stand inside the structure and tell the
townspeople of what they saw. He wanted the Fourteen Pillars to do
their job and send a message – fear to those who would dismiss
Solwyn, and pride for those of Solwyn. The Pillars, as Wynter would
later tell people, represented how men believed so much, they
sacrificed themselves for this edifice and for the idea that was
Solwyn.

In the weeks following the rise of Castle Solwyn the glowing
beacon of the great blue north tower also did its job, as people
flocked to the town, drawn to the curious blue light that stood still in
the sky above the lake. Men who came to the castle were welcomed
and urged to return home, gather their families, their wealth, their
weapons, and as many supplies as they could bring back as their
price for joining the burgeoning community. Tradesmen, shop
keepers, farriers, blacksmiths, miners, fishermen, seamstresses,
surgeons, cobblers, tinkers, tanners … over the course of weeks they
all returned with their families and trains of carts loaded with their
possessions and everything else they could find, scrounge, or steal.

As the people arrived, Wynter spoke to Nethyal as behind
them several oxen-drawn carts made their way across the worn path
into town. "More will come in the spring. The minor nobility, the
land-lords, and inevitably, the militia."

Nethyal didn't ask the question out loud, but he turned to Wynter, his eyes seeking explanation.

"As people arrive here, the lords lose their tax payers, their workers, their shops, their servants, their food, and their own comfort." Wynter's gaze never left the town as he answered. "The only reason they don't come now is because the crops are in and they will be well-fed until spring. But, come spring, they will ride here to reclaim their property." Wynter thought about how he could welcome his guests and turned to face Nethyal and smiled. "We must prepare for them before they gather together to prepare for us."

As Solwyn grew workers engaged themselves in building the necessary infrastructure. All worked with enthusiasm and in concert with one another under the shadow of the Cobalt Tower. Nethyal found men and women able to organize people into teams for farming, foraging, fishing, construction, and other work and, by Wynter's design, Nethyal told each team of their duties under the watchful gaze of Kelmenth and the rest of the Fourteen Pillars. Those who saw the Pillars were moved by the sacrifice of the Fourteen and were in awe of the grandeur of Wynter's new order.

Before the first snows came every man, woman, and child walked through the castle entrance and into the throne room beyond to witness the spectacle of the Fourteen. Six men held hands to encircle one of the massive ice towers and everyone who saw the pillars gazed into the open eyes of those encased within. Wynter greeted everyone who came to see what he built, and he lavished praise on the men and women he said so heroically offered their strength to Solwyn.

"Each of the Fourteen pleaded with me to be allowed this honor," Wynter told the townspeople, digging deep into his wellspring of charisma, choking back emotion. "I could not have done it without them. The strength of the people of Solwyn will always rest here as the foundation of our town, ennobling even the lowest among us. And I see the same strength as I look across to the city you are building even today."

"Do you think you're pouring it on a bit thick?" Wynter's wife was never much for speech making, and thought her husband was over-selling pride.

"I could rule by fear alone, but this is so much more useful," Wynter responded smoothly. *"People want to feel useful and they want to be part of something special. When I need them to take up arms and kill their enemies, there won't be one here who won't gladly do it – to live forever in memory in the same way as the Fourteen. No, I am not overselling pride. I'm planting pride and it will be the single greatest crop of my kingdom. It will grow quickly and spread like a weed."*

As the days grew shorter and colder families joined together to ensure everyone in Solwyn was housed. All able-bodied men, women, boys and girls were put to work, and Nethyal ensured people were warm and fed. For the men and larger boys, basic weapons training was begun, and the forges of Solwyn rang out a staccato of metal on metal that went on for hours after the sun had set each day.

"The people work hard and they long to see their king." Nethyal repeated a phrase he had first uttered some weeks after Wynter had raised his castle. He was a wonder, this Eifen; he was efficient and smart and asked for nothing. It was this last thing that gave Wynter cause to wonder. What was it, exactly, the warrior wanted? Certainly, he wasn't fulfilled being an administrator – though, to his credit, he was the finest Wynter had ever seen. His role as a protector was rarely needed. With his wife back and speaking to him only when he allowed, Wynter found tasks that routinely taxed him to exhaustion, rarely caused him more than physical pain and almost never incapacitation. Still, there was too much to do to worry about Nethyal's needs. When the time came, Wynter knew, he could deal with the warrior.

"Why do you think they need to see me?" Wynter asked. The massive throne room had been softened and warmed with the addition of polar bear pelts and rich wooden desks and furniture crafted by some of the finest artisans in the north. It occurred to him that Bayside might be a step down from the Cobalt Tower. But his plan was about power, not a better house.

"You are their king, and they look to you," Nethyal did not disbelieve it. In his own town the chief was an integral part of the community and was expected to take part and be part of life with the people. He believed even a king should be seen by his people.

"Yes, they do," Wynter said, looking at the blue-green vaults spanning the distance between pillars. The warrior stood like a pillar himself, his back as straight as his gaze as he met Wynter's eyes. "And if I were to go out among them each day and work by their side, there would be no mystery," Wynter continued. "By making them wait, it becomes a celebration when I go into the town. I can bestow gifts, and congratulate, and if need be, set an example. But, as you say, it seems it might be time. I will come to the town tomorrow."

As Nethyal left, Wynter turned his attention to his desk. On it was a rough map of the small towns and villages strung out along a line from the Frostspine mountains in the west to the shores of the great ocean to the east. These were the former homes of many of his subjects. Some had also come from the south, but Wynter had learned much about these northern towns from his people, some of it by talking to those who passed through the halls of the castle, and some from Nethyal who spoke frequently with men and women in town. He learned about the towns' defenses, their land, their resources, their crops – in short everything he would need to determine which towns were worth collecting as part of his northern kingdom, and which he could safely ignore. These latter were not worth fighting for and as Solwyn became the major power in the region, he knew they would quickly beg to be part of his new kingdom.

To the south, lay Bayside, one of the smallest of the capital cities of Eigrae of which he was aware. In his former life Wynter had seen far grander, more opulent places - places that didn't yet have a space on his map, but that had a place in his schemes. "Yes," he thought to himself, "Bayside will be a fine trophy, but it is a mere trifle."

"*What of the girl?*" The voice of his dead wife didn't annoy him as it used to. He had been practicing how to shut her out and he could do so as easily as lighting or extinguishing a candle. She was only in his head because he allowed her to be and when he was by himself, he often allowed her access, if only to have someone to discuss his ideas with. It was, Wynter thought, a marvelous way to tell a secret and rest easy that it would be kept.

"The girl with green and blue eyes. I have not forgotten about her. In fact, I hope this will bring her to me. She has something I want."

"Could you not just find her and take it? How hard could it be to best her with your power?"

"If she were any other girl, you would be correct. But she isn't. She has the same power. Nethyal said she had not realized her potential, but it would be unwise, after all this time, to assume that remains the case. She will have harnessed some of this power – how could she not? Still, eventually, she will come to me. She will see her world being altered and she will try to save it."

"How can you be so sure? Is it because she's a woman, and you don't think she's strong enough to fight you openly?"

It was insulting, this line of questioning. Wynter didn't see male or female; he saw potential and skill and cowardice and courage. He knew a bowstring pulled by a child or a woman was as deadly as one pulled by himself.

"It is because she is a human-being," Wynter said. "I've watched many people down the shaft of an arrow or through a crack in a wall. People don't like change. They don't like war. They'd don't like what they can't control. Even the most cowardly among a group of people will stand up when everything they know is being threatened. She will stand. And she will act, and that will be her undoing. She will play by the old rules. Because she does not understand the new rules."

Wynter shut his wife out before she could reply and went to a window in his great northern tower that overlooked his castle and the growing town before him which was spreading west so that the work going on was nearby his fortress. Below, workers were busy constructing an armory, stables, and barracks. Everything was being done by lamplight and fires. Work was slower in the winter with limited sunlight, colder weather, and heavier clothing, but everywhere the town was alive with activity. In his heart, Wynter was proud of what he had accomplished and of the people who were making his goals real.

"You are a proud people," he said out loud to himself as he watched logs and stone being unloaded. "And you shall be named anew. From tomorrow you will begin your own race, and you will be known as the Kelmen." With a smile, Wynter's magic moved stone and logs to their places where workmen had been laboring for hours to shift the articles and would have labored hours longer until it was done. The group of men turned toward the great blue tower and placed their hands to their hearts in thanks. Wynter lifted his right arm in response. His left side was a hanging weight, tingling from his fingertips to his toes. Even his mouth had gone slack and he could feel a small rivulet of saliva forming at the corner.

Magic, he had come to understand, was limited by distance. The further away one worked magic, the more difficult it was. Taking the small towns to the east and west would be more challenging with this limitation as he would have to travel with his small force. At that rate, it might take a year or even two to overthrow all the towns from the eastern shore and west to the mountains. Still, half his face smiled. He dragged his body across the room to his bed, and as he lay down and closed his eyes, he heard the faint echo of 'Hail, Wynter King; Hail, Solwyn.'

The blustery wind and rain foretold of a cold night in the thickening of fall, and the group rode quietly until they arrived at the crater. Wae Relin, seeing the wreckage of the forest for the first time, was in awe how anyone could have lived through such devastation, but none of the women wanted to discuss that night again – not now, not here. Lydria stopped and knelt quietly by her father's grave. They were close to Eifynar, and on horseback it wouldn't take long. All of them were thinking of a warm bed and hot food, but they gave Lydria privacy and waited for her before moving forward.

"Lydria, strangers have passed this way recently. Several, on horseback."

Lydria relayed the message and before the echoes of her words had faded both Wae Relin and Haidrea were off their mounts and moving forward looking for tracks. Lydria moved to stand near Haustis and the two waited until the Wae Relin and Haidrea returned to their horses.

"We should move more slowly from this point," Haidrea said. Her defenses were up. Wae Relin agreed and the two prepared to walk ahead of the horses.

"No," Lydria said finally, with an authority she did not entirely feel. "Kimi is ahead of us, and he will let us know what we might find. It is getting late, it is cold, and we are all prepared for food and proper rest. If trouble comes our way, I think we can dispatch a group of highwaymen. Soon we will be close to Eifynar where they will be watching as well. I'd rather move quickly toward that destination than linger here. If there are people in front of us on horseback, it stands to reason they will remain so. If they are headed to the village, it is also best we be there as quickly as possible in case our help is needed."

Haidrea looked to Haustis who motioned for her and Wae Relin to regain their saddles and move forward.

There were no sentries to meet them as there were when Lydria first made her way to the town. The trees had lost most of their foliage and with the sun spreading its last rays in front of them, they could see the woods to either side of the path were clear. Kimi, despite his warning of the travelers, wasn't concerned and that made Lydria feel easier, but not at ease. *"Who do you think it might be,"* the woman asked from the quick trot of her saddle.

"I have no idea. They were few and they were not in a hurry. If there was trouble, there would be signs in the forest. The other animals would be wary and quiet. There is no sign of birds who follow violence."

Lydria for a moment, felt like a child re-learning lessons from her father. A battle or large loss of life inevitably brings carrion birds, and quickly. The skies here were largely empty. Soon, Haidrea dropped back from her position at the front with Wae Relin and leaned in to speak with her friend.

"It is not often we have travelers. Those who do find us, do so largely by accident, as Eifynar is far away from the main trails," Haidrea confided. "Yet it seems they know the way here and the tracks show a consistent movement – not the halting and turning you would expect of someone who might be lost."

Without more to add, the group rode along silently until they were able to make out the telltale sign of a fire – a faint orange tinge among the treetops, brightened against the darkness. There were people in Eifynar and when Lydria and Haidrea entered the village, they found Wae Ilsit and Drae Ghern waiting for them with a man of Wesolk. He was old, but not like Drae Ghern. His back was straight and his eyes clear. He looked up when the group came in and smiled in a way that was both warm and welcoming but made Lydria suspicious just the same. *"Kimi, do a circuit of the village and see if there are more men or horses about."*

"I will. But if it makes you feel better, I sense no tension here, but I smell deer and … is that partridge? I love partridge. They are devilishly hard to catch…"

"Kimi!"

"I'm on my way."

In Wesolk, Lydria was sure this man would have stepped forward to be greeted, but he didn't as much as flinch in their direction. He obviously knew the customs of the Eifen and seemed to be comfortable maintaining them. It was Wae Ilsit who moved first to greet his daughter as the travelers dismounted. Following what she had learned, Lydria was next and hugged the man warmly, proceeding then to Drae Ghern who seemed very happy to see them. Wae Ilsit greeted Wae Relin and when told of his lineage, hugged him for a long time before standing the younger man to his right, so that he might introduce the last guest to all.

Even with the revelation that an Eifen of the west was amongst them, the people of Eifynar were not as excited as they soon would be. The western Eifen were largely unknown and it had been generations since the name Eigraenal had been spoken openly, and so, Lydria watched Wae Ilsit, with a formality and stiffness that she understood, introduce Haustis. The entire town reacted as if a god had been dropped in their midst and it was some time before Wae Ilsit could restore calm. While he was doing this, Haustis reached out to Drae Ghern, holding him by both hands and staring at him for long moments. It seemed like ages before she pulled away and looked toward her son.

"Honored Haustis, Daughter, friend Lydria, and Wae Relin of our kin of the west, I would have you meet Krieger, a friend of mine for many years, and a steadfast and true ally of the Eifen in the kingdom called Wesolk, to the south."

TWENTY-FIVE

"Well met." Krieger spoke smoothly and with the assurance of an old friend. He was polite and met each of their eyes as he spoke, smiling the entire time. His voice was firm but not demanding, and like his body, his voice gave away none of the years evident in his skin and hair.

For a man of his age, a fair bit older than her father, Lydria believed, Krieger's hair was thick and long even while being more white than black. He wore his hair in a small braid extending to the top of his shoulder blades and tied in the same fashion as Haidrea's. In fact, it was tied remarkably well for someone not of Eifynar. Lydria wondered for a moment, if it was tied for the same reason – for stealth and combat. Certainly no one would take so much time for vanity alone. After a few moments, Krieger reached his hand out to Haustis and shook it as in the fashion of Wesolk and said, "It is good to see you again, Haustis," and then he moved toward her to greet her in the fashion of the Eifen.

"You don't know me…but you must be Lydria." Krieger moved toward her and reached out a gentle hand to her shoulder. "I knew your father Cargile very well. We never spoke more than once or twice but reports from the guard often featured his name and it was well respected within the castle. He was a good and honest man with integrity and he is sorely missed."

Lydria didn't know what to say. She hadn't expected the compassion or that this man would have known of her father. "Thank you, sir," she said. Her father had always taught her that if she didn't know the rank, she should always assume there was one, and assume it was higher than her own.

After greeting Haidrea and Wae Relin, Krieger looked around as if searching for something else. After a moment of doing this, he turned to Lydria and asked the whereabouts of the most exceptional member of their company.

Assuming from Drae Ghern's smile that Krieger must have been told about Kimi, she offered that he was hunting.

"That makes sense." Krieger smiled again. It may have been a trick of the shadows caused by dancing firelight, but Lydria was almost sure he winked. Before she could decide, however, Wae Ilsit was motioning everyone to the great hall where Lydria had first spoken to the chief and Drae Ghern.

The hall was more comfortably appointed than it had been previously, Lydria noted. Many of the benches and boards had been removed and there were rugs and soft cushions laid out. There was food prepared and distributed on platters resting on low stumps around an area near a fire at the far end of the room. It was obvious where Wae Ilsit expected his guests to sit while they spoke.

"You have traveled far and must be hungry," Wae Ilsit said. "Please eat your fill while we speak. We may be here long. Many stories will be told this night and not all of them pleasant."

As they settled Drae Ghern was smiling warmly at Lydria, but his eyes seemed sad. Occasionally, the old man glanced at Haustis, as if to be in her presence was his greatest wish. Looking at Drae Ghern and knowing the secret Haustis kept, Lydria felt sad and slightly ashamed that she knew the secret Drae Ghern did not. A look at Haustis, and she felt sorry for her as well – it was evident the gathering was uncomfortable for everyone. The sidelong glances Haustis stole toward Drae Ghern, who seemed so much her elder, were as if she were trying to absorb as much of him as she could while nearby, but helpless to make her feelings known.

Lydria looked to her hands and pressed the stump of her finger against her palm, hoping for a small tingle of pain in the healed skin to help her focus. There was no pain, but she felt as though she could bend the knuckle that no longer existed and watched the empty space where she could feel the missing fingertip moving back and forth. For a moment, she wondered if magic could make it whole again.

Krieger sat cross legged on a large rug to the side of the fire, his back to the wall and facing the entrance. Lydria laughed inwardly at how he surveyed the room and even amongst friends took the most defensible position. Lydria wondered how much time he had spent with Wae Ilsit and how well he knew the Eifen to be so comfortable among them.

Haidrea took food from a platter near her shoulder and passed the plate to her left. In this way, all the plates soon found their way amongst the guests. While they ate, no one spoke, and many of the men took off what garments they could as the fire warmed the room. Finally, Drae Ghern clapped his hands and raised his eyes to the rafters above, invoking the spirits to watch over the group and provide wise counsel. What guidance he sought she could not yet guess.

Wae Ilsit broke the silence that followed. "We are here to discuss the wielder Wynter and the threat he poses to both Eifen and the people of Wesolk. Many days and nights have passed since Nethyal and his warriors went north into the land of ice and snow, and we have heard little from travelers and none directly. It is my hope Krieger will have a more useful story that will set us upon a path of celebration, rather than a path of war."

Krieger nodded his appreciation for the introduction and scanned the room, judging his audience and taking note of their attention.

"Thank you, friend, but my stories are not cause for celebration. My stories are full of sadness and betrayal. The future shown me by the tidings of my agents throughout these lands is one of death and misery should we sit idly by and wait for danger to pass."

Krieger softened his tone and continued, pacing out his words like an old man telling night time stories to his grandchildren. "There were reports some months ago of a man wandering north on his own. He was a ragged beggar many thought, mumbling to himself and nervously looking about as if waiting for some unseen enemy to collapse upon him. I gave the reports no notice. There are many paranoid wandering beggars and most only get a second counting when they are found dead in a ditch, the victim of crime or starvation, or cold, or drink. In time, however, the beggar appeared in the stories of others. The new stories told of how he had taken a companion, a strong warrior who walked along, sometimes carrying him, sometimes tending him, but always by his side."

Krieger paused for several seconds as the men and women in the lodge stared at their hands and looked tentatively at one another.

"Stories have come more recently from travelers from the northern provinces that mention a new master of a small village by the shores of a great bay. This village has always been a small place where fishermen and hunters brave the cold, follow the herds, fish through holes in the ice, and who live a simple, plain, and rough existence. The new master of this village gives his name freely. By you, he is known as Wynter. The people of the village called him lord for a time. They now call him king. The people have even taken a new name for themselves and their town – the Kelmen of Solwyn." Krieger took a small puff from a pipe offered by Drae Ghern.

"The name, Kelmen is not unimportant, and chosen, I think, to send a message. One of my informants was a man named Kelmenth, and I have not heard from him in a long time. That he is now involved in Wynter's plan is what we are being led to believe. My information now comes from outside Solwyn, in the form of letters from land holders, mayors of paltry villages, and minor nobles whose towns have been devastated by the flow of people moving toward Wynter and his new kingdom. The letters to Bayside request help – troops and weapons to put down this man who upsets the balance in the north."

"And the other, who walked by the side of Wynter through the frozen north?" Wae Ilsit spoke with stones in his voice. He barely breathed, and his jaw was clenched as he forced the words through his teeth. Lydria understood that he knew, and a quick glance to Drae Ghern, confirmed he knew as well. His head hung low and his eyes, barely discernable in the harsh glow of the fire, were red and glistening with moisture.

For his part, Krieger was hesitant to give a name; not because he didn't know, but because he did not want to cause pain to Wae Ilsit. Spy or assassin or politician, Lydria decided, Krieger was genuinely fond of Wae Ilsit and Drae Ghern and would rather they be spared his stark appraisal of the situation. But there was no other way.

"His name is Nethyal. A name he also has not hidden. I am very sorry, my friend." Krieger reached his hand toward Wae Ilsit but was stopped by a small motion from the chief.

"And his companions – what have you heard from them?"

Here the entire company leaned forward slightly, for no one had heard what had become of the warriors who left the village with Nethyal. Krieger paused, trying to find an alternative to words he again did not want to speak. "They were found during the last moon, lying in a camp not six days march north of this place. They had been killed in their sleep." Krieger opened his pack and took out a fox pelt and handed it to Wae Ilsit. "These were found near the men." Wae Ilsit lifted the burnt orange covering to find three small weapons, gifts from fathers who would never see their sons again.

"It is so." Wae Ilsit's voice broke once as he muttered the words and then fell silent.

"I would not think Nethyal capable of such treachery," offered Haidrea, to console her father.

Wae Ilsit looked up briefly and smiled at his daughter, acknowledging her grief, but it was Drae Ghern who spoke. "The shadow of power is upon Nethyal and has been for many seasons. When Lydria came to us, Nethyal above all thought to use her power for harm. He sees in Wynter an opportunity to bask in that power even though it does not belong to him."

All eyes in the hall moved from Drae Ghern and made their way around the room, silently appraising each person as if they could determine simply by looking, whether such treachery lurked behind the eyes of their fellows. At last each set of eyes turned to Krieger, a man they did not know who, despite his apparent familiarity with the Eifen, was not of them.

Wae Ilsit saw the glances and stares and looked at Haustis who nodded, and the chief straightened his back, raised his head and looked at the legendary woman.

"Many seasons ago, soon after I became chief, I was granted an audience with the gentle Haustis who sits beside us. It has always been said that Haustis greets each new chief, but I thought it was a tale, a legend that could not possibly be true. When she came, however, I knew the truth of it, and together we spoke to each other and with the spirits for several days. We spoke as we hunted, as we ate, before we slept; we spoke at great length and shared our stories from the spirits. Within these stories there was a warning, that there would come a warrior who would betray his people. For years I was wary and stood guard against this thing, but our warriors were true and strong and there was no need to fear them. Even as I sent Nethyal on his way north, I did not see in him the evil of which the spirits spoke – the man who chose to pursue power above all else.

"And I must carry that shame and burden as the father and chief of a traitor to his people. For now, however, we must all be open and tell our stories. Only then can we hope to work together to avenge our fallen warriors and bring them peace."

The room was quiet as Wae Ilsit finished and Lydria wasted no time in beginning her own story, which all had heard except Krieger. For a long while she spoke of the meeting of Wynter in the forest, the death of her father, of finding Kimi, and a description of magic and her ability to use this new power. To Lydria's relief, Krieger did not interrupt. He did not ask her to perform magic. He did not ask what things she could do with her power. He said nothing and showed no expression as she spoke.

When she finished her story, Krieger cleared his throat and thanked Lydria. "As you have been so open with all of us, I feel it is time that I am open with you."

TWENTY-SIX

Krieger's story took a long time. Food was eaten, pipes were lit, smoked, and refilled. Fires were kept alight, and the story was well told. Only Wae Ilsit, it seemed, was privy to more than portions of Krieger's story, but everyone was encouraged by his candor. By the time he was finished, it was time to sleep, for it had been decided that in the morning Krieger would travel south to Bayside with Lydria, Kimi, Haidrea, and Haustis. Wae Ilsit and Drae Ghern both deemed it a wise decision and even Haustis conceded the people of the south needed to be aware of the danger they faced. Lydria did not agree it wise to travel south when the danger lie to the north. Nor did she think it wise to deliver the power she wielded to the king of Bayside.

As they made their way toward their rooms for the evening, Krieger took Lydria by the arm and spoke softly so only she could hear. "I know you are hesitant to show your power to the king, and that is wise. I ask you, I beg of you, do not use your power, any of it, in Bayside. If he will abide, put Kimi on a leash and we can say he is a tamed pet you raised – if not, he should remain in the forest until we head back to this place. I have worked many years to keep the peace in our kingdom, I don't want to provide Ahlric a weapon of conquest that will start another war."

Lydria smiled warmly in acknowledgement and breathed in relief that Krieger understood her hesitancy and was working on her behalf. As she was ready to thank the old spy, he spoke again, this time leaning in even closer. "And don't mention Captain Branch either." Krieger paused before saying more, judging the questioning expression on the woman's face. "Has Branch not spoken to you of his lineage?" Lydria shook her head and told Krieger of Branch and Weaver's intention of going to the king after returning to Steven's Folly.

"I see. Thank you for telling me this, Lydria. We need to trust each other, because if we don't, we will end up fighting amongst ourselves instead of paying attention to the threat Wynter poses. The politicians will attack each other like vultures if we don't stick together. Politicians are good at one thing Lydria, they are good at looking no further than their next meal."

"Are you not a politician, Krieger?"

"No. I am a spy and an assassin who plays at politician because the hours, the food, and the expectation of seeing the morning are all much, much better. Good night." Lydria watched the man walk away from the rooms allocated to them and back to Wae Ilsit's home. She knew he would not sleep for some time.

The next morning four horses and a bobcat were heading south through a patch of thick forest, quietly at first and their mood and tongues lightening as the sun filtered through the nearly bare canopy of trees. Wae Relin stayed behind in Eifynar for a time, to discuss his people in the west for scriveners who would record his account. Then he would head back to his camp to prepare to go home, or to go north.

"A leash? Are you serious – he actually said a leash?"

After more than an hour of this Lydria was still somewhat amused by Kimi's ability to be affronted for so long. *"You know, you don't have to, you can stay in the forest outside of town, but it's a very large town with lots of people – people who aren't used to seeing bobcats and who would send arrows in your direction if they thought you were after their livestock."*

"Well, I hate to admit it, but they'd probably be right. Still, would you subject yourself to wearing a leash?"

"Kimi, we will make it very loose, so you can get out if you need to. But I can carry you if you'd like and so long as you were still, you would hardly notice, I don't think."

"Fine. But I agree to this only because you have such terrible senses and I think the idea of going into this town and castle is madness. You'll probably need me before we're out of that place."

With his moaning complete, the cat wandered away from the horses and into the forest. Lydria occasionally would look through his eyes for practice and to see what lie ahead. They had found that the more they shared their senses, the less unpleasant it was for each of them, despite Lydria's inadequate sight and poor hearing.

"Will we head straight to the castle or stop for the evening and arrive in daylight?" Lydria asked Krieger, who was slowing his pace to ride next to her. Krieger moved back and forth along the small line of horses all day, spending time with Haustis, Haidrea, and Lydria, learning more about them and giving them some insight into himself as well. If nothing else, Krieger was a resourceful and well-traveled man who knew people across Wesolk and into several other neighboring kingdoms.

Before he could respond, Lydria asked a question that had been on her mind since meeting the spy. "How did you know Wynter?"

"Yes, I thought we'd come to that." He looked off into the distance as if he were searching back through time and a way to answer the question.

Krieger took a deep breath before beginning. It was the same look she'd seen on her father's face as he told a soldier's wife that she was now a widow. It was filled with distaste and remorse underlined with duty and understanding it was the right thing to do.

"Wynter enters my story many years ago when I was a spy. He was a young man with few prospects apart from petty theft, prison, and most likely a noose. I took him in out of pity. I had been in the places he was heading. Being so young, he didn't question morality, only whether something was necessary to achieve a desired end. He was one of the finest bowmen I've ever known. For a time, when his apprenticeship with me ended and he could take up work as a spy in his own right, he decided to follow me into the next turn of my life – the dark world of a king's assassin. But that world is a small place, and those who live there are best left alone, so we went our separate ways; but always I would watch and listen for signs of his passage.

"As my network of allies grew, the results of his work would turn up as footnotes in messages sent to me. His range was vast, far beyond Wesolk, and beyond bordering kingdoms as well. He traveled lightly and quickly and with no more thought to family or hearth than for the lives he took.

"But, after a few years, word of his work came less often, and it was more difficult to find news of Wynter. I was concerned and went searching for him. The man I found was a miserable thing. He had finally discovered some sort of morality. It was an earnest morality, not the type of casual flirtation with the concepts of good and evil found at the bottom of a wine bottle. This new awareness caused a real conflict within him.

"As it turns out, he had fallen in love. As all men do who fall in love, he started to question many things connected to life and death. We spoke for a long time about the future. He was getting older, and my beard was already growing in patchy, and my eyesight not so good for sighting anything at long range. He told me then that he was done. He would marry and settle somewhere and no longer live in the shadows. His only remorse lay in not having made the decision sooner in life. He felt he was behind and he needed to make up for lost time; to settle down properly and have a family, and that's what he did. He moved to Thrushton, married his love, had children, took up a trade as a bowyer and never looked back."

Lydria stared at Krieger for a moment and after a few seconds, he returned her gaze.

"You are aware Wynter had a family?"

"We were unsure." Lydria told Krieger of the boy they had found in the water and how they guessed he may have been connected to Wynter.

"Well, let me provide for you what you are missing." Lydria was aware that all through his talk with her, Krieger's voice had opened to include Haidrea and Haustis. His story, it would seem, was something he believed was important and wanted everyone to know.

"When the forest was destroyed, and the sky rained ash, I came north to see what had happened. When I arrived, I found a new helmet set upon a grave overlooking a remarkable catastrophe. Eventually, my travels took to me to Lem, the ferryman, who told me many stories of his own, which I won't go into here for it would take another two days to hear all the old man's ramblings. But he told me of a boy who had been pulled from the lake and the connection he believed the boy had with Thrushton and Wynter. After such a time where I believed it safe, I went to the island and found Wynter's wife and daughter. The houses on the island were untouched and the loss of life total. Wynter's family lay where they had fallen. There was an arrow through the woman's chest, but the signs of plague upon her were unmistakable. When I returned to shore, I continued inland, following leads and whispers. A family many miles from the shore had met a nasty end - their house had been burned around them, but I don't believe it was fire that killed them.

"Wynter's skill is such that with a bow, some arrows, a good vantage point, and a little time to plan, he represents a very real danger. With the power I'm told he has, he is quite possibly the biggest threat any kingdom has ever faced."

Lydria felt suddenly cold as she considered what someone like Wynter could do with the power she wielded. "I have seen the madness in his eyes, Krieger, and I know some of what he is capable of. I agree with you – he is a threat, not just to the kingdom, but to everyone in Wesolk and all of Eigrae."

The party continued riding, each considering a world where Wynter was king, and before the sun fell behind the trees, Lydria smelled wood smoke, and called out to Kimi.

"There is a cabin up ahead. No one is there, but there is a fire and there is fresh food hanging from a tree."

Lydria slowed her mount and relayed the information. Krieger smiled and pushed ahead. "Let us rest this evening, my friends. There is a house ahead where we can eat and prepare ourselves, for soon we visit a king."

TWENTY-SEVEN

Krieger's safe-house was remarkably comfortable. The stone fireplace was large enough to cook on and provide heat for the entire building. There were soft furnishings and comfortable sleeping quarters and as Kimi had pointed out, there was an abundance of food on hand.

It took Lydria's eyes a moment to adjust to the firelight, but when they did she was aware not only of the warmth and homeliness of the cabin, but of the weapons everywhere she looked. Her father had been over-protective and made sure she knew how to handle a variety of weapons, and he had placed small knives and other implements at strategic points throughout the house, so regardless of where she was, a weapon was rarely more than arms reach away. So it was with Krieger's safe house. From short daggers to polearms, almost every type of weapon Lydria had ever seen had its place on the walls or shelves of the cabin. Some weapons were hung as decoration, but all were well maintained and serviceable to anyone familiar with their use.

"If there is anything here that suits you, please take it as a gift and use it well," Krieger said, as he watched the women take in their surroundings. There was a smile playing at his mouth, Lydria thought, as if he were showing off a new baby or an especially fine horse. "It's likely we will need sturdy weapons in the days ahead, but here you are safe. Please make yourselves comfortable and I will cook."

When Krieger opened the door he stopped, frozen in his tracks and whispered, "Lydria, I believe your friend would like to come in."

Standing opposite Krieger, his mouth clamped around a large rabbit, Kimi stood and looked directly at Krieger and made no move to flee. "Krieger meet Kimi, my very hungry friend." Krieger stepped aside, and Kimi moved casually forward, never breaking eye contact until he was safely over the threshold, where he made his way toward the fire and began to eat.

"Well, at least one of us is fed. I will see to the rest of us then." Krieger was smiling widely with both his mouth and eyes as he turned from the door and made his way to a hanging deer carcass nearby.

Krieger soon had meat sizzling on a spit and he turned aside to pull out a pipe and offer it to all. Haustis took a long pull from the thick and elegantly carved pipe and exclaimed her approval when she finally exhaled. "That weed is wonderful, Krieger. Where did you come by it?"

"That, my dear Haustis, is what happens when you have connections in far-away lands. A former employer of mine sends me a tub every fall without fail. I can't hope to smoke half of it and you're welcome to take as much as you'd like. As to its particular blend I cannot say, and I dare not ask. Some secrets are best kept, I think."

Krieger accepted the pipe back from Haustis and produced another from the same small chest that held his weed which he filled and offered back to her as her own.

From her experiences with the Eifen, Lydria knew the long draw Krieger took on his pipe was the first act of preparation, calming his throat with smoke before beginning a story. When he finished, he held the bowl of the pipe in his left hand and gently cradled the stem which was easily a foot long and slightly curved, between the first two fingers of his right hand, slowly releasing the smoke from his mouth in short, crisp rings.

"I find myself in the uncomfortable position of breaking with tradition," Krieger said. "I know it is customary to provide a story with a meal, but I find myself instead wanting to ask a question. A question that has been on my mind for many days." He looked carefully at each woman before settling his gaze on Lydria. "Is Wynter's power real?"

Lydria expected the question and having watched the recent exchange of pipes between Krieger and Haustis, she realized how she could show the potential for power possessed by Wynter.

Looking at the pipe in Krieger's arms, Lydria squeezed her palms together and thought carefully of how the hollow stem of the pipe opened into the bottom of the bowl and how the outside of each instrument could be crafted and carved by those who had taken the time to learn the art. Slowly, she pulled her palms apart, revealing as she did a blue light that stretched from palm to palm, curling up her right hand as if pinching something with her index finger and thumb and then the light dissipated, leaving in its wake a clean, white bone pipe with a bowl finely etched in black with a prowling bobcat. She handed the pipe to Krieger who was unable to put his thoughts into words, and who wasn't aware that if he had spoken, Lydria would have been unable to hear him.

Kimi, I can't hear anything!

"Relax, Lydria, I can still hear, and I can relay what is said. Better yet, why don't you borrow my ears for a time? The practice will be good, and you may gain some insight through the experience."

While Krieger gathered his thoughts for his next question, Lydria quickly moved her thoughts to Kimi and a wall of sound came back, causing her to flinch slightly, drawing quick glances from Haustis and Haidrea. The two women began to speak, commenting on the craftsmanship of the pipe and drawing Krieger's attention away from Lydria.

Every word spoken came to Lydria as if it were spoken inches from her face and sounds she had never been aware of entered her consciousness as if they were nearby. It was all she could do not to constantly turn her head to try to pinpoint the new noises.

"It will take some getting used to," Kimi assured her. *"Your ears, like your eyes, are not suited to taking in all the clues the world presents. It amazes me how your type has done so well given its basic deficiencies. Focus on the voices of your friends."*

"But what are all these other sounds? They seem so close like they are all around me."

"They are." If bobcats could smile, Kimi most certainly was. *"What you hear is the noise of the animals your kind is ignorant of. There are snakes below this building, squirrels and chipmunks outside, birds of course, and several smaller insects and creatures you'd probably rather not think about. We*

can discuss all this another time, but for now, you need to concentrate on the people in front of you."

It was easy to focus on her friends, but it was difficult to not wince at the volume. They all seemed to be yelling, and Lydria nodded to Haustis and looked at Krieger who held the new pipe in one hand, raised his eyebrows to Lydria while holding a pinch of weed in the other. Lydria nodded eagerly and Krieger filled the pipe and handed it toward her.

"No, friend Krieger, you must be first, as the gift was made for you." Both the offer and the refusal were traditional amongst the Eifen when a gift of importance was bestowed. Krieger smiled like a child presented with a toy and when he lit the weed and pulled his cheeks together he nearly coughed out loud.

"It pulls so easily, it is effortless." Krieger lifted the pipe again and pulled more gently, filling his mouth with smoke and again releasing it in tight circles. He looked up to Lydria when he finished, his face serious once again. "How can it be?"

Together with input from the others, Lydria told Krieger all she knew. It was a gamble, as Kimi's voice reminded her often, but Lydria explained to the bobcat that Krieger did not feel untrustworthy. *"I have bent my mind toward his truthfulness, and while I'm not sure whether or not magic can help with judging the intent of people, he feels as a friend would feel. I don't know how to explain it better."*

As Haidrea explained how Lydria had healed Kimi, Lydria presented to each their dinner cut and served on wooden plates, without ever moving. Through it all, Krieger did no more than give slight facial clues as to his surprise when presented with a new feat of magic. When both dinner and the stories were finished, he broke his silence.

"Practice all you can, and let no discomfort stop you. I will send word to Bayside that we are delayed, and we will stay here for a time. But we cannot over-delay our audience with the king." Krieger slowed his speech and lowered his tone, though to Lydria he still might as well have been yelling directly at her. "What you have shown me is incredible. I am at the same time envious of you and sorry for you. Your gift can cure many ills, but at every corner I see

179

the potential for its ill use. No one else in Wesolk must know what you can do, and that includes the king. When the time comes, you will tell your story of Wynter. Others will fill in what they know of his abilities. If you are known to have this power, it will be beyond me to save you from the machinations of ambitious men."

"Krieger, I am grateful, but what of this?" Lydria reached up and touched her blue collar. It was not natural and could not be explained away by chance. That both she and Wynter could be the only two who bore such a mark surely would connect them in the minds of people for their abilities as well as their looks.

"It is an easy thing to hide, with a scarf and hood." Haidrea reached for a bag and pulled from it a delicately woven strip of cloth. "It is a gift from home and it would not be unseemly in these colder times for you to wear it for warmth. Do as Kimi does and cover your mark with fur."

With the matter taken care of, Krieger turned his attention back to his new pipe and then Lydria. "The things I have seen these last few minutes fill me with wonder and make all the weapons in this room dull with age, but still, I wonder, are they the extent of your power?"

The question started a lengthy discussion on the possibilities magic presented. It was late in the evening when Krieger and his guests turned to their beds, eyes newly opened and wide to the potential ruin that stood before them.

TWENTY-EIGHT

Throughout the winter and into the spring Wynter continued building his community. Whereas in fall his kingdom consisted of little more than a series of huts near the bay, the town was now broad and wide, encircling the bay to the west and passing by the front gates of the castle to the east.

Emissaries had started to arrive from some of the larger villages strung out to the east and west of Solwyn, and even a few from sizeable hamlets and small villages to the south, along the edge of the tundra and forest that marked the boundary between Wesolk and the officially unclaimed north.

Wynter made sure the heralds of these towns were appropriately welcomed and shown how much had been accomplished in Solwyn in a year. He met with each emissary in his throne room, regaled them with the story of the Fourteen, and impressed upon them the opportunities available in a growing kingdom such as Solwyn, and the need for men with political aspirations. He made sure they and their servants spent time in establishments where stories of his abilities were told and exaggerated so much he was himself doubtful he could perform the feats credited to him.

For a month, each minor functionary who visited was feted and charmed and sent away with a small token to placate their disgruntled lords. But the stories they took back were the weapon Wynter counted on to bring his enemies to his doorstep. By summer, word reached Wynter some of the lords would visit the Cobalt Tower to, as the letters grandly stated, "wish well upon the North's new shining star."

"Do they think I'm stupid?" Wynter scoffed at the first such letter and threw it on his desk, looking at Nethyal for an opinion, not an answer.

"They are careful with their words, and they come as a group, each with his servants and men at arms. A large force will come upon this place." Nethyal stopped his thought short and paused for a moment. "When the Eifen have need of a new chief, a leader is called forward. Then, the people may decide to put forward another, or several others to be considered as chief as well. When this happens, the people must agree on how the new chief will be chosen. In the past, this was often accomplished by combat."

"Often, you say, but not always?"

"Not always. It is rare for a challenge to be made, but the man who is first named chief is traditionally offered the right to choose the challenge."

Wynter looked at Nethyal and smiled. The space of his missing tooth soon showed again, and he started to laugh. "Well, then Nethyal, we shall give them a challenge. Prepare stables and billets for the men and begin preparing for a mid-summer feast. I shall prepare a letter of welcome and we shall need a walled arena to fete our guests."

Throughout the spring the Kelmen worked from dawn to dusk - even as the days reached into the evenings. On the northeastern side of the castle, opposite the bulk of town, a new building emerged, a rectangular series of walls that could be closed at one end with a giant gate. Where most of the townspeople expected to find lists and targets and the paraphernalia of combat or a contest inside the building they instead found nothing, simply an open field. As the walls went up benches were added along the two long sides and a wide platform raised on the closed end. In the middle of the field, more benches filled about half the space until it looked like the entire town could easily find a seat. Even Nethyal was not entirely sure of what Wynter had planned.

The arrival of the lords did not disappoint. They entered town a full week early hoping to test Wynter's resourcefulness, but they were met and welcomed as if they had arrived as agreed. There was more than score of standards flying by the time the last group staggered into Solwyn from the town of East View, on the shore of the great eastern sea. The lord there had made a fortune on fishing and, some said considerably more on coastal raiding. Far to the west was the large town of Brookfield that sat under the shadows of the

Frostspine Mountains, and other smaller towns that were large enough, or had resources enough, to warrant a titled ruler.

The lords brought men at arms, servants, slaves, animals, priests, what tradesmen they had remaining – everything, Wynter believed, designed to overextend the resources of his small town.

Wynter and Nethyal met the newcomers outside the castle while the Kelmen met with squires and servants and slaves and took away horses and baggage quickly and efficiently. With more than twenty nobles and their advisors, Wynter thought the odds were falling into his favor.

"Welcome, Lords and Ladies, to Solwyn. On behalf of the Kelmen people, I, King Wynter, welcome you to the Cobalt Tower."

Wynter's words had the desired effect. While they all stared openly at the blue collar on his neck, some still laughed quietly at Wynter's use of king, an honorific that would place Wynter above themselves and in direct contention with their benefactor in Wesolk. While none of the towns of the north were officially part of Wesolk, many had accepted Ahlric as their king, to facilitate trade and stave off would-be conquerors who wouldn't dare incur the wrath of Wesolk. Effectively, the nobles gathered in Solwyn were the heads of territories that belonged to Ahlric in all but deed.

Wynter inclined his head in a gesture of equanimity toward the outbursts while Nethyal took careful note of who did not laugh and who, if any, may have inclined their head in recognition of Wynter's claim.

"Would you please join me in the great hall so that we can become acquainted and be refreshed," Wynter said before turning his back on the group and heading toward the castle gates.

Since its construction, gates had been created from black oak that had traveled for months from a kingdom bordering a desert far away to the south and west. Wynter had been there once and was struck by the hardness of the wood and its durability against fire. To fell a black oak often took days and required special tools and skill. As such, crafting such large and magnificent doors was slow and expensive. The effect, however, against the blue-green ice walls, was stunning. When the castle was lit from inside, the doorway looked like a mouth of darkness from which none could escape.

The sight of the massive doors caused a small murmur from those who understood the woods' value, but it was nothing compared to the gasps that greeted Wynter's ears when they entered the great hall. "So, it is true" was a phrase that resonated from the mouths of several lords.

"My Lords and Ladies, it is my pleasure to introduce to you, the Fourteen. The men and women who gave their lives so that Solwyn might be fortified by life itself." Wynter made a show of bowing and throwing his arms out to his sides as a gesture that invited his guests to move about the space freely. They needed little encouragement to mingle and without exception they all ran their hands along the perfectly smooth pillars, some walking completely around them, their hands never leaving the surface.

"They look like they're still alive," one of the ladies commented to no one, but close enough to Wynter that he believed she meant it for his ears. Moving closely to the woman and leaning in so he was sure no one else could hear, he whispered, "they are."

***

Every attempt to discuss politics or the resettling of people to his kingdom was waved off for the better part of a week. Wynter instead spent his time engaging each of his guests in turn and answering questions about the castle, the tower, and his unusual collar. He answered each inquiry with patience, as if it were the first time he'd been asked a question he longed to answer. He was thoughtful and companionable, and he spent as much time as he could with his guests, until, by the end of the week, everything was in place.

On the morning of the eighth day, Wynter gathered the dignitaries in the shadow of the Fourteen and said, "My Lords and Ladies, I know you have all traveled a great distance and that we have business to discuss. As much as it pains me to put aside this pleasantness, I fear we must at last move on to the reason for your visit, and to the political necessity at hand. However, I'm sure we can quickly come to agreeable terms and continue our festivities."

His speech was well received and when he suggested making their way to the arena, the entire group cheerfully filed out of the castle toward the enclosure. Solwyn had begun a festival that very day, with stalls selling treats and delicacies from the north. Banners and bunting were draped across posts and buildings leading the way to the arena where, as Wynter and the lords entered, they were greeted with cheers. The benches were filled with men and women gaily dressed and those who couldn't find seats inside stood in the space of the open gate. Banners representing the twenty lords were hung along the walls and chairs had been placed on the stage at the closed end of the arena.

Nethyal and Wynter walked to the stage as the nobles and their wives were escorted to seats in front of the stage.

"My Lords and Ladies, thank you for coming," Wynter began. As the audience settled, he lifted and extended his hands out and drew them toward him as if telling unseen workmen to close the great gates. Those standing in the space moved inward and as Wynter's hands fell to his sides and the massive wooden gate closed almost silently. The arena was now enclosed, and all attention was on Wynter.

"My Lords and Ladies you stand here today in the court of Solwyn accused of crimes against your people. Of causing suffering and anguish on others to the aggrandizement of yourselves. You stand charged of the ownership and or unlawful servitude of your people, the unjust taxation of those entrusted to your care, and the inability to provide for those who look to your leadership. How do you plead?"

TWENTY-NINE

Wynter's proclamation brought cheers from the crowd and looks of abject horror from the front rows. For the men at arms, servants and other members of the lords' households who were left outside the arena, the cheering sounded as if a great contest were underway. Men roamed the lines of benches to randomly encourage cheering, but Wynter's announcement needed no such goading.

The assembled lords and their ladies rose almost as one and started clamoring for Wynter's attention. Their noise was pitiful amidst the din of the town.

Nethyal who was by Wynter's side for the entire theater, whispered to him the name of a lord who had given a signal of allegiance when the nobility first heard Wynter call himself king. Wynter pointed and called him forward.

"Belarth, do you believe you are a good lord to your people?"

"Yes, sire."

The honorific was immediate, and its tone of obeisance was not lost on Wynter. "Why, then, do they leave you in droves to come to a cold, desolate place?" The arena was quiet now and a row of Kelmen spearmen had herded the nobility back to their seats where they understood silence was all that stood between their life and a blade in the throat.

"Because they have found a truth here, sire. They say they have found a place where people can live together, none richer or poorer, and all well fed and cared for."

Wynter looked to Nethyal, surprised the lord had spoken to his people who had moved to the town. The Eifen lifted an eyebrow and nodded, confirming Belarth had spoken to his former subjects.

Belarth was the lord of East View, the largest town of the north and the last to arrive. He, more than the rest, had much to lose and was in a constant struggle to maintain his station, living as he did on a seaside town that could be the target of everything from storms to pirates. The loss of his people would hit East View more significantly than most.

"You will take your men and go back to your town. If there are those who wish to go with you, they go so with our blessing and with our assistance. East View will become the capital of the Eastern Reaches and you shall be Governor of the Eastern Reaches. No other title shall you, or anyone else have lest it be given by me. There is one king and one lord of the North, and he stands before you. Do you agree to these terms?"

The man knelt at once and waited for his king to bid him stand. Wynter raised his voice to the crowd. "Join with me in congratulating Belarth, Governor of the Eastern Reach." The applause was thunderous, and the assembled nobility looked at one another in grave concern. By giving this man title to the Eastern Reach, they were sure several towns, their towns, would now fall under his governance, begging the question of what would become of them.

"Governor, before you take your leave, which man among this group do you feel is most worthy of being granted governance over his people?"

The question came as a shock and the governor's lip twitched as he realized the significance of what he was being asked, but he looked across at his former peers and considered each conscientiously, before offering his answer.

"My liege, if I may speak openly, there is no man here who is most worthy of such an honor. Rather, there is a woman who ensures the people of her village are cared for and babes not go hungry even during the cruelest winter. Grettune of Goose Landing has looked out for the people of her village since the passing of her father. When crops fail, she opens her kitchens; when winter is fierce, she has space by her fire. She does it all under the nose of the so-called lord who does nothing for his people."

Wynter asked him to point the woman out and he looked to her. She was still quite young with red hair and a fair complexion hidden beneath too much face paint and outlandish clothes. Her husband, if indeed that was who he was, was at least twenty years her elder, soft around the middle, bald of head, with thick jowls and bad skin. No one who lived in these northern conditions should be so well fed they go to fat in this way, Wynter thought.

Calling the woman forward he pronounced Grettune Governess of the Western Reaches to be situated in the western town of Brookfield under the shadow of the Frostspine Mountains. The announcement was met with more thunderous and genuine applause. To those few more who had not scoffed at the king, Wynter awarded new lands in the southern crescent, a series of hamlets and farming villages that ran in an east to west string south of Solwyn between the Eastern Sea and the Western Reaches. These former lords would become earls and report to the governors who would report directly to Lord Nethyal.

These small posts would be given priority for men and equipment for they were to be the eyes and ears of Solwyn as well as the larder of his kingdom, inhabiting mostly arable land with forests and space for grazing. When the time came, Wynter thought, they would also be his fodder, slowing the advance of the enemy Wynter hoped would be on its way.

When the cheering had died down for the earls, they along with the governors, were escorted to the rear of the arena. Wynter looked to the rest and slowly shook his head.

"You were given control of men and could not control yourselves. What should a king do with such miserable subjects?"

The lord who had openly laughed loudest when they arrived spoke quickly, his voice quavering, "exile us, oh, king." The others around him nodded solemnly. Exile, they thought, was an excellent way to spare their lives.

"You do a grave dishonor to the memory of the Fourteen Pillars. Who among you would so willfully give yourself for the betterment of the rest?"

The question was met with silence and uncomfortable movement. The crowd erupted in applause again, maintaining the illusion of sport. Laughter was prompted at some point and all the noise only added to the discomfort of those on trial.

"Do you have champions?"

The question drew hopeful eyes from the floor. "Do you believe that's wise," offered Nethyal into his king's ear.

"Oh, very much so. Killing these few would be easy but there are several hundred armed-men outside these gates. I would like to keep as many as possible. Our people will fight, but we also need real soldiers."

Wynter returned his gaze to the twelve faces staring at him and called out the first, a lord who was weak, pale, and had most likely inherited the estate of his father. He was sallow, reeked of perfume and wore more face paint than his wife – probably to conceal a skin disease, Wynter noted. His was also the largest remaining holding with the most men at arms. Wynter and Nethyal left the platform and stood in front of the man.

"You are Grummond?"

"Yes," was all the man said before Nethyal's blow to his unprotected stomach buckled his knees causing him to gasp out a, 'yes, sire' as he knelt before Wynter, vomiting his breakfast, and plotting a revenge he would never see.

"I make you an offer Grummond." Wynter did not give any indication he realized the man had been hit or that he was nearly prone. "Send for your champion. When he arrives, he will choose whether to fight me. If he fights and wins, that is, if he kills me, you will become King of Solwyn. If I kill him or spare his life, then you shall die."

"If I refuse?"

"I shall kill you now. There will be no exile." Wynter raised his head as he made the statement, being sure to catch the eyes of the remaining lords.

"I offer now one chance for the consorts and households of those who stand accused to step away, renounce their relationships, and stay here in Solwyn to take up the profession that best suits them and be useful members of our kingdom. If you have children, they will be brought here to join you. Who will join us?"

Laughter and cheering spontaneously erupted among the benches as the consorts, wives, lovers, butlers, servants, and households of all the remaining lords rose as one and moved to the back of the arena with the governors and earls. Mostly they cried, and only a few made anything approaching a loving parting with their spouse. *"Maybe their husbands will join them again after they're dead. Do you think so, my love?"*

"I wouldn't wish it on them. Go away."

Wynter and Nethyal moved back to their seats on the platform and twelve chairs were brought up and arranged on either side of the two men. The former lords were encouraged to climb the stage and take their seats and a runner was sent to gather the men at arms of each lord. They marched into the arena fully armed and armored and formed ranks in front of the benches along the arena walls. The large end doors remained open and a crier called forward a champion to represent each lord and the rules of engagement were read allowed for all to hear. The lords, each in turn, agreed to the conditions of the contest and an enormous shout went out again from the arena as Wynter rolled up his sleeves and walked to a cleared space in the center of the field to await his first challenger.

THIRTY

Grummond's man answered the call quickly, stepping forward with an ease and presence that caused some discomfort among Wynter's following. It was an interesting juxtaposition that the weakest lord should have the bravest champion - and the two could not be more different. The man towered over everyone in the building, Wynter guessed he had to be nearly seven feet tall. He was huge and surely could kill a man simply by falling on him. Taking his place in the center of the arena, the giant man nimbly grabbed his sword off a back-scabbard and planted the point in the dirt in front of him. For any other man present, the sword would have required both hands, but this man moved the massive piece of metal with such fluid grace it seemed weightless. With a practiced nonchalance the larger man casually placed his left hand on the pommel and his right hand on top of the left and waited. There was no arrogance in the movement, Wynter noted. He was merely doing as he had been trained.

Wynter looked to Grummond and gave him an appreciative nod. "Your champion is stunning, Grummond. My compliments."

The little man, used to having his way, sneered his response. "I will take your castle and piss on it until it melts." He turned back to his champion and smiled, sure he would live to see the end of the day.

"That makes this so much more fun for me then." Wynter turned back to the champion and applause broke out again and continued until he waved to his people and lowered his hands, entreating them to remain calm.

Wynter extended his hand to the man, who had to look down to see him properly. "Good afternoon. I am Wynter, King of Solwyn, and you are…"

The champion was taken aback by Wynter's casual nature. "Sire?"

"Your name, man. What is your name?"

"Sir Keldon, sire, in service to Lord Grummond."

"Do you enjoy being in service to Lord Grummond?"

"Sire?"

"Look, Sir Keldon, let's not make this more difficult than it needs to be. Lord Grummond is a puffed-up little fop who wouldn't last two minutes in a tavern brawl, much less be able to put on armor. Does he treat the people of your village well? Does he treat you well?"

Sir Keldon didn't respond right away but Wynter noticed his eyes shift subtly to his left, and following that glance, he saw the woman who came as Grummond's wife. Looking at her and then at Sir Keldon, he decided to try a new approach.

"Sir Keldon, would you like to have that woman as your wife; legally and for the rest of your days?"

"Yes, Sire, more than anything else."

"Then you have to make a decision. You can fight me and die, and never see her again; and believe me Sir Keldon, you most certainly will die." To reinforce his threat, Wynter caused the chest and back plates of the giant's armor to constrict upon themselves, causing the champion to feel how easily he could be crushed.

"Or, you can renounce Lord Grummond and kneel before me and accept me as your king. I will allow you to retain your title, I will give you land, and I will make you the Captain Commander of all Solwyn's forces. Does this sound agreeable to you?" Wynter released his hold on Keldon's armor so the man could breathe easily again and respond.

For his part, Keldon never flinched at the discomfort he felt, and Wynter was sure only the two of them were aware of what had happened. "You are exceedingly kind, sire, but it seems, somewhat...dishonorable?"

"Sir Keldon, your time is now. Honor is a great thing for the living. Accept my offer and live and you may be as honorable as you like."

With only a second's hesitation, the giant man knelt before Wynter. The applause was deafening. The woman who had drawn Sir Keldon's attention was smiling broadly and openly weeping, clasping

192

her hands in front of her face. When the applause died down, Wynter turned to Nethyal who grabbed Grummond by the arm and led him down to the arena floor.

Grasping the hilt of Sir Keldon's enormous sword, Wynter imparted a small bit of magic allowing him to easily lift the monstrous steel blade with a single hand, earning him much respect and credibility from the soldiers in the arena. He moved the blade until the point rested above Sir Keldon's heart announcing that Sir Keldon of The Cobalt Tower rise and be recognized as the First Knight and Captain Commander of Solwyn, reporting to the king alone.

As the man made his feet again, he smiled triumphantly and looked toward his love.

"As the First Knight and Captain Commander of Solwyn, you may ask a boon of me, Sir Keldon and I shall grant it."

"I should like to marry, my king."

"Bring the woman forth."

As the giant went to claim his bride, Grummond began to yell. "That is my wife, you cannot marry my wife!"

The crowd, upon hearing this roared its approval again, causing Grummond's face to go red like flowing blood. What the crowd did not hear was Wynter's response, "it's not illegal for a widow to remarry, Grummond."

With Sir Keldon and his bride-to-be before him, Wynter knew there was still the matter of removing Grummond with enough of a show as to bring the other champions in line as well.

"*Ask the woman how to do it. My bet is this Grummond creature has treated her cruelly. Ask her how she would like to see the wretch removed.*"

It was, Wynter thought, an excellent idea. "You are, Malai, currently the wife of Grummond." The woman nodded. "While I would see my knight commander happy and my vow to him fulfilled, it is impossible that he marries someone who is already married. So, Malai, by way of a wedding gift, how would you become a widow?"

The woman, who Wynter had thought was shy and demure, showed more mettle than her husband. Her eyes and face pricked up at once as she realized what was being asked and Wynter could

almost see the wheels in her head turning with possibilities. Malai
leaned forward and lowered her voice so only Wynter could hear and
asked if what he had told her about the Fourteen were true? It
dawned on him then, that it was Malai who had asked if those inside
the pillars were alive when she saw the Fourteen for the first time.

Wynter laughed aloud and put his hand on her shoulder.
"Why, Malai, you are a treasure among women, hidden away with
this feeble wretch Grummond. Good people," Wynter turned to the
audience, "Malai asks if she could be widowed by creating a
Fifteenth to join the Honored Fourteen."

The crowd applauded loudly and Grummond blanched, his
face moving from the red of embarrassment to the white of shock in
a moment. The other eleven lords started to rise out of their seats
and with a flick of Wynter's wrist, the wooden chairs grew limbs
which ensnared the lords and brought them back to their seats,
firmly tied. The crowd did not miss this bit of magic and grew quiet.
It was not unknown for their king to use his power, but they knew it
was not used idly.

Wynter felt another tooth dislodge from his gums and
fought back the urge to gasp in pain and surprise. If this keeps up, he
thought, I will look like a leper and not be able to be seen in public.
He steeled himself and swallowed the tooth and a mouthful of
blood, motioning to Nethyal to bring him a skin of water.

Moving close to Malai he spoke softly so as not to open his
mouth too much and to minimize the air rushing across the fresh
gap in his jaw bone. "If I make him the Fifteenth Pillar, he will
remain alive, and technically you will not be widowed." She nodded
and stepped back to Sir Keldon's side.

To the crowd, Wynter spoke, not caring if blood flew from
his mouth as he did; the effect, he thought, would be a good one.
"This man is not fit to be made one of the Pillars of Solwyn. He is
not a Kelman and he is entirely unworthy of such a glorious sacrifice.
But, if Malai would have him become ice, there is no reason she
should not have her wedding gift." He looked to the men who
tended the fishing boats and said, "take him to the shore, prepare a
boat and sail north to the ice. When you arrive, cut from the ice a

hole, and lower him in." The crowd roared their approval again and Grummond was taken from the arena cursing and screaming the entire time.

"Bring the next champion."

"My king, we beseech you, do not play with us so; have mercy upon us." The call came from among those lords tied to their seats on stage.

Wynter looked at them and at the soldiers amassed before him. He ran his tongue across the sensitive hole in his jaw and, when the crowd's silence was at its height, he replied. "I will retire to the castle for an hour to think upon it," Wynter proclaimed. "If I can divine a reason to spare your lives, perhaps I shall."

To the men at arms in ranks along the arena's edge, Wynter looked next. They could see which way the wind blew, he knew, and it wouldn't take much to have them all join his cause. They respected the giant Keldon if nothing else, and Wynter believed they would follow him.

"Sir Keldon, please offer a place in the forces of Solwyn for any among the men at arms who would renounce their former lords and stay here or be deployed to the Eastern and Western Reaches as needed."

Sir Keldon bowed in salute, spoke briefly to his soon-to-be wife, and made his way across the arena. He quickly and quietly took command of the corps in front of him and after his voice died away, each company of men replied in turn. Sir Keldon then led the fully formed and equipped army of Solwyn out of the arena.

Wynter stood for long minutes watching the arena empty until only the retainers, servants, slaves, cooks, and concubines who had followed their lords to Solwyn remained, having nowhere to go without their lords. They bowed respectfully as Wynter and Nethyal walked past them out the great gates.

"You have one hour. See Lord Nethyal when you are finished, and he will find you work and lodging." As they continued to walk Wynter turned back to a former slave and pointed out a small pile sticks, rope and stone. "Please clean up when you're done." As he and Nethyal walked out of the arena, Wynter ensured the gates crashed closed behind. Moments later as they walked toward the castle, Wynter and Nethyal could hear screams from inside the arena walls. Wynter smiled and didn't care who saw the blood fall from his lips.

"We have conquered the north in an afternoon, Nethyal. It cost us a tooth."

THIRTY-ONE

Krieger's camp was their home for nearly a month as Lydria honed her magical skills under the watchful eyes of Krieger and Haustis. Haidrea and Kimi spent much of their time in the forest hunting and when in camp, they did their best to help Lydria recover from her work.

During her training sessions, Lydria learned that using magic to incapacitate an enemy was more effective than killing, as it took less of a toll on the wielder. They also discovered that magic was better at close range, losing its effectiveness with distance, while the impact to the wielder remained the same regardless. It was interesting to Lydria, that when Kimi stood away from her, closer to her targets, her magic seemed to be more potent at greater distances.

"That your magic has limitations is good," Krieger said. "If Wynter is to attack Bayside, he will have to travel with his armies to do it which means while he is powerful, he is not invincible. As to why your magic retains its power when Kimi is afield, I am at a loss, but unless Wynter has such a helper, it gives us an advantage."

Krieger's schedule continued every day with Lydria practicing magic, building up her abilities with small tasks and increasing the intensity and repetitions of tasks as the days passed.

"Kimi, I feel this is all I have done for the last year." Lydria did not often complain, but the effort was taxing, and she was tired and sore.

"It is important. You've told me before how your father did things without thinking because of the countless hours and days he had trained to do those things. It is the same with you now. You are following the path of your father, and like him, you will see the reward of your work."

It was Haustis who ended the training one morning after Lydria used ground vines to ensnare the legs of Krieger and Haidrea and pull them to the ground.

"Krieger, it is time." The old woman looked at the man lying on the ground and he returned her gaze in a way that made it apparent they would travel as soon as he could be untangled. "The vision I have recently seen is unlike anything I've ever witnessed. There is a shift of power coming to the world. It is not clear if it is Wynter or of Wynter's making, but we cannot wait longer." Without another word, she turned to the cabin and started gathering her things. Lydria limped after her and when Haidrea returned from the woods, her horse was saddled, and they started toward Bayside.

It was mid-afternoon, and the light frost of early morning had given way to a sharp, but sunny day. Krieger had provisioned them with warmer clothes from stores in his cabin. The city, he told them, despite its buildings and fires, was often cold and without sun as the stone walls captured the cold and held onto it like a lover until forced by fire to let it go.

The journey to Bayside would only take a few days, but Krieger insisted on traveling to the east and entering town through the eastern gate.

"It may seem overly cautious, but I have never traveled with such important cargo as I have with me today," he nodded toward Lydria. "I have friends to the east of Bayside who can tell me the temperament of the city before we enter. Arriving from the east puts the sun at our back in the early morning. When we arrive, we will have a better view of the town than they will have of us."

"You speak as if we are entering an enemy city, Krieger." Haustis' voice raised slightly, and she looked at the man with something akin to suspicion. "Is there something you are aware of that you're not telling us, my friend?"

The others remained silent as they watched Haustis and Krieger, neither of whom gave away much in their words or motions. Even Kimi, with all the sensitivities of his kind, found it hard to fathom any deeper meaning in their words.

"For years I have kept many secrets my dear Haustis, but never have I had the opportunity to keep one from you. No, there is nothing I am aware of, but we have time to be cautious. The city of a king is a fickle place and court politics often change overnight. Many a man has been woken by the pounding of the guard at his door even though he was at peace when he went to bed. My caution stems only from the importance I give to my mission."

The exchange seemed to be enough for Haustis. Kimi traveled apart from the horses and planned to stay off the paths as they rode, and outside the walls and boundaries of the city when they arrived. *"I will meet you tonight,"* he told his friend, and Lydria gave him a mental hug as he bounded into the forest.

The travel was steady and easy going. For a time, Krieger continued to drill Lydria to perform small magic, and to goad her into action he threw stones at her from the saddle. Her first reaction was to use magic to hurl the projectile back. The tactic was successful, as several bruises and small cuts to Krieger's arm and cheek testified, but the weakening effect it had on Lydria was considerable.

"Unless I sit here pelting you with stones for weeks on end, you will be able to fend off only a few such attacks before your own body betrays you."

Lydria asked Krieger to throw one more and this time the stone bounced away before it hit her. To Haustis and Haidrea, traveling on either side of Lydria, it seemed as though the rock simply stopped before it reached her and fell to the ground.

Krieger smiled broadly. "Does it hurt you to do this?"

"I think I could possibly do this all day, but I'm not sure that I could do anything else besides."

Haustis looked to Krieger and back to Lydria. "As she is not acting upon the stone, she uses less magic. If she were to hurl the stone back at you, as she did before, the force for the movement comes from her magic. She has recreated a steel shield in magical form. To a soldier, holding a shield, while not effortless, is a chore he can manage all day. Well done, Lydria."

As the afternoon wore on, Lydria experimented with moving the magic shield between herself and Haidrea and Haustis, encompassing both herself and her horse, and extending the shield further from her body. While these tasks were possible, they proved to be difficult, at one point nearly causing her to fall from her mount before Haidrea moved along side and held her in the saddle.

At camp it was all Lydria could do to eat before she was asleep.

The next morning was clear and brisk, with a wind coming down from the north that brought with it a dry, stringent but odorless feeling in the back of the travelers' noses. "Snow will fall soon, you can smell it on the air," Haidrea said. The first snow of the year was almost never heavy, but it began the cycle of freezing the ground so that deeper, longer-lasting snows could follow. For Krieger, the snow and its inevitable melt meant mud and prints that would last for days.

"Do you think anyone is following us?" Lydria asked the question of Krieger but it was Haidrea who responded. "There was someone shadowing us for a time yesterday. They were behind us and slightly to the north, but they did not account for the modest breeze yesterday that foretold of the wind today. They were never close and perhaps were just meant to watch?" She looked directly at Krieger. It wasn't so much a question to answer as a statement to confirm.

To his credit Krieger did not seem surprised by the response. "Your people are a wonder to me even after all these years. I have friends in these parts and they keep an eye on who travels this path and many others. If we were anyone else, I'm sure they would have approached more closely to try and discern our business. As it is, we must be more cautious now and not practice Lydria's skills any more while on this path."

"If we are to travel, we should be going." Haustis spurred her horse to a trot and looked impatiently for the others to follow. When they arrived at her side she told them, "Last night the spirits showed more treachery and peril. While I don't know the time or place, I feel we should be on our way, to either avoid those omens, or be done with them quickly."

The threat of snow did not disappoint and as it began to fall, a wind from the north pushed the flakes at their sides. As the day progressed, so did the wind until the last of the leaves were blown from the trees and tiny pebbles of ice and dirt combined with the snow to lash at their faces forcing them to push onward with their left eyes closed and leaning heavily to the left to stay upright. Even the horses were slowed by the weight of the wind.

On an impulse Lydria conjured her rock shield and was mildly surprised when she found it protected her from the wind and its assorted small projectiles as well. She was quickly enveloped in a quiet warmth. The wind no longer reached her ears and the sudden lack of ice made her face feel warm. Her reverie was interrupted by Krieger who trotted up beside her and leaned his face inside her shield so that he could whisper to her.

"If you are trying to show the world that there is something different about you other than your blue collar, I couldn't think of a better way to do it. The wind and snow collide with your shield as if there were a wall by your side. If you were to stand still, there would be a drift at your feet in minutes."

Reluctantly, Lydria let the wind and ice hammer back at her face. Before burying her head in her traveling cloak, she turned to look at Krieger and smiled.

Krieger smiled back.

THIRTY-TWO

Lydria's party spent the first night outside in the open and then pushed through the following day and into the early evening before arriving at another cabin. Inside they made a fire and put a large iron pot over a tripod and soon, a rich venison stew filled the small space with its aroma. Haustis dipped a finger to taste the gravy and Lydria watched as she closed her eyes and smiled, drawing envious looks of anticipation from Haidrea and Krieger who had just entered from tending the horses.

Lydria reached out her thoughts to Kimi but the bobcat wasn't nearby. It worried her when she couldn't be with him and she wondered if parents often felt the same way about their children. He was clever, Lydria knew, and could take care of himself and his thick mottled orange fur would keep him as warm outside as they were inside.

Haustis motioned for Lydria to help Haidrea lay out their things to dry and busied herself collecting the bowls and wooden spoons sitting on a small shelf under a thin, high window. The window's position, Lydria noted, allowed the fading light of day to enter the room and a similar window on the opposite wall caught the rising sun. But the windows were set high and were too narrow for any but a child to squirm through. Seeing that this cabin too was bristling with weapons, she wondered if anyone would be foolish enough to attempt robbery.

When Krieger settled by the fire they ate and Haustis asked them to join her to seek out the spirits' advice. Despite the fine weed and pipes, no new omen came to them and Haustis accepted that her earlier vision of peril might be the last she would see.

"Tomorrow we will enter the town early. The gatekeepers are known to me and will not hinder our passage and we will go straight to the castle. Lydria, it may be best that you keep a scarf around your neck and a veil over your eyes while we travel. You and your father are not unknown and while news of your father's untimely death was met with grief in Bayside, the lack of news concerning your whereabouts has led to speculation and gossip."

"Gossip?"

"People are strange, you know this. Anything they don't know for a fact they will gladly entertain any number of foolish stories to satisfy their curiosity. As I have heard, you have been trapped by foreigners and hauled off to the southern deserts; you've been kidnapped by the Eifen to teach them our language; you've run off with Lem and are having his children..."

"Lem?" Haidrea smiled behind her hand and finally laughed out loud and even Lydria was forced to join in.

"When we are there, what is our plan?" Haustis asked, ever mindful that being inside a castle was akin to being in a prison for her.

"I have an audience with the king before midday," Krieger said. How he had managed to contrive an audience after being so long away was curious, but a quick rocking motion of Haustis' head cautioned Lydria against pursuing the question they both longed to have answered.

Krieger continued, "We must make the king see that Wynter cannot be trusted and has a powerful weapon at his disposal which could endanger the entire kingdom. The trick is that we can't mention what this weapon is, we must be vague and yet still provide enough information to make the situation undeniable. Your meeting with Wynter, Lydria, will be important. The facts, as you are to relay to the king, are that Wynter ambushed your party, and as a result all were slain, and a great furrow has been torn from the wilderness. You do not need to say Wynter was responsible, but you should imply he was."

"You leave out a great many details, Krieger." Lydria felt as if she'd somehow been asked to swindle an old lady out of the contents of her larder.

"The key, Lydria, is that you must not lie. There are men in the king's court who can spot a liar; I, myself, am quite adept at this skill and any could be trained if they knew only the clues. But we need not lie, we just need to present the facts in such a way as they will result in the king doing what we want – and making him feel like he is the one who wants it."

"What is our job during this charade," asked Haustis, motioning with a finger between her and Haidrea who sat straight and quiet as ever, watching and listening to the machinations being built around them.

"You are here as representatives of the Eifen. The king respects your people regardless of what many believe. Some do not believe the Eifen exist, but he knows, and he has been made to appreciate your bravery and ferocity as warriors. He also understands Eifynar lies somewhere in the forests along his northern border. Further, he likely knows a member of your people gives aide to Wynter. He will take a great interest in the Eifen."

"Will he not be angered by such treachery," Haidrea's voice was hard and she barely opened her mouth to utter the short sentence. Her brother had been very close to her, Lydria knew, and his betrayal Haidrea took upon herself. "Will the king not look at Eifynar and see it as a place that gives aid to an enemy?"

"No, he will not." Krieger's tone was certain which gave some comfort to Lydria but seemed not to have the same effect with her friend. Krieger noticed it as well. "Treachery and betrayal is not unknown among either of our peoples, Haidrea. In fact, it is far more common amongst our own than it is among your people. But your father's disavowal of Nethyal has traveled far and word has almost certainly reached the castle and the king. One thing Ahlric understands very well is that for the leader of any people to publicly disavow a member of his own kingdom is a serious matter. For that disavowal to be made against his own son -- that is practically unheard of. Your father has too much to lose to not make amends."

Haustis reached out and gripped Haidrea's left hand with her right. Haidrea did not flinch from the affection, but Lydria saw she gripped the older woman's hand back. It was a moment Lydria did not try to join. As close as she had become with them, there was something about this moment she knew needed to be between Haidrea and her grandmother.

"How long will we stay?" Lydria asked, hoping for an answer that would see them back in the cabin the next evening.

"We must stay until the king makes a decision. It could come swiftly, it could take days. Sometimes the king makes his own mind and issues orders to be followed immediately. Other times, he delays and seeks the advice of his ministers. In most normal events, I find the second way the best course of action. But we are not dealing with normal events. I will urge quick action. Still, we may be some days in the castle and when we leave it again, we may be among hundreds who travel north."

Lydria looked to the others. Haidrea and Haustis had let go of each other's hands and where Lydria would normally expect to see a woman in Haidrea's position wiping away tears, she saw only a steely resolve. She had seen it before in soldiers under her father's command, usually after they had watched a comrade die and accepted the fate of the dead man as their own. Men like that often became impetuous in battle and performed acts that many called heroic and courageous. They led desperate charges and fought against long odds. Cargile had always told his daughter that these men sought death as the only sure way to ease their suffering minds and hearts. Calling them heroes eased the minds and hearts of those who wanted to live. For her part, Lydria hoped that Haidrea was stronger than those men.

THIRTY-THREE

For all Krieger's confidence that getting into Bayside would be easy, it turned out they were treated no differently than any other traveler or trader who came through the gates. He admitted he had miscalculated the number of people who arrived for market and so the four of them tried to blend in with those waiting for the eastern gate to open. Only when they arrived at the gate did Krieger open his cloak slightly to show a pin with Ahlric's insignia that picked him out as a member of the royal household. From that point, they moved swiftly.

The early morning streets were quiet, and the rising sun did little to clean them. They traveled in the middle of the road to avoid the splash from the chamber pots being emptied from the second-floor windows over-hanging the street. Small brick ditches were built into the sides of the cobbled street, but little care was taken to ensure the contents of pots landed there. Even when they did, the splash often found its way to those who traveled too close to the road's edge.

The main road from the gate, Lydria knew, was one of two cobbled roads in the city. It crossed from the east gate to the west gate overlooking the bay after which the city was named. A second road ran from the castle, at the northernmost point of the city to the south gate, both converging at the center in a large square cobbled space where traders and farmers gathered each day. In the square criers could be heard remarking on the news, or delivering royal decrees, or pronouncing the schedule for the administration of justice. At this time of the morning, however, the only noises were the shuffle of feet along the dew-slick stones, and the grumbling of people who weren't fast enough to evade the intermittent rain of human waste.

Market stalls were being set up along the intersection of the two roads and noise from the sellers was creeping up as if following the sun. Slightly to the north of the square to the east, there was some gallows off the main road so as not to interfere with the view of the castle, or from the castle. Because of this, royals who wished to witness an execution, came to the square which resulted in a robust day for traders.

The castle itself had been under construction of some kind for as long as Lydria could remember. Every day hundreds of men pushed and rolled enormous granite blocks through the streets on logs that were moved from back to front by men and horses. The stones came from quarries to the south and the location of the town, Cargile had told her, was the result of the location of the quarry. It was a straight line from the quarry to the castle – and the quarry doubled as a defensive measure. Masons pulled stone from the quarry carefully, digging the massive trench in such a way as to force any army from the south to squeeze through a gap between the quarry and lake on one side, or the quarry and a small series of rugged hills on the other.

As Lydria entered the center of town, the group turned north past the gallows. Lydria told Haidrea what she knew of the building as she seemed in awe of its size. "The foundations have been dug very deep and rest on the bedrock below the dirt. Granite and stone are used to build the foundations and walls you see."

"Is it all stone inside?"

"I've never been in the castle. My father had, though, and he said it was a very fine place, and that it would be a bloody job to make your way inside unasked."

"Your father was correct," Krieger joined. "The men who laid down the castle so many years ago, used all their knowledge of defense and built all of it into this space. What you can't see from here is the amount of space there is inside the hills to the north of the castle. The occupants of this castle could withstand a siege for years."

"Is this building not finished?" Haidrea asked, never taking her eyes from the walls which grew larger with every step.

"It is finished enough to stand fast against an enemy, but it would not yet endure long against a determined foe with time and men to spare. The thing about castles, Haidrea, is that they are built to withstand all known weapons, but it takes several generations of men to build a castle. It takes far less time to devise a better weapon. And we will never have enough time to make a building defensible against the likes of Wynter."

With the name of Wynter still lingering in the air to remind them of the seriousness of their task, they continued in silence, and were motioned through one guard point and then a second on the far end of a bridge that connected the castle to the path. The bridge was a thick wooden structure designed to hold the weight of wagons and stones from years before when the foundation had been set down. It would be nearly impossible to throw down such a bridge, thought Lydria. The space under the bridge was deep and cut out of the ground with straight steep sides that would be nearly impossible to climb. This was the first pit that provided stones for the castle, Krieger told them. At the bottom were jagged rocks embedded in the earth. There was some water at the bottom as well, but the ravine was a long way from becoming a moat, if that was indeed the intention of the space.

After crossing the bridge and moving under the raised portcullis, Krieger pointed out the defenses in the stone archway they passed under before continuing through another raised portcullis to the courtyard beyond. The courtyard was vast, with stables and houses, farriers, blacksmiths, bakers and other buildings built along the inside of the wall. Seeing Krieger, a boy ran out from a stable and took the horses allowing the three women, and Krieger to enter the castle proper through a small, guarded tunnel to the side. Lydria looked to Haustis who was pale and looked nauseous as she moved deeper into an unnatural world. Seeing Lydria's concern, however, the older woman smiled and nodded that she was fine.

Inside the castle it was, as Krieger had anticipated, cold. They made their way, single-file up a narrow winding staircase that seemed to go on for an unnaturally long time before arriving at a platform with a locked door. Using the small light from a narrow hole in the wall above them, Krieger opened the door with a nimbleness that suggested he could have done it as easily blindfolded. The doorway emptied into another landing with a stone wall to the left and front and a locked door to the right. Through this door more stairs curled upwards in the opposite direction and Krieger motioned for them to remain silent. This time, the climb was quick and through one more door at the top, they entered a large chamber where Krieger told them they could drop their gear and rest on one of the many cushioned chairs and benches.

The room had three doorways including the stairwell they had just entered, which from inside, looked like a solid stone wall. Lydria marveled at the skill that could make a door disappear so completely. Krieger saw Lydria examining the wall and showed her a stone which she could only reach with help, that could be pushed to activate a latch allowing the door to open. The other two entries were sealed with heavy wooden doors reinforced with iron bands.

"Welcome to my home," he said. "Through that door is the castle and through the other you will find a sleeping area. You are welcome to make yourselves at home here while we wait. I will have food sent up and prepare for our visit to the king."

Lydria and Haidrea began to put their things away, but Haustis motioned for them to stop. "We do not know what to expect here. Carry your belongings with you always. The spirits warn of danger and I think we should listen carefully until at least we are out of this place."

A banging on the door startled them all, including Krieger. On the other side a voice rang out as he began to unlatch and open the door. "Lord Krieger, you and your guests are requested to join the king in his quarters at once."

"Thank you, Lyle," Krieger said to the red-faced boy on the other side who had obviously just run up all the steps. "Sorry, milord," the boy said, "but the guards told the king you had entered the castle walls and he's in ever such a hurry to see you. It appears there's mischief afoot up north."

Sending the boy on his way, Krieger looked at Lydria. "Remember, not a word other than what we discussed." He motioned for the women to precede him out of his room and he smiled at Haustis as he saw they carried all their small belongings with them. "You would do well in court, Haustis."

"Not for one hundred of your tubs of weed," she replied and walked stiffly past him.

As they walked down the hall toward the king's chambers, Lyle intercepted them again. "Milord, the king has bidden you come to the throne room." After delivering his message the youngster sped off down the halls again. Krieger stopped for a moment and raised his eyebrow before continuing.

"Is there something wrong with the throne room?" Lydria asked.

"No. Probably not. However, it is an odd place to meet. Normally only the council meets in the throne room. I requested a private audience and I would hope this will not be a council meeting. Keep your scarf on, Lydria, we are almost there."

Rounding another corner and down a quick flight of wide, straight stairs, Krieger paused briefly before a pair of guards watching over a set of double doors. Judging by the guards' shiny metal halberds and ceremonial armor, it was evident the room they guarded was Ahlric's throne room. With a quick look to Haidrea, Haustis and finally Lydria, Krieger nodded to the guards who swiftly and smoothly opened the doors. On the other side, as if he knew they were coming, a herald announced the arrival of his Lordship Krieger, King's Counselor, Surveyor of the Royal Territories, and Captain Commander of the King's Emissaries.

Krieger went ahead and bowed to the king. Lydria followed with the Eifen and the three stood abreast, bowing as one to the monarch.

Lydria took in the room as a reflex as her father had taught her. Always, he had said, be aware of how to leave a room, and how many potential foes might be in any room with you. As she surveyed the throne room, she noticed a dozen armed guards. Four moved to positions in front of the doors they had just entered, four more lined the aisle to the king's right, behind Haustis, and four more opposite them behind Haidrea. They were far enough back where it would take them only a few seconds to draw their weapons and lunge toward them.

The weapons and armor worn by the guards was not ceremonial, Lydria noted. They were clean and polished, but the scabbards were worn so the weapons could be pulled smoothly.

Turning her attention to the king, Lydria realized for the first time he was shorter than her father. He wasn't old, but he looked unwell and Lydria had to force herself not to run to his side to more closely inspect him. While all around him soldiers showed signs of heightened tension, Ahlric was slumped in his chair listening to Krieger. His back was bowed, and his eyes half closed, red, and wet as if Krieger were telling him a sad tale. His shoulders were curved forward, small and weak, and the king's hands rested on his legs like claws with nails as black as night.

As Krieger spoke privately with the king, Lydria stood on the thick rug that led to the slightly raised dais that held Ahlric's throne. Light came flooding in from windows that ran nearly the height of the walls. There were at least ten painted windows on either side showing scenes from the founding of Wesolk and the early kings, but all were narrow and the light they provided was augmented by torchlight from sconces along both walls between the windows. The colored sunlight reflected dust in the room, and narrow banners hanging high above the sconces showed the noble houses of Wesolk and gave the room a softer feel than the stone interior warranted. The throne itself, largely concealed by Ahlric and Krieger, was not the ornate piece of furniture she had anticipated. It was small and had a cushioned seat with a back that only went as high as the middle of a person's back. It was a practical piece of furniture made for conducting business, not creating impressions. Other than the throne, the only other furniture were several unused benches lining the walls under the windows.

When Krieger finished speaking with the king, he came back to Lydria and told her to answer the king's questions honestly, as discussed.

"I would speak to the one who goes by Lydria," said the king with a voice that was both weak and tired, confirming to Lydria that Ahlric was not well. She turned to face the king and stepped forward, bowing again. "I am Lydria, your highness."

"You are the daughter of Cargile?"

"Yes, your highness."

The king's chest heaved as he fought to bring air into his chest. His face, despite his weepy eyes, seemed genuinely sad as he mentioned Lydria's father's name – she was struck that he should be so moved by the loss of a common soldier.

"Your father was a clever man and highly thought of within these halls. I've been told that your loss has also been felt within your father's company. I make it a point to try to speak with men who return from battle and who have suffered injury. Many times, have I heard of your extraordinary skills with a needle, and when needs be, a blade." Ahlric smiled at Lydria and lowered his head knowingly, as if he had heard some of the stories of her run-ins with drunks at taverns. "It is a comfort to the men knowing such as yourself serve alongside them, and I'm happy to have you returned to us, although I wish your father were by your side."

Lydria felt her face flush and a tear form and she quickly bowed again in grateful acknowledgement of the king's kind words.

"Sadly though, it appears we cannot linger long to remember the fallen. Krieger tells me there is mischief up north which may find its way south. To this, I know the truth, as my agents tell me that more than a dozen small hamlets and villages far to the north have come under the sway of a man called Wynter who pretends now to be a king. A king of frozen fishing villages."

The guards allowed themselves a quiet and quick chuckle that made its way around the room, starting with the guards by the door to those closest to the throne. Neither Lydria, nor Krieger joined their laughter nor did Ahlric who only allowed himself a broad smile.

Krieger took a half step forward and added, "sire, Wynter may also be known to you, for he and I share a common past. You may not have known him by name, but in your name, he performed certain…delicate matters that were most beneficial to the kingdom."

The mirth in the king's face dropped noticeably. He understood the abilities a man such as Krieger possessed. "Were you a compatriot of this man then, Krieger? What do you know of him?"

"His skill, sire, was without equal in our rare profession. He came to his power young and has worked in many lands to the far south, and even once or twice beyond the eastern sea, I believe. I know not what connections he might have in any of these places, but his awareness of the greater world beyond Bayside is beyond question. It is not known if he is in contact with people in those lands, but he is not averse to doing what he must to achieve his goals." Ahlric looked at Krieger as he finished the report and its meaning was not lost on the king.

Ahlric had been on the throne for many years and while he had no children of his own, or even a wife, he was a likeable enough man and a capable monarch. Krieger explained that where some heads of state were dim and needed to be spoon-fed information, Ahlric was quick to pick up on intrigue and made sure he had information from multiple sources. Krieger's information was the best, of course, but Ahlric was careful to not rely too heavily upon any one advisor. It was, Krieger believed, perhaps Ahlric's defining trait, and one that had served him remarkably well.

The king moved his head slowly from Krieger until he was facing Lydria again. His voice had lost the light-heartedness of a moment before. "Krieger tells me you have met Wynter…"

It was her invitation to speak and she dutifully recalled the killing of Josen, the flight of her father and Bracknell to capture him, and the odd way in which he spoke to himself as if holding a conversation with someone else. She spoke of the destruction of the forest and how he had walked away down the ruined path of felled trees and tilled earth; and how she was finally rescued by an Eifen warrior. Ahlric looked up and smiled as Haidrea inclined her head toward him. Lydria did not speak of the blue stone, the blue collars she and Wynter shared as a mark of their abilities, a bobcat, or the power she and Wynter possessed.

"Do we deal simply with a madman, then, Krieger?" the king asked when Lydria's story was finished. "A crazy person who speaks to voices in his head and calls himself king of the north because he's manipulated a group of peasants to do so? Am I supposed to march an army into the north for a simple lunatic who holds sway over land that is barely arable and mostly useless?"

Before Krieger could respond, Haustis cleared her throat gently and stepped forward. "Noble king, if I may, might I be permitted to speak?" Krieger introduced her.

Ahlric, upon hearing the name Haustis made a small effort to push his shoulders back and sit up straighter while continuing to lean forward. "I have heard the name Haustis. Even some within the kingdom have heard this name and the legend of the Woman of the Woods, as she is sometimes called. How comes it to be that she stands now before me? Please, lady, proceed."

Haustis told of her first meeting with Wynter in the woods north of the desolation of the forest and how she could feel something out of place. "The spirits sensed that this man is more than a typical man," she said to him. "The spirits showed me a vision of him calling fire from the sky and walking unharmed through a forest of spears. He is not a natural man, good king, he is a man to fear and the spirits tell me he must be destroyed before he has gained his full power."

"Does he threaten me, Krieger?" The king's question was calm and even but Lydria could feel the soldiers at the back of the room take a nearly silent step forward.

"He threatens us all."

"And what say you, warrior? What is your position on this mad man?"

Haidrea did not expect to speak and Lydria quickly realized the king knew this. Ahlric was clever. He wanted as much information as possible and he was going to get it.

With all the pride of an Eifen warrior, Haidrea walked to the center of the rug before the throne and nodded respectfully toward Ahlric. "Great king," she began. "If it please you, I will speak for my people. When I witnessed the destruction of the forest, I saw two people rejoin the living – Lydria and Wynter. There should have been three. It was Wynter who took an arrow's point and ended the life of the soldier Cargile who, though wounded, still drew breath. More still, it is my ... former ...brother Nethyal, who now tends to

214

Wynter and stands by his side. I would, on behalf of the Eifen, like to avenge the pride of our people."

Ahlric sat quietly until the motionlessness of the room became uncomfortable. Ahlric and Krieger were used to such tricks to put others off their ease, but Haidrea spoke no more. After long, tense moments the king raised himself up and walked to the back of his throne, resting his fingertips on the low back, and looking down at Krieger, Lydria and the two Eifen women, he smiled, raised his chin and said, "I do not believe you."

The guards inched closer, the eight not by the doors fanning out in an arc behind Haidrea and Haustis. Lydria saw a subtle shift of Krieger's clothing as he prepared to reach for a weapon. The training of Cargile was not lost on Lydria but as she calculated the best way to escape she realized, there was no best way. There was no escape.

"My lord? Everything we have told you is truth...."

"Krieger, everything you have told me is rehearsed half-truth. I have other eyes and ears that stretch from the upstart north where Wynter makes his home, to the great Southern Deserts. You have told me true, but you have left out a great deal. What of Wynter's power? I have heard how he has made food appear to the starving, made stone move with a wave of his hand, and how he has single-handedly made a castle of ice appear from the ground - in a day.

"Hundreds have labored here for years, and their fathers, and their fathers before them and still my castle is not complete, while a great Cobalt Tower surveys the northern wastes. Is this the work of a madman? There has been no mention of his power that has not also included mention of the Eifen who stands by him day and night. It is also said that Wynter wears an impenetrable collar of blue around his neck." Ahlric looked to Lydria and his eyes moved to the scarf wrapped around her own neck. "I think these things are connected, don't you?"

Ahlric moved his gaze slowly to Haidrea. "I don't believe you want to harm your 'former' brother. I believe you want to join him and take over Bayside and become masters of this land. And you, Haustis. Yes, I've heard your name and legend, it is filled with tales of spirits who work on behalf of the Eifen but never on behalf of my people.

"I may ride north against Wynter, but first I will have you taken in chains until you decide to tell me the other half of your story." Ahlric nodded to his men.

The soldiers lowered their spears. Haustis and Haidrea moved down the aisle so that all four were huddled together in front of the king's throne. Haidrea took Lydria by the wrist moving between the wielder and the wall of blades in front of her. The soldiers had collapsed their arc and formed a tighter line three wide and two deep with a man flanking to either side. The guards by the doors had not moved, but their weapons were raised and ready.

For a moment the room was deafeningly quiet as everyone considered their next move and it was Haidrea who moved first. Lydria watched as if everything were slowed. A soldier's spear was already moving toward Haidrea as her right hand reached back to draw a long dagger, her left still gripping Lydria's wrist. There was a crack and a sucking noise as the soldier's spear buried itself in Haidrea's chest. The Eifen's lithe body was thrown backward, her shoulder crashing into Lydria as a jet of crimson splashed across the spear shaft in front of her.

"No." Lydria screamed the word and threw her hand around her friend as the others moved toward the falling warrior. From Lydria's body a burst of air like a storm wind blew across the throne room scattering soldiers and kings alike into walls. Spears, swords, shields, helmets, anything not a part of the castle was hurled away.

Krieger and Haustis reached Haidrea and Lydria at the same time, before they all crashed to the floor in a blinding flash of light.

THIRTY-FOUR

Winter in Solwyn was hard. With the additional population who had moved to be near the security of the Cobalt Tower, work continued unabated as building continued.

Nethyal chose able men and women to administer the growing kingdom so that he and Wynter could focus on the battles they were certain would come.

"Would it not be best to fight in the winter, sire?" Nethyal asked. "They would not expect it."

"That is true, however it is not my intent to bring the fight to them. Our power is here. Let them drag their provisions across the wastes and meet us on our field."

"You know then, that they will come?"

"Ahlric has spies here and they tell him enough to make him worry. Soon, they will tell him more and make him paranoid."

"Spies? You know this? Should we not root these people out and have done with them?"

"If we were unaware of them, yes, I should say so. But I know who they are and knowing this I can use them to my advantage. In fact, you can help me – I'd like you to go into town tonight and tell the people about your sister and her friend with the green and blue eyes. Specifically, I'd like you tell the people there is another who wears the blue collar of magic, and that she covets the throne of the south."

"Why give our enemy news of this weapon?"

"Because our enemy is a king and a king's biggest concern is always about remaining king. Ahlric is no different. He has his assassins and spies and he strives to know what goes on beyond his borders. But when he finds out there is someone capable of such power within his borders, he will try to own that person or destroy them. This Lydria and your family, they are not an army, and they know that to be rid of me, they will need one. They will go to Ahlric. We need to be sure we have his ear before they do. With Ahlric looking within, we might buy ourselves an extra year in which to prepare."

Nethyal looked at Wynter, sitting on a throne covered in furs and smiled. "I will see that it is done." He walked away with no more emotion than had he crushed a fly. Nethyal had become indispensable to Wynter's project and it bothered him to so freely admit this limitation. *"I knew he would be necessary to watch over me for a time, but without him now, I would be buried under meeting with villagers, and sorting out petty squabbles."*

"Is it so bad to need someone, husband?" Wynter let his wife enter his thoughts more often as the cold weather and darkness embraced the north. She was a useful sounding board for his plans and provided a way for him to speak to himself and know his own mind in a different way. She was useful.

"It's not bad to need someone. It's deadly, however, to rely on someone."

"You could make him regent and live in your blue tower and plan your conquest of Wesolk. There is no need for you to personally approve of everything – not now."

"I have considered such an arrangement, but I need to wander by myself for a time, to see with my own eyes what happens to the south."

"Will that not be dangerous?"

"There is very little to the south, or in any direction, that is a danger to me. Only one person in this world is a danger to me and she must be removed. I made a promise to her."

"You made a promise to me…"

Wynter cut off the conversation. Every time he spoke with her, it ended this way; eventually she spoke as if she were still alive, or she would bring up some past mistake of Wynter's hoping to open old wounds. No. Soon, he would travel south – if for no other reason than to see the sun again.

***

To Wynter's relief spring came early. War would come, even if he had to start one himself. Until then, he engaged his people in the defense of Solwyn. The Eastern and Western Reaches were under new governors and the word from his spies in those lands gave him more hope than he had dared to believe.

The governors of the Reaches maintained exceptional communication with the earls south of Solwyn and carts of supplies and food were clogging the tracks in either direction. Grettune had taken it upon herself to put men to work building a proper road between Brookfield and Solwyn that was wide and well patrolled. The road encouraged the growth of settlements and increased trade and wealth. If his spies were to be believed, everyone was getting along well, and the people were happy. Seeing the utility of Grettune's road, Wynter at once put men to work on a similar road heading toward East View.

"Such roads will make it easier for an approaching army to travel here," Nethyal said, with a voice that conveyed no concern one way or the other.

"Indeed, I hope so." Wynter waited to see if the Eifen would figure out his plan, and when he gave no indication of doing so, he continued, "A kingdom army is a mighty thing, with horses, wagons, provisions, weapons, and men, followed closely by a second army of camp followers, cooks, tinkerers, armorers, wives, harlots – everything you need, in fact, to make war. A road makes marching easy and fast. But mostly, it brings them from a single direction – along a set path where we can disrupt and harass them for miles. In the meantime, the roads make our lives much easier. There hasn't been an army yet that hasn't yielded to the temptation of a road.

"Send word to Grettune that I will begin my tour of the kingdom with the Western Reach and pass on my congratulations on her achievement. We shall call it the Western Governess Road from Brookfield to Solwyn, in her honor."

Nethyal provided the townspeople with news that the king to the south grew jealous and threatened war upon them. The Kelmen were well fed, happy, and motivated to protect what they had built. They would die happily for their king, Nethyal reported, and the thought made Wynter eager to for Ahlric's arrival. And the arrival of Lydria.

Leaving Nethyal in charge, Wynter headed west on his own, traveling light with only his bow. He had maintained his skills as an archer over the cold winter as much for something to do as for the good it did his body. His travels, he assured Nethyal, would not require the warrior's skills. Wynter would see to his people and gather what intelligence he could on his own. He promised he would not go beyond Brookfield.

He lied.

THIRTY-FIVE

Wynter left Solwyn by the Western Governess Road and made sure he was seen as he made his way alone out of Solwyn. He didn't hurry, putting his easy manner to good use in building his reputation as a king of the people. Everywhere he went he was treated with the respect and deference a king should be shown – even one who walked along the road and inquired into the lives of his people. But soon after the last farmhouse had been passed, he moved toward the south, toward the track he had taken to arrive at Solwyn, amidst the scrub growth and open frost fields.

Where his earlier trip had been cold and hungry with a watchful eye over his shoulder, this time he stood tall and walked like a man who did not care if he were seen or not. In fact, Wynter quite hoped he would be seen. Ahlric had spies everywhere but spies were rarely assassins. If his movements were noted by Ahlric, perhaps then the assassins would come, but his deeper hope, was that Lydria would hear of his travels.

Months earlier Wynter's own spies had told him Lydria and Krieger, along with two Eifen had been seen entering the castle in Bayside. Shortly afterward alarms rang, and the guards were scrambling. The gates of the city were closed, and a search was made for 'treasonous spies'. Life in Bayside since then had taken on a peculiar rhythm of tension and suspicion. Guards were sent off in each direction from the city on their search and rumor had it that men were being marshalled for an expedition that summer. The problem, for Wynter, was that he didn't know if the army would march on Solwyn, the Eifen, or another unsuspecting kingdom to the south or the east.

Somehow, Lydria and her friends had escaped. Wynter thought it most likely they were holed up with Krieger, probably still within the city's walls. It didn't take much of a description from his network for him to surmise that they were with Haustis, the old woman who had left him in the clearing so long ago; and the other Eifen was almost certainly Nethyal's sister.

After several days walking, the frost line receded. Spring was coming in full to the kingdom and Wynter realized he was near to the crater where he had found the stone.

Several days later he found it. The long line of destruction looked like it had always been there. Shoots of green appeared from under the blanket of forest debris and ash, but the devastation made him shiver involuntarily. Looking to the west down the clearing he saw a great mound of earth forming a small wall marking the crater's furthest edge. There, in that hole in the ground, he had promised Lydria he would find and kill her. He walked back down the path he had hobbled from more than a year earlier and walked around the crater itself, which had been partially filled by leaves, debris, and dirt from the crater walls. Outside the crater, along the western edge, Wynter noticed a small marker had been placed in the ground. Surely, that was the soldier whose life he had mercifully ended, for his was the only body visible in the wreckage of the forest.

Wynter still remembered the face of the broken man, covered in his own blood, beaten and punctured by wood splinters like daggers. His eyes found Wynter and he had managed a rasping, bubbling request, 'kill me.' It had been the second time someone had asked Wynter for death to spare them from pain, and he didn't hesitate. Using an arrow lying nearby he silenced the man before rummaging through his belongings to find what he could and moving to the crater where he found the stone and the woman, Lydria.

As he reached the grave it dawned on Wynter that Lydria must have known this man if she took the time to bury him – for who else could have done it? He could have been her husband, or brother, or father… it didn't really matter. He had killed the man, and as he had left the instrument of his demise buried in his neck, it was likely Lydria guessed at Wynter's part in his death.

"Why is it you are always around when people cry out for death?"

Wynter had kept his wife from his thoughts as he walked from Solwyn, but walking through the trench and crater, he had let his guard down. He answered out loud, as he did when they spoke the last time they were in this place.

"Maybe because it's my job, and I'm very good at it," he replied smoothly. "Think of how horrible your death, and his, would have been if not for me. You should both be thanking me." And he shut her out again before she could reply.

Wynter picked up a helmet near the burial site and wondered how it had come through the destruction so unscathed. He was ready to drop it when he paused and raised his head in time to see a rabbit darting through the underbrush and Wynter laughed to himself wondering if he were starting to hear things. He dropped the helmet and turned to head back to the crater but stopped again almost immediately.

"So, you are Wynter." It wasn't a question. "I told you that you would regain your ability to walk. Have you decided finally, to turn away from the north and death, and move south?"

Wynter smiled. "Haustis, is it." Again, not a question, just the repetition of formalities. "The north has been a welcoming home to me. I've made a fine life there and if you visit, you'll find the people of my kingdom are happy and prosperous. I've swept away the charlatans and overlords who would keep people starving and poor, and I've created a new society. Why ever would I look to the south?"

Haustis was surprised both by his candor and his words. If it were true, perhaps she had misjudged him. But, she knew what Wynter was capable of and the spirits had been telling her for months the world would be a better place without him. Still, she sensed no dishonesty in his words.

"You have not been to the north since I've remade it, have you? You still judge me on what your spirits told you. But, as you said yourself, the spirits are only guides. Why don't you see for yourself before you condemn me?"

"You speak as one trying to convince a father that he is fit for their daughter. It does not sit well with you, Wynter. The spirits, they still hold that your loss would be but a good thing for the earth."

"Are you here to kill me then?"

"Are you deserving or desirous of death?"

"We are all deserving of death, Haustis. You know that. Each of us in our turn, sneaking up around your circle, doing things that we ought not. The question isn't whether we are deserving of death, but whether at what point we deserve death. I think I still have much to do before I pass. More to the point, I don't think you are the one who will call me from this place."

Wynter shifted slightly but didn't move his feet, preparing himself for her next move. What he didn't expect was an invitation.

"Will you share a pipe with me, Wynter, and join me with the spirits?"

THIRTY-SIX

Lydria heard the world around her but could not communicate. In fact, she thought, hearing the world might be too much – she was generally aware of it. The way she viewed the world through her mind was how a traveler viewed the distance through a thick fog. The noises she could hear were slowly starting to reveal themselves as voices and she concluded by their tone, they were the voices of friends. Krieger at least, she could identify by his rich, deep, voice. She could not hear Haidrea but could feel her presence close by. Anything more specific than this was closed to her senses.

From the point where she recognized Krieger, it felt like days had gone by before her mind snapped open to a new intrusion.

"Lydria. Lydria. If you can hear me, let me know."

The voice was sad. It sounded defeated, as if it were asking the question out of habit. Lydria strained her senses to hear more but no more came until days later when the same voice said the same thing, but this time she felt something else as well – compassion, love, fear.

"Lydria."

"I hear you." It was all she could think to answer, but she couldn't put the thought into words. Lydria felt as though she were only a thought with no body, mired in a haze.

"You can hear me!" The voice jumped into her consciousness and slowly Lydria began to remember Kimi, the owner of the voice and her lost spirit soared with happiness. Kimi was still with her.

"I can't move, Kimi!" She was about to tell the cat to stop licking her face, but the sensation was so overwhelming she let him continue, allowing the scrape of his rough tongue across her cheeks and eyes fill her with awareness and the joy that came from being able to feel once more. *"What's happened, where are we?"*

"I have only recently found you. But it appears you've been gone for a long time."

Lydria considered his use of 'a long time' and dismissed it as the panic at seeing someone you love wounded or hurt. She had seen many women in the camps claim they had watched their husbands die for weeks when often it was no more than hours or days. Time passed differently for those who waited, Lydria thought.

"Lydria, you have been lying here for a half-dozen moons, at least," the bobcat told her. *"When you left for Bayside the winter had not come on full – and now spring is giving way to summer."*

Months? She repeated her question to Kimi and didn't wait for a response as she demanded to know what had happened, where they were and what was going on with the king and Wynter. *"Slowly, my friend, slowly. First, I must make the others understand you are with us. Things are … complicated."*

"Fine." Lydria's voice was a whisper. She could feel herself going back to sleep and pushed rest from her mind willing herself to stay awake. *"I am tired, my friend. What's happening?"*

There was a pause, as if Kimi were trying to best decide how to answer the question. Short chirrups, purrs of happiness at having his friend back, cut off as he prepared to speak, only to start again as he hesitated.

"What do you remember, Lydria?"

Lydria thought she could feel that cat's weight resting on the back of her shoulder, as if he were whispering in her ear. *"I remember…Haidrea!"*

Reliving her memories of Ahlric's throne room caused a wave of nausea to wash over Lydria, but she persisted, providing all the detail she could recall and waiting until Kimi's next question helped trigger more. When she was finished, it was as if she had cut down, chopped and moved the wood of a great oak by magic. She was exhausted, emotionally and physically.

"Now I need to tell you what happened next."

Kimi told the story well although it was nearly impossible to believe. The blast in the throne room had not only knocked back the soldiers moving toward them, it had taken Lydria, Haidrea, Krieger, and Haustis from that place to the outpost where they had first met Wae Relin.

But what of Haidrea?

"I think it's best if we speak of that when everyone has arrived. I need to try to make it known that you have returned and are with us once more. For now, sleep, my friend. Sleep to regain your strength." And she did.

When Lydria woke again, she was groggy and sore, like she had engaged in combat practice late into the evening – and lost. But she could hear now. Sounds of the room, muted and dull were coming to her as if spoken behind a wall. Krieger was with her and Kimi as well. Haidrea, it seemed was nearby as well, but Lydria could not hear her. Still, it was some relief to feel that her friend was alive.

"Kimi, I need your eyes and ears."

Hesitantly, Kimi acquiesced, knowing of no better way to pass information to his friend, who had still not opened her own eyes. Lydria blinked the cat's eyes out of habit as she got used to the light that streamed into her own head and reacquainted herself with the different arrangement of colors she enjoyed while part of the bobcat. The first thing she noticed was Haidrea, laying on her back, her head resting on cushions. There was a cloth covering her chest, and a bright light seeping out from the folds. Lydria saw her own left hand under the cloth, her three and half fingers pointed up toward Haidrea's chin, her palm resting just beneath the warrior's ribcage. Seeing herself lying with her face against Haidrea's leg was odd, as her own right hand was trapped under her as she rested partially on her stomach and on her left side.

"No one dared move you for fear of breaking your contact with Haidrea."

Lydria looked up and saw Krieger, Wae Relin, and Branch, all of whom were watching Kimi with interest. Krieger smiled and said, "welcome back, Lydria."

"Lydria, it is Wae Relin, can you hear me?"

Lydria had Kimi move to Wae Relin and put a paw on the man's knee to signal that she could hear, and the warrior continued. "Haidrea is alive, but only just. We believe your magic has been keeping her alive and that if you remove your hand…"

Lydria reeled at the explanation and immediately withdrew from Kimi and set her mind to looking inward at the magic that flowed through her hand. As she started to make the connections and feel the power flow from her, she knew it to be true. She gently shifted her focus to her own skin and as she regained the sensations of her flesh, she focused outward. Straining to see, her right eye opened slightly, months of disuse built up like a fog across her sight, but she was able to make out the outline of Haidrea's chest rising and falling in a slow rhythm. With a steadying thought, Lydria moved her attention to her arm and left hand where three and half fingers formed a barrier below Haidrea's ribcage. Under the warrior's skin, she felt a shard of metal and the foulness of disease that reached through her magic and assaulted her nose as if she was amid a battle tending wounded men.

"Kimi, I need your help. I need you to remove this cloth from Haidrea's chest."

Kimi quickly grabbed the cloth with his teeth and pulled it away, drenching the room with a warm yellow light emanating from Lydria's hand and the wound in Haidrea's chest. The others drew back out of reflex but just as quickly moved forward, turning their attention back to Haidrea, where between Lydria's half-index finger and her middle finger, a piece of metal began to emerge. Branch reacted first, kneeling and drawing the metal out and pushing Lydria's fingers back together again.

Glancing quickly with Kimi's eyes, Lydria saw the metal removed and then withdrew to her own eyes and waited long, anxious minutes for Haidrea's breathing to return to a steady, even pace.

With that finished, Lydria turned her attention to her surroundings and saw a fire pit close by with a stew pot and bowls her friends had likely used to feed the two women for months. Further away from the fire pit was Lydria's spirit bag.

"This metal you have taken from Haidrea, Lydria, it is well you have removed it, but I do not think that is what ails her now." Wae Relin spoke directly to Lydria, and to the others as well. "We have you back, and you must work to regain your strength, for we have lost much time and as summer begins, the movement of men starts in earnest."

"Does he think we should let Haidrea die?"

"No, Lydria. He believes she is already gone. He believes her spirit has started the journey to join those of her ancestors. While you hold on and while Haidrea draws breath, there is a connection between those two worlds – Haidrea is still held here, unable to journey on. It is a connection, he thinks, that does not do well for a soul to linger in."

"He wants me to let go?"

"I do not think he wants you to, but while you hold on to Haidrea, you both remain helpless. War is coming, if it is not already here, and you are needed."

"Haidrea is needed as well. By me. What of Haustis, where is she and what does she think?"

Kimi rested his chin on her shoulder and purred softly. He was a fully-grown bobcat now and Lydria could feel the weight of his head. No longer would he ride happily around her neck.

"Lydria, Haustis has joined the spirits herself. Early in this spring, she set off to the east, back to where you found me and there she met her end. I found her lying next to the burial mound of your father. She held only this," and Kimi withdrew to fetch the necklace Haustis had used to explain the concept of Grey to her and others.

"How, Kimi?"

"I smelled the odor of another there, Wynter, and I believe they sat peacefully together for a time before they fought. I can tell you Haustis did not leave Wynter unharmed. If he did not have magic, I am certain he would be dead now. Despite her end, Haustis looked calm and serene."

"Are you sure it was Wynter, Kimi?"

"Yes. His smell awakened something in me – he smells, in some ways, like you. The magic becomes a part of those who wear the collar and it lingers in you in much the same way as any strong scent."

Lydria looked at the necklace Kimi had dropped in front of her. "Kimi, is my bag from Drae Ghern here? Bring it to me."

Seeing the bobcat dragging the bag toward Lydria, Wae Relin hurried to help and opened it quickly, taking out each item in turn and placing them before Lydria so she could see each. Kimi pawed a parcel wrapped in bearskin and Branch reached down to unwrap it, revealing a stone, similar in hue to the one Lydria took from the crater. But it was a river stone that had been polished and worked so that it was hollowed out, deeply, like a thimble. The outside was carved with a delicately detailed hand print but with half an index finger, and it was topped with a jewel.

"It is a clever and beautiful thing that is very finely done," said Wae Relin with sincere appreciation for the craftsmanship of the piece. "The etching shows this was meant as jewelry for your finger, perhaps to protect the naked stub. The women of Eifynar thought very highly of you to have made you such a gift."

Lydria's heart swelled at the thought of Eifynar, of the women and children there who were in danger from Wynter, and possibly even from Bayside. They were caught in the middle of two armies – in a battleground.

At a thought from Lydria, Kimi pawed at the clean white bone of Lydria's finger until Wae Relin picked it up as well and looking at the two items, he knew what Lydria wanted him to do, so he put the blue stone on the larger end of the finger bone and with a little effort, it stuck in place, as if it were made to fit there. It was clearly too small for the stump of skin on Lydria's hand.

Following Lydria's orders, Kimi picked up the necklace of Haustis and dropped it on Wae Relin's knee. It required some back and forth but eventually, with the suggestions of Branch and Krieger, who had both become very interested in the silent conversation taking place, Wae Relin secured the finger within the necklace so that the circle was complete, with the blue thimble-stone resting between the black and white stones, and the point of Lydria's bone finger resting in the center of the circle.

"Kimi, place the necklace under my hand."

Wae Relin, watching Kimi's pawing of Lydria's left hand, gently lifted the glowing hand and placed the necklace under Lydria's palm and watched.

"What will happen?"

"I'm not sure, Kimi. I hope my finger, being a part of me, will do for Haidrea what I cannot do forever."

Kimi stared into Lydria's eyes and finally moved back to the items still on the floor. The cat moved his paw to the blue stone from the crater and gently batted it toward Wae Relin who picked it up and stood frozen, his eyes fixed on a point above both Lydria and Kimi for several breaths, and then placed the stone gently under Lydria's hand and on top of the necklace, and then he covered them both with Haidrea's hands.

As the stone was put in place Lydria felt a surge of power through her arm and looked up at Wae Relin and then to Haidrea, whose eyes cracked open in the onslaught of golden light.

Haidrea looked at Wae Relin and then Branch and smiled. She looked down her body and saw the face of Lydria and said, "Sister, there is not much time."

THIRTY-SEVEN

"What were you thinking, joining that woman in the spirit world? You had no business there and she knew it. It was a trap and you're lucky to be alive."

Wynter willed her to go away but she wouldn't. He had taken Haustis' pipe and smoked her weed and saw visions that made even his skin crawl. And while he stood in a foreign land of surreal colors and inexhaustible horrors, a demon came for him, forged of fire and on a pair of giant wings. The great beast was unlike anything he had ever seen, scales like armor lined its body and its mouth an elongated snout not unlike a dog, but so much larger. It had teeth like swords and when it roared, it was all he could do to not wet himself, so much did it shake his insides. Two legs like the trunks of oaks ended in wicked feet the length of his body and topped with talons so large they could slice open a buffalo with ease. But despite the wind of its wings and the dread of its teeth, the true terror was when the beast reared back and drew breath, for then it sent forth a stream of fire and death, melting the rocks it touched.

Wynter was petrified at first, and as he was thrown toward the beast he reacted instinctively, and it saved his life. Without a weapon, he called upon his magic to block the fire – or most of it. Despite his best efforts, the heat was so intense he was surprised he had not melted.

Fortunately for Wynter, the beast was not free. It was chained to a gigantic block of pure white stone. The beast strained and snapped its massive jaws in Wynter's direction, but the chain held. And what a chain it was. It was in darkness what the block was in white. A black so pure that even the flames seemed to be consumed by it. Where the block and the chain met there was nothing, as if the connection did not exist.

"But I am alive. I have survived whatever horror that was, and Haustis is no more." That was his first thought after he realized his shield had held.

But was it true? Wynter's recollection of his fight with the beast was cloudy at best and he closed his eyes to remember.

Seeing the chain, he realized the beast was not angry at him, but angry at being captive. He remembered wishing he had his bow, and it appeared. Surprised but delighted, he immediately thought of arrows and they appeared as well. Using all the considerable skill ingrained in his muscles and mind over a lifetime, Wynter sent arrow after arrow straight at the beast, aiming for the softest spots he could find. Not a single arrow reached its target. They were incinerated before reaching the creature and so Wynter began to move. With his bow he was in near-constant motion, taking in the details of the scene around him, that included the beast in its center surrounded by a debris field of boulders and rocks, the burned stumps of trees and a blackened ash that was once ground. Wynter was desperate to find a way to silence the beast, or escape.

Escape, running away, was always an option – it always had been. But when he tried to run he was thrown back toward the beast by an unseen force that pushed against his chest so hard he tumbled backward. And so, he moved to hide behind the largest stones and look at everything again and again until he formed a plan.

His eyes kept returning to the dark chain and ivory block and he thought of an arrow fashioned not of wood and steel, but of the midnight darkness of the chain. The arrow arrived in his hand in an instant and in a single fluid motion, Wynter dropped to his left knee, knocked the arrow and held his breath. He drew the arrow back slowly, the feathers, unlike any he had used before, were stiff and scraped across his face and the arrow head seemed to only exist as an edge of waves, such as one might see rising from the desert floor. When he let the arrow fly, the feathers drew blood from his cheek.

Wynter shuddered to remember that instant, as if time stood still. The arrow left the string and twisted slightly upon release, a fine mist of blood from his face following the shaft and, it was impossible to be certain now, but he remembered seeing his blood absorbed into the feathers as the arrow sped on its way, straight to the point where chain and block met.

The seconds it took for Wynter to draw the string and fire the arrow seemed to drag on for minutes. The only thing Wynter heard was a single beat of his heart and then the arrow struck home, and the result was immediate and devastating.

The arrow collided with its target and created a wave of power like Wynter had only seen once before, in the forest where he had found the stone. The force of the air threw him onto his back and forced even time to regain its natural speed. The beast roared again, pulling at his chain but finding no resistance. With a brief look toward Wynter, the beast pushed his massive wings and left the ground, the air from its wings nearly as violent as the blast that forced Wynter to the ground, and it flew off into an unseen sky trailing a ribbon of darkness.

Staggering to his feet, Wynter looked to the ivory block and saw it split in half as cleanly as a dagger drawn across a throat.

"Perhaps the spirits were correct. It seems I should have killed you when you were motionless on the ground."

Wynter searched for the voice of Haustis. His bow was gone and wish as he might, it did not come back.

"This is your spirit world then, old woman?"

"No. This is yours. I have to say it is different than I expected. What was that creature?"

"This is your nightmare, not mine. Call it what you will."

"You freed it. Why?"

"I wasn't trying to free it, I was trying to kill it."

"Was it a threat to you, chained as it was?"

Wynter considered not answering but continuing the conversation might allow him time to find Haustis or a way from this place.

"Did you not feel the heat? I call that a threat." In truth, the heat was horrible and Wynter knew for certain that only his magic kept him from being burned to ash. He reached a tentative hand to his face and felt the wetness where blood still seeped from a wound on his cheek and then, as the rush of battle left him, he started to feel the pain. He gingerly moved his fingertips around his face and felt a stickiness that told him his skin had been damaged. The backs of his hands and fingers too were ravaged from the heat, large welts and blisters forming as he watched.

He could only imagine the damage the heat had done and was furious. Wynter was not a vain man, but he knew people put trust and faith in a person based as much upon how they looked as how they acted.

"The people of the north – are you 'freeing' them as well?"

Wynter spun around on the spot, fed up with whatever game Haustis was playing, and moved toward the ivory block. The surface was perfectly smooth and shone like glass. Where from a distance the stone seemed as pure white as a fresh snow, up close it reflected his image clearly. What Wynter saw did not please him and he hurled his answer to Haustis' question into the air.

"They are free! I have given them hope and security and equality and they have made me their king. I have made a veritable paradise from a frozen and wretched place."

Haustis' voice was on the air before Wynter's last syllable faded into the echoes. "So, you are working for their benefit alone? It is your intention to build a free, prosperous and happy kingdom among the wastes of the north?"

"She toys with you, husband, cut her down."

"Do you not think I would have done that if I knew where she was?"

"Think! Is this a real place you have been before, or do you sit next to her in a world that makes more sense? She is within your reach. Think!" And she was gone. She left on her own, forcing him to plan his next move carefully. Haustis' patience would not be eternal, of that, he was certain.

"I build my kingdom for the reasons all kings build," he said, letting the words fall from his mouth without much to indicate where they were going. He needed time and he was making the most of trying to get out of this place; to be the first to make it back to the world he and Haustis inhabited. "Kings build to create a society where the best can rise and the rest – well, the rest – they exist to do our bidding. It is the same in every society – there are farmers and muckrakers, and there are those who build, create, and help a society become powerful. I am creating a kingdom of the latter; but one where everyone takes a portion of their time to rake muck and make food. We all need to eat, you know."

Wynter's pulse slowed as he turned his mind toward reason. He needed to be calm when he smoked with Haustis to reach this place, it stood to reason he would need to be calm to leave. He continued reciting platitudes about equality and nobility when he found his way out, returning in time to see Haustis raising a blade to stab down at him, aiming for the soft patch of skin between his collarbone and neck. The strike would have resulted in a swift and silent death, at least, but he raised his arm and blocked the killing stroke. Haustis' knife imbedded itself between the bones of his forearm, as his right hand reached out to grab the old woman's throat.

"You're right, Haustis. You should have killed me while I was lying motionless on the forest floor. But you're too late. It is too late. I will rule everything your eyes have ever seen before I'm done. Maybe someday someone will stop me, but it most certainly will not be you."

Wynter's fingers, weeping puss and scarred from the heat of the creature in his spirit world, or possibly from the fire nearby, cried out in pain as he forced his thumb and fingers together from either side of the woman's throat. She made pitiable sounds, but her eyes never left his. And with a final act of defiance, the old woman managed to lift her own right hand and bring it down on the hilt of the dagger in his forearm and drive Wynter's limp left arm and the blade into his belly.

Haustis didn't hear Wynter's scream. As the knife plunged into Wynter, he released his grip on the old woman's neck, but he had already crushed her windpipe. As he brought his right hand to his side to stem the flow of dark red blood, the old woman's last act was to smile, before falling over sideways, dead.

THIRTY-EIGHT

It was nearly a week before Haidrea and Lydria had regained strength to move. The amulet Lydria made had fused together, the circle had shrunk and met her finger bone below the stone cap and the tip of the finger rested tightly on the bottom of the circle as if forged there by a blacksmith. It was harder than any bone and it was wholly as deep blue as the sky just after dusk. As it rested upon Haidrea's smooth skin, it gave off a soft yellow light that pulsed slightly, in time with the woman's own heart. Lydria could feel the power in the necklace but shuddered to think what might happen should it fall from Haidrea's neck. Still, Haidrea was alive and Lydria could rest and as if sensing her friend's concern, Haidrea slipped the disc under her leather tunic where only the faintest light cast a warm shadow on her neck.

Lydria told the others of how Kimi found Haustis' body lying near the grave of Cargile as the cat made his way west to find Lydria, and how he took the necklace that was near her fallen body. Kimi's story also noted the deep, dark earth near her which he said smelled strongly of Wynter.

"He is wounded, but not dead," Krieger said. "If he and Lydria share power, we gain no advantage by his wounds, but we should make preparations to travel as soon as we may."

Weaver arrived the next day and brought news that families were leaving Steven's Folly; persuaded to move north by word of Wynter's new kingdom. "They now live in Brookfield under a governess named Grettune, who holds authority over several smaller towns. But the real power seems to be a tiny fishing village called Solwyn, which has, if you can believe it, a castle with a great blue tower."

The party smiled, and Krieger even laughed a little before they confirmed all they knew to Weaver. "That explains the extra manning at the fort, then," Weaver told them. Soon after the escape of Lydria and her fellows, a detachment was sent to Steven's Folly and a new commander was put in charge who sent patrols to look for Branch, who had left the fort in late winter, and a group of traitors. "They say Captain Branch was conspiring with Eifen renegades against Ahlric."

Krieger sat down as Weaver spoke and raised his head and looked to Branch. "Though we need to move soon, I think it may be time we hear your story Edgar." Branch nodded silently and found a chair which he casually turned so he could hang his arms over the back as he spoke. Haidrea moved to a seat close to him and smiled, which seemed to reassure the man. When everyone had taken their seats, Krieger started to take out his pipe from his coat, but Branch held up his hand in refusal.

"There is no need for a pipe, my friend, for my story is short." Branch looked at everyone and drew a breath before beginning. "You know me as Edgar Branch, captain of the forces of Wesolk. My birth name, however, is Cambric, son of Nobric, nephew of Ahlric, and rightful heir to the throne Wesolk, as his last nephew. Nobric was Ahlric's youngest brother, the seventh son of Charic. I too, am the youngest, and the seventh child, but I am the only son of Nobric. Of my sisters I know nothing but what Krieger has told me. All who live are married to traders, merchants, or others, but I have no memory of them. Before I could walk, my father, believing I might be in danger sent me away to a tiny hamlet south of the Swinton Flats, and over the hills that mark Wesolk's southern border with the free territories Between Wesolk and the desert kingdoms of Dar'Ahlmon far to the south. I grew up with people of learning who taught me to read and write. As I grew, Krieger came and taught me to fight and ride. Otherwise, there were few visitors, save an Eifen woman – Haustis, who taught me of her people, her language, her stories. She said the spirits sent her to find me, for what purpose she would not say.

"When I was old enough, Krieger told me my story."

The room was still for several breaths before Krieger nodded to Branch who stood and left the room. "The proof of Edgar's lineage and claim to the throne exist in the village where he grew up. If it is ever needed, we can find it there. But despite Ahlric's treatment of us in his castle, it is not our intent to throw down the ruler of Wesolk. Our focus needs to be fixed on the north. But the danger from Wynter is not the only danger – not for some of us at least."

With no more to be said, Krieger began to discuss their next steps.

"We must assume the roads to the east and the paths to Eifynar will be watched, so we cannot go there. There is only one way, and that is north. We will stay until Lydria and Haidrea can ride, and then we will make haste to Solwyn.

In the days that followed Weaver headed north to the Folly, to do what could be done to mislead the new commander there and keep them out of Krieger's way. While Lydria and Haidrea gained their strength, Krieger left for hours at a time, to meet with his informants or find what information he could from the sources he still commanded.

Branch and Relin, who had asked they forgo his title as he was no longer the leader of his expedition, spent hours honing their skills outside, and learning, Relin revealed one night, that Branch was an accomplished bowman. Haidrea spent much of her time deep in thought and communing with the spirits, which she was now able to do without pipe or smoke. She believed the amulet helped her to find her path to the spirits. Lydria, after spending two days doing little more than sleeping and eating, went into the forest to practice her magic, Kimi by her side.

"Are you ready, Lydria?"

"To practice magic again, after so long? Yes, I suppose it's time."

"No. Are you ready for Wynter? You must realize it will be you who must face him – the power he wields would overcome any other before they could raise a weapon against him."

"I will do what I must do." Lydria said no more but casually motioned her hand from left to right as if to sweep a small branch from their path. As she made the motion, the branch flew with distinct force and shattered into a nearby tree. Lydria stopped and looked at the remains of the stick and with surprise at Kimi.

"Do more," the cat urged.

Looking through the trees, Lydria saw the top of a large stone buried in the dirt. Moving the stone should, she thought, leave her limping back to the camp barely able to stand. She stared for a moment and the stone shook as if loosening itself from the soil and lifted from the ground. It was enormous. The top of the stone was barely a portion of the whole which was easily the size of a cow. Lydria moved it through the trees and dropped it close to where she and Kimi stood and waited for the ground to rush up to meet her.

Seconds ticked by before Kimi spoke. *"Are you well?"*

"I feel … fine. I have a dull ache in my shoulder, but otherwise…"

Lydria and Kimi spent the afternoon performing such magic as she had already learned and finding she was largely unharmed by the effort. As they made their way back to the camp, they silently discussed what might have happened.

"I cannot heal freely, and while it takes little from me, Haidrea's wound was no simple cut to mend. The months of keeping Haidrea alive must have worked in the same way my training has," Lydria said in a rushed voice when everyone had gathered in the cabin.

Krieger was the first to ask her to do a task. "Ready yourself, Lydria." With no further warning he threw a chunk of firewood at her. Instantly, Lydria shielded herself from the wood. Krieger raised an eyebrow and looked to the others. Within seconds everyone was throwing whatever they could find in her direction. Lydria easily blocked objects and moved items around in the cabin to knock over her assailants. As the onslaught reached the point where Lydria knew someone was bound to get hurt, she simply yelled for everyone to stop. And they did.

"What have you done, Lydria?" Kimi was on his rear legs, front paws in the air and mouth opened as if he were about to jump on Branch, who stood holding a bed roll he was swinging toward Lydria's mid-section. Haidrea, who had not joined in the fray, walked calmly among and between the men, pushing Krieger lightly with her finger to see if he would move. He did not. He stood as a statue with his right hand resting on the hilt of his dagger, his left hand balled into a fist moving toward Lydria's nose.

"This is interesting Lydria," Haidrea said as she completed her navigation of the room and stood in front of her friend. "Why am I still moving?"

It was a sound question. "You were not involved in the fight and I was not thinking of you as a threat when I spoke."

Kimi chimed in again with the same question he had had earlier in the woods, *"Are you well?"*

Looking to Kimi and back to Haidrea, Lydria replied aloud. "I feel remarkably well. A little tired and very hungry, but I'm not in any pain."

Haidrea sat and indicated Lydria should do likewise. "In my recent travels in the spirit world, I have seen many things that did not make sense, until now. I moved in a place, through a room of statues. The people were still as if carved of stone, but they were alive – they felt alive. They could hear and see and feel. I daresay if you punched Relin in the face now, he would feel it, but would not move. I believe they can also hear us.

"I can," Kimi provided. *"I can smell and as my mouth is open, I can taste the smoke from the fire – I can do everything…except move."*

Lydria relayed the bobcat's message and then asked Haidrea what else she had seen in the spirit world.

"I have seen a great blue tower that glows brilliantly in a land that is at times engulfed in light and at times covered in darkness. It sits as part of a fortress of ice built upon the souls of those who can see, and feel, and hear, but cannot move. They are angry, and they blame their masters who they believe sent them knowingly to their fate." Haidrea paused and ran her fingers along the necklace she wore through her tunic, tracing a line around the now solid horse hair circle to the capstone on top of the bone finger that were alike in their hue. She inhaled deeply and looked up at Lydria, "You cannot free them. They must be freed by their captor. But they must not be freed. Their captor must not be allowed to free them. You must do what we could not ... you must kill Wynter."

"What do you mean, 'they can't be freed' and 'what we could not'?"

Haidrea laughed lightly, recalling a memory for Lydria of when they first met, and she heard that distinctly feminine sound. But the sound was tinged with concern now. It was a laugh that was not carefree. "I am the Haustis now. Through the spirits, I have some connection to all the Haustis of the past, and with the power that flows through this amulet, I can reach more of them than any Haustis before – and they can speak to each other in that realm as well. It was the job given to the previous Haustis to kill Wynter, and she did not do this. You must."

THIRTY-NINE

Wynter couldn't savor his victory as he held the knife in place trying to assess whether the wound would be fatal. He had put enough knives in people to understand that a stab didn't necessarily mean death. He also knew, that depending upon where the blade landed, the result could be worse – a long, slow, painful death.

"Are you stupid? Heal yourself."

Would this woman never leave him alone? But, she was right, there was no reason he should not be able to, and so he turned his mind toward his body and remembered the bodies cut by surgeons who let him watch as they opened his victims. He knew he would have to mend his body to minimize the blood loss. Leaving the blade in his side helped stem the flow, but it had to come out. He focused his power on his stomach and slowly drew the knife away from his body. The pain was excruciating.

"I am with you – and I will help you keep your senses."

Wynter, for once, was grateful for her presence; surely without her, he would have passed out and likely bled to death. As the tip of the knife cleared his skin, he threw it aside and reached in his pack for a cloth to use as a dressing for his wound. His magic had helped stop the bleeding at least, but he had lost a tremendous amount of blood. He was dizzy and disoriented, and his skin burned. He wasn't sure if those feelings were from loss of blood, his fight with the beast, or his use of a type of magic that he had spent little time learning.

Wynter lowered his head to the dirt and breathed heavily, staring at the blood pooled by his feet. The bleeding had stopped, and he was sure he would live, but he was a brutal mess. A mouth full of holes where teeth used to be; a face, arms and hands burned raw in Haustis' hellish nightmare; and a long march back to Solwyn still in front of him. He forced himself to sit up and looked at the old woman lying cold on the ground. If it were possible, she was staring at him. She had died with her eyes wide open and her mouth curved up in an almost unnatural smile. He reached down and ripped the necklace from around her neck and scoffed out loud. "There is no Grey, old woman," he said. "There is only power" and he tossed the circlet back to land near her body.

The walk home for Wynter was unlike the last time he had made the trip north. Despite his pain and scars he feared nothing. The magic he used was for food, fire, or sometimes to numb the pain his burns caused. The price of this magic seemed to be negligible for him as it cost neither tooth nor excess pain, although any small pain it might cause would be buried under the agony that was his skin.

"Perhaps," he pondered, "I have grown strong enough where new magic does not cause me pain any longer." He didn't believe it.

The people he met on his walk gave him wide berth until he called out to them directly. Some wanted to run, but he used his power to pull them toward him. It was taxing, but not debilitating. The people he chose to bring to him were small and weak creatures who only required a bit of a pull before coming to him of their own volition. It might have been done with his voice alone and a surety of presence, but his visage initially repulsed people. They were afraid, he knew, that he might be a leper or have plague or some other equally deadly pox. Only the band of blue around his neck confirmed to them that they were in the presence of Wynter, King of Solwyn.

In that way Wynter learned much as he marched north. News and gossip knew no borders and Ahlric was preparing to march. By high summer, many believed he would take his army from Bayside by the North Gate.

Wynter was pleased to hear his own army was taking shape under the leadership of Sir Keldon. The roads were being built rapidly and many expected they would be finished within a few years. Trade was moving between the Eastern and Western Reaches, and even the southern outposts were doing well. Fine weather and motivated people will do wonders for the harvest, Wynter thought.

With each traveler Wynter received not only news, but also food, shelter, or whatever he needed. It seemed that despite his appearance, the name of the king still commanded some respect on the open road. Wynter bade each of them to stop at the Cobalt Tower when they returned north, and he would reward them for their generosity.

Slowly Wynter made his way into his own lands and returned to Solwyn during the narrow window of darkness in high summer. He did not stop but made sure he was seen returning to his throne. By morning the entire town would know he had returned.

Wynter entered his castle and was met by Nethyal. This man didn't sleep, it seemed. But his resourcefulness was commendable and Wynter was weary and grateful for Nethyal's presence.

"My king, you are hurt?"

Wynter smiled. "I was, but I am better now that I return to my home." Wynter thought it an odd thing to have said but realized he did feel better – physically better. "But I am much better off than the men of Ahlric who ambushed me."

Nethyal's eyes went wide with surprise and Wynter delivered to him a story that would wind its way through the town with the speed of a winter wind. How Ahlric's men had found him and attacked while he slept and how he had managed to fight them off without a weapon. At the end of the battle, with only one man left standing, King Wynter had showed mercy upon the wretch and told him to return south with a warning to Ahlric. "I told him to tell his king that if the men of Ahlric step foot on the soil of Solwyn or its territories it would mean war." He looked at Nethyal and offered a smile. "I have left open the door for peace, my friend. Let us see if they take it or repay mercy with treachery."

Wynter asked Nethyal to leave him, knowing he would filter the message to his most trusted gossips in town. He wasn't even sure Nethyal believed him, but it didn't matter, Nethyal did what needed to be done. The Eifen was very adept at picking up how the men of the kingdoms behaved, and he was even more adept at using that information against them.

"Is this why you keep him, husband? As a messenger?"

Inwardly, Wynter bristled at the word husband, but took a moment to answer. The warrior had been useful to him as he learned to harness his power. He had been useful to him as an intermediary with the people and as an administrator to his growing kingdom. But he was still an Eifen – the same breed of people that spawned Haustis.

"I keep him because it pleases me to have him do the work of a clerk; and because by my side, I know where he is at all times."

The last, Wynter thought, was probably more-true than the rest. The question of what to do with Nethyal would require more thought, but for now, Wynter knew, he remained useful.

Throwing off his traveling cloak, Wynter surveyed his great hall and looked at the Fourteen Pillars of Solwyn. The ice, he noted, had lost some of its clarity around the edges, and had taken on a tinge of the blue-green that made up the rest of the structure. But still, the faces of the Fourteen could be seen clearly and he went to their leader in the first pillar by the great doors and placed his hand on the pillar of ice and spoke slowly and deliberately, the words falling unbidden from his mouth as if they had been rehearsed.

Wynter could see the result he wanted in his mind, and he maintained that focus as he moved from pillar to pillar, invoking a similar mantra to each of the Fourteen before dragging himself to the nearby dais and collapsing on his throne. His bones ached, and his skin felt tight on his face, the burned flesh on his arms tingled – the first sensation he'd felt in them since the blisters had subsided during his march north. His arms and hands were largely scar tissue now, red and bright except for the white line in his forearm where Haustis' knife had wedged itself. The arm was largely healed thanks to his magic, but his burns would not heal. They were magic burns, he knew, and he would never be rid of them. Looking at his bow by one of the black doors, he doubted if he would ever be able to hold the weapon steady again or endure the force of a drawn arrow.

Still, Wynter smiled. He had no more need of bows or arrows or any weapon of steel. He had just planted the seeds of his finest work. He was exhausted and in pain and he felt alive because of it. The magic demanded he sleep, and he closed his eyes happily, grateful to be home.

FORTY

The journey north was as pleasant as early summer could make it. Lydria, Krieger, Haidrea, Relin, and Branch were all on horseback. They needed time. Getting to Solwyn before Ahlric would require being very fast and lucky, skirting to the northwest past Steven's Folly before heading north and then northeast toward Solwyn.

As the group prepared to travel, Krieger determined the bulk of Ahlric's forces were already on the road and Eifynar would be the first to feel the army pass.

"We must help them." Haidrea said it plainly and without emotion, as a prudent course of action.

"We cannot help them," Krieger replied. "I have sent word to Wae Ilsit to move his people from that place at first sign of Ahlric moving. That was done before the message of Ahlric's movement came to me. If Ahlric chooses to fight the Eifen and Wae Ilsit sees fit, he will stall the army for as long as his warriors are able. I believe, however, that he will choose a better course and leave the town. We may yet meet him upon our road, but our road is what we must follow."

The trail the group had to follow was not easy. They were on the western bank of the lake south and west of Steven's Folly. They would have to move through the woods, avoid the soldiers of the Folly and make their way across the flatlands to the north toward the Cobalt Tower, and Wynter.

They traveled quickly, knowing they would have to travel long hours with short rest. Ahlric's army would be in no hurry, knowing their force would overpower the northerners easily. They would travel slowly, gathering with wagon trains, and equipment each night. Starting each morning would be a long affair in the best of circumstances. Only small groups like Lydria's moved quickly. But still, they traveled through the forest, whereas the army would travel through open land and perhaps on roads.

The canopy of trees had not yet filled in completely and some light made its way to the forest floor allowing the companions to see well into the distance. Kimi ran ahead looking for soldiers and suggesting paths to Lydria who rode at the head of the column with Krieger by her side.

During their first day, Branch informed them of the routes normally taken by soldiers from the Folly as they scouted around the fort. They were rarely more than a half-day's march from the safety of the outpost, and rarely in groups larger than two.

"You're saying they won't openly attack us then," Krieger surmised. "But, being seen is as dangerous as being confronted, and we don't know what changes have been made in the routine of the outpost. We will need to travel further west of the fort to ensure we are unseen."

They urged their mounts forward stopping briefly for sleep and to rest their horses. Within two days, Branch judged they were west of the fort and nearly out of the area where patrols might ride. Krieger looked to Lydria who told Kimi to start heading to the northeast. Several days later, Kimi called an unexpected stop.

"Lydria, there is something in front of our path."

The cat let out a small growl to let Lydria and the rest of the company know he was with them. *"These are not men of the outpost, but Eifen and mixed among them a more familiar smell I can't quite place. They have passed this way earlier today and are still moving."*

Lydria relayed the information to Krieger as the rest of the group listened a horse length behind. "I will go," Haidrea said. "If they are Eifen, it would be best that they see me first."

The warrior waited for no response or permission but moved ahead and opened her horse's gait to catch whomever might be in front of them.

Before Lydria could form the words, she heard Kimi's voice in her head, *"I will go too – and get ahead of her."*

The rest of the group moved on, remaining behind until they could learn more from either Kimi or Haidrea. When several hours had passed with no word, Krieger stopped and dismounted.

"We may as well take the opportunity to refill our water, feed the horses and eat," he said. He didn't need to explain their situation. Lydria understood that given their circumstances, a long, fast road might be in their future. It was wise to rest while they could.

They tended to their horses before sitting in a circle that allowed each to keep a watch on a different piece of the forest. They ate in relative silence, broken only by a short word of gratitude to Lydria for heating their food with magic – saving them time and the smoke from a fire.

Lydria was still trying to make sense of her ability to use magic in these small ways and feel no effects. It had taken her months of unconsciousness doing a single task to become so proficient. It made her shudder to think of what a person who was willing to dedicate the time and pain necessary to master such power could accomplish. They went to their bedrolls silently and drifted off slowly.

Lydria had first watch and as the deepest part of night passed and the moon shone high in the sky, she felt a familiar tingle that told her Kimi was trying to reach her but was too far away.

"Krieger. Get up. Kimi is coming. I don't know what message he brings."

Krieger nodded his understanding and woke Branch and Relin. "Is there reason to expect the news is bad?" he asked Lydria. With a small shake of her head, he moved to stand with her behind a large tree away from the camp and the horses.

"Lydria. The familiar smell – it was Weaver. He is with the Eifen now. Come quickly."

Lydria told the others and minutes later they were mounted again with clear skies and a bright moon to guide them. Along the trail they met Haidrea who had turned back soon after arriving to lead her friends quickly. They arrived at the camp before dawn and were immediately shown to a small, smelly hunting lodge made from animal skins and held up by poles tied together at the top to make a covered space large enough for several men.

Lydria entered the lodge first and found Haidrea, Drae Ghern and Wae Ilsit waiting. Branch, Weaver, Relin, and Krieger were all invited in as well and when they had sat down, Wae Ilsit spoke first.

"Well met," Wae Ilsit said. "We have no time for stories. This is a council of war and our stories must wait."

Lydria spoke for the party and told all she could, leaving out only what they had learned of Haustis. She was followed by Krieger, Branch and Weaver who understood by Lydria's omission that they were not to not tell Haustis' story. That was a story for Haidrea, who spoke last.

"Grandfather, father, all you have heard is true but there is some news I must tell," Haidrea spoke carefully and slowly, but did not become emotional. She spoke as Haustis and not as Haidrea. "Wynter, in addition to his betrayals among the kingdom, has struck the Eifen as well. The woman you knew as Haustis rests now with the spirits by Wynter's hand. I am now Haustis and through Lydria's gift, I continue to draw breath and through her magic I remain connected to the spirits as easily as I speak with you."

She withdrew the circlet with Lydria's finger from beneath her tunic and showed it to her father and grandfather. "There is one last thing, dear Drae Ghern. From the Haustis most recent, she begs me tell you, she has always loved you and it hurt her gravely to leave your side all those seasons ago. But her path lay with the spirits and they would not be denied."

The small lodge went still as a stump as everyone's eyes turned slowly to Drae Ghern, who was motionless as a single tear rolled down his cheek. His mouth opened only enough for his lips to part, a thin white film still straining to keep them together, and he breathed in slowly and closed his mouth again.

"Father," said Wae Ilsit, slowly turning to the old man and gently cradling his weathered hand in his own. "I am so sorry that you must know this. So many years ago, I guessed the riddle of Haustis and she made me take an oath on the spirits that you could not know."

Drae Ghern turned slowly to his son and reached his arms out to hold Wae Ilsit by either side of his head and kissed him slowly on each cheek. "My son, I too had guessed at Haustis' riddle many years ago and wanted only to tell you, so that you would know your mother lived and loved you. I understand the will of the spirits, and it will not be long before we are together again."

The room breathed for the first time in what seemed an eternity and Lydria noted that everyone was warmed by the secret both father and son had contained for so long; even Kimi began a slow, even rumble that reached the ears of everyone in the lodge.

"Now, Haustis," Drae Ghern's eyes were still damp with happiness, but his manner turned stern once again as he faced Haidrea. "Let us tell you how the world fares to the east."

For nearly an hour Drae Ghern and Wae Ilsit described how Eifen scouts reported a great mass of horses and men gathering on the plains to the east of Bayside. They rode north, a small party detached from the front to scout their own path. That path brought them eventually to Eifynar.

"We were fortunate to have heard from Krieger several suns earlier," Wae Ilsit nodded his thanks to the man. "We sent the large part of our people to the west, some for refuge and others, to prepare to fight."

"The problem," Krieger interrupted, "is who do you fight?"

"Our people will want to fight Ahlric," Drae Ghern added. "We left only a small force in the town and several scouts. The kingdom men came and sat to take food and smoke and speak with our people. The kingdom men had sent in a force for talks and while they did so, others crept into the village and set upon our warriors with arrows and knives and burned Eifynar until all that stands now are black stumps. Our people were killed like dogs." Drae Ghern's fury flushed his face so that he appeared decades younger and Lydria was sure that given a weapon, he could at this moment, fight with any kingdom soldier and be left standing.

"Ahlric is ill and sees foes at all sides."

Krieger's statement was said so that all those who heard his voice knew his statement to be true. He said it as a fact; as a fact he

251

had known for a long time but was determined to ignore, to pretend wasn't true. The massacre of Wae Ilsit's people, however, proved even more than he could allow.

"For many years Ahlric has been a sensible, some would say enlightened, ruler. He opened up Wesolk to new ways of thinking, he judiciously avoided war where possible and met it with fierceness when necessary. In his early years he was a friend of the Eifen in court and changed the minds of many lords regarding our brothers of the woods. In many respects, he has been everything the people have needed. Of late, however, he shifts between the old Ahlric, and a sick, fearful, at times ponderous man who finds conspiracies at every corner. Within the court, we hide his less wholesome nature as best we are able. If word got out that a king without an heir was ill, the lords would start taking sides.

"While we were in his court, we saw Ahlric at his weakest and it is this face of the king we have tried to hide. In the sickness' grip, he appears weak and feeble, he coughs and the cloth he carries with him is now often covered in blood. His mind, however, is sharp, but in it he sees only the carrion birds waiting to carry him away.

"He was becoming paranoid when only swords and men threatened him. When he heard of the power of Wynter, he became sure the throne of Wesolk was the target. For the better part of a year, Ahlric has waited for an invasion from the north that has not come and against all council, he could not be deterred from moving north to meet this new threat.

Krieger turned to Lydria and lowered his eyes. "In his court, when the king and I spoke privately, it was then he asked me to renew my allegiance and put a knife in your back. He knew of your power, for he has spies of his own and Wynter is clever to use them to his own ends.

"Regardless of what he knew or thought he knew, he was correct," Krieger continued. "Even without seeing your collar, you presented a threat he could see and dispatch without the cost of an armed expedition. Since our unexpected departure," Krieger smiled before continuing, "I have had scant information from Bayside. You can be assured that if you walked into the city today with your collar visible, your story would be well known, and the people would fear you."

There was a lapse of several moments before Branch, who sat patiently next to Relin, broke the silence. "Would Ahlric then not send a force to the Folly? If he knows we have traveled together, and given my former position, would he not want to ensure the outpost doesn't represent a threat on his western flank?"

"It is possible, but I think Ahlric focuses his vision to the north and the north alone. He is not all together wrong to believe that Wynter threatens him. He would do us a favor to kill the man," Krieger said.

"I sense you have misgivings about this course." Wae Ilsit was looking carefully at Krieger, his own instinct as a commander, putting the pieces together.

"The only misgiving I have, is that he may do it. We all know the power Wynter commands." Krieger spoke slowly to reinforce the seriousness of his belief. "Wise and noble kings have marched for less than the threat Ahlric perceives from the north; although none have marched against a greater threat. Killing Wynter would be a just result, but the costs could be staggering and then where does it lead? Does he search the countryside for Lydria? He won't simply stand down his forces knowing she's out there.

"And there's an outcome that will bode ill for all Wesolk - win or lose, Ahlric's forces will be depleted. By this season's end, word of Wynter and Lydria will have made its way beyond the borders of Wesolk. Some may think it is only a story to scare children, but some will believe it. All of them will have their soldiers ready. If word gets out that Ahlric has defeated Wynter at great cost, those armies may march on Wesolk."

Everyone could appreciate the consequences of such a war. With the bulk of Ahlric's troops to the north, Wesolk could, at best, lose large parts of its eastern holdings.

"What do you recommend, then, friend Krieger?" Drae Ghern spoke softly but directly, his old hands still and firm on his knees.

253

"Wae Ilsit, Drae Ghern, we have known each other for many seasons, and you know the respect I have for you both and your people. I ask no such thing lightly, but we must be the ones to kill Wynter. We must arrive in Solwyn before the armies of Ahlric. Your warriors can move like spirits in the forests and harass his forces. Strike quickly at the back of the train and sparingly at the scouts. Within a day, they will change their traveling tactics to protect the carts – it will slow them, but they travel with an overwhelming force, so the delay will be prudent to them.

"There are those close to Ahlric who do not understand, or believe, the power of Lydria and Wynter, but they will have heard stories of what happened in the castle. Every unseen attack from the woods will instill in them the fear of that which they do not understand. They will travel slowly, some may run. This all works to our advantage."

"Drae Ghern, Relin, Haustis," Wae Ilsit looked at those he had called and commanded the attention of the entire lodge. I tell you this because you should know all as we prepare for war. I have known Krieger for many seasons, and it is I who am his ears and voice within Eifynar; for I too, have consulted the spirits with Haustis, my mother, and they showed me that this man stands in the middle of the Grey, between peace and chaos. But only now do I understand how he does so. But Krieger is correct, we cannot allow Ahlric to battle Wynter. The destruction of Ahlric's army would invite invasion and we have no understanding of the men who would come. Our people would be hunted like deer and fare no better. We must try to do what Krieger says. It is the only way."

FORTY-ONE

The company moved the same day leaving Wae Ilsit and Drae Ghern before the sun had reached its height. Weaver remained with Wae Ilsit to help delay Ahlric's advance.

With the camp behind them, Lydria's group moved swiftly through the forest. Kimi maintained a connection with Lydria and she shared his eyes and ears as he pointed out landmarks and trailheads. The collaboration made for a remarkable pace and soon the woods thinned, and they continued to the northeast.

"In this thin forest hiding will be impossible," Krieger said. "We must travel in the open and make for the most western town along the ring of villages Wynter has taken under his domain, Brookfield. It lies in the shadow of the Frostspine Mountains and used to be little more than a small village of farmers and those who wanted a quiet life away from cities. In a short time, it has become a large town with trade and a road being built east to Solwyn."

"Perhaps we can blend in with the people who have migrated north in the recent months," Lydria suggested. "It would make our journey easier if we could use the road from Brookfield and travel openly."

"*What about me? I'm hardly able to travel through town without attracting some attention.*"

Lydria gave voice to Kimi's concerns and with the cat lopping alongside the horses, Lydria closed her eyes and pictured Kimi – but not Kimi.

Haidrea was the first to notice Kimi no longer seemed so out of place. Instead of a fully-grown bobcat, their road was now shared by a large tom cat with ragged and dirty orange fur and a perpetual scowl. By the time Kimi himself realized what had happened the others were all trying to suppress laughter.

"*What have you done to me? This is not acceptable – this is degrading and humiliating...*"

"Oh, pretty puss, would you like to ride on the horse?" Lydria felt sorry for Kimi but felt that the magical deception was worth it as Kimi's eyes and ears were far keener than any of their own. To leave him on his own in such a sparsely vegetated place would make him a target for hunters. *"There are many more people nearby now, Kimi, and they need to eat. We do not need you avoiding arrows at every turn. Come up here and ride with me."*

Kimi watched the horses walk down the trail before sprinting forward onto the horse's back, realizing as he did that his body felt no different than it had before, and that his movements were not impeded by the spindly legs and insignificant claws he saw. When he landed on the horse's back, the animal huffed and started to rear before Lydria calmed him, and when he took his place in front of Lydria, she said that he felt as heavy and fat as ever. Kimi pushed as much of his weight as possible against Lydria's bladder and went almost immediately to sleep.

"Lydria, this magic, does it pain you?" Haidrea had been watching both Kimi and Lydria for the last several minutes, trying to discern if there were any physical difference in her friend.

"I feel none, but situated as I am, that may not be the case. If I got off this horse, I might find that my legs will not hold my weight – but as far as I can tell, there is no effect."

"Could you try that on all of us," Relin suggested. "It may be wise if we need to conceal ourselves quickly; but if you cannot, it would be best to discover this now."

He was right, and so Lydria looked closely at Branch who was closest to her and within a second, she heard gasps and saw that where sat the former Captain Commander of Steven's Folly, now sat a crone of considerable age with blackened teeth and rotting gums. Lydria started to laugh and turning to the side, threw up.

"Serves you right," Kimi muttered and continued to purr.

"I am well," Lydria said. "My stomach is upset but I think it will pass soon. At least now we know."

It was two days later when Branch, returned to his normal self, saw a group of travelers heading toward Brookfield from the southeast. There were about a dozen of them in carts and wagons, with several horses.

"Kimi says there are eight men and at least four are armed," Lydria told them. "They are not soldiers. They have some small collection of livestock following behind. There are women as well, perhaps as many as the men, but they show no weapons."

"It is time then, that we make some friends," Krieger said.

Lydria thought for a moment and all of them looked dirtier and more ragged than they had a moment before. Even the horses looked less well fed, as if a good day's work might be the end of them. Again, her stomach complained, but not as badly as when she had changed Branch's appearance. The only appearance she had changed noticeably was her own. On the suggestion of Relin, Lydria had changed herself so that anyone who looked saw only a plain girl with thin hair and brown eyes. The blue collar of the stone, however, would not be concealed by magic, so Lydria wrapped a light scarf around her neck to hide that which only she, Wynter, and beneath his fur, Kimi, wore.

Krieger rode out alone and slowly to the travelers heading north and stopped to speak with them for some minutes before motioning his comrades to join him as the group moved slowly forward again.

"My friends," Krieger announced, "this is the extended family of Lem the ferryman. They make their way to Brookfield and away from the devastation that makes its way north. They have agreed we can join them, but we must ride up front and set up a camp."

Lydria and the others nodded thanks to the ferryman's family and set off at a trot to distance themselves somewhat from the wagons and Krieger described the family's move north. "The youngest of the lot, Lem's grandson, I believe, came south to find the family and bring them north, claiming there was work and food and people who were well looked after in Brookfield. There is a governess there who is in charge and is said to be an able and fair woman. We can stay with these people tonight and be in town tomorrow."

"Is it wise to enter an unknown place with so much at stake?" Relin asked. Branch nodded his agreement and Krieger started to speak before changing his mind and turning to Lydria and Haidrea.

"What do the spirits say, Haustis?" Using her formal title told Lydria that Krieger not only accepted Haidrea as Haustis, but also that the spy believed her information might better help them with what was to come.

"Speed is our friend and the enemy of Wynter," Haidrea replied. "Going to the town makes sense if we are posing as travelers. We can ask there about the road to Solwyn and whether it remains open against the coming of Ahlric. But more than this day we cannot delay – we must arrive at the Cobalt Tower soon. It would be unwise to believe that Wynter is not ready."

The track for several miles into Brookfield was a forest of stumps. As far as they could see, the only signs of trees were saplings and those upon the mountains. Every tree that could be used to build had been hewn down.

"The animals have left to the west and to the mountains," Kimi told Lydria. *"I can smell fear – and not just from the wonton destruction of the forest."*

They arrived at the new wooden gates of Brookfield late the following day. To call it evening would be incorrect, because as summer approached the sun stayed in the sky for many hours longer than they were used to in Bayside.

Krieger and Branch studied the fortifications that were being constructed around the city. Men and solid women, worked in homespun or leathers, pulling logs, cutting, hauling and nailing. The sounds of hammers maintained their pacing like an army's drummer, and everywhere it seemed people moved quickly. They weren't just working, they were actively engaged in building. Despite the dirty and scuffed up, often blood smeared appearance of legs and arms, it was beyond doubt these people were happy – as if they were hurrying to build their wedding night roost.

The wall surrounding the town was simple. Thick and sharpened stakes were planted in the ground at various angles along ditches and earthen mounds. This is how all walled cities started, Krieger told them. Relin was fascinated and wondered out loud where all the trees had come from, because despite the deforestation outside the city, it was obvious much of the wood here was from larger trees, and from more than had been cut nearby. His question was answered from a guard who had stepped out of his shelter to meet them.

"The wood is a gift from his grace, King Wynter," the man said, straightening as he invoked his monarch's name. "He pulls it from the ground with his hands and loads it into carts without so much as moving," the man supplied. "I've seen it...well, I know those who say they've seen it. Who are you then, and where do you go?" The guard quickly shifted to his task of guarding the city entrance.

"We travel from south of Bayside, having heard of a great new kingdom to the north where we can work as free men and be treated as such," Krieger said, perhaps a little too loftily for Lydria's thinking. "May we find lodging here for an evening before making our way east to Solwyn?"

"Aye, that you may," the guard said. "But I will have to inform the governess of your arrival. She likes to welcome travelers who make for Solwyn. But I warn you, after you meet her, you may well stay here and travel no further. Least wise, that's what has happened to many who now call Brookfield home."

"The governess will meet us?" Krieger's voiced went uncommonly high in surprise and wondered when the meeting could be arranged. "But whatever will we wear, we are not attired to meet with the nobility, certainly," he threw the guard a look that served as an honest plea for advice.

"Go to the Ice Pillar and there you'll find rooms and there the governess will find you when she's ready," the guard supplied happily. "Don't worry about your clothes, all kinds come through here and none are better dressed than yourselves."

With a perfunctory discussion of town rules, the guard rubbed Kimi under the chin and waved them on their way.

FORTY-TWO

As the season progressed, Wynter's informants from the south reported Ahlric was on the move, slaughtering what remained of Eifynar and reaching the first of his earldoms along the southern rim. Nethyal did not seem surprised or concerned when the destruction of his home was announced so casually, and he motioned for the informant to continue as he looked concerned he would be punished for bringing such news.

People from the south were already arriving with carts and crops. Wynter smiled. The earls he had chosen had done well and the people arrived with everything they could carry – denying all sustenance to Ahlric and his men. At first sight of the advancing army they had destroyed the wells and killed the animals they couldn't bring north. He smiled inwardly when the report concluded that there were no soldiers among the refugees.

Wynter dismissed the short, thin man and as his grey cloak disappeared from the doorway to his hall, Wynter said, "they fight, Nethyal. You see, they fight because they believe."

"Yes, sire. But their deaths in small groups will serve no purpose. Would it not be better that they gathered here to face the forces of the south?"

Wynter smiled and shook his head. The Eifen, for his formidable bravery and skill as a fighter, did not understand the tactics and strategy at the foundation of human warfare. "They buy us time, and as importantly, they buy us heroes."

The statement left no impression upon Nethyal and so Wynter tried again. "The people will hear the stories of those few soldiers and how they valiantly defended their homes against overwhelming odds. That will make them stronger, and they will fight even harder to be as worthy as their countrymen."

Nethyal nodded his assent and agreed the plan was sound in theory before Wynter sent him from the castle to find someone to make a song about the dead.

"I still don't trust him, husband. He is using you."

"For what? What could he possibly use me for? Safety, security, power, wealth? That is what I offered him. He does not use me. I use him, and I will hear no more of this."

Wynter sat back against his low backed throne of ice. It was covered with furs and comfortable despite its material. For more than a week before news of Ahlric's movements had reach him, Wynter had taken a daily walk around his town, past the crude stone walls taking shape and the guard posts. He went alone, despite the pleadings of both Nethyal and Sir Keldon, and now he smiled, knowing the defenses of Solwyn would be ready.

As useful as Nethyal was, Wynter believed Keldon extraordinary. Since taking over as commander, the forces of Solwyn had grown steadily in both numbers and efficiency. The giant studied and absorbed all he could from Nethyal about Eifen fighting styles and he listened to his men. He had created a training regimen that produced competent soldiers from farmers in a relatively short time.

Being a new town, trade was still in its infancy and so able-bodied men were put to work building, farming, or hunting, but only after they had first spent time learning to fight. The women were taught to pull a bowstring or perform tasks that would be useful in combat. Many women carried short swords, and all were given basic instruction in how to hold and use them. Those men and women who were especially adept stayed as soldiers while the rest carried on with their appointed jobs.

When Ahlric's army came, they would be met by the entirety of Solwyn. To reach the castle they would have to be prepared to kill women and youngsters along with the men. These thoughts kept Wynter occupied as he made his daily walks around town after receiving the news of the advancing army. He retraced his steps along the arc of the city and stopped often, kneeling and touching the ground and smiling. When he got tired he would rest, and then carry on until he was ready to return to the castle, greeting his people as he passed.

Despite Wynter's recent disfigurement, his people still smiled at him, and would often ask him questions about Ahlric, or just to thank him. They did not, he noted, still smile as they once did. There was a pause now as they surveyed his scarred face. Only his blue collar showed no signs of damage, further highlighting the reddened and burned flesh above and below. Perhaps they saw the burns as a weakness, that he was not impervious to injury. Or perhaps it was pity. Wynter hoped it was the former. The former he could deal with, for he was sure there was no weakness in him. Pity, however, he could not stand. It was the weak, mewling, fops like Grummond who hungered after pity.

"Sire." It was Keldon who pulled him out of his reverie the day before after making his rounds outside the boundary of the city. Keldon knelt and waited for his king to acknowledge him. Keldon was used to the injuries caused in battle and had not once averted his eyes away from his king. Of all the nobility gathered in his arena the previous year, none came close to the nobility of the giant knight.

Wynter nodded and indicated Keldon should rise, which the man did, but not to his full height. "Sire, I have word from our scouts. Ahlric's forces are advancing and will be here within a fortnight. It appears, however, that a group of them have split off to the west; for what purpose we don't know. It's thought that perhaps they go to Brookfield."

"What do you think, Sir Keldon?"

The man hesitated and rose fully to tower over his king. Wynter smiled inwardly at the knight, who alone of his advisors knelt rather than bowed. It was the soldier's only way to not stand above his king. Indeed, even kneeling Wynter barely saw above his head. But Wynter made it clear that he should stand after making his report.

"It makes no sense, sire. The group was not large enough to take even Brookfield, and the tundra that surrounds us means no force will flank us unseen."

Wynter considered his commander's position and wondered to himself the reason for the detour when he spied Nethyal walking toward him from behind Keldon. When Keldon repeated his thoughts to Nethyal, the warrior said nothing while considering the report.

262

"They seek to hunt down the remnants of Eifynar," Nethyal said coolly. "Or they seek the men of Steven's Folly to take Brookfield and deprive us of their trade."

Wynter studied Nethyal's face and found it stoic, as always. Turning to Keldon, he told his commander to send a small party toward Steven's Folly. "Don't send too many, though, Keldon," Wynter said with a smirk, "The Folly is only worth keeping an eye on, not fighting for. Send only fast men with good eyes."

The two soldiers took their leave and Wynter continued across the hundred yards of empty space between the village and the castle. A single flight of steps separated the town from the castle and the arena to the east, but in the flat space around the lake, a dozen stairs may as well have been a cliff. As he approached, a guard labored to open the massive black door enough for Wynter to enter. Inside was bathed in a blue-green light as the sun reflected off any surface not covered – including much of the roof, which made Wynter's stronghold vibrant and light.

Wynter walked past a servant offering refreshment and into his main hall. He needed to visit each of the Fourteen Pillars.

For the past ten days, this had been his routine – walking an arc around the town and retreating to his throne room and stopping for several minutes to speak with the men and women encased in pillars of ice. He looked into their faces, their eyes open and mouths closed, and he could sense the awareness buried deep inside the ice. Just as he had been aware but unable to do anything while lying upon the ground after leaving the crater, so the Fourteen stood now. Rooted to the spot by ice and magic, giving up a very tiny piece of their essence each day to maintain the fortress around them. The Fourteen would not last forever, Wynter knew. A hundred years, certainly, perhaps two hundred, but as mere shells of the men and women who stood before him now. Three hundred years from now the castle would fall in upon itself. "That's right," he said to a woman in the middle pillar along the right side as he walked toward his throne. "You will stand here for another two hundred years until there isn't enough of you left to maintain the magic."

Wynter thought for a moment that the woman's bright blue eyes widened in surprise or terror, but certainly, he knew that could not be.

Wynter looked past her dark hair, which still grew, he noted, and now included a streak of white that reached from her right eye to the back of her ear, in a single line. It was, he thought, a rather pleasing look. Over her shoulder, however, he noted the pillars continued to change – losing their clarity as a vibrant, blue-green wrapped its way up from the floor and was now about waist level with the occupants of the pillars. The colors appeared solid from the back only, still making its way around to the front of the pillars in wisps of sky blue that reached out their tendrils toward the front of each pillar, preparing to hug their occupants in a dark embrace. Soon the Fourteen would be lost behind a wall of blue-green like the rest of the castle.

Sitting on his throne, Wynter looked down the corridor made by The Fourteen. Wooden beams and stone were lying in well-organized piles in the aisles between the columns and the main walls. After his war with Ahlric was over, Wynter would have craftsmen come and build wooden walls and ceiling buttresses next to the ice, and floors of marble and stone. When the ice failed, the castle of Solwyn would continue to stand, needing only to be mopped dry.

Wynter wasn't sure how long it would take before he could no longer see or show off his prized Fourteen, but it wouldn't matter. His plans for the Fourteen didn't involve them staying in their icy prisons. He had already started the incantations to reveal his true intent and it required only a few more words and a single item to set in motion. Until then, he waited for war to reach his gate.

FORTY-THREE

The Ice Pillar was a stunning achievement in a town so utterly devoid of trees. It was a two-level wooden inn that, like most buildings in Brookfield, was built very recently. From the narrow mud track that passed as a street, the Ice Pillar filled Lydria's vision. Inside it was comfortable, clean, and busy. A stable boy took their horses to a shelter nearby and Krieger gave him a copper piece for his trouble. The boy looked at the coin and thanked Krieger before moving away with the horses in tow.

"Well, at least Wesolk money is still good here," Krieger said as he opened the well-oiled door into a bright and fragrant common area. Meat, stew, and fish all made an appearance on waves of odor coming from patrons' plates. Fresh vegetables and bread were in evidence and beer, apparently, was consumed far more moderately than in many taverns Krieger had visited.

"They have venison, and rabbit, and ... moose." Kimi was nearly standing on Lydria's shoulder now and several tables were looking toward them and smiling at the orange cat as it strained its nose in the air.

"Sit, down, Kimi. You're very heavy. We'll get you food – maybe even some moose." The bobcat did as he was asked but not before drooling down the back of Lydria's tunic for good measure. *"Hurry,"* he added.

Krieger and Branch were already at the bar as Relin, and Haidrea made their way to an open section of a long table. "This is good. It reminds me of home, where we sit together to share food." Relin was looking around the room, as if he were searching for someone, while Haidrea sat quietly beside Lydria.

Haidrea leaned to her friend and whispered. "Does this not seem odd to you? This place is so clean and light and with so little drunkenness and so many women."

Haidrea was correct, and Lydria realized that fully half the patrons were women. They were not only with their husbands, but on their own, wearing leather breeches and with dirt on their hands and faces like many of the men. Everyone, it appeared, was in work clothing, dirty and stained with sweat, but not ragged. People regularly came in and replaced those who had left, and all seemed to be on good terms with the man behind the bar. It was a brisk business so early in the evening.

"Is this not a good thing? Would you rather be in a dark, smelly hole of a tavern with filthy men belching and grabbing at you as you walk past?" Lydria pushed her friend with her shoulder and smiled, but the more she thought about it, the more she realized Haidrea was correct. There was something odd about the tavern.

Haidrea had not spent time in dark taverns like Lydria described, but she had been younger once among warriors or hunters who drank late at night and became loud and spoke with their hands. The Eifen were not prone to drunkenness, but it was not unheard of. "Perhaps I worry too much, but this place unsettles me."

Krieger and Branch returned to the table along with a serving woman – all of them laden with plates and mugs which they distributed around the table. Kimi, who stood up immediately upon seeing the food, jumped to the table and snatched a piece of meat from the nearest plate and growled defiantly as he hunched over his dinner. The patrons nearby laughed good-naturedly, but none reached out their hand to pet him as he ate.

Krieger and Branch sat and soon everyone was enjoying the first hot meal they'd had in days not prepared by magic. "I have two rooms for us at the top of the stairs at the end of the hall. We'll discuss our traveling plans after we eat. Until then," he lifted his mug and raised his voice and shouted, "King Wynter!" The room echoed the sentiment readily and many people turned toward Krieger and raised their own mugs in appreciation of his recognition of their sovereign.

Throughout the meal, several people clapped Krieger on the back as they walked past, but none stopped to talk as the group ate. As they were finishing their meal and preparing to head to their rooms, the front door swung silently open, and a small, clean-shaven man stepped in and looked toward the barman and said simply, "Grettune approaches."

The buzzing common room went silent and those who sat nearby the party quickly removed themselves to the far corners of the room so there was at least one empty table in all directions around them. Those patrons who moved quickly found places at other tables as diners and drinkers squeezed tight on their benches and made space for the newcomers. Several looked toward Lydria and smiled warmly. Whatever was going on, she thought, did not seem to indicate trouble. In fact, more people were coming into the room from lodgings both above and below the stairs.

The barwomen quickly moved to the vacated tables and cleaned them, straightening the chairs as they left, while the barman selected a clear wine glass from a case behind his bar and retrieved a corked bottle from beneath its heavy wooden frame. He poured the glass half full of a deep red liquid and placed it upon a small silver tray he had taken from another area under his bar top.

Without a sound the man who gave warning of the Governesses' arrival, for Lydria believed such a reaction could only result from the Governess herself visiting, opened the door again and stood to the side and within seconds a woman with long, red hair, curled at the ends, entered the room. She beamed as she came in and almost as one the gathered guests greeted her as a long-lost friend. "Madam Governess Grettune." They almost sang it, so casually did it fall from their mouths, and Lydria could see they meant it as well. As Grettune moved about the room shaking hands and making pleasant idle talk with various people, Lydria watched, fascinated, by a type of ruler she'd never seen before.

Grettune was dressed in a tunic and leggings, much like Haidrea's but far more finely crafted, with beautifully small stitching and flower patterns that largely hid the seams down each side. Her tunic was pulled in tightly around her thin waist emphasizing her relative frailty amongst the more sizeable women who were the norm in this harsh land. The tunic, however, didn't open as Haidrea's – tied by gut from mid chest to the bottom of her neck; it was tied up to her throat with a material that was wide like gut, but finer, and her sleeves extended down to her wrists where they were delicately tied with what looked like lace. The clothes, with minor modifications, would be suitable to work in if one didn't mind dirtying expensive clothing. Grettune's clothing was far more practical than anything Lydria had ever seen women of wealth or power wear in Bayside where colorful, ornate, and delicate dresses were the garments of prestige. Here, all it took was some fine needlework.

"You must be our newcomers, welcome to Brookfield."

Grettune took turns shaking everyone by the hand and offering a small hug to the women and a generous stroke to Kimi's up-turned tummy, before motioning for Relin to move over so that she might sit down. When she did, she had hardly settled in before the glass of wine was in front of her and the conversation in the Ice Pillar picked up again.

Grettune gave them some general information about the town including where they should visit and what the shops and stalls might have of interest. She was very proud of how much they had accomplished since all the newcomers had arrived and after several minutes of this, she paused to look at each member of the party before stopping at Lydria whom she asked what plans the group had about settling down and work.

"I had hoped to find work with a healer, or perhaps a seamstress," Lydria replied smoothly.

"Your skills with a healer may be more in demand than you might think." Grettune looked genuinely saddened by the prospect and hung her head for a moment, long enough for Lydria to reach out and grasp her hand. The warm yellow glow that poured between their fingers surprised everyone and Krieger looked up quickly to Lydria who responded with a shrug of her shoulders, as confused as everyone else. Grettune didn't seem to see the light which was hidden by her body from the rest of the room, but her visage changed noticeably. Her head came up and her eyes went wide, her mouth opened slightly, and her jaw went slack as if she were staring into an unimaginable expanse. Lydria removed her hand and the light faded. Grettune's mouth closed slowly, and her lips crept up into a smile such as one might get upon sipping a hot drink after coming in from the cold.

"What did you see?" It was Haidrea who asked.

"Perhaps we should talk elsewhere," Krieger said softly, nudging Grettune's foot with his own as he did so. The governess quickly regained her composure, and delicately sipped her wine.

She raised her voice slightly so that she would be sure to be overhead by others in the room, none of whom seemed to have witnessed anything out of the ordinary. "You are all very well met and welcome to stay in Brookfield for as long as you wish. Indeed, I would take it as a singular honor if you would visit me tomorrow that we might have a morning meal together and you can tell me of your plans. Hopefully I can convince you to stay. She smiled brightly at the group and pushed her chair back quietly before retracing her steps around the room, wishing a good evening to all and, perhaps most shockingly to Krieger and Branch, paying for her drink before she left, a stream of well wishes following her out the door.

"Well, there's something you don't see every day," Branch said. "A titled ruler who shakes the common person by the hand and then pays for her own drink."

"Not just her own, but yours as well." It was the barman who had come to deliver the news about their drinks. "You have your rooms. If it please you, I would like to come up for a chat after closing."

Without allowing time for questions or a response of any kind, the barman shuffled off to wipe up tables and clear dishes just as his servers had done earlier.

Without further conversation, the group finished their food and left the common area to head to their rooms. On their way up, they enthusiastically returned good evenings and fare-thee-wells wished by the remaining patrons of the tavern.

Inside the room at the end of the hall, Krieger stood as the others sat on the edges of the three pallet beds that occupied most of the room's space, while Relin and Branch sat on the floor, Relin to the side of the door and Branch across the room opposite it.

"What say the spirits, Haidrea?" Krieger asked. It was apparent he had an opinion on what had happened, but he wanted all the information possible before committing to his course out loud.

Haidrea was still and no one interrupted her. The only sound in the room, was the breathy purr of Kimi, who had curled up on the lap of Lydria content to be petted.

"The barman and the Governess have spent time in each other's company. They smell of each other."

"Are you suggesting she spends a lot of time in the tavern?" Lydria thought it was a curious place for a governess to spend much of her time.

"Not at all. I suggest that these two have a far more intimate space where they each spend considerably more time than she spends here."

"Do you think the others are aware of their relationship?"

"I can smell things, I can't read minds." Kimi scoffed at the thought. *"I will say, though, that there isn't much that would surprise me here. Everyone is happier than in any other human settlement – even Eifynar wasn't like this. They just seem very satisfied and fulfilled with what they've accomplished."*

Before Haidrea could provide an answer for Krieger, there was a light knock at the door and Relin opened it cautiously. The barman squeezed through the doorway and motioned for it to be quickly closed behind him.

"My name is Perryn, I'm the landlord here and Grettune wishes that I speak with you." Perryn looked around the room, sizing up each of those who stood before him and realizing, with a definitive sagging of his shoulders, that should things go poorly, he wouldn't leave alive.

"Sit, Perryn, and tell us what you have to say." Krieger was now in his element. As a spy there was a certain statecraft employed and the kingdom man did it with a grace and ease that Lydria could only marvel at. His tone with Perryn confirmed to everyone that he was in charge and they shouldn't interrupt.

Perryn was not an old man, nor was he like the overweight, stained slobs Lydria was familiar with from visits to inns and taverns and bars with her father. He was older than Lydria but not as old as Krieger, and beneath his apron his torso was still lean and solid. If his forearms were larger and better defined, he could pass for a blacksmith; but as it was they were modestly muscled and attached to a somewhat sunken chest that hinted perhaps at a poor ability to engage in vigorous activity. His hair was full and brown and his face accustomed to smiling often. Even his eyes seemed happy – wide and without the darkness underneath that were hallmarks of the poor, tired, and oppressed.

Lydria caught the eye of Haidrea who nodded and smiled, signifying the man could be trusted. Her glance did not escape Krieger who assumed a more relaxed posture as well, sitting on a bench across from the man and leaning in to give more attention to his story.

"Grettune ..." the man licked his lips, unsure of how to go on. "She wants your help. She believes you might be able to help her and Brookfield in the coming war. War is coming, if you didn't already know. Even now the army of Wesolk rides north to Solwyn. Grettune believes you may be able to help save the lives of many people."

"How are we to do that? And whose lives are we to save?" Krieger kept his questioning short and left little room for anything other than answers that would give him information.

"The lives you save may be your own. To do this thing, you need to reach Solwyn before Ahlric. You need to kill Wynter."

FORTY-FOUR

The Palace of the Governess was more title than building. It was a stunning structure compared to the simple single-story buildings surrounding it, but it was nothing special other than that it was made of stone and brick. Most buildings were mud and sticks, so the Governess' home seemed palatial.

Inside, it was far more splendid with rugs and tapestries and furnishings that must have come from far-off kingdoms.

Grettune met them and led them inside through a series of doors to what Lydria believed to be the center of the building.

"We're not alone here are we, Kimi?"

"No. There are small holes somewhere in the walls – I can feel the air on my whiskers. I would guess they are there for defense rather than fresh air."

"I'm very glad you've come," Grettune said, indicating seats that had been placed very specifically in a semi-circle around a large desk in the middle of the room. "Tell me, what happened when you touched my hand?"

The woman was direct, a trait Lydria appreciated and was sure that Krieger would think highly of as well. There was no reason for pleasantries – if Grettune didn't find out what she wanted it was almost certain they would be dead. Lydria raised her head as if to try to explain, but Grettune held up a hand to stop her.

"No. I don't want to know. I feel much better because of it, however, and clearer of mind. My husband, Perryn, tells me you treated him well and were gracious guests. I expect, based on what I saw when you touched my hand," Grettune looked at Lydria with warmth and thanks, "that you may be able to help my people, and possibly those of Solwyn, and even Bayside. Perryn has told you what needs to be done."

After several seconds where it was obvious Grettune would say no more, Krieger ventured a cautious nod. "The people seem to love their king, and their governess. Why do you believe this needs to be done?"

"Despite all the good that has been done in the north, there is danger." Grettune smiled when she saw the looks of confusion on her guest's faces. "Yes, he has done remarkable things in a short time. He has rid the people of the north of minor lords who behaved as tyrants. He has freed the people of unfair taxation, allowed them to work for themselves and the betterment of their communities; he enriches individuals and allows those who do well and treat others fairly to flourish, while making examples of those who would get rich and lazy off the backs of others and use people as slaves or chattel."

"Why does a man such as this need to go? Why not let him continue to build this wonderful new country?"

It was a bold statement and one that could get them all killed, but Lydria knew Krieger did not ask it lightly.

Grettune smiled again. Smiling was natural for her, it came easily, and it fit her face. She and Perryn were well matched, Lydria thought, but the barman's wife had a core of steel that he might not possess.

"Because he's mad. He wields power that is unlike anything you've ever witnessed. Much of the success of our own town has come because of his power. There are those who think he is possessed by a demon. He calls his power magic, but the name of the demon doesn't matter. His power is absolute, and he treats us well, but an observant child could see he merely plans to use his people as willing fodder in this fight against Ahlric. But the people are so well treated, they don't observe, they smile and rejoice in the savior of the Cobalt Tower. But, when he has his war, and wins – and he will win - how many more battles will there be?"

"Your people have certainly been used as fodder before – against their will. Why is this so different?" Branch leaned closer, nearly sitting on the very edge of his seat, almost impatient to hear her answer.

"What happens when he wins? Do you think this pleasant lie will continue?"

"Why us? How did you know you could trust us?" Haidrea spoke before Krieger could get out the same question, but from Haidrea it resulted in a softening of Grettune's posture.

"Because, when I touched her hand," Grettune pointed to Lydria, "I felt warm, and whole. I could see you, Haustis." The use of the title took everyone by surprise being hidden as they were behind Lydria's magic. "I could see you all riding to Solwyn and throwing down the Cobalt Tower. I could see Ahlric's army riding only to find defeat."

"Is there more?" Haidrea asked as if she knew there were more.

At this Grettune shuddered. "I saw the fall and rise of two great kings as the pillars crumbled. And I saw two men made whole. Other things I saw as well, but those things, I think, are for another time when we meet again."

"The spirits have shown me these things as well," said Haidrea. "Also, a second path should we fail. That path leads to war far beyond Bayside."

"Well then, Governess, we should be moving." Krieger's tone indicated for his part the conversation was through, but he looked to the woman to see if there were more she had yet to say.

"Yes, that would be best. There are those, even in Solwyn, who will aid you in your quest." Grettune opened a drawer in her desk and took out a fine eagle-feather quill and presented it to Haidrea. "Before being chosen to lead these people, I was a teacher of the young and have let that experience guide me. By this sign, those you shall meet will know you and you can speak freely if they present you a vial of blue ink."

Grettune stood and escorted the party outside to their waiting horses. "I will do my best to send only those who would help you along the Governess' Road and hinder the travel of all those who would fight for Wynter or his cause."

"Grettune," Lydria stepped forward and held out the small stone sphere indicating the governess should touch it. For a moment Grettune's hand lingered over the stone before she pulled it away. "This too, I have seen. When Wynter has been cast down, I will consider this gift, but now is not the time."

FORTY-FIVE

The road to Solwyn was flat and hard and the horses stretched their legs and made admirable time. Very little trade was taking place as the communities readied for war and travel along the road was largely heading toward Solwyn instead of away from it. By this, they realized Grettune was true in her estimation of Wynter's use of his people.

The road, they knew, should be flooded with people trying to escape the nightmare that awaited a city under threat by a larger army. But there were no wagons filled with children or women or the sick or infirm heading west. The wagons they passed heading east were full of foodstuffs, weapons, and men. But they were too pitifully few to be of much assistance.

With hard riding, they soon joined a small group of farmers bringing their early crop in from the fields. All around the city, fields were being harvested early to deny Ahlric sustenance and increase the city's stocks. Despite the impending battle, the gates, such as they were, were hardly guarded. The men pressed to matters such as reinforcing the small, new walls and drilling archers. The army, when it arrived, would be visible for a long time before reaching the walls. Full deployments of guards at the gate were unnecessary. When Ahlric's host showed themselves, the gates would be sealed.

The group was waved through with no more than a passing glance at Krieger and his party who, thanks to Lydria, still looked like farmers themselves. When they entered the city, they were struck at once with how new everything looked. The lumber and logs for the dwellings, as well as the rocks for larger buildings, walls, and fortifications, were not from the local area and must have been transported dozens if not hundreds of leagues to reach a point so far north.

With the castle their only destination, they continued east through the sparse market where fresh fish and meat were among the main offerings. Heavy clothes made from elk, and seal, some spices from the south, carvings made of bone – these indicated a population continuing with life as death marched toward them. The only indication of trouble ahead were the echoes of hammers on metal that rang out continuously from every direction and the smell of blacksmith furnaces - the number of which seemed to be enough for a city many times its size.

"These people may look like they are going about their business, but they are preparing for war, there is little doubt." Krieger's tone was ominous but accurate. Looking at the people, Lydria realized almost everyone – to include the women – were armed. Swords, daggers, small shields, leather bracers, gauntlets, and leggings. If Ahlric expected to sweep these people aside or march into town as its citizens ran away, he and his men would pay for their misplaced expectations in blood.

Kimi, who had been running free since entering the city in his tomcat disguise, was ahead of the group and watching from a rooftop when he spotted the Cobalt Tower. It was easily the tallest structure in the area, but as the sun rose in the east, it was so well hidden by the blue sky, it seemed to simply appear on the horizon. The castle it anchored was not easily missed either, sunlight glinting off its icy surface, but it was perhaps only half the height of the tower and not nearly as grand as castles of the south.

"Wynter certainly isn't trying to hide." Kimi's thoughts reached Lydria as she made her way past a group of soldiers led by an enormous man – a soldier of rank. The soldier's gaze swept over them as his eyes adjusted to the light after coming out of a barracks to their right. He continued to walk but stopped and looked toward them again, focusing his attention on Krieger.

The enormous man told his lieutenant to bring men south to reinforce the patrols and posts, and then he turned his full attention to the group as they tried to skirt past.

"Hold there, strangers." He did not bellow the command but there was no denying it was a command. "Do I know you? Something of your walk is familiar, yet your face is not." The soldier walked toward Krieger, his question directed at him alone. "What is your name?"

For the first time, Lydria knew Krieger wasn't sure exactly how to respond, but it was apparent he was aware of who this man was. Several tense seconds of silence followed as the soldier reached for a dagger that would suffice as a short sword for many of more moderate size, when Krieger broke the silence and stayed the man's hand.

"It is I, Keldon – Krieger of Bayside. But no longer in the employ of the king who marches toward your gates," he added quickly. "How long has it been, my friend?"

"Friend, he says. Ha! How long since you stunted my growth with the beating you gave me as a boy? And you have retained your skill at subterfuge. Even for a farmer, you are the roughest I have ever seen."

"Keldon, to be fair, you were taller than I even at such a young age, and I've had help with my disguise."

The giant reached out and grabbed Krieger by the shoulders and pulled him to his chest even as Haidrea, Branch, and Relin reached for weapons. The hug was strong enough where Lydria heard Krieger's spine crack as Keldon lifted him into the air.

Finally, he put Krieger down and turned toward three sets of hands hovering over weapons still sheathed. "I suggest you move your hands, before someone sees you and thinks you mean to kill the Knight Commander of Solwyn." Keldon smiled as he said it and waved his hand to unseen forces behind the group. His voice was gentle and its inflection one of welcome and kindness.

"So, what brings you here? Are you here to fight against your king, Krieger, or do you just happen to be walking about the country-side with a family of well-armed farmers?"

Haidrea stepped forward and held forth a piece of wood wrapped in corn husks. "We bring a gift to you, Keldon, from the Governess of the Western Reaches, with her compliments."

Smiling widely, Keldon opened the package and his face fell. For the second time, Lydria wondered if they had made a mistake and called to Kimi to find her, the panic in her voice unmistakable.

"Come with me and say nothing," Keldon commanded, his voice lowered. "Do exactly as I tell you." As they walked through the streets he said nothing more to Krieger nor any of the others and trusted that they followed his long strides. As Kimi caught up, Lydria told him to stay vigilant and nearby.

"Commander Keldon." It was an officer of the guard who looked to the group before turning again toward his commander.

"Speak, sub-commander. They are no concern of yours."

The sub-commander spoke briefly and quietly to Keldon before saluting sharply and heading off at top speed.

Keldon led them through the city, returning west until they reached a group of several larger but still modest homes that shared a dirt path along the back of each dwelling. The alley was full of garbage and being near the shore of the lake, stank of fish. Keldon opened the back door to one of the houses, ushering them inside.

"I told the sub-commander that I would be busy interrogating you and that he is to tell no one. But Ahlric will be here within a few days. Please, sit while I get my wife and find you food and drink."

He left them in the back room of a house with only a single small window opening into the alley. Before anyone's eyes could adjust to the shift in light, he came back, carrying no food or drink, but only a small bottle.

"I hope this gift is well received," he said as he presented Haidrea with a vial of blue ink.

FORTY-SIX

"Sire, Ahlric's forces will be here in two days' time, perhaps sooner." The report was delivered by Nethyal in his even tone. That he had grown accustomed to anticipating Wynter's questions, was evident as he nimbly shifted from fact to fact. "The people are armed and ready. There are no idle hands in the city and Sir Keldon has increased the patrols. We await only an enemy."

"And what role will you play when the fighting starts, Nethyal?"

"As ever, my role is to be by your side and protect you. Should your magic incapacitate you, I will be here to see that you are safe until you have recovered."

"When is the last time I have required your assistance?" Wynter had changed his tone to see how his protector would react – to see if he could detect anything in the warrior's visage that would give him cause to heed his wife's caution. But he was disappointed if he thought he would find a sign in the Eifen's face.

"When you of late returned from your trip abroad having rid us of the crone Haustis." Nethyal's voice showed no signs of smugness or arrogance. It was in fact, true, that Wynter had asked for his assistance as he dealt with the physical pain of his burned and scarred features. True also that Nethyal had assisted him with pains that were more mental than physical through his unflinching devotion and his willingness to look Wynter in the face and not change how he interacted with him.

"They will have no need of you on the field when Ahlric and his dogs come, my friend. I have seen to that. They will die in droves before they touch so much as a cobble within the town. You shall be by my side to watch the destruction of Ahlric's forces. When we're done, and I take up a residence in Bayside, I will need someone to watch over the north and rule from the Cobalt Tower."

"Will you not continue to rule over the north, sire?"

"Would you not be satisfied to be a king, Nethyal?"

"I have no desire to be anything of the sort, sire. The duties of a king would not suit me."

"They suit you like the clothes you wear, Nethyal. You would make a fine king. When I make my home in Bayside, you will become King of the North, bowing only to me, your emperor. No man will dare stand against me."

Wynter's gift of the northern kingdom did no more to excite a response from the Eifen than did notice of dinner. "Go and send runners along the eastern and western roads to bring in any provisions that may be stranded. If crops still stand, see to it they are burned. Leave nothing for Ahlric to eat and no stone for him to hide behind." With that order Nethyal nodded, turned and left.

Wynter reached into a pocket and pulled from it a blue stone. He had retrieved it from the center of floor in the Cobalt Tower and now he slowly touched it to the larger stone he held. As they connected the smaller of the two melted into the larger and it reformed, the lines on its face disappeared and then returned, streaking bands of silver marking out fourteen sections on the face of the sphere.

The pillars were almost completely opaque now and so Wynter flicked his wrist, more out of habit than necessity, and heard the satisfying crash of the doors to his throne room as they closed. Still holding the stone, Wynter walked to the end of the room and looked at the first of the Fourteen, Kelmenth, the leader of the traitors who fed information as Ahlric's spies.

For a long time after imprisoning them in the pillars, Wynter considered if they might have been more useful had he fed inaccurate information to them to report to Ahlric. But, after sitting in this room day after day and especially after his fight with Haustis, he was certain their captivity was the right choice.

The ice in the first pillar was almost entirely blue – so blue in fact, it was almost black and only by holding his hand against the ice could he impregnate it with enough light to see the man inside. Today he could only see the man's eyes.

"Are you scared now?" Wynter asked out loud. "You've had a front-row seat to the growth of an empire, and now I'm going to give you what you've wanted all this time – I'm going to give you your freedom."

Wynter held the blue sphere in his left hand and pressed it over his head against the ice. As he was somehow sure it would, a piece detached from the sphere and moved its way through the ice to embed itself in the forehead of the man inside. The result was immediate – an intense flash of light that caused even Wynter to flinch.

The light burned his skin anew and racked his body with pain such as he had never felt. Every fiber of his being, from his hair to his guts was on fire, but he never let go of the pillar and he never lost sight of his vision.

When the light faded Wynter could feel the sphere reshape itself and knew that when next he looked only thirteen segments would remain.

Thirteen of the pillars remained blue with a window to the face of the man or woman inside. The first pillar, however, had changed. It now stood emerald green and the man inside would be all but invisible to any who did not know he was there. So well did his skin now blend with the ice that Wynter was only sure he existed when Kelmenth opened his eyes.

The eyes were larger than human eyes and they blinked three times before they stayed open. Wynter saw then the long, thin, vertical pupil that convinced him he had succeeded. A collar of blue scales encircled the creature's neck and shone like a beacon, pulsing like a heartbeat for several minutes until it eventually slowed and dimmed. Taking a step back, the only thing that suggested the green pillar was more than it seemed was the now steady but dimming glow of the blue collar.

Wynter was tired, but he was out of time. He needed to complete the Fourteen, so he went from pillar to pillar repeating the process, calling on his wife to help him endure the worst of the pain, and never relenting as he looked into the eyes of each of the condemned and promised them freedom before instilling his power into the ice and giving birth to the beasts of Haustis' nightmare.

Finally, he returned to Kelmenth. The creature inside the pillar was much smaller than the beast he had fought in the spirit world. It was a young creature shaped from the form of the man inside, but it would grow, Wynter knew, to rival the beast he fought.

Where fourteen pillars of blue ice had stood, the room was now awash in color. Four green, four blue, and six red pillars, each reflecting a small dim blue glow from within. The colors were meaningless to Wynter, it was the creatures he coveted.

"Do you hear me?"

"*What have you done?*" The voice in Wynter's head was so much different than that of his wife. It pulsed with life and a vibrancy the dead woman's voice did not possess. It was nearly tangible in his mind, a thing he could reach out and touch.

"I've freed you. Soon you will leave your ice prisons and join me as I sweep aside the armies of this world like the pathetic fools they are. We will be kings of all we survey."

"*You are merely asking us to exchange an ice prison for another prison of your making.*"

"I have fought the mother of all your kind in the spirit world and emerged victorious. I have created you in this world. I am your maker and you will do as I say."

FORTY-SEVEN

The relief on everyone's face was immediate – even Keldon breathed more easily realizing he was among friends. "My wife goes to gather another who will be crucial to our task," Keldon said. "When they return, we will make our plans."

With the need for secrecy removed, Lydria removed the disguises and Keldon was momentarily caught off guard. Krieger smiled to put his friend at ease and Keldon looked at them all again for the first time.

He looked to Relin and Haidrea before speaking. "I'm afraid my friends, that we will have no time for proper introductions; though it seems there are stories that could be told that would last us through even the long winter of the north. Our mission must be completed tonight, before Ahlric's forces arrive in numbers."

While they waited for Keldon's wife, he explained that the situation in Solwyn was not what most in the community believed. Keldon realized it almost immediately and had seen in Grettune a person who shared his concern for the people and recognized the danger Wynter represented.

"My former lord was not a good man, nor was he fair to his people. However, he fell well short of wholesale slaughter, which is what Wynter proposes for all who live in Solwyn, although they do not know it. Wynter's power is great, and there is no denying what he has done and what he is capable of, but we believe his ability to fight an army is more than even he can accomplish. Malai and our friend have been discussing a plan that would end Wynter's threat to us – but we are only three and would be hard pressed to succeed – yet still, we will try. Your arrival gives me hope that we might tax Wynter's power so much that we can defeat him and negotiate on more peaceful terms with Ahlric."

While they waited, Keldon told them of the purge at the arena the previous year and how he and Malai had married, how she was widowed, and how it was apparent even then, that crossing

Wynter meant almost certain death – unless you were one of the Fourteen, who, rumor had it, were not dead at all.

"The people flocked to Wynter's banner because there is freedom here. To anyone who has lived under the rule of lords who tax heavily, pay poorly, and laugh at the idea of free men – for them, this is the best they have ever seen." Keldon barely paused as he constructed his tale of the perfect society. "Wynter has everyone working, and everyone eats from the same plate. We all have shelter of our own making, we all have food of our own tilling and hunting; most have more than they would have ever dreamed possible before."

"And what is the price you must pay for this paradise?" Krieger was unimpressed with Keldon's description no matter how good it sounded. Doubtless he had heard it before and knew how it ended.

"The price we pay is unknown to most. All members of the community are trained with some weapon," Keldon continued. "Everyone knows that when invaders come, we will all have to fight. And, of itself, this is no bad thing. People should fight for what they have; to protect it if needs be. But the walls, the training, all of it is just for show. We may slow Ahlric's advance. We may even stop him for a time. But there is no outcome other than total and utter ruin for the people here. But they are so happy with their present lot in life, that they fail to see the map on which is played the larger game. Most in Solwyn are ready to die to be thought worthy of the Fourteen."

"These fourteen you mention, is it true they volunteered?" Branch could not help but show his skepticism of the claim and yet, there was something in his manner that seemed to Lydria like he admired their spirit.

"I know only what I've been told, and if you ask a market full of people how they came to be, you will hear but one answer – that they begged the king to allow them the honor of supporting his reign."

"What of Wynter? All men have a weakness. What is his?" Relin wanted to move the conversation to things that might help them kill the wielder king.

"He speaks to himself like there is another person nearby." Lydria's voice escaped her, but Keldon nodded his assent surprised to find she was aware of his eccentric habit.

"This is true. How do you know it?" The large man sat with the rest of them but still towered over them, the shapes of his legs and arms visible through the tight mail mesh that enveloped them. Only on his chest did Keldon currently wear heavy plate armor and it rose and lowered smoothly with his breathing as he waited for an answer. Lydria told him of the short time she had spent in Wynter's company and as she finished the door opened, and they listened to footsteps approaching.

It was Malai, and she whispered quickly into the ear of her husband.

"I will need to go back to the barracks. Malai will tell you all she has said to me, and soon you must make your way to the castle. We may yet meet there." With an enormous hand, Keldon drew his wife to his side and kissed her, before inclining his head to the company and making his own way out the front door.

Malai looked at everyone and sat down. She was not a delicate woman, but she was not hard either. She was pretty, Lydria thought, with short, dark hair and distinct cheeks. She was carrying a short sword like many women of the town, but she had chosen to continue wearing a dress. When she saw Lydria staring, she offered that as wife of the knight commander, she had a certain role to play in the town as well as her husband, and that it would never do to try to maintain that role in breeches.

Still, Malai smiled and seemed to spend an especially long time looking at Haidrea. Her eyes dropped somewhat as she did so, but eventually she drew herself up, and relayed the plan.

"There are so few of us there isn't much we can do. Some of you are known by Wynter," she looked to Lydria and questioningly to Krieger, who nodded his agreement, "and some of you may be known by others in the king's court. Know this, Wynter is the only enemy in the castle. It has been his habit of late to make a trip outside and around the perimeter of the town – for reasons we do not know," she said. "He has not made that trip today, but from Keldon and others we know that he has taxed himself heavily.

"He was in a fight in the spring; a fight that has left him scarred and ravaged. The blue collar around his neck is untouched, but his face and arms are red as if burned by fire. How he stands the pain, we are not sure, but he does.

"He continues his plans to build his castle anew from the inside, with wood and stone, and this we find curious as the Fourteen Pillars stand strong. Keldon has said that it is because he wishes his castle to be more comfortable. But that cannot be true. From the moment he raised it from the ground, the castle and the Pillars have been his pride.

"It has been hinted at, however, that the Fourteen are no more. When I first arrived in Solwyn, I witnessed the Fourteen – each encased in a perfectly clear pillar of ice. You could see their eyes and you would swear they were alive. However, no one can see them now. The pillars have taken their own colors."

"Malai, what will the people do if they discover our mission?" Krieger's question was asked, Lydria was sure, so that everyone would be aware of the dangers of the mission.

"They will kill us – if we are lucky. If we are not lucky, they will take us to Wynter."

FORTY-EIGHT

Wynter sat upon his throne motionless. He could move, of that he was certain, but the effort it took to finish the Fourteen was more than he expected, and so he was not displeased to see Nethyal. Despite the late hour he carried no lantern – the short night with a large moon took on the aspect of early morning. He carried, however, a plate of food and a skin of water and Wynter realized how hungry he was.

As he entered the room, the only suggestion Nethyal made that something might be amiss was a single, quick glance at the pillars. He accepted the color change without question.

"Are you well, my king?" Nethyal's pace did not increase to more quickly be with his sovereign nor did his tone take on any hint of concern. It was a question Nethyal had asked so many times as to be a formality now and Wynter smiled at the man's consistency.

"I am, tired and nothing more." Wynter sat up in his throne, but the effort was far more difficult than he was willing to admit. "Do we have word from our scouts?"

Nethyal set the food down on small table he moved to Wynter's side from its position behind the throne. The water skin he handed directly to Wynter and indicated that he should drink.

"By this time tomorrow we will be invaded, or we will have defended successfully."

Nethyal's comment came without criticism. "I have spoken to the knight commander and suggested he increase the watch and prepare his troops."

Wynter couldn't suppress a short laugh. "I'm sure he appreciated your assistance." Since inviting Keldon to be the knight commander, Nethyal had been nothing but cold to the soldier. At every opportunity he would make suggestions to the larger man, and Wynter knew, from having known soldiers all his life, that the sight of Nethyal coming in his direction bothered his giant knight. The animosity was not bitter, but it was there, and it served the king well,

Wynter believed, if his two advisors were constantly seeking an edge against the other.

"Husband, you fool…"

Wynter closed his eyes and tuned her out almost immediately. It was indicative of his state that she made it through at all, and food and rest were needed. "I think I will take some food and then head to my rooms – would be so kind as to help me and bring my dinner, Nethyal?"

The Eifen nodded mutely and collected the food and offered a hand to Wynter's elbow.

"Why have the Pillars changed colors, sire?" Nethyal asked the question as they moved past the last pillar before moving up the stairs to Wynter's private rooms. The question was out of character and it sent a tingle down Wynter's spine. He lifted the water skin as if to drink.

"No! Don't drink that, you fool. Kill him now!"

Instinctively Wynter used his remaining strength and pushed himself away from Nethyal, who not being prepared for such a move stumbled backward to the throne but managed to reach for a small dark knife before his movement fully stopped.

"So, is this how it's to end, Nethyal?" Wynter lifted the water skin and sniffed. "Snowberry? Poison seems rather beneath you."

Nethyal wasted no time talking and attacked with the small knife in his right hand and another knife in his left, lunging straight at Wynter with each hand carving through the air so as not to present an easily parried target.

No stranger to knives, Wynter moved backwards carefully, blunting the Eifen's onslaught by binding the man's clothing, a simple use of benign magic, but one he felt nonetheless in his weakened state. Using one knife to cut the clothing that bound his legs, Nethyal threw the larger steel blade toward Wynter with a speed that caught the king entirely off guard. The blade embedded itself in Wynter's shoulder and the pain reinvigorated the assassin's instincts. With tremendous ease, Wynter lunged forward and caught the wrist of his attacker and crouched under Nethyal's chest, hurling him across the floor to crash into a blood red pillar closest to his throne.

With the blade still in his shoulder, Wynter smiled as he approached, throwing up his arms and pinning Nethyal to the floor with invisible hands. The magic was taking its toll and Wynter could feel himself grow weary, so he grasped the hilt of the knife in his skin and twisted, gaining clarity and power through the pain scorching through his arm and chest.

"Why now, Nethyal? Why? The enemy is nearly upon us and our glory is at hand."

"People deserve better than to be fattened like cows for slaughter." Rising on his left arm, Nethyal lunged from the floor, using the pillar to help propel him toward Wynter, the black knife edge leading and pointed toward the wielder's heart.

"You were right, come to me now."

Nethyal's momentum couldn't be stopped as a small wall studded with pointed daggers of frozen water broke through the floor and the Eifen's body slammed into the surface, impaling himself in a half dozen places. The warrior's blood coated the deadly sheet of ice in a red that seemed brilliant against the larger pillars. Nethyal hung in the air supported by fist-thick icicles and watched the last of his breath spread out before him. He turned his eyes toward Wynter, who stood behind the wall as if he too had been impaled, and then his ears tilted back against the side of his head and Wynter heard him utter only, "sister" before the steam of his breath ceased.

Wynter looked at the man as he registered Nethyal's final word and dropped to the floor, narrowly escaping the arrow that crashed through the space he had just occupied. He immediately created a small wall in the middle of the throne room - wood and stone stacked nearby flying of their own volition to impede the progress of any intruder. The diversion allowed him to reach deep into the ice and with his wife's help, call forth the First Pillar.

FORTY-NINE

Keldon met the company at the castle and sent Malai with Relin to parlay with Ahlric's forces while Branch and Krieger guarded the entrance to the castle. "There is no place for you in this fight, my friend," Keldon said to Krieger as Lydria and Haidrea followed the giant, using his body as a shield.

The throne room was everything they had been told and more as 14 enormous pillars of green, blue and red lined the central aisle. Hastily erected wooden beams stood next to the Fourteen serving as additional support for the arched roof above, and stacks of stone and wood lined the aisles on either side of the pillars. Keldon fired a crossbow bolt down the middle of the room as he burst through the door, tossing the heavy weapon aside as stone and wood flew from the sides of the room and assembled into a crude wall in front of them. Seconds later the floor began to shake and a green pillar to the left of Lydria cracked like a tree being felled. Without thinking, Lydria put up a shield around the three of them, protecting them from the ice shards that flew from the wreckage of the first pillar a heartbeat later.

Keldon slipped to the left to put himself between the new danger and Lydria and Haidrea, giving both women time to traverse the wall in front of them and hunt down Wynter. Haidrea was already scaling the wall which was about the same height as Keldon, and when she reached the top her eyes focused on a small tributary of blood that she followed to a small pool underneath a man who could only be her brother.

"Nethyal?" Haidrea didn't shout the word, but Lydria heard in her voice the same trembling disbelief she had heard so often when she was young. Men who had fought together for years, watching one of their fellows fall, and despite seeing the truth of it, not being able to believe their eyes.

Torn between chasing Haidrea and helping Keldon, she called out to the large knight who had taken the enormous sword from his back and was circling with a green beast half the size of a horse with the wings of a bird, a long tail and a snout full of dagger-sized teeth. Amidst the green scales of its skin, shone a blue collar like her own.

"Go," shouted Keldon, sensing her hesitation. "Find Wynter and kill him if you can. I will deal with this beast." Keldon's enormous sword was in front of him now and his eyes were wide. Keldon was in his element as he brandished his mighty sword, and as he began his first swing Lydria removed her shield and climbed over the barricade, forcing herself not to look back.

Forward was no better. Haidrea knelt on the blood-soaked floor near a man who was clearly dead, several large spikes of ice protruding through him and holding him off the ground. Haidrea looked up and urged her to find Wynter. "I will help Keldon – I know this beast he fights though I know not how it came to be here."

Haidrea stood and held Lydria's right wrist and placed a deep black knife in her palm. It was the knife Wae Ilsit had gifted Nethyal when he left to find Wynter, Lydria realized, and it was warm in her hand. "Nethyal was holding this when he fought Wynter," Haidrea explained quietly, "This is a Farn'Nethyn blade, there is none finer." Haidrea squeezed Lydria's shoulders and ran back to the wall to help Keldon.

Lydria looked quickly at Nethyal and turned to the single dark doorway where Wynter must have run. She raised her shield again, holding the black blade in her right hand and calling forth a small sphere from her left, providing a low but cheerful blue light that seeped into every corner of the hall. Taking a calming breath, she moved into the Cobalt Tower.

The tower was very tall, but not wide and there was but a single stairway ringing the outside wall. In a tower such as this, the light would only serve to warn Wynter of her arrival, so she extinguished it but kept her shield in front of her, quietly and carefully navigating the steps with her left shoulder to the wall and moving slowly to peer over each landing as she passed.

The tower was obviously meant solely for Wynter as there were no corridors or even other staircases. As each landing revealed its purpose but not its occupant, she continued. Only after passing three landings did she notice a window on an otherwise empty floor and she stopped to look to a sky lightening toward dawn. The red mound of the sun was peeking above the tundra to the east and sparkling off the still water of the lake. It would be worth sitting to watch the sun rise. It was calming, but after a moment, she squared her shoulders and started back up the staircase, confident in what must be done and knowing that she alone could do it. "This is what it must feel like to be the first upon a castle's walls," she thought. "It is very liberating."

A window near the stairs showed her a glimpse of Ahlric's army. Hundreds of small fires dotted the tundra, just below a small rise visible only from her current height. The fires suggested a large force, but they burned uninterrupted. No soldiers crossed in front of them to make them flicker. The army, she knew, still slept, but with the sunrise, the camp would start to move, and when it did it would come north.

As she approached the final landing, the stairs ended. Looking up, Lydria could see the curved ice beams that held up the pointed roof of the tower. All of it was a deep blue, which reflected the growing light into patches of dark shadow matched only by the blade in her hand.

Moving more slowly, she peered cautiously over the threshold of the floor and saw Wynter staring out a window, also looking at Ahlric's army, she guessed. The room was thick with rugs and furniture. A large desk, several chairs, a lounge, a bed, and several empty cages on the floor following the curve of the wall near the stair opening. There were windows in the walls here, looking out in wide views from the cardinal directions. They were wide windows, not tall and narrow as the windows below and they were covered with what must have been a thin, perfectly clear sheet of ice, as no sound reached them from the outside.

Lydria put her first foot on the landing and the room was instantly bathed in light. Lydria could see at once this must have been Wynter's private quarters. There were clothes in neat piles, and a bow hung on the wall like a trophy with a quiver of arrows hung on an ice spike beneath it. Where Wynter stood, in front of the window, however, there was nothing, and without turning he spoke.

"So, what will you do now Lydria? Will you kill me? Do you think you can?" Wynter turned to her and she recoiled slightly, looking not at his face but at the knife still embedded in his shoulder. He smiled and grasped the knife handle and twisted slightly curling up his face in exquisite pain that brought the feeling of power flooding back to him. She could see the ravaging burn marks and scars on his face and wondered how he managed to walk, let alone run a kingdom. Men with burns such as Wynter's generally did not live long. The pain was immense and when the pain didn't kill, the infection such wounds brought, did. Lydria put the black blade in a belt at her side.

Wynter cocked his head slightly. He was used to the looks people gave him when they looked at his face and he could discern between pity, and horror. What he saw now, however, was not something he had seen before – sorrow. *"She is weak. Look at how she sees you, she thinks you are in pain and she wants to help you. She's even put away her weapon. Let her approach and kill her!"*

Wynter answered his wife out loud, never taking his eyes from the green and blue eyes of the woman before him. "I knew she would come to me, my dear. I told you she would."

Lydria knew he was not talking to her but spoke as though he were. "How did you know?" Lydria sidestepped her way into the room, away from the hole in the floor that led to the stairway and into the center of the room.

"Of course, you came." Wynter bored his eyes into Lydria and he spoke every word as if it were a spear aimed at her heart. "That old crone, Haustis, she came for me and died in the attempt. You will too."

"Haustis arrived at your gates with me."

The comment caught Wynter off guard and he reached up to twist the knife in his shoulder again but instead drew it out and threw it at Lydria, not like one would throw a knife, but like a random object, out of spite and malice. It stopped a foot in front of Lydria's chest and fell to the ground. Wynter laughed out loud. He was impressed and genuinely happy to have someone with whom he could discuss magic. "How long can you do that?"

"How long can you throw knives?"

Knowing the woman hadn't followed him to talk about their powers, he folded his arms in front of him, the white scar on his forearm visible and shining against the redness of the rest of his arm. "What makes you think you can harm me? I have brought to life the greatest creature this world has ever seen and even now, he dines on my commander in the throne room below.

"Haustis. Keldon. Your... father? Was it? They all died by my hand. You will be no different."

Lydria had moved very slowly forward, coming closer to Wynter. In his condition, she reasoned, a close-in fight might be more favorable to her. Wielder or not, he could be stabbed, or hit, or his scarred face and arms handled in such a way as to leave him a writhing mass of pain. All the options were agreeable to her and upon hearing her father's name, it came as only a small surprise to both, that Lydria sprang at Wynter and clutched her hands on either side of his face.

The pain from his burns immediately raced to his nerves and he screamed, while at the same time, pulling items from the room and smashing them uselessly into Lydria's shield before finally causing the floor beneath her feet to melt away and re-freeze, locking her in place with ice above her ankles.

"Now you have her, husband. Finish this."

Unable to move, Lydria could feel her grasp on Wynter's face and neck failing as he moved away, her fingernails drawing blood as she desperately tried to maintain her grip. If he moved away, she might not get a second chance. Wynter continued to move backward, grabbing Lydria's wrists, but the scraping of her nails was torture to him. As Wynter started to move up to get her away from his face, Lydria's fingers slipped as they crossed the collar on Wynter's neck, and she knew that to defeat him, she could not let go. Desperately holding to his neck, Lydria watched as Wynter's eyes shifted as if he were listening to the voice in his head again. It was a motion she had seen before, from other men as they called out for their mothers before they died, and she knew what needed to be done.

Locking eyes with Wynter, Lydria focused her magic and nine long nails grew from her fingers and plunged into her enemy's neck, holding him tight, causing him to redouble his screams and loosen his grip on her wrists.

Lydria realized she couldn't kill Wynter with magic.

"Perhaps I can heal you instead." As Wynter screamed, Lydria encased him in a pure golden healing light that flowed from her fingers directly into his head.

Lydria followed the light with her thoughts, swimming down a tunnel of light into his head as images screamed past her eyes, replaying scenes from Wynter's life. She saw images of his first kill, of him sighting an arrow, of a young Krieger showing him how to dispose of a body, of watching bodies being cut open slowly and deliberately. She saw him laughing with a baby, and working in his shop, she saw him put an arrow in a woman, and she watched the fingertips of a young boy recede under the water. She saw Wynter cry, and she felt the rage build in him until at last the movement stopped and she found herself in a boundless room of light.

"What are you doing here? How did you get here?" A woman's voice reached out to Lydria through the connection they now shared in Wynter's mind. Her voice was rasping, as if she couldn't get enough air to flow across the dry leaves of her lungs. She sounded hollow and bitter.

"I'm here to help Wynter, to heal him." Lydria knew from the information flowing into her as part of Wynter's subconscious, that the speaker was his wife, the woman sitting on the bed with the child – the woman Wynter had killed. She was like a shadow in Lydria's sight; a spot of darkness untouched and unharmed by the healing light she poured into Wynter. The room the two women shared in his mind seemed more real than the one shared by Lydria and Wynter where the assassin still screamed out in pain, while

desperately, vainly trying to remove the nine needles from his face and neck.

In her battle, Lydria threw magic spears at the dark shape of Ellaster and they dissolved; she tried crushing the shape with conjured boulders and the darkness seeped between them. Anything Lydria tried, simply passed through the darkness.

"You can't defeat us. Even now, while you're here, Wynter is preparing to sever your hands. But by coming here, you've given me a wonderful idea of what we'll do with you. I don't think you'll die; I think we'll keep you here and feed off your power – I will break your mind and then you can defend this forsaken wasteland as a mindless, handless, but living reminder of what happens when you cross us. We'll leave you buried knee-deep in ice while we go south and create an empire."

Outside, Lydria could see Wynter working through his pain and pulling out a small knife, preparing to make good on Ellaster's threat to cut off her hands. Slowly, Wynter was digging the blade past her shield and she felt the first prick of its bite as it made its way through the skin of her left wrist.

In desperation, Lydria reached out to Kimi and through his eyes saw he was running to the town. She watched the early morning shadows fall back as the sun rose in the sky and still he ran, trying to reach her.

Remembering the light that had surrounded Kimi when they met, Lydria lowered her shield and focused all her attention and power into healing Wynter, oblivious of the grinding metal blade that scraped its way across her wrist to the bone.

The warm golden light that had for a moment surrounded Kimi and for months nurtured Haidrea now burned as bright as the sun, illuminating all of Wynter's mind. As the light reached its peak intensity, the grinding knife stopped attacking Lydria's wrist. The deepest parts of Wynter's mind became clear as the shadows and crevasses into which Ellaster crept blinked out, one by one under the relentlessness of her brilliance.

Ellaster had no place to hide as Lydria continued to pour the light into Wynter. She fought light with darkness, screamed out for her husband's power, but Wynter's mind was awash in healing light and he had no strength to give her. Screaming obscenities and vowing revenge, the lingering smudge of darkness that had moved to the corners of Lydria's vision faded and then went away completely with a faint pop, like a frog diving into a pond.

Despite Ellaster's defeat, Lydria kept pouring light into Wynter until she felt his body go slack and fall underneath her. Only then did she retract her finger nails and release her grip on his head.

Lydria wanted to fall to her knees, but the floor still held her feet fast above the ankle. She looked at Wynter lying on the floor, and then to her left hand which was still attached but bleeding profusely. She healed the jagged gash and reached toward Wynter to heal the gouges her nails had made, followed by the knife wound in his shoulder. When she was finished she saw Wynter the man, looking peaceful, his expression relaxed, his muscles loose, and she couldn't help but think he looked as if he were enjoying his first restful sleep in years.

Lydria freed herself from the ice and then knelt next to Wynter and looked at his burned face and arms, wondering if she could ease the pain he suffered at the hands of Haustis. She reached out her hand and moved the sweaty, matted black hair from his face, noticing the blue collar, and the threat it represented.

Sitting on her heels, Lydria reached for the black blade of Eifynar. She held the knife by the handle and pointed the blade toward Wynter, considering whether to show mercy and spare him a life of misery and pain.

The blade hummed in her hand, and the black blade seemed to fade, presenting a shimmering, fog-like edge. Without quite understanding how or why, she lowered the knife to Wynter's neck and as the blade touched the blue stone, the collar shifted and swirled, moving back and forth as if trying to remove the knife from its surface. Lydria placed the entire flat of the blade against Wynter's throat and the collar pulsed and raised itself from his skin, becoming a real necklace of shining blue gems. She inserted the point of the Farn'Nethyn blade under this new collar and gently twisted the knife as if prying a board loose. The blade hummed and with a whiff of burnt flesh, the knife came lose and the collar turned to mist, leaving a small black stone lying next to the sleeping Wynter.

Lydria reached down and picked up the stone and returned her gaze to the disfigured form of Wynter. There was a pale band of unblemished skin around his neck, where the collar had been; it was not scarred or disfigured but lay bare as a perpetual reminder of his defeat.

Looking at his burns and his collar of fresh, pink skin, Lydria touched the scarf she wore around her own neck and thought of her father and Josen. Of Haustis. Of the boy in the lake. She took off her scarf and carefully wrapped it around Wynter's neck, hiding his healthy skin. "We all carry pain," she whispered to the sleeping man, looking at his burns. "You will wear yours."

She pocketed Wynter's stone and bound him, reinforcing his bonds with magic. Wynter was subdued but there was still a war that needed to be stopped.

FIFTY

Haidrea and Keldon met Lydria as she was descending the stairs. Both were sweaty, and their chests heaved with exertion, but still they were running toward her - Keldon armed with a short sword, and Haidrea with nothing more than a large knife.

"Lydria." It was all Haidrea could manage before crushing her friend with a hug. She pulled away with moist eyes, smiling like a new bride. "Have you killed him, then?" After being hugged by Keldon, Lydria looked at her friends and could only tell them the truth.

"I could not. But, his threat is diminished." She held the stone she had picked up from Wynter's side and added it to her own and the three of them watched as the small stone was absorbed by Lydria's. The sphere reformed, and fine lines glowed briefly, outlining thirteen segments.

The three made their way to the throne room where the dead man Haidrea had been with when Lydria rushed up the stairs was laid out on the floor, away from the stained ice. Lydria turned to Haidrea, not knowing what to say. Her friend surprised her by turning her lips up into a smile.

"The Lord Nethyal died trying to kill Wynter. He has been working with Malai and I since shortly after we arrived in Solwyn." Keldon saluted the prone figure by placing his right balled fist over his heart. "He said he originally sought out the power of Wynter, but it took him only a few suns to realize the madness in him and the folly of controlling such power. Lord Nethyal had considered killing Wynter several times, while he was weak, but said that he sensed an unseen force that protected the king. As time passed, Lord Nethyal watched the good that came of the king's power; the people who were helped and freed from misery and given a chance to live as free people. So, he maintained his position, believing he would have the opportunity to kill him should he follow through on his mad plans of war. As he watched Wynter's power grow, he became aware that magic had never been used to kill a human. The act of killing a person with magic, he believed, would all but do the same to even Wynter. So, Lord Nethyal helped Wynter and waited – he waited for allies, he waited for war, and he waited for the right moment to weaken Wynter so much that someone else might be able to finally kill him. He told me once that he hoped the spirits would receive him well when he died."

Keldon raised a hand to his nose and sniffed before turning away, giving Lydria and Haidrea a moment to speak between themselves.

"My brother has been welcomed by the spirits." Haidrea's eyes glistened with tears and she turned to her friend. "When I came here, my one intent was to kill my brother. It was an awful burden, and one I am happy to be without. Yet, I wish I would have known, so I could have fought by his side."

Lydria hugged her friend and turned to the entrance where Keldon stood over the body of the beast he had killed, his massive sword still buried in the creature's neck. He reached to retrieve his weapon and a tendril of blue mist lit the room, curling up the blade and wrapping itself around the crosspiece. The three watched as the wire-wrapped crosspiece and hilt slowly changed from cold steel to warm blue stone.

As the mist subsided, they looked at the dead creature and around its neck, brilliant against the dark emerald scales of its body, they saw a ring of human skin where the collar had been. "This creature then is one of the Fourteen." Keldon's face dropped as he looked to each of the remaining thirteen columns before turning his attention back to the beast at his feet.

As the knight touched the blue hilt Lydria watched his eyes, her own full of expectation as to how he would react when he came into contact with the stone. His eyes flickered and widened but only for a moment. Keldon casually lifted the blade, surprised to see none of the creature's viscous green blood staining the metal, but instead a shining radiance as if new – or Lydria noted, more than new. The blade shone with its own light, a light neither Keldon nor Haidrea seemed to notice, a blue shimmering iridescence from the crosspiece to the tip of steel, that was as visible to Lydria as her own hand.

"There is nothing like a good fight to make a sword feel lighter than normal," Keldon mused as he swung the blade over his back. "We may still have need of it, I'm afraid. I have heard nothing from beyond the gates – we know not where Ahlric's forces stand.

"*Lydria!*"

"*Kimi? Where are you?*" A wave of relief swept over Lydria as she rushed toward the castle doors which she opened with a thought. Kimi launched himself into her arms and she had to use a small bit of magic to lift him easily. Kimi wasn't in his disguise and Lydria's collar pulsated a dim blue, visible to the crowd that had gathered outside the castle doors. A small group of guardsmen formed a line between the castle and citizens awaiting news of the nearby army. None outside the castle knew of Wynter's defeat, but many had seen the light from the tower, and guessed their king was working to defeat the forces of Wesolk. The ringing of hammers on metal which had been so constant since Lydria had arrived in Solwyn had gone eerily silent, only the single biting report of a lone hammer rhythmically falling on metal remained, highlighting the stillness in town – the calm before the storm of battle.

Lydria looked past Branch and Krieger to a group of dirty, stern women who waited patiently, peering between the uneven line of soldiers in front of them. In their eyes Lydria saw the same look she had seen too many times in the past – the look of those who knew they were going to die. They weren't sad, but resolute in their belief. Lydria smiled warmly and scratched her neck, drawing the women's eyes to her blue collar, hoping that if they knew they were protected by magic, they might feel more hope and less inevitability.

Turning to Branch and Krieger Lydria caught them up on the matter of Wynter, Nethyal, and the pillar before Krieger summarized the work left to be done. "We still have two problems – Ahlric and a citizenry who are going to be displeased that we committed regicide." Lydria looked at Keldon as the leader in a town where, regardless of Lydria's power, he alone held any sway.

"There is only one prudent course of action," Keldon, standing fully upright with dark green blood smeared across his chest and face, looked down at the others who were immediately worried that the kingdom's virtuous Knight Commander would ignite a riot. "We lie."

"Good people hear me now and carry my words to those protecting our city," Keldon's voice shifted coming from deep in his chest and projecting across the streets, and without warning, Keldon pulled his sword from his back and touched the tip to the rock steps of the castle. Almost immediately Lydria felt calm and ready to listen to whatever Keldon might say. It was an odd feeling and one that passed quickly, but a glance to Krieger and Haidrea and then to the townsfolk, confirmed she was the only one so dispossessed.

"Is Keldon a wielder now as well?" Kimi looked up suddenly as if startled when the sword met the steps.

"He does not wear a collar; but note the hilt of his sword. Do you think magic could reside within the blade?" It was a rhetorical question as both Lydria and Kimi looked to Haidrea's necklace, its pale golden light just visible on her neck for those keen enough to look for it. The pair waited to see what Keldon would say, and whether his words would mark him as friend or foe.

"Wynter is no longer king of Solwyn. He has broken trust with you and the Lord Nethyal discovered this treachery and fought a beast that Wynter conjured from some nether world, a beast unknown to man, and terrible in its countenance. The beast has been beaten by the blade before me, and Wynter taken captive and removed of his magic by the might of the Lord Nethyal and this wielder," he motioned to Lydria who held up her chin to more fully expose her blue collar for all to see. "Wynter is imprisoned in the Cobalt Tower. He is no longer a wielder, and he has no claim to your servitude or your loyalty."

Keldon's last words were inflected so that all knew he was finished speaking. As heads in the crowd began to bob with understanding, the knight casually swung the sword around his back and into its scabbard and almost at once the silence was broken by murmuring amongst the crowd. "All Hail King Nethyal," shouted one man, who was followed immediately by a dozen others.

"The Lord Nethyal, died fighting the beast and Wynter." Keldon's sorrow was genuine, but he quickly regained his composure and rallied the people. "The only king nearby is a foreign king who would take our land and enslave us. Look not to kings, but to your own arms and the love of your families." With that, Keldon swept off the steps of the castle toward a horse his lieutenant had waiting for him.

The crowd, understanding the danger had not passed, went back to positions along the walls or on the rooftops, or back to their homes, or whatever they were needed. The crowd dispersed quickly, and horses were brought for Lydria, Haidrea, Branch, and Krieger.

The ride beyond the gates was fast and their approach was noticed almost immediately. Ahlric's army was stopped on the tundra several long bowshots from the town and Keldon lifted a flag of parley as they rode forward and down a small hill where sights of war were laid out in front of them, the stench not yet diffused into the air, but the birds already descending upon their feast.

While largely flat, the tundra had several small, shallow gullies and it was in one of these that Ahlric had placed his men. It was a good location, Lydria noted – it provided some shelter to hide the actual size of the army and provided a natural break in the terrain that would allow for some basic staging and maneuver out of sight from the city – and a place to retreat if it came to that. Currently, however, the only thing the small hill hid was devastation.

Along an arc several furlongs in either direction, men and horses were laid out along dips in the ground that were not part of the natural landscape. Their blood pooled on the easily saturated tundra and the pathetic groans of fallen horses and their riders rose from the ground as they passed, while blood flowed into puddles like the babbling of a small stream. The stench grew thick and Lydria held back a tear for the men who were taking swords to horses and trying to remove the wounded. One of these men, as Lydria watched, moved to the front of the line of downed animals and fell to the ground. She couldn't see what happened but the spray of red mist that rose from where he fell made it clear his body would soon be collected with the others.

Lydria dismounted and moved to the nearest casualty and held her hands to his chest. A thin spray of blood documented his heartbeat and the man, turned his head to her and said, "Is that you, mother?" before his jaw went slack and the spray of blood became a seeping trickle. She stood and turned to take in the carnage. The risen sun played off tack, armor, and blood, creating a kaleidoscope of twinkling light which was mesmerizing and sickening in turn.

Haidrea joined Lydria by the horses and together they knelt to the ground and placed their joined hands on the dirt. "Feel Eigrae, wielder, feel what Wynter has done."

Lydria followed her palms into the ground and saw that Wynter had created dozens of shallow pits and filled them with stakes and ice blades and covered them with a magical image of the surrounding land. It was a classic pit trap made many times deadlier by magic. This is how one can kill with magic, she thought, just like the ice wall that killed Nethyal, these pits were harmless. But if a person fell upon them, they were deadly. The magic didn't cause the death, but it created the instrument of death, which meant Lydria's magic could not heal those few who cried out their last breaths in pain. Reaching out further, Lydria felt more traps still covered and pushed her magic through the ground until yellow light sprayed up from a dozen new pits that opened in an arc around the town.

As she finished the two women stood in time to see a single rider approaching. The man, in chain leggings and light chest plate, had been up long before sunrise, and was possibly drunk. His face was ashen, and his eyes met Keldon's and then each of the others in turn, lingering on Lydria, her neck, and glancing to either side where shafts of yellow had only moments before reached out toward the sky. He straightened in his saddle and offered Keldon a salute as crisp as his bruised and bandaged right arm would allow, calling the Knight Commander of Solwyn out by name. Keldon's size had made him well known even among soldiers of Bayside. "Sir Keldon, I am Captain Manlar – do you come under flag of parlay and agree to the traditional terms of such a flag?"

"We do."

Manlar nodded and yanked on the reins of his horse, joining Keldon as they made their way past the pits of devastation through an area of relative calm, where only trampled short grass gave notice of anything amiss. In the center of camp, well away from the dirty white tents of the common soldiers, there was a grand tent with gilt threading. It was large enough where Keldon could easily stand inside with several men and their horses. The king's standard, however, did not fly. *"Did Ahlric not take the field?"* Kimi, again in the guise of an orange tom, sat alertly on the saddle in front of Lydria.

Keldon noticed the lack of standard as well and asked Manlar who they would meet.

Manlar said nothing as the horses slowed. Squires collected their horses and Manlar held open the tent flap. Inside on a feather bed lay the body of Ahlric.

"He died leading the first group toward Solwyn," Manlar said. "He had told the men he would be back shortly with the head of a traitor. He didn't make it halfway there. It grieves me deeply to lose four score men and half as many horses."

Manlar was informal, as soldiers who consider themselves peers were likely to be. Lydria had always found it so with her father among others of his rank. When a superior or inferior came to the room, however, the formality reappeared instantly. Waving them to take a seat, Manlar poured wine and quickly drank some himself.

"What happened?" asked Krieger.

Manlar started, only then recognizing the figure before him and starting to stand, resuming his seat quickly at a gesture from Krieger. "My lord, we were told you had been killed by the Eifen."

"You were misinformed. What has happened, captain?"

Manlar told them of how several hundred men had formed that morning in good spirits and preparing to be back at the camp by lunch, the town securely in their control. The first wave ascended the hill and the flats to either side and seemed to be swallowed by the ground.

"They simply rode into their graves. There was no way to know they were there, and no way to avoid them." Manlar passed an icicle about six inches long and two inches wide at the base to Keldon who passed it to Lydria.

"So, this is what Wynter has been doing these last weeks," Keldon said. "I am sorry for the loss of your men and I would avoid more bloodshed."

"As would I," Manlar said, "but Ahlric had no heir and as word of his death spreads, the loss of eight score men will be only the start of the killing. You know what an open line of secession means." Manlar was pouring himself another glass of wine and Keldon reached out to stop him.

"It means you need your wits about you. And it means we need to figure out where the power bases are within Wesolk to prevent civil war. You will have more potent enemies than Solwyn now, and you cannot afford to have your army range far from home."

Manlar nodded in agreement but cradled his glass in his hand all the same. "Who is fit to lead?"

"There is a rightful heir to the throne of Bayside." Krieger said simply.

"That would solve all our problems and deserve another drink." Manlar lifted his glass again. "Who is this 'rightful heir'?"

"Are you familiar with Captain Edgar Branch from Steven's Folly?"

FIFTY-ONE

The Lords of Wesolk had, under the rule of Ahlric and his forebears, grown rich and prosperous. They had no desire to engage in an expensive, and self-destructive war amongst themselves. Keldon, with sword drawn, sat down with them to arrange a peace, which was agreed quickly and without a portion of the hostility and gamesmanship Krieger would have expected.

Unable to help heal the soldiers of Bayside, Lydria used her power to bury them and mark their graves.

Within a day, the people of Solwyn and the troops of Wesolk gathered in the tundra and Branch was announced as rightful heir to Bayside and his birth proclaimed by Krieger. Knowing the documents of which Krieger spoke would be produced to verify the claim, the ministers who traveled with the king quickly agreed and Branch quietly assured them their services would continue to be required under his leadership.

Lydria saw at once that Branch held the respect of the soldiers as well as the lords and none believed King Edgar would threaten their power or property. Most of all, they were acutely aware of the danger should he not be accepted. The lords conceded, even without the drawn blade of Keldon, that Edgar's rule would be more advantageous than the alternative.

"As my first act as King of Wesolk then, I would make a long-lasting and fruitful peace between the people of Solwyn, the people of Eifynar, and the people of Wesolk. Wesolk will relinquish any claims real or implied to the cities of the north, and work to maintain a prosperous and mutually beneficial trade with Solwyn."

Wae Ilsit stood by the new king's side and held him by both shoulders. "On behalf of the Eifen, we are encouraged by this offer. However, our home is no more, and we will return to the west."

"Your loss has been most grievous, Wae Ilsit, is there nothing I can do?"

"You are a king now. I am the leader of my people. We will go west and tell our stories and then, we will come back. Perhaps, in time, we can build a peace between Wesolk and the far western city of my ancestors. But I will come back, and we will rebuild Eifynar."

"The city of the Eifen shall be watched over and treated as a sacred place until your return," Edgar pulled the man to him and hugged him long. As the two separated, Edgar lifted his head so that all could hear, "The Eifen are now, and will be forever forward, steadfast friends and allies of the people of Wesolk. Eifynar, and the woods from the sea to the great lake will be their home, whenever they shall return." Wae Ilsit smiled and bowed his head in thanks.

"Who speaks for Solwyn?" The crowd grew silent waiting to see who would step forward, when a voice from the back spoke. "I would have Sir Keldon be King of Solwyn with Malai as our Queen."

The cheers from the people of Solwyn gathered on the tundra were instant and boisterous. Those near him pushed Keldon forward, his head towering above all the others so that everyone might see the humble man blush by such acclaim. Even the soldiers of Wesolk joined in the shouting, happy to see another of their own so elevated.

"I speak for Solwyn, and if they will have me, I consent to be their king," Keldon said as he was greeted by both Branch and Wae Ilsit, all of whom were engulfed in a tremendous roar of approval.

FIFTY-TWO

The next morning, after the formalities of signatures sealed a treaty of peace and cooperation between the three lands, the soldiers of Wesolk began their march back to Bayside while Wae Ilsit, Relin and Drae Ghern prepared to head west.

Lydria approached Wae Ilsit with a small leather wrapped parcel in her hands. Looking into her eyes, Wae Ilsit unwrapped the gift to reveal the Farn'Nethyn blade he had given his son.

"Thank you Lydria." Wae Ilsit's eyes tightened and his lips rose to a smile born of sunshine and happiness. "You must keep this gift. Because of you, I know my son did not die in dishonor and that he has atoned for his youth at the price of his old age. You are my daughter now. Haustis belongs to all the Eifen, and so the Farn'Nethyn blade passes to you." Wae Ilsit placed the package back in Lydria's hand and laid his palm across it, squeezing the stump of her finger and smiling again before turning away, leaving Drae Ghern alone with the wielder.

"The Farn'Nethyn is more than an interesting ore," Drae Ghern said. "Until recently I have given very little thought to the darkstone blade. For years, we have searched for this ore because it was rare, and valuable, and held properties steel blades could not match. However, the spirits have of late shown me visions of a blade of night and a blade of fire."

"Do you know what it means?"

"I do not." Drae Ghern smiled, took Lydria's hands, pressed them to his lips and turned to walk with his son.

Lydria and Haidrea returned to Solwyn with Keldon, the people filtering back to their farms and homes, and the hammers picking up the rhythmic pounding of previous days but with less intensity and foreboding.

Watching the people return to their homes, a rending series of cracks filled the air, and the people of Solwyn turned as one toward the castle, where red, green, and blue shapes were flying through broken panels of the ice roof. The pillars had shattered, and within seconds, the ground started to shake as the castle crashed down upon itself. Chunks of ice the size of boulders flew to the west, smashing into the arena.

When the air around the building had cleared, only the Cobalt Tower remained. The entire town followed Keldon, Lydria, Haidrea, and Krieger toward the tower, but no one spoke. When they arrived, the townspeople stood respectfully by the stairs, not willing to encroach upon the home of their king, even if it had fallen to the ground.

"Would you like me to stay and help you build a new castle of stone and wood," Lydria asked.

Keldon never had the opportunity to answer. A large, hairy man wearing a leather smock and carrying a hammer nearly as long as Lydria's arm spoke first. "If it's all the same by you wielder, I think we'd prefer to make our king a proper home, and again, with respect, I think we've had enough magic for a time."

Keldon turned his head to Lydria so that his smile couldn't be seen by the townspeople, and lifted his eyebrows, and then turned to walk back into town, offering to buy them all a drink.

Lydria, Haidrea and Krieger stayed in the ruined building, helping Lydria look for something that they found under a pile of wood. Lydria lifted it with magic and brought the scaly green body of the man who had been Kelmenth to the base of the Cobalt Tower where she prepared for it a tomb of magical construction. On a glossy black stone covering the remains, Lydria thought of etching the man's name into the stone, and when she opened her eyes to see her work, she was surprised to see a fading green light and words carved in silver, "Here lies Kelmenth, first of the Dragons."

"At least we have a name for the creatures now," Krieger said, reaching out his hand to help Lydria to her feet. Climbing the stairs to the main floor of the castle, Lydria sealed the Cobalt Tower, creating a prison for Wynter that only the sword of Keldon could unlock.

In town Lydria and Haidrea bid farewell to Krieger who was to return to Bayside and his new position in the court of Edgar.

"I am to be the king's personal counselor," he said sheepishly to Lydria. "I hope you will visit us soon." Krieger hugged the women in the Eifen fashion and knelt to scratch Kimi's ears. "I will miss you too, young Kimi. You are a most inspirational feline." Reaching into his pocket, Krieger took out meat he had gotten from a butcher.

Krieger left the women and made his farewell to the king and queen, who had joined her husband outside the tavern, where most of the town gathered to drink.

As Lydria and Haidrea came to make their farewells, Keldon said, "I will watch over Wynter and see that he is treated well. For all the ill he intended, he has done great good for many people of the north. While I cannot forgive his sins, I also cannot forget his work. It has provided me my queen, my throne, my people, and the very lives of many of these people." Keldon was a wise king already, Lydria thought, so much more than many kings became in a lifetime.

"Such as it ever is amongst the Grey," Haidrea said. "Works done in the service of evil often turn to good." Haustis smiled at her friends and reminded Lydria that it was time to head west to speak with Grettune.

Both women promised they would return for the coronations of Keldon and Edgar the following summer, and Lydria would check in on the prisoner from time to time.

"Until that time, King Keldon, keep your sword with you and please let me know if you see any sign of the remaining thirteen... dragons."

***

The peace of the Cobalt Tower, even in the dark winters, was calming and Wynter watched from the windows as the construction of a great house was begun for Solwyn's new king on the footprint of his former castle. The town continued to grow and prosper and in the dark evenings he looked to the north, to watch strange lights in the sky, but what they were he could not recall. The question nagged at him and he felt as if he should understand the riddle but each time he came close, the answer slipped away. Grasping at the edges of his memory he could feel an intense heat and fear but could not recall what caused either.

Somehow, Wynter retained some of his magic, although it was only of a kind that was both beneficial and personal, and even that seemed to leave him altogether when Keldon left town.

Months later, as the town moved through spring and prepared for the coronation of Keldon, Wynter drifted into sleep where he walked in a place of cold whiteness along a cobbled path with white-barked trees and colorless flora. He was entirely unaffected by the cold and enjoying the serenity and motionlessness of the place. He longed to sit and soak in the quiet and was relieved to see a stone bench near a bend in a path some distance away. When he sat, he closed his eyes, hoping to dream within a dream, and perhaps never to return to the prison of his tower. His desire to not wake from such a lovely dream crashed to a halt when he heard a young man's voice.

"Hello, father."

****

98497565R00185

Made in the USA
Lexington, KY
07 September 2018